"The lady wil[l] [see you now.]" [The Fibian]
pulled aside the cur[tain.]

Raeder and his party moved forward. Then he lifted
his head and saw her. . . .

She was enormous, huge, gigantic, easily twice as big
as the Fibian males who accompanied them. The males
were around five feet tall, give or take three inches, which
made the lady who towered over them at least ten feet
in height. *And I thought the huge front door was just for
show*, Raeder thought.

The lady was slung in a huge web hammock that hung
from the ceiling high above them; it creaked slightly with
her every move. Gems that looked like emerald, diamond,
and tourmaline were woven into the fabric of it and
glittered in the soft, omnidirectional light. Behind her was
a large screen from which the queen Fibian appeared
to be looking the humans over.

Raeder wondered if the queen was really that much
larger than the lady Sisree, or if it was merely an illusion caused by her appearing on vid—some sort of
holographic protocol.

He and his crew held their hands in the position of
the first degree of respect that they had been taught,
and bowed their heads courteously. Lady Sisree extended
her pedipalps to her guests. This gracious gesture was
usually only offered to Fibians in the highest favor. Sisree
offered it in this case because she wanted to know more
about these aliens. Their skin, for example, and *hair* were
very intriguing to her, and her mother the Queen was
most interested in their simple-looking eyes.

Her great head rushed forward and Raeder had all
he could do not to jump back at the suddenness of the
movement. He could almost feel his heart bump up
against the top of his skull from the shock.

JAMES DOOHAN

THE INDEPENDENT COMMAND

S.M. STIRLING

VOLUME **3** OF THE FLIGHT ENGINEER

BAEN

THE INDEPENDENT COMMAND:
VOLUME 3 OF THE FLIGHT ENGINEER

This is a work of fiction. All the characters and events portrayed in this book are fictional, and any resemblance to real people or incidents is purely coincidental.

A Baen Books Original

Baen Publishing Enterprises
P.O. Box 1403
Riverdale, NY 10471
www.baen.com

ISBN: 0-671-31851-9

Cover art by David Mattingly

First paperback printing, December 2001

Library of Congress Cataloging-in-Publication Number 00-058664

Distributed by Simon & Schuster
1230 Avenue of the Americas
New York, NY 10020

Production by Windhaven Press, Auburn, NH
Printed in the United States of America

THE INDEPENDENT
COMMAND

PROLOGUE

Excarix entered the presence of his queen with terror thrumming in his thorax. Like all queens Syaris was easily twice as large as he was, her pedipalps capable of severing his head from his body in one neat snip, her temperament such that this was an all too likely conclusion to any interview. Therefore the abject fear instinctive in a male of his species when approaching the most puissant female of the clan was greatly increased.

Over time he had, perforce, learned to ignore his feelings. But a private audience, like this one, arranged for a male of no consequence, like himself, strengthened his terror almost to the point of pain.

Yet no sign of his turmoil was apparent. He moved with solemn dignity, holding his pedipalps in a position of worshipful subservience.

Syaris seemed unaware of him as she idly stroked

1

a writhing, silk wrapped bundle suspended from the ceiling. That she was not hungry was apparent to Excarix by scent. But not to the bound prey that mewled in terror as she tapped its cocoon to make it spin.

As he drew near to her desire grew in him and added its own rhythms to the disturbance within.

So beautiful, he thought as the power of her pheromones began to work on him.

It was not merely the influence of her scent that made him find her ravishing. By the standards of his species the young queen was indeed very lovely. The exquisite shape of her head at the end of her unusually long and graceful neck, the subtle shadings of her gleaming, reddish-brown body, the slender length of her legs, the charming placement of her eyes— especially the anterior dorsal pair, the "gates of the soul" as the poets put it—all this made her a bewitching sight.

At this point he would have found it very difficult to withdraw from her presence, even if he were actively threatened.

She wants me, he realized in dawning joy, and felt distant surprise. For he knew that she had been trained by her mother queen to have great control over the passion inducing secretions. The release of these particular pheromones implied permission to approach the queen and receive one of the highest honors a male could achieve.

The simple privilege of mating with a female so beautiful was worth aspiring to. But to deposit his seed with the *queen*! He had plans and hopes, of course he did, but there was no reason at this juncture for her to anticipate and agree to them. Even in his own somewhat arrogant estimation he had not earned such an honor.

And yet . . . by his own unmistakable reaction she was deliberately arousing him.

Excarix struggled to maintain his impassive appearance even as her scent caused his throat sac to swell with sperm. He struggled to resist the urge to stroke her slender body and to spin silk around her delicate limbs.

Excarix stopped at a respectful distance from the queen and lowered his fore-body submissively.

After a few more spins of her bundled prey she turned her gleaming eyes upon him.

"Yes?" she asked in a voice both musical and indifferent.

Excarix rose to a speaking position.

"It has begun, my queen," he said, noting with dismay the lustful depth of his voice.

The queen's chelicerae adopted a position of pleased amusement.

"Our forces are . . ." he said, his voice trailing off helplessly. He struggled to maintain his focus, to dispense his message with appropriate dignity.

"Come closer," Syaris purred. "I would see you better."

He approached, embarrassed to hear his breath hissing audibly. Inhibition slipped away like an illusion. Without her permission he reached forward and stroked the delicate down on one of her legs.

She made a pleased, sighing sound. "Closer," she invited.

With a nimble leap Excarix found himself upon her back, stroking her abdomen with all of his limbs. All thought of restraint was forgotten as his spinneret whipped back and forth, spinning strands of silk to bind her to him.

"Bold," she cooed and fell onto her side, allowing him freer access to her larger body.

Disbelief prompted him to caution and he rose over her, slowly, so as not to startle. Carefully, carefully Excarix stroked her tender underside, moving ever closer to the dainty hairs of her genital opening, just below the juncture of her last pair of legs. Syaris hissed her pleasure and with this encouragement he moved forward. Using the very points of his clawed hand he traced the outline of the inviting, forbidden zone. Boldly he reached out and sank the sharp tip of one claw into the tender inner flesh.

The queen's legs thrashed helplessly, then began to stroke his back as she encouraged him with a wordless murmuring. He continued to stroke and tickle her as he gathered a droplet of his sperm in his chelicerae. She opened to him and he leaned forward, intoxicated by her scent.

Excarix struck the wall with great force. For a stunned moment he feared that he might have cracked his chitin. Then she was upon him, his slender neck held in her powerful pincers.

"Ambitious!" she sneered, her chelicerae still showing pleased amusement. "But as yet you've done nothing to make you worthy of such an honor, have you, Third Minister?"

"I . . . I apologize for offending your majesty," Excarix stammered. "I misunderstood."

"Y-esss, you did misunderstand, Third Minister." She straightened, lifting the smaller male by his neck. "You were being invited to give me pleasure. And you gave me precious little of it before you made a grab for what you wanted, didn't you?"

"I was foolish, Majesty, I am truly sorry to have offended you."

"You have done worse than offend me, worm." She dropped him in contempt. "You have disappointed me."

She slashed him several times with her tailwhip, each strike depositing a healthy dose of acid on his chitin. The humiliation was worse than the pain.

"Leave me," she said, turning her back on him. "I don't want to see you again until you are whole."

Excarix slunk from the room, smoke writhing around the holes in his carapace. It would be months before he would be allowed into her glorious presence again. And he had not delivered his message.

CHAPTER ONE

Commander Peter Ernst Raeder gazed contentedly at the scenery flashing by, sipped his perfectly chilled champagne, stretched out his long legs and crossed them at the ankles.

The mag-lev train on which he was a passenger was an antique, a feature of travel on Come By Chance, and the most luxurious method of travel he'd ever sampled. The extra cost of first-class private accommodations was well worth the money. The seats were wide and comfy, the leg room ample, the windows enormous and the company . . . Raeder glanced at Lieutenant Commander Sarah James and caught her watching him instead of the lush mountains they traveled through.

He smiled, she smiled; warm, fuzzy, blissful, idiot happiness infused the air. Raeder could care less about anything just now but the rightness of things

7

as they currently stood between him and Sarah James of the rich russet hair, the smooth lips, the . . .

They clinked glasses and gave each other the conspiratorial grins of people in love. The glorious forest-meadow-mountain vistas of Come By Chance came in a poor second to the limitless horizons they saw in each other's eyes. The scent of pine and spring flowers went by unnoticed.

Suddenly Peter began to chuckle.

"What?" Sarah asked.

"Oh, it's just that this," he gestured around him with his glass, ended by tipping it in her direction, "is a switch."

Sarah gave him a look of smiling confusion.

"A switch from what?" Her eyes betrayed the flash of thought, *Us?*

"I'm not under suspicion, on suspension or awaiting trial." He leaned in closer. "Or alone." Her lips twitched in acknowledgement. "In fact," Peter continued, leaning back with a slightly smug smile tugging at his lips, "everything is going incredibly smoo—"

There was a jerk, and the ear-torturing, inhuman screech of metal scraping against metal with phenomenal force. Raeder and Sarah were shaken and tossed like dice in a box, flung back and forth against each other and the sides of the compartment. The bellow of ripping steel struck the ear like a blow; so loud that Raeder couldn't hear his own voice when he shouted Sarah's name. . . .

Things are back to normal, he thought. *All screwed up. And here I thought the gods had relented.*

Memory scrolled through his mind. He hoped it wasn't the end-of-life flashback you were supposed to get; at least it wasn't his whole life. Just the start of his latest planetside leave. . . .

❖   ❖   ❖

Raeder gripped his carryall a little tighter and squared his jaw. He exited the tiny shuttle to find himself at a landing area so small it barely existed, just a circle of cerement large enough to hold the shuttle and a few antennae. He walked towards the security shack, which was no more than a roofed cubicle for the soldier on duty, and handed over his ID and Dr. Pianca's invitation. With a wordless salute the soldier took them and began inputting a query.

It had been a brief and uneventful trip from Marjorie Base, on Come By Chance's lone moon, to Camp Seta, Star Command's hospital/convalescent center on CBC itself. Raeder would have welcomed a delay somewhere along the line, but wheels had turned with miraculous smoothness and here he was in incredibly short order. Luckily, he was completely superfluous on the *Invincible* while the dockyard crews worked her back up—a fact that they'd made abundantly plain.

The guard in the security shack handed back Peter's documents with another salute and Raeder walked out into the open. The warm, moist air held a delicate scent of spices and flowers, making it a pleasure just to breathe.

Peter gazed about himself. The camp was set in a verdant valley cupped between craggy, snow-capped mountains, under a clear sky full of wings— most too far away to show that they were scaly leather instead of feathers—and it had an aura of serenity about it. The buildings were sleek and modern with large windows and colorful native woods bright against the white stucco architecture. Each ward-complex had its own unique fountain and brightly flowered courtyard. The foothills beyond were lush with tropical vegetation; many of the trees were a species of giant bromeliad and the colors varied from a green so deep it was almost black to hot pink, deep red, rusty orange and good old Earth green. Beyond the buildings, just visible between two low, green hills, the hint of a lake sparkled, fed by a waterfall that leapt from stone to stone down a tall, narrow cliff in a glittering white cascade.

As though resisting the charm of this place a vague anxiety stirred within him concerning duties left unfinished on the severely damaged *Invincible. Belay that,* he ordered himself. *You've left Main Deck in very competent hands.* Now what did he do about his anxiety in regard to this visit?

Sarah James' doctor, Regina Pianca, had called and invited him to visit her. "She says she misses your sparring matches," the doctor explained with a smile.

The physical or the verbal ones? Raeder had wondered.

But just the idea of visiting Camp Seta, universally known in the service as Camp Stick 'Em Together Again, gave him the collywobbles.

Spent too much time getting repaired at one of these myself, he thought.

Which was true, but unreasonable in this case. He wouldn't be visiting Sarah in the burn ward, covered with pink, regenerating goo. He wouldn't see her in the reconstruction section, struggling to master a new electronic limb. He'd be visiting her in the psych unit.

Well . . . maybe that's what really has me scared. The doctor hadn't gone into detail regarding Sarah's problems. But the fact that her physician was making the invitation seemed ominous to Raeder.

When she'd shipped out for Camp Seta Sarah was holding herself together by sheer willpower. The

Mollies hadn't had her in their hands long, but it had been more than long enough to torture her.

Raeder remembered the last time he'd seen her— she'd smiled at him, her voice had been controlled, her hand steady as she saluted the captain. But her eyes had told a different story; wide and shocked and wild. It made him glad that Star Command policy was to send anybody recovered from Mollie captivity for psych evaluation.

He looked forward to seeing her; he dreaded seeing her.

Dr. Pianca had told him that they'd taken Camp Seta over from a very exclusive spa. "No sense in trying to keep it open with the wartime travel restrictions in place," she'd said. "The environment is wonderful for the patients, and the Commonwealth is paying the owners a pretty good rent."

Raeder noticed that each building was so positioned that it would be difficult, if not impossible, to see into another's windows.

Leave it to rich people to insure their privacy, he thought.

"Commander Raeder?"

Peter turned to find a young medic at his elbow.

"Warren Bourget," he said and held out his hand. "Welcome to Camp Seta."

Civilian, Raeder thought.

"Where's Doctor Pianca?" Peter asked, shaking Bourget's hand.

"Unfortunately she's been delayed by an emergency, Commander. I'll show you to your quarters and give you an escorted tour, if you'd like, while you're waiting."

Raeder struggled against imagining the type of emergency a psych specialist would have.

"When do I get to see Lieutenant Commander James?"

"Ah, well, Dr. Pianca would prefer to brief you before you actually see the patient," Bourget said with a smile.

Raeder's features hardened.

"Why, is there a problem?"

"No, no, Commander. I should more properly have said, *debrief* you, sir. Then, when you've spoken to the lieutenant commander, the doctor will want to interview you again. It's standard procedure, nothing more, I assure you."

Raeder gave him a look. Then smiled and nodded.

"If you'll show me to my quarters," he said affably, "I'll just unpack and then maybe wander around for awhile. Then I'll check back to my quarters to see if you've left me a message. How's that sound?"

Bourget hesitated.

"Very well, Commander, that sounds fine. I'd just like to caution you that Doctor Pianca would like to speak to you before you see her patient."

"I'll bear that in mind," Raeder murmured.

Sarah was bored and restless and getting fed up.

She'd been through an awful experience, she'd been ashamed of herself for getting caught, for being tortured, she'd had issues about being in control. But she'd talked it all out, understood the advice the doctor had given her and was trying to incorporate it into her behavior.

The fact was that what she really needed was to get back to work. Instinct told her that only time could help now, and useful work would help that time pass constructively.

If I could only convince Regina of that, Sarah thought glumly. She turned off the music, part of her therapy, and rose from her couch. *I've got to move around,* she thought. Slipping on her running shoes, she went out for a jog.

As she trotted down the manicured paths of Camp Seta bits of the music the doctor had assigned flitted though her mind and she found herself humming. The sun felt good, and the soft, warm air against her face, the racing of her blood, all felt wonderful. Realizing she was happy just to be alive, Sarah smiled. *If you're happy and you know it clap your hands,* she thought and laughed.

She stopped and looked nervously around, pretending to take her pulse. *Laughing without visible cause, what would my shrink say about that?*

"Sarah!"

She spun on her heel and stared openmouthed at Commander Peter Raeder.

"Peter?" she said, unbelieving.

"Lieutenant Commander?" he responded with a lopsided grin.

"So they finally bagged you," she said, laughing, reaching out her hands to him. "Don't worry, when the doctors are finished with you you'll be as sane as anybody in the military."

He took her hands with pleasure, enjoying their smooth warmth.

"Oooh," he said and winced. "That bad, huh? We'd better spring you from this place PDQ, then. I wouldn't want you *that* sane."

Raeder watched as a weariness came over her and took the sparkle from her eyes. Though she still smiled and stood proudly erect he could see it was an effort.

"So," she asked, elaborately casual, "what brings you to Camp Stick 'Em Together Again?"

"Your doctor. She wanted to talk to me, presumably about you. But now that you mention it . . ."

Sarah grinned. "It's good to see you, Peter. Let me show you around."

Peter glanced around them, looking a bit furtive.

"Um . . . The good doctor wanted to talk to me before I saw you," he said. "Maybe we could go somewhere private and you can fill me in on your adventures in psychiatry."

"How about here?" She sat down on the grass, long tanned legs out before her.

Peter looked around. They were in a little fold in the path, surrounded by foliage. No one was visible and there were no sounds that indicated people were nearby. So he followed suit and they sat awhile in silence until he began to feel awkward.

"It's beautiful here," he said at last.

"Umm." Sarah shook back her hair and closed her eyes as the breeze caressed her face. "It is that. I'd love to vacation here someday." Then she turned to look at Peter. "But right now I'd like to leave."

"The doctor disagrees?"

"She does." Sarah grimaced and shook her head. "I honestly don't understand what else she thinks she can do for me. I want to work, I want to contribute. I've always been like that, but she thinks it's some sort of manifestation of guilt. I'm willing to concede that in some small way there might be a little truth in that. What I don't understand is, what good is it going to do anybody, especially me, keeping me here bored out of my skull and frustrated? I know I could be useful on the *Invincible*, and I sure as hell don't want to lose my berth on her." She turned to Raeder. "Think you can help me?"

"Well, I was gonna tell her what a wild woman you were, and that you'd managed to keep it out of your official record through a combination of blackmail and bribery. But I guess I could tell her the truth instead."

She punched him in the arm, then laughed.

Raeder looked serious. "Violent behavior and inappropriate laughing. What would the good doctor say about this?"

Sarah's mouth and eyes widened in dismay and she gasped.

"Whoa," he said, frowning. "You're really worried, here, aren't you?"

Her shoulders slumped, then she shrugged.

"It's just that it's all so subjective," she said in near despair. "I'm not well until Pianca clears me, no matter how I feel about it. And frankly she seems to me to be dragging her feet." Flopping back on the grass she grumbled, "She's one of the owners of this place, y'know. Maybe she's trying to keep it full for the government pay."

"She mentioned that the Commonwealth was paying a good rent."

"The government also pays a pretty penny per patient as well," Sarah told him. Then she sat up, waving her hands as though to erase what she'd just been saying. "Pianca's a good doctor! She really *has* helped me and I'm grateful. I just feel she's holding on a little longer than she needs to."

"I'll do what I can," Raeder promised.

Sarah smiled, her eyes warm. "I know you will."

At that moment Raeder's stomach expressed itself loudly and they both laughed.

"Let me show you to the restaurant," Sarah said, rising and brushing off her bottom. "It's much too elegant to be called a mess."

Doctor Regina Pianca was a short, dark woman with an aura of capable efficiency about her. The gray in her hair placed her around sixty—early middle age—as did the lines on her face that indicated humor. She eyed Raeder quietly; her direct gaze seemed to encourage him to speak.

They'd already talked a great deal, about him, about Sarah and the *Invincible*.

At last the doctor said, "Well, it's obvious you've already spoken to the lieutenant commander. I'm sorry you didn't give me a chance to speak to you beforehand. But no harm done." She gave him a gentle smile. "It's also obvious that she means a great deal to you. Personally."

"She's a fine officer," Raeder said sternly.

The doctor laughed out loud and Peter felt a blush rising, which annoyed and embarrassed him both.

"I'm sorry, Commander," Pianca said. "Yes, she is a fine officer. Your captain called me to tell me so, and to indicate that he wanted her cleared for duty before he left Come By Chance. She's getting pretty twitchy, too." The doctor looked at him sidelong, with a crooked smile on her full lips. "So what do you think, Commander?"

"She seems fine to me, Doctor," Raeder answered instantly. "And the *Invincible* can certainly use her abilities."

"Yes," Pianca said dryly. "I'm sure it can." She sat forward in her chair and folded her hands before her. "The thing is, Commander, with what she's been through, and the tension and stress and all, the girl's exhausted. She's a great deal better rested than she was, but I think that the lieutenant commander requires at least another two weeks before she returns to duty."

"The lieutenant commander is very concerned about losing her berth on the *Invincible*, ma'am."

Pianca nodded judiciously. "I'm aware of that, Commander. Sarah has been very forthright with me." The doctor looked off into the distance and seemed to be suppressing a smile.

"She has a way of expressing herself," Raeder said, slowly, remembering a few choice examples.

Pianca grinned openly, her dark eyes sparkling.

"That she does, my boy, that she does. So," the doctor slapped her hands down on the desk briskly, "I have requested your assistance from your captain, who most reluctantly agreed to spare you."

"Ma'am," Raeder protested, "that will leave the ship short two officers . . ."

"Yes it will, won't it? I calculate that it will set things behind for at least two weeks."

"Easily, ma'am," Raeder agreed with a short, disapproving nod.

"Excellent," Pianca said crisply. "I'm pleased to be able to tell you that for the next two weeks the lieutenant commander's therapy will consist of vacationing with you at government expense. At the end of that time, which I'm instructing you to fill with fun and frolic, Commander, I will release her to return to her duties." She gave him an evil grin. "By which time all necessary repairs should have been accomplished and you can all fly off to glory."

Raeder sat as one poleaxed.

"Thank you, ma'am," he said numbly.

"You're welcome, Commander," Pianca said with a smile. Then more seriously she explained, "Exhaustion is a very real condition, Commander. My patient would recover all on her own in time. She's young, and flexible, so there's no doubt of that. But I'd prefer to send her back to her duties completely recovered. It will be easier on everyone that way."

"Yes, ma'am," Peter agreed.

"I'd keep her here for another two weeks anyway." She raised a finger to forestall his protest. "But by then your ship would probably have left, the rate you're accomplishing repairs. Not to mention the agonies of tension that would put Sarah through. However," she pointed at him, "with you here things will be considerably slowed down on the *Invincible*. Your captain assures me of it. Knowing this, and with your, no doubt excellent, company to take her mind off things I expect the lieutenant commander to finally relax." She laughed outright at his expression. "Go on," Pianca waved a hand, "have some fun."

Raeder stood and was halfway out the door before he remembered to say, "Thank you, ma'am!"

"You mean I'm cleared?" Sarah asked. Her eyes were wide and her voice told of her astonishment.

"Yep." Raeder looked smug, heck, he felt smug. *You'd think you'd arranged this instead of just passing along the news.*

"But the *Invincible* . . ." she protested.

Raeder waved his hands, his expression that of a big spender with plenty of credits.

"Not our problem," he said generously. "The doc says you're suffering from exhaustion. Yeah, I know," Raeder said in answer to her wry look. "I don't get it either. But because of it, our assignment is to vacation for the next two weeks."

"Whooo-HAA!" she shouted and threw herself into his arms. "Do you know how to water ski?"

"No."

"Can you ride?"

"Yeah . . . a little."

"Do you like hiking? Do you play tennis? How about golf?"

"Whoa, whoa slow down. Yes, yes, not yet to that last bunch," Raeder said, grinning.

"What do you want to do first?" Sarah asked, fairly buzzing with repressed energy.

"Lunch!" Peter said. "That's too many decisions to

make on an empty stomach. Besides, we have two full weeks to show Doctor Pianca what exhausted really looks like."

"Hedonist," she sneered.

"Jock," he responded.

Clear moonlight silvered the falls and lake below. Peter and Sarah lay side by side on a verdant hillside, the remains of a sumptuous picnic beside them. The last ten days had been wonderful, fun, full of pleasure and good company.

Sarah lifted herself onto her elbows and leaned her head back to gaze at the stars. Raeder, lying beside her on the grass, gazed at her instead, admiring the graceful curve of her throat, the fall of her auburn hair on her bare shoulders. He took a deep, grateful breath and turned on his side.

"Smell that?" he asked.

She turned to look at him, her face going into eclipse, but he could see the sparkle of her eyes. Or imagined he did.

"Smell what?"

"Grass, trees, flowers, water, soil—*life*. I love it!" She grinned.

"Don't get me wrong," he said hastily. "I could never be a ground pounder. I love the *Invincible*. But sometimes . . ." He paused, gazing up at the stars. "Sometimes I miss this."

Sarah took a deep breath and let it out with a loud sigh.

"It is beautiful here, isn't it?"

He answered with an "mmm," and they lapsed into a comfortable silence. She lay back down, resting her head on her crossed arms and Peter looked at her through half-closed eyes. She was so much improved from the pale, nervous creature she'd been just four weeks ago. Camp Stick 'Em Together Again had certainly worked its magic on her. Sarah looked like she could take on the world again.

"Oh, look," she said and sat up.

Raeder sat up and looked where she pointed. The moonlight glinted off the rainbow scales of a school of aircod, little organic blimps, as they floated over the surface of the lake.

"Yum," he commented softly, then grunted when she nudged him with her elbow.

"Pig," she muttered.

He chuckled, genuinely pleased at her spirit. But the little fishlike organisms were tasty. They were a delicacy and widely exported. He knew better than to say so, though.

Still, they did make a pretty and peaceful sight drifting along beside the waterfall. From a distant hillside came the sharp *bep!* of an airseal on the hunt. The little school of aircod broke apart, scattering like droplets.

"Oohhh," Sarah said, sounding vaguely disappointed.

Impulsively Raeder leaned over to kiss her cheek. She turned to face him before his lips touched her and they looked at each other, breathing in one another's breath. Sarah moved first and Raeder welcomed her.

"Well," she said, smiling shyly, "that was a long time coming."

"Worth the wait," he told her and kissed her again.

After a long, sweet moment they broke apart. She rose to her feet, cleared her throat, then asked, "Um, wanna go for a swim?"

"I don't have a suit."

With a slow, mischievous grin Sarah turned on her heel and headed for the lake below. She glanced over her shoulder at him and waggled her brows.

"We need suits?"

✧   ✧

Raeder sat before Doctor Pianca's desk, feeling very uncomfortable. No matter how he twisted in the chair he still felt . . . compressed somehow.

"Do you think this was the right time to enter this new phase of your relationship?" the doctor was asking. Her expression was neutral, tending towards disapproving. But that could just be his interpretation.

"Yes," Peter said. He spoke confidently, and he believed he was right. But he was uncomfortable with the doctor's questions. In fact he was uncomfortable that the doctor *knew* about the intimacy between him and Sarah. *How did she find out?* he wondered. *Did someone see us?* There was genuine horror in back of the question. He really disliked the notion that they'd been spied on. *But . . . we were out there in the open. . . .* No, they'd done nothing wrong. And Sarah had made the first advance. *Wasn't that a good thing?*

"Yes," Pianca agreed as though she'd read his mind. "It is good that she made the first move. But," the doctor reached out to him, "you must remember that she is upside down."

"What?" Peter asked, thunderstruck.

"Can you hear me?" Pianca demanded.

"Yeah, I can hear you," Peter muttered. It was surprisingly hard to say so, though.

"Can you move?" the doctor asked.

"Uh . . ."

"Peter, you're stuck. I need you to help me get you free. Can you hear me? Answer me, Peter!"

He shook his head, opening his eyes slowly. He found himself looking down at Sarah's anxious face. Her hair was wild and there was a spot of blood on her cheek. Slowly he reached down and touched it.

Sarah let out her breath in a weak laugh.

"That's your blood, buddy. Can you move? Are you hurt?"

Raeder became aware that he was crammed upside down into a corner of what had been the ceiling of their train compartment. Sarah and someone whose feet he could see behind her had apparently just succeeded in dragging part of his seat off of him. He closed his eyes and took stock of himself. He tasted blood in his mouth; apparently he'd bitten himself, and his head hurt, but the rest of him seemed functional. Meanwhile, the position in which he had landed was becoming unbearable.

He shifted and squirmed and managed to extricate himself from the cage of metal around him. Suddenly he dropped and Sarah caught him, bearing him to the floor in a controlled fall.

"Looks like he's okay," said a voice from the doorway. "See ya."

"Who was that?" Raeder asked.

"His name's Lao," Sarah said. "On leave, like us. Right now he and some of the others are trying to help."

"What happened?" Raeder asked.

"We don't know yet."

Peter sat up, then cautiously got to his feet.

"Let's go find out," he suggested and staggered out of their compartment.

CHAPTER TWO

"Talk about a train wreck," Raeder muttered. He licked his lips, tasted blood, and brushed back his hair. "Will you look at that," he said to Sarah.

From where he stood, leaned really, at one of the large picture windows lining the corridor outside their wrecked compartment he could see almost half the train dangling from the elevated mag-lev support.

The first car had landed on its snub nose and crinkled like a pig's snout. It seemed to support the other two cars above it, though the center one had bent in the middle. The third car in the pileup was just before the one they were standing in.

"How many people are left in this car?" Raeder asked.

Sarah shook her head. "All, I suppose. But how many that might be, I've no idea." She leaned against the window, straining to see behind them. "No sign of emergency ladders being deployed. But it hasn't been that long, Peter. You were only out a couple of minutes."

"Let's see if we can find Lao," Raeder suggested. "See what he's up to. Then we'd better start getting people out of here."

She nodded and led him down the car.

It was quiet, but then each compartment was soundproofed. Still, anything like loud cries for help should be audible.

Maybe the quiet's a good thing, he thought.

About halfway down the car they found that the emergency phone safe had been opened and the unit lay discarded on the floor. Sarah picked it up and put it to her ear. She shook her head, then pressed a few buttons and tried again.

"It's dead," she said.

"Well," Raeder said, "if it was intended to communicate with someone in the forward cars . . ." He shrugged.

Sarah winced, then nodded.

Peter indicated that they should keep going. The next two compartments were empty, and the third held a man who was obviously beyond help. Lao suddenly popped his head out the door of the fourth compartment.

"I need some help here!" he said.

They entered the compartment to find a very groggy man with a rising lump on his forehead trying to comfort three stunned-looking little girls, their eyes huge in pale, elfin faces.

"In here," Lao said and gestured to the miniature bathroom.

They crowded the doorway of the tiny lavatory to find a young woman wedged between the commode and the wall, bleeding copiously from a head wound.

Sarah squeezed in and knelt, touching the side of the woman's neck.

"She must have hit her head on the sink." Looking over her shoulder at Lao she asked, "Where's the med kit?" Lao handed it over. "Her pulse isn't bad, so it's probably not as awful as it looks," Sarah said. "Head wounds always bleed like crazy."

"I just couldn't get at her," Lao said apologetically.

Raeder looked at the man's broad shoulders and big arms and didn't doubt it. The woman's head was below the level of the commode and her shoulders were twisted in a way that made him sure one of her arms was dislocated. Even with Sarah to help dislodge her it was going to be a job getting her out of there.

"Hope she stays unconscious until we can get her up," Peter muttered.

Lao rolled his eyes and grunted in assent.

"Okay," Sarah said, passing back the kit, "that should hold her."

Sliding one arm beneath the unconscious woman she began to try nudging and pulling her out of her corner. After a few tries Sarah stopped and let out a frustrated breath.

"She's really stuck," she said through clenched teeth.

"Want me to try?" Raeder offered.

Sarah considered it, looking him up and down, then shook her head.

"I don't think you can," she told him.

"Maybe we shouldn't move her. She might be more seriously hurt than we know."

"Maybe you're right." Reluctantly Sarah stood and brushed herself off. "At least we've dealt with the bleeding."

Raeder turned to the man comforting the children. "You okay?"

The man nodded slowly.

"My wife?" he asked.

"Still unconscious," Sarah told him. "But she seems stable. We think we'd better leave her as she is until help comes."

The man looked at them for a moment, then motioned to Sarah.

"Would you mind looking over my girls?" he asked. "I'd like to talk to you fellows outside."

Sarah blinked, then shrugged and said, "Sure."

The three girls looked at her like she was an ax murderer and at their father as if they couldn't believe he was leaving them alone with her.

"I'll be right back, kids," the man said. "Be good."

Outside he gestured to the two men and led them a little ways from his compartment, reeling a little as he walked.

"You sure you're okay?" Lao asked.

He nodded, then put his hand on the lump as though regretting the gesture.

Handing a com unit to Raeder he said, "I tried calling out for help. But this is dead. It was fine about an hour ago—now I can't even raise a beep when I hit the keys."

A chill feeling hit Raeder as he listened to him. He put his hand on the man's shoulder and gently pushed him back upright.

"Maybe it was damaged when we crashed," Peter suggested, hoping he was right. "Listen, we're going to keep checking the rest of the car to see if we can help anybody else. Maybe someone here does have a working unit. If we find one we'll let you know."

The man leaned forward again, eyes wide, and spoke softly. "I don't think anyone's coming. I think it's up to us."

At that moment a door opened at the back of the

car and a small party, led by a woman in a conductor's uniform came through. "Everybody all right in here?" she asked.

"This man's wife is unconscious and wedged into a corner of the lavatory," Raeder said moving towards her. "We think she might have a dislocated shoulder too. And we have one dead, but we haven't finished checking this car yet."

The conductor and her party came towards them—suddenly, with a shriek, the car started slipping forward, then stopped with a jolt. Everyone grabbed for something to hold onto. The slipping stopped and they all froze in position, looking at one another in horror.

"Maybe we'd better not come in any further," the conductor said in a shaking voice.

Slowly Raeder, Lao and the man with the lump moved back towards his compartment.

"Girls," the man called out, "I want you to go with these people to the back of the train."

"Actually," Raeder said quietly to the conductor, "shouldn't there be an escape ladder of some kind around here?"

The conductor nodded. "Yes, of course. Every car has one."

"Maybe we'd better start lowering them, and getting people to the ground," Raeder suggested. "When can we expect help to arrive?"

"I don't know," the conductor answered. Her broad face was pale and her eyes perplexed. "No one seems to have a working unit and none of the train's com equipment seems to be functioning either. Don't worry," she said, reading their expressions, "this ought to have registered back at the station as soon as it happened so it shouldn't be more than an hour. Less, actually."

Peter nodded, then took a deep, thoughtful breath.

"We thought we should leave Mrs. . . . ?" He turned to the man beside him.

"Lisa . . . uh, Faron," the man said. "I'm Carl."

"Mrs. Faron where she was in case she was more seriously hurt than she seemed. But with the car slipping, we'd better get her out now. Meanwhile, you'd better start getting the other passengers down from the train. Starting with Mr. Faron's little girls."

"I'll do it," Faron said.

"No!" Sarah and Peter said as one. They looked at one another.

"The girls are fine," Sarah said, addressing their father. "Shaken up, but they're okay, not even a bump on 'em."

"Look, Carl," Raeder said, placing his hand on Faron's shoulder, "you've got a head wound and you're still woozy. You can't take the chance with your children's safety. And we're more than willing to help you." He gestured at the others, who nodded gamely.

"They're scared," Carl said dubiously, his mouth working, "and their mother . . ."

"One thing at a time," Raeder said. "First we get you all safely down to the ground. Are there any medical personnel on board?" he asked the conductor.

"Not officially," she said. "If there is anyone they'll probably volunteer." Turning to the group behind her she asked, "Any of you?"

One young man raised his hand. "I'm a corpsman."

"Would you please check Mrs. Faron?" Sarah asked gesturing behind her.

With a calm, "Sure," he followed her inside.

"What about the cars behind us, have you folks checked them all for injuries?" Raeder asked.

"Uh huh," the conductor said. "There are approximately a hundred and eight people back there. We've got some broken bones, but not nearly as many as you'd expect. We've been lucky, it was a slow day."

"Anybody helping them?" Peter asked, frowning. *Must be,* he assured himself. *I can't see a corpsman walking away from someone with a broken bone.*

The conductor knotted her brow. "Now you mention it, yes. People did seem to be helping out. I asked for doctors. . . . Didn't even think of nurses or corpsmen." She shook her head ruefully. "Everyone injured seemed to have an attendant though. I should have known. I was just so worried about what we might find forward, and grateful that it wasn't worse."

"Things'll be worse in the forward cars," Sarah said, glancing out the window."

"We'll worry about that later," Peter advised. "Right now why don't we get our ladder down. Is there any sort of emergency sling?" he asked the conductor.

"Yes."

She led them to the back of the car and pulled down a handle marked EMERGENCY EQUIPMENT. Inside the exposed cabinet were flares, a large flashlight, an extinguisher and what looked like a net. When unfolded it turned out to be a sort of hammock-chair with a piece of netting that fastened over the front. The conductor had taken out several pieces of metal and was putting them together while they watched, then she attached a roll of slender, plastic-encased wire.

"A winch," she said, holding it up. "You slide the feet in there to brace it." She indicated several slots in the deck.

Then she turned to a hatch labeled EMERGENCY EXIT, yanked a lever, and pushed and pulled the door out of the way, passing it to Raeder who placed it behind him. The conductor then lifted a panel out of the floor, grasped the mess of netting inside, lifted and tossed out a construction that opened out to a tube made of strong synthetic cord.

"Now you know how it's done," she said to the passengers who'd followed her, "you can go back through the cars and help get the others out, if you would."

"Mr. Faron," Peter said, "why don't you get started down so that you'll be on the ground to meet your girls."

"Sure," Faron said. He swallowed visibly and turned like a condemned man towards the emergency exit.

"You sort of leap into it," the conductor said. "Don't worry, you can't fall."

Faron gave her a wry look, then closed his eyes and leapt out. The tube, reinforced with flexible hoops, caught him and in no time he was safely on the ground. He waved at them, grinning.

Raeder waved back and the conductor gave a satisfied nod and went into his compartment.

It took both Sarah and the conductor a good deal of maneuvering in the tiny space to free Mrs. Faron. Mercifully, she remained unconscious.

Meanwhile, Raeder took the girls out with him and talked them through the process of escaping from the car. The youngest looked like she was going to cry, but the older two seemed too stunned to care one way or the other.

"Look," Peter said, encouragingly, "there's Daddy."

The middle child, who might have been five, leaned out, saw him and waved. Then she turned to Peter and reached out for him; Raeder took her into his arms.

"Now you two stay here and watch," he said to the other girls. "Hold onto one another's hand and wait until I get back to help you down. Okay?" The eldest nodded, mouth open. The little one's face worked like she was about to explode. "Okay?" he asked again.

Neither girl said anything so Peter turned to the opening.

"I wanna go! I wanna go!" the youngest suddenly shrieked, leaping towards Peter.

"Whoa!" he cried, grabbing her by the back of her tunic just before she went headfirst down the chute. "Wait a minute." He pulled her back. *My heart should be starting again any second now,* he thought. He took a deep breath. "Okay. Here's what we're gonna do. You," he said to the oldest, "go back in the compartment and see if there's anything valuable, like mommy's purse, that you can take with you. Then wait for me to come back. Can you do that?"

The girl nodded, turned and rushed back into their compartment.

"Now, you," he pointed a finger at the middle child, "get on my back, piggyback and hold on tight."

The kid climbed aboard, folding her small arms directly across Raeder's windpipe with astonishing force.

"A little looser," Raeder gasped out. "Not so tight. Loose. . . ." He took the little arms in his hands and positioned them so that he could breathe. "Like that. Okay?" A nod from over his shoulder. Then Peter opened his arms to the smallest one, who suddenly seemed shy. She looked back into their compartment.

"Mommy?" she said, lower lip trembling.

"She'll be down soon," Raeder assured her. "You'll want to be on the ground waiting for her, won't you?"

He'd caught just the right tone of adult/parental confidence and the toddler came forward and grabbed his shoulders.

"This is going to be fun!" Peter told them, then jumped into the chute with a shrill, "Wheeeee!"

It was in fact an easy trip except for the first few

moments, when tiny fingers dug into his muscles like steel spikes. Before they hit bottom though the older girl was whooping and her little sister was laughing. Peter handed them over to their relieved father. Then made the arduous climb back up.

He flung himself onto the car's floor with a *whoof!* and opened his eyes to the sight of a small pair of shoes. Looking up, he saw a huge pocketbook held by a very earnest little girl.

"Ready," she said grimly.

"We will be too," Sarah said from the doorway. "When you get back."

He gave her a thumbs-up and held his arms open for the oldest girl, who draped Mama's purse over his arm then clung to him like a limpet, her eyes squeezed tightly shut. He leapt out, and she began to shriek, never letting up until they touched the ground. Then she went silent, released him, took the purse and went to take her father's hand.

I can't hear out of my left ear, Raeder thought, still a little stunned by the sheer volume the kid had achieved.

Aloud he said, "Your wife will be down next." *Am I yelling?* he wondered. Then he turned and began climbing again.

When Raeder got back up to the car Sarah was waiting for him.

"We've got her in the chair," she said. "We're gonna need you to lift her over the edge."

"Fine," Raeder gasped. "Anything. Just don't make me climb this thing again." He hauled himself up to a sitting position. "Hey, why don't you throw down some blankets and pillows while I'm catching my breath. They're gonna need 'em."

"Good idea," Sarah said and moved off to gather them up.

While he was waiting Raeder had a brainstorm. He went into the Farons' compartment and folded down one of the upper berths. *Ah, guessed right, the mattress will come off.* He dragged it over to the emergency door and, catching Faron's eye, waved him off and dropped the mattress down. *Better drop down a few more,* he thought. *The conductor said we had some injuries.*

"Good idea!" Sarah said when she saw what he was doing. She wrapped the pillows and blankets in a sheet and tossed them out the door. "When we get back we'll throw out the rest of them. Who knows how many injured there'll be eventually?"

"Back?" Peter said, dropping a mattress.

"We're going to have to help Mr. Faron with his wife, Peter. Not only is he injured, but he has those kids to look out for." She gave him a sympathetic grin. "You can do it, sweetie. Think of it as a mountain-climbing course."

Raeder grinned and groaned. They'd taken a mountain climbing lesson at Camp Seta, taught by a man so outrageously enthusiastic, "Aw, we can make this little bit," that by the time they returned to sea level they were convinced he was a torturer in training.

"We'll just break it down into steps," Peter said heartily.

"One step at a time," Sarah agreed cheerfully, "that's how you reach the summit!"

"This is going to kill me," he muttered, picking up the still-unconscious Mrs. Faron. "I know it will."

He gently lowered the emergency chair out of the car to let it swing slowly in the open air.

"Oh no, man, you'll be fine," Sarah said in a nasal imitation of their teacher. "Go for it!" She started the winch moving. "You'd better go down to meet her,"

Sarah advised him. "We wouldn't want Mr. Faron to drop her."

"On my way."

Faron had already set up the mattress to receive his wounded wife, well away from the train. When Raeder returned to the escape chute he saw that Sarah had been busy. The ground was littered with mattresses and among them were three dolls which were greeted with cries of joy from the little girls. People were descending from the other cars in considerable numbers now.

Peter walked over to a man in a conductor's uniform.

"We've thrown down some blankets and mattresses over there," he said, pointing to where the Farons were gathered around Mrs. F. "But we'll probably need more when we start getting people off the forward cars. Could you have people still on board strip their cars for blankets and pillows and mattresses and such?" It was phrased as a question and spoken like an order. Peter glanced over at the fallen train. "Oh," he said, grabbing the conductor's arm. "Maybe you or some of the more hale passengers could see if you can help out some of the people in that first car." He couldn't be sure, but he thought he saw some motion through one of the windows.

The man said, "Yessir," and sprang to it.

Raeder walked over to the chute and looked wearily upward. *It's only about fifty feet*, he thought, squinting. *That's not so far.*

Of course, gravity was a complication, as was climbing up something only meant to be climbed down. He sighed and allowed his shoulders to slump. *Okay*, he thought, *that's enough whining. Get going.*

Sarah watched him climb with a rueful smile. *Poor Peter, what is this, the third climb? Well, honey, it's gonna get worse before it gets better.*

She'd opened the door between their car and the one in front of them. It was at a slightly less steep angle than the cars below it, but they were still going to need rope.

"Oh boy," Raeder said, flopping his front half down on the deck beside her. "I'm gettin' too old for this stuff."

"Train wrecks?" she asked, grabbing him by the belt and hauling him aboard. "Have you done a lot of these?"

"Heck, no!" He gave her one of his choirboy looks as he rolled onto his back. "Lieutenant Commander, this is not my fault."

"Y'know, Raeder, every time you give me that look, I just get so suspicious."

He gave her the raspberry, then slowly stood up and clapped his hands.

"Well, let's do it."

"We'll need some rope," Sarah said, rising also.

Peter picked up the chute and began hauling it in.

"That'll work," she said and moved to help him.

Together they pulled in the whole apparatus. It was permanently attached, so they dragged it to the other end of the car, dropping it through. It only reached about a quarter of the way down.

"We'll drop their escape chute down the middle of their car. No way are most people going to be able to climb up to it," he said, thinking out loud. "We'll probably have to make slits in the fabric here and there to get people into it."

"I'll get our med kit," Sarah said.

Peter began hauling in their emergency chair. From the look of the crumpled metal and plastic of the other cars he knew they were going to need it. He dislodged the winch from its mooring. Then he leaned out the door and looked at the fallen cars.

Is it my imagination, or is that middle car more bent than it was?

Suddenly the conductor's voice saying, "There are approximately a hundred and eight people back there," struck him. There were three cars behind this one. And three before.

Don't panic, he told himself. *There were only us, the Farons, Lao and the dead man on this car. Maybe the forward cars will have fewer people still.*

The rear cars were less expensive, but the seating was open back there, like on a shuttle. The luxury compartments on the forward cars took up a lot of space. There were only eight on this one, four singles, suitable for two passengers, and four doubles, suitable for four adults each. But the first car . . . wasn't it an observation car . . . more seats?

Sufficient unto the day is the evil thereof, Peter warned himself. *Don't go borrowing trouble.* There was going to be more than enough to go around.

"Look out the window," Sarah said as she came up to him. "Looks like they're trying to get people out of the bottom car."

Just as Peter reached the window he saw one of the conductors pull himself through one of the train's broken windows.

"Good," he said. "That leaves us with just the top two."

Sarah smiled at his confident tone.

"Well then, let's get started," she said. "I don't like the look of that middle car at all."

Raeder climbed down the outside of the chute to the next car's emergency exit. Once there he braced himself between the outer wall and the wall of the next cabin below his feet. Sarah tossed him the winch and he set it into the slots in the decking. Then she climbed down to join him. Together they pulled out the escape chute and tossed it down the length of the car.

Heads popped out of compartments along the way as it bounced down.

"Is anybody hurt?" Peter called.

"Bumped and bruised," a man called back, "but we're okay."

"Good," Sarah said. "Can everyone here manage to climb down the chute to the next car?" Sarah shouted.

"My wife can't," an older man called back.

"Don't worry," she called. "We've got an emergency sling."

Raeder had reached their compartment and swung himself inside. The lady was rather frail looking, but her eyes were bright and her smile was game.

"I'll help as much as I can," she said.

Peter grinned at her. "Good," he said encouragingly. "First let's get the riffraff out of the way." He leaned back out of the compartment and shouted to the people above him. "I'm going to climb down to the next car and let down their emergency chute. When it's ready I'll call out and then we'll evacuate from the top down."

"I'm going first," a man said from just below Peter. "I can't wait any longer." Beside him his wife compressed her lips, but said nothing.

"If you want to open the door and pull out the chute that's great," Raeder said. "Thanks."

The man gaped, his mouth opened and closed twice, then his wife nudged him and, with a sour look on his face, he reached out, grabbed the chute and proceeded to climb clumsily down to the next car. Peter looked up at Sarah, who slowly winked back at him.

"No," Raeder said as one or two people moved to

join him. "Wait until the door is open, there's no room down there for more than two people to stand." Hands withdrew, but anxious passengers stayed at their doorways.

Growling and complaining, but obviously aware that the rest of his fellow passengers were watching, Raeder's unwilling helper wrenched open the door to the next car and dropped the chute through, then continued on his way.

After a few minutes he shouted, panting, "I can't budge this door. It's jammed."

"Right there," Raeder called back and climbed down to join him. "Whoa," he said when he saw the door.

The frame had buckled, just slightly, but enough to make it part of the wall as far as getting through it was concerned. *It's supposed to open inward,* Peter recalled. *So I guess we can't kick it out either.* He looked down the car.

Where it had bent there seemed to be very little space to get through.

"Hmmm," he said. "I'm going to check further down the car. Maybe we can get through the exit in the forward car."

"I doubt it," the man said sourly. "I mean, two cars landed on top of that one. So what're the odds?"

"Good point," Raeder conceded. "Well, we can probably go through one of the windows," he mused, then nodded. "Let's do it."

Together they gathered up the chute and dragged it into the empty compartment next to the useless emergency exit. The safety glass of the window was already crackled and ready to fall apart. One sturdy kick from Peter's boot and the frame was empty. They pushed the chute out and the man watched it fall.

"Oh, my God," he said, visibly paling. "I can't climb down that, I'll kill myself."

Raeder pulled out his knife and cut some of the netting.

"You can't fall if you're inside the chute," he said. "I've already been down and back up several times, it's completely safe."

"Yeah, but you cut it!"

"Any one of these threads is calibrated to hold someone three times your weight," Peter lied confidently. "There are more than enough left to guarantee your safe landing."

"You sure?" the man asked, licking his lips nervously.

"Yep. You might as well go ahead," Raeder told him. "It'll give everyone else confidence."

That won him a glare from the man. He was an extremely reluctant hero at best and would have vastly preferred to see Raeder precede him down the chute.

"Thanks," Peter said and, reaching out, began to climb back up to the other car.

"Yeah, sure," the man muttered as he wriggled through the hole in the chute.

"Okay, everybody," Raeder stood beside the door at the bottom of the car, "starting from the top, in twos. We had to put the chute through a window in the compartment right next to the emergency door. Mr. . . ."

"Cramden," his wife shouted.

"Cramden has gone down ahead of us to test it. So everything is all right." *Or as all right as things can be in a wrecked train. And, of course, assuming Mr. Cramden actually made it down safely.* Which he must have. He looked like a screamer and Peter hadn't heard one, so . . .

They'd been lucky with this car. The occupants were

all adults and all pretty fit, except for the elderly couple Peter was with.

Sarah came through the door, pulling the sling chair in after her. With the husband's help, she fitted the old lady into it.

"Peter," she said quietly to him after she'd finished. "Why don't we take out this window and let her down from here? It'll be easier than maneuvering her down to the next compartment."

"Good idea. Cover them up with something while I get to work on the window."

Sarah and the old couple huddled in the corner of the compartment under a blue blanket, monogrammed in bright red with the line's initials. The lieutenant commander watched Raeder balance himself, gather his chi, and strike out at the glass with his booted foot and a mighty shout.

He rebounded with such force that he was halfway out the door before she snagged his trousers and halted his flight. His hands appeared on either side of the doorway and he pulled himself back in, his teeth gritted with effort.

"Man," he said, "that's some glass!"

"Nice to know something on this train is doing what it's supposed to," Sarah muttered.

"You'd better help me with this." He stood and positioned himself again. "Two's got to be better than one."

Sarah lined up beside him and they kicked at the window in unison. Ten, fifteen, twenty strikes. She sat down in a heap and pushed sweat-damp hair off her brow.

"This is supposed to be the easy way, right?"

Raeder flopped down beside her and peered at the recalcitrant glass with narrowed eyes as though taking the enemy's measure.

"What we need to do," he said, "is pierce it somehow. That'll weaken it enough that a few kicks will take it out."

Sarah nodded her head judiciously, looking like she was in this for the long haul.

The old couple looked at one another dubiously, but said nothing.

Raeder came to his feet.

"Maybe just a few more kicks," he muttered and bounced on his toes a few times.

The train lurched and the old lady screamed, her cries echoed from further down the car by other voices.

"We're losing sight of what we're supposed to be doing," Sarah said. "I'll go up and work the winch. Sir, you go down to the first cabin and wait for your wife." She grabbed the netting and swarmed up to the top. "Ready!" she shouted down.

She and Raeder anxiously watched the old man descend, slowly, painfully. Sarah could have sworn she felt micro-tremors beneath her feet and prayed that the man would be standing on something solid if the train slipped again.

At last he stepped into the compartment they'd set up for escape.

"Ready," he called.

Raeder guided the bundled elderly lady out of their compartment and, as he'd instructed her, she grasped the netting, holding herself firm until he could get into position. When he was in place Sarah began lowering her. Peter told the woman to let go and he caged her with his arms and legs, preventing her from bumping against the walls on her descent. When they reached the escape chamber, Raeder lifted up his hand and Sarah locked the mechanism. Once they had her in the compartment Raeder put his hand out the door and signaled. Sarah lowered more line until he clasped his hand in a signal to stop.

After a moment he reappeared and signaled her to lower away. Sarah complied and slowly lowered line for what seemed an eternity until Raeder returned to signal, "enough."

"Finally," she muttered and climbed down to meet him. "Is there anybody left aboard?" There had been one or two passengers in this car that had gone down with the others, she'd seen them.

"I don't know," Raeder said. "Let's find out." Moving to the door of the compartment he shouted, "Hey! Anybody left in here?"

"Help!" a woman's voice cried. "Can you hear me? Help, I'm stuck!"

Peter and Sarah turned to one another with *Oh, great,* expressions on their faces.

"We're coming," he said aloud. "Make some noise so we'll find you."

The thumping the woman made led them to the bend in the car. That last little slip had narrowed the gap until not even Sarah, slender as she was, could fit through.

"Hello?" Raeder said.

"In here," the voice came from the narrowest part of the bend.

Peter could see that the door to her compartment was also folded. *Well, she won't be leaving through that.*

"Looks like your door is jammed," he said.

"Well, duh! If it wasn't I wouldn't be stuck, now would I?"

"Good point," he agreed. "Look, I'm gonna see if I can reach you through your window. Hang on, don't worry if you don't hear me for awhile. I haven't gone away, I'm just checking out other options."

"Well, hurry up!"

Sarah suppressed a laugh and started up the corridor, Peter behind her. The door to the next compartment was also jammed shut, but discreet knocking brought no answer.

"Why are you tapping so softly?" she asked.

"Because I don't want to start Boxcar Bertha bellowing."

She snickered. "Y'know, Bertha suits her."

The third door was open and the window badly crackled.

"Yea!" Peter said softly. He and Sarah looked at one another and with a cry of "Yeeee-AH!" they knocked it out of its frame with simultaneous kicks.

"What happened?" Bertha almost screamed. "Hello?"

"We had to break a window," Peter shouted back.

"By screaming at it? What are you people, *nuts*?" The lady was getting really tense.

"Hang on," Sarah shouted back. "I'll go get the sling," she said.

There was no point in making this woman climb in and out of windows. Besides, she might be hurt.

"Is there enough slack to get her to the ground?" Peter asked when she brought in the sling.

Sarah shrugged. "Close enough for government work."

"I don't think that's what she wants to hear," Peter said dubiously.

"Tough," Sarah said under her breath.

"She's a corker, all right," he said, quoting his mom.

He rigged a harness for himself from the line connected to the sling chair and sat backwards in the open window. At this point the drop to the next window was almost vertical. The window to the compartment beside them was smashed, but the one below was untouched.

"Damn," Raeder said wearily.

"What?" Sarah leaned out the window beside him and saw the perfect shield of safety glass. "Damn," she said.

"Couldn't have said it better myself," he agreed and began to lower himself. *Maybe I can get up some power by pushing myself off and hitting it with both feet,* he thought.

At the edge of the window he did just that, slamming both feet into the glass, bouncing back out into space. He did it again, and again, trying to hit the same spot.

"What the hell are you *doing*?" Bertha screeched, pounding at the window with the flat of her hand. "Get me outta here!"

Raeder's mouth dropped open and he hit the window with his feet, then angled himself so that he lay sideways to the glass. The woman was obviously a heavy-worlder. Short, which was common among them, muscular and almost square in shape.

There's no way she's going to fit in the sling chair, he thought. *Heck, I'm not sure she'll fit through the window.*

"I'm trying to break the glass," he shouted to her. "It's the only way we can get you out. But it's real hard to break."

"Oh, for crying out loud!" Bertha snarled.

She shoved her elbow through the glass just in front of Peter's chest. He stared in astonishment at the pale, muscular joint as she withdrew it.

"Damn!" she snapped. "That stuff's not supposed to cut you and look at that!"

Blood was trickling slowly from a tiny scratch just above her elbow.

Raeder took a deep breath and got himself in position.

"Okay," he warned, "stand back, face away from the window, I'm coming through." He stamped several times and pieces flew into the compartment.

"Thanks for the warning," she said, brushing safety glass from her hair. "Name's Beryl," she added, thrusting out a large hand.

Peter took it, grinning like a fool. He'd been positive she was going to say Bertha and then he would have laughed like a fool. *Which, based on what I've seen of her temperament, she wouldn't have taken too well at all.* He finished hauling in the line and displayed the sling attached to it.

Beryl looked at it, looked at him, then back at the sling.

"I can't fit in that thing," she sneered.

"Um, no, guess not," he agreed. "Uh, what about if we made some kind of harness for you? Could you let yourself down that way?"

She picked up the line and shook it at him. In her hands it looked like a piece of string.

"What do you think?" she asked, her eyes smoldering.

"It's a lot stronger than it looks," Peter assured her.

"This thing," Beryl said, holding up the seat, "was not designed to carry someone of my bulk. I think it's fair to assume that the line isn't either," she said, enunciating each word as she flung it aside.

We could pull the chute down . . . he thought briefly. *Hmm, maybe not.* For one thing he doubted her fingers would go through the mesh. *Besides, they're not really designed to take your whole weight. They're more for controlling and breaking your fall from the inside.* And to get Beryl inside they'd have to cut the thing almost all the way through. *Which brings us full circle.* He sat down.

Beryl gave him a disgusted look and went to the

window, just managing to catch Sarah's feet before they hit her in the stomach.

"Oh!" Sarah said. "Hi."

"Oh, hi yourself," Beryl said, pulling her in.

"Good," Peter said. "We can either combine these seats and lower you using both lines, or you can hold on to both and climb down."

"I look like a mountain climber to you, buddy?"

Raeder looked at her. *No, you look like somebody who shoves mountains out of her way.*

"Look," he said aloud, "we don't have many options. And none of the options we have are really all that good. But the worst option you've got is to stay here until rescue comes."

She looked at him. He shrugged.

"You're right," she said and swallowed hard. "I'm just so damn scared."

Sarah gave her a pat on the shoulder. "You can do this," she said.

Raeder showed her how to rig an emergency harness, and with much biting of lips she managed it.

"You're strong," he told her. "You can do this."

"And it's not that far," Sarah reassured her.

"I can do this," Beryl repeated in a shaking voice.

They nodded at her and Raeder helped her to sit on the window sill.

"Oh, God," Beryl said as she looked down. "I think I'm going to be sick." Then she glared at Sarah. "It is too a long way down."

"You can do this," Peter said calmly. "Just remember what we told you."

Beryl took a deep breath and swung out, her eyes went wide as her feet touched against the side of the car.

"Hey!" she said. "This is easy!" She swung out and down again. "This is fun!"

Peter and Sarah smiled at one another and yelled encouraging words at their unwilling student. In an amazingly short time Beryl was on the ground waving at them enthusiastically. They waved back.

Then the train began to fold. Peter and Sarah leapt out and grabbed the two swinging lines as the car above them came down, forcing Beryl's car to bend towards them. The falling train left them both descending rapidly, out of control. They found themselves climbing frantically upward, in through the window of one of the cars. There was a pause in the car's fall and they both dived back out, sliding down the rope so fast their palms were cut.

Looking up over his shoulder Raeder saw the car above them poised, balancing by some trick of gravity on the top end of Beryl's car. They hit the ground and started running just as the car overbalanced and fell.

Sarah looked back and pushed Peter sideways, he fell, she tripped on him and they began to roll down a steep incline, screaming their heads off.

The ground shook as the fifty-foot-long car struck— glass exploded and trees and bushes snapped, a choking cloud of dust rose accompanied by a cluster of panicked avian life. It looked like someone had blown a huge cloud of multicolored bubbles.

When the dust cleared they could see that their car had broken off clean, leaving two cars still attached to the mag-lev track. They also saw that they had landed a mere five feet away from the fallen giant.

"Oh," Sarah said and hugged him.

I don't think I can be that articulate, Peter thought as he dazedly stroked her back.

CHAPTER THREE

An hour and a half later things were beginning to look organized. Many of the passengers turned out to be military, so the injured were laid out in precise rows being tended to, food and water were in one area, uninjured civilians in another.

"Things are looking good," Sarah said approvingly.

"Yeah," Raeder growled. "But where is everybody? Those rescue crews are *late*."

The conductors had told them that the train tripped certain telltales as it went along to show where it was at any time. Not to mention satellite information. By now the station had to know that something was wrong, despite the strange loss of communication.

And still no one came.

They were passing what they'd come to consider

the civilian enclave when the middle Faron girl skipped up to them and fixed adoring eyes on Peter.

"Does your daddy know where you are?" he asked.

She nodded, smiling happily.

"How's your mom?" Sarah asked.

Instantly the little girl's face fell.

"She's crying!" she confided, obviously devastated. Moms weren't supposed to cry.

"Well," Peter said calmly, "that was quite a bump on the head she got. You'd cry too, I bet."

The girl looked dubious. "I'm brave," she said.

"True. She is," Peter said to Sarah. "Very."

"Piggyback?" the kid said reaching up.

"O-kay." Raeder sounded dubious now. "Where's your dad? I'll give you a lift over to him."

Her brows came down in an impatient little curl and her lower lip slid out.

"Well, *he* said I should go play." Her voice implied that Dad didn't care if he ever saw her again.

"When was that, honey?" Sarah asked.

The look she gave Sarah left no doubt as to what she thought of this *woman* butting into a conversation with the object of her adoration. An adoration that was beginning to have a pretty shaky foundation with all this talking and no piggyback ride in sight. She shrugged, in a way that indicated the usual devotion to time of a five-year-old.

"Okay," Raeder said, squatting down. "Hop aboard and we'll go look for him."

"Yaaay!" She ran around Peter and threw her arms around his neck in her own patented choke hold. "Giddyap!"

"Remember before," Raeder rasped out, rearranging her hands. "Gotta give your horsie some air."

They left smiles in their wake as they hip-hopped towards the injured section. Once within its borders though, he started walking and saying "Sssh," to the enthusiastic girl on his back.

"Demi! Where've you been, honey?" Her father came up and pulled her from Peter's back.

"Hi, Daddy."

"Thanks for finding her," Faron said. "That's, what, four times you've come to our rescue today? Come meet my wife," he said before Raeder could answer.

"Oh, no," Sarah said. From where she stood she could see Lisa Faron, who looked bruised and exhausted. *Nobody in that condition should be forced to meet anybody.* "We've got to go talk to the conductors." She grabbed Peter's arm. "We better get moving, sweetie."

Raeder shook Faron's hand, waved to Demi and took Sarah's arm.

As they walked away Peter said, "Conductors?" out of the side of his mouth.

Sarah grinned. "It was an excuse. I just didn't think the poor woman was up to meeting people."

"That's what I figured," he said. "But I liked the sweetie part." He put an arm around her and gave her a squeeze. "Actually, I'm trying to restrain myself from bugging the conductors again."

"Yeah," she agreed with a sigh. "They don't know any more than we do." She kissed him. They were several moments into it, when they heard, "What the heck was that?"

They opened their eyes and saw nothing different.

"What?" Raeder shouted over his shoulder.

"That white flash?" an older man said. "Came from over that way." He pointed off northeast.

Peter and Sarah looked at one another. That was the direction of the spaceport. *Naw,* he thought.

"Fusion bomb?" Sarah said, her lips stiff.

"Airburst," Raeder agreed. He turned to look at

her. "Something in the five-megaton range, I'd say. We've got to get to Marjorie Base. Soonest." To the *Invincible*.

He looked around and, seeing a rocky outcropping, climbed up and put his hands to his mouth.

"Attention!" he shouted. "Attention! Any uninjured military personnel rally to me." Raeder repeated it again. They came running, worried frowns on their faces, many of them bearing bruises and bandages. They were followed by a crowd of able-bodied civilians.

"I'm Commander Raeder of the C.S.S. *Invincible*. This is Lieutenant Commander James. We've got to get back to Twillingate and the spaceport."

"What about us?" one of the civilians piped up. "You're not going to just leave us here, are you? What about the injured?"

"To be honest," Peter answered, "you may well be safer here than in a city. Once we're in Twillingate we can find out why no help has come for us. In addition, our leaving leaves more food and water for you."

"Are you thinking of walking out of here?" one of the conductors asked, a tinge of horrified disbelief in her voice.

Raeder grimaced. Under perfect circumstances they were a full day's hard march from the city. And the country they'd traversed to this point, while beautiful scenery, was lousy for foot travel. One major river, some swamp, lots of ravines and plenty of unfriendly wildlife.

He opened his mouth to speak, then stopped. "Listen," he said.

Over the rustling breeze and chirps of insects could be heard a high-pitched whine. Definitely mechanical and growing nearer and louder as it continued.

Everyone scanned the skies, finally focusing on the northeast. There a pair of tiny black dots could been seen; they swelled with astonishing speed into two rescue boats. The boats hovered, found a viable landing space and came down slowly. People rushed to greet them, turning their heads from the upflung leaves and dirt the craft's old-fashioned, but powerful, rotors stirred as they landed.

A single door opened on the side of each vehicle and ramps were deployed. Men and women in pale blue uniforms disembarked, carrying med kits. An older man stood at the top of one the ramps and signaled for silence.

"Due to circumstances beyond our control, at the moment we will only be able to take the most severely wounded victims of the crash," he said.

There was a universal sound of distress from the waiting crowd.

"What circumstances?" a woman called out. A chorus of, "Yeah!" echoed from the crowd.

"Communications are down," the blue-clad man told them. "I really don't know the full story. All I know is that we won't be able to return here for a full day at the very least."

Now the crowd made a sound of alarm.

"We have tents, cots, blankets, food and water," the aid man said. "You'll be in no danger. And we will be evacuating the most injured among you. As well as leaving behind some of our qualified medical personnel. By tomorrow we hope to have more emergency vehicles available to come for you."

Raeder had stood listening with his arms crossed over his chest, backed by the military personnel he'd gathered together.

"Well," he said grimly, "I guess it's up to us, people. If we're getting back to Twillingate any time soon we're going to have to make this train—" he glanced up at the track above them "—what's left of it, run."

There was an affirmative mumble in response.

"Do we have any engineering personnel among us?" Peter asked.

Three hands went up and Raeder found he had one full lieutenant and two second lieutenants.

"Okay, people." The commander pointed upward. "How do I make that work?"

"Well, sir," said Lieutenant Tiffany Shelton, obviously thinking on her feet, "that last car up there has a set of controls, just like the first one that crashed. We'll need to lighten the load first. I'd estimate that there are only about eighty of us, so we can easily squeeze together in one car."

"Okay," Peter said with a nod. "We decouple the second car, remove the seats and anything else we can get rid of. How do we make it go?"

The three engineering types looked at one another, changed position, rubbed their chins and noses, nodded and grunted, then turned as one to Raeder.

Shelton said, "There are emergency batteries on every car. We can scavenge those and cobble together a sort of localized mag-lev system. The batteries are supposed to last twelve hours, but this will drain them in at best five." She looked doubtful for a moment, silently consulted with her fellow engineers. "Actually, more like four," she admitted.

Raeder shrugged, then shook his head.

"Better than walking all the way," he said.

The trip had taken six hours to reach this remote spot. But they'd been traveling very slowly. Still, even if they had to walk cross country for the last leg of the trip it would save them at least eight to ten hours.

"Okay people," he said to his group. "Let's get to it. Sarah, talk to the conductors, find out how to

decouple that car. Then take a team and do it. You,"
he pointed out several men and women, "you, you
get the emergency batteries disconnected from those
downed cars."

He sent someone to the emergency aid crew to
scavenge any tools they could to remove the seats.
Then Raeder climbed up to the mag-lev track for, he
hoped, the last time to help with the work.

It was pitch dark when she woke. The first thing
Second Lieutenant Cynthia Robbins was aware of was
the hissing sound that had wakened her. The second
was the complete darkness around here, a darkness
that could only be a closed compartment with no
lights at all, like velvet lying on the surface of your
eyes, with only the strobes and flashes of your own
retinas to light it.

The third was a slightly musky, mildly astringent
scent. She knew that scent. It was Paddy. And though
she usually enjoyed the scent of the man she loved
this was a bit too much of a good thing. He lay upon
her so that she could hardly breathe.

She meant to say, "Paddy?" but it came out,
"Pdddg?"

That's when she remembered. They had been on
their way to a meeting with the quartermaster to
wrangle over a lost parts order. The *Invincible* was
lodged at the repair facility over at what had been
a civilian luxury liner's berth. Nothing at the military
site had been able to accommodate her.

It was inconvenient being miles away from head-
quarters and being required to slog over almost every
day for some meeting or other. She and Paddy had
been grizzling about it as they trod down the long
tunnel leading from the underground shuttle to the
military base.

"Bad enough," Paddy had been saying, "that we have to ride over here two and three times a day." Which was wild New Hibernian exaggeration at its finest. "But this bloody tunnel is two miles long if it's an inch!"

More like half a mile, but that's pardonable.

"Couldn't they at least have a moving walkway?" he demanded.

"They probably want us to get our daily exercise," Cynthia remembered telling him.

And then . . . and then she woke up with Paddy on top of her, crushing her, in fact.

"Pad," she managed to say, shoving at him weakly. "Mmm-ove."

After a moment she felt him jerk, then shift slightly. "Wha?" he asked.

"Move," she pleaded. "You're crushing me."

He slid away from her, and she shifted onto her side, which seemed to give them more room.

"Where?" the big man said plaintively. Then she felt him stir, as though he had lifted his head to look around. "What the bludy hell happened?"

"Gas?" she suggested, still hearing that nerve-wracking hiss. "Some sort of explosion?"

Cynthia waved her arm around above her head and met no obstacle. She sat up cautiously, suppressing a groan as she moved. Whatever had hit them had left her feeling one hundred percent bruised. Continuously waving her arm above her, she carefully got her feet under her and started to rise. When she was standing straight the lieutenant stretched to her full height and found the ceiling. It seemed to have a tentlike shape, a bit asymmetric; it was hard to tell in the pitch darkness.

"I think you could stand up if you're careful," she said.

"Oh, darlin', I don't think I want to stand up at all."

"Are you hurt?" she asked in alarm, squatting down and reaching for him.

"Well, I've felt better, acushla. But if I am hurt it's nothing that will kill me."

Cynthia found his face and cupped his broad cheek in her small hand.

"Then call me Lieutenant." There was relief and a smile in her voice though she spoke crisply. "We're on duty."

Paddy grinned in the dark.

"Aye, Lieutenant, me love. Though I think we're alone here and no disgrace to anybody but ourselves."

There was a sliding sound, as of debris shifting, and a light went on, almost blinding them after the intense darkness. In a moment they could see again and beheld a face, discernable only by the whites of its eyes staring out of the dirt.

"Help," said the captain's dry voice.

"Civilians in uniform," Mai Ling Ju, the executive officer of the *Invincible* muttered.

She maneuvered the all-terrain tractor over the rim of a crater as bits of conversation drifted in and out of her mind. A smile stretched her full lips as she remembered the captain saying: "Sir, the Romans didn't conquer the world by holding meetings about it, they did it by killing all those who opposed them. I must excuse myself now because it is my duty to prepare my ship to fight the Commonwealth's enemies and time is growing short."

Rear Admiral Covil's mouth was still opening and closing in silent, flummoxed outrage as Knott strode from the meeting room. That Ju remained in his place had done nothing to mollify Covil.

But what else could Knott do? There had been so many useless meetings that the crew of the *Invincible* had been forced to conclude that the so-called officers on this out-of-the-way little base found some sort of cachet in rubbing elbows with real fighting commanders.

Then, in the middle of Covil's diatribe the roof fell in.

Fibians, Ju thought. *From the cut of their craft.* The energy footprints had been quite distinctive—not too different from Commonwealth or Mollie spacecraft, the laws of physics were universal—but distinctive. She found herself intrigued and excited by this exotic enemy. Wary too—they were efficient killers, the Intelligence reports said.

The matter of how they'd managed to get the drop on a military base was a question for another day. Their first pass had done extensive damage, burying a number of the connecting tunnels that honeycombed the mostly underground base.

"Sir!" a young rating had called out to her officer as they'd entered the command center. "Section seven is calling for ammunition."

"Tell them the tunnels are collapsed in that area," her commander had answered. "We'll have to send it overland."

"You can't do that," the rear admiral had spluttered. "It would be suicide! I absolutely forbid it."

Ju heard the young officer in charge of section seven say: "We're down to making obscene remarks and antic gestures out here, sir, and it's not working!"

She doubted that the rear admiral heard her; the commander had spoken over her comment to say, "Sir, section seven is responsible for covering this part of the base. If they don't get some ammunition we, and they, are going to be easy meat for the bu—enemy."

Nice save, Ju thought. *I'll bet the rear admiral would have lambasted you for twenty minutes for saying bugs instead of enemy.* Not that Covil was a bad man, but he was a civilian administrator, hastily promoted, not a battle leader, and he was out of his depth.

She kept the jouncing train of missiles in the shadow of the crater's rim as long as possible. The Fibians could see into the ultraviolet range without the need for mechanical aid. So they could see her in the shadow just as well as out of it—better perhaps. But there were Mollie pilots among them, and the rim provided some protection from attack. Besides, it was instinctively the right choice.

Her insides squeezed with a raw terror that her mind kept at bay. Ahead of her was the low dome that marked her destination. There was the occasional burst of laser fire—visible due to the guide-beams, and an occasional flare as dust drifted into the pencil-thin columns of energetic photons—but no missiles launched. Because she had them. She'd make a beautiful explosion if some bug looked down at the wrong moment and targeted her.

"I can't ask anyone to take that risk!" the rear admiral had insisted.

"That's what we're here for, sir," Ju had said into the silence that greeted that remark. "So civilians won't have to take those risks. I'll go." To the commander she'd said, "Where do I suit up?"

"You can't!"

"I can, sir. I must." Then she'd left him.

She was rather proud of that *I can and must* remark, it would make a great epitaph. *Hey,* Ju warned herself, *no negative thinking.*

In any case, she'd rather die trying to save herself than be squashed by the bugs because Covil couldn't bring himself to order people to risk their lives. If that was negative thinking, so be it.

Ahead something struck, a bomb or a kinetic-energy missile, throwing up a fountain of moondust and rock that fell with eerie, silvery slowness. Coolly she veered around the new crater, hoping it was an accident and not a direct attack on her slow-moving little vehicle. Before her, perhaps five hundred yards away, she could see the jet-black opening that led into section seven. Laser fire cut the ground directly in front of her.

Not a mistake, then, she thought.

Paddy and Cynthia had dug the dirt away from the captain's chest and shoulders to find his waist pinched by a large slab of masonry. The masonry itself would have been fairly light, being made of foamed syncrete, but it supported tons of earth and only a miracle had kept it from slicing Knott in half. Paddy and Cynthia supported it to either side of the captain with pieces of the same stuff, then dug around him, letting his body down inch by inch with painful slowness. When they pulled on his shoulders Knott cried out.

"I'm stuck!" he said. "And I think whatever it is, it's lodged in my leg."

Paddy and Cynthia looked at one another, a silent, *Oh, shit,* passing between them.

"Which side, sir?" Cynthia asked.

"Right," Knott said. He closed his eyes.

Cynthia wasn't sure whether he'd passed out for a moment or was just being incredibly stoic; she redoubled her efforts at digging out his legs. She and Paddy had taken off their shirts to use them as bags for the dirt she dug and passed back to him.

"How long, d'ye think, before they come for us?"

Paddy asked her, whispering as though the captain couldn't hear him.

Knott politely kept silent, but thought: *Hopefully before the air goes bad or escapes.*

"One thing at a time, Chief," Cynthia said. "Let's get the captain free first and do some first aid on his wounds. Then we'll worry about digging our way out."

It made Paddy grin. Both the use of his rank before the near-unconscious captain and her assumption that they'd rescue themselves.

"Right you are, Lieutenant." He packed his answer with all the warmth he felt for her, and in the dark of the tunnel she was digging he thought he saw the twinkle of her smile.

They'd taken their time over uncovering Knott, pausing every now and then to shore up the accidental roof overhead. And also in the hope that they wouldn't damage him more by moving him too soon. At last Cynthia had reached the place where the captain was caught.

She swallowed hard. A long piece of steel had plunged through the meat of Knott's calf just behind the bone and into the ground beneath. It was bleeding, but not pulsing, which she took to be a good sign. But she felt utterly helpless. They couldn't remove it, they couldn't bandage the wound, a tourniquet would take constant tending.

She crawled out of the hole she'd made.

"We can't pull him out," she told Paddy. She put a hand on his arm and squeezed lightly. "We've got to get out of here."

Paddy rubbed the back of his neck and looked around their tiny shelter.

"Which way?" he asked, sweeping his arms around, smacking his hand on the wall. "Ow!"

Her eyes widened and she looked around. Which

way had they been heading, how far from the station, how far from the shuttle? With an effort of will she forced herself to remember where she'd been when the captain had turned on his light. From there she could remember how she had been lying before she stood. Had they fallen backward or forward? She glanced at the captain.

Okay, the captain was walking towards us. So, that means that if we dig towards his feet we should reach the station. She suppressed the thought that they might have been thrown around in the blast. *It must have been an explosion, at least. Accidental? Some sort of enemy attack?*

"That way," she said. "I'll keep digging away from the captain's feet, that should get us to the station."

"I'll pack the dirt in there," Paddy said, indicating the deeper side of their cubby.

He didn't argue about who should do the excavating. Her small form meant there would be less dirt to move, and given the small space they had for it, that was a factor. Once Cyndy reached help they could pull dirt out the other side. He tried not to think of what would happen to all of them if, beyond the captain's feet, Cynthia dug her way to the moon's surface instead of the tunnel.

"Section seven, this is Mai Ling Ju, XO of the *Invincible*. I'm approximately five hundred yards from you now, towing a shipment of seekers and antimissile missiles. Would you be so good as to lay down some covering fire for me, please?"

A relieved grin split Lieutenant Sese Ortega's dark face.

"Yes, ma'am," she said over the com. "I see you, Ms. Ju, we will cov—"

Overhead, something went by fast enough to be

a blur against the stars. The beam that struck downward was visible in vacuum, probably a plasma cannon. Rock gouted, and part of the left rear corner of the hindmost cart in her slow-moving train was hit.

"What happened?" Ortega demanded.

"By some miracle, while that hit, it only struck a glancing blow," Ju answered. "But my helmet readout is showing a big, big jump in radiation. Cracked casing on a warhead, probably. So if you people aren't already in your suits, get into them now."

Sese frowned. "Ma'am, I can't allow a damaged bomb into this facility," she said.

"I completely understand your position, Lieutenant," Ju said calmly. "However, while there is a cure for radiation poisoning there is none for being blown to bits. Which you most certainly will be if you don't get some munitions in there." The XO felt a sensation of heat coming from behind her, and a prickle on her skin like sunburn. Totally imaginary; it would be hours before the symptoms manifested themselves, protected as she was.

Sensing the lieutenant's hesitation Ju said, "We can decouple the damaged bomb and shove it back outside, which should mitigate the damage somewhat. But right now, I am ordering you to open that crash door."

Well, thought Ortega, tapping in the command on her console, *it's a direct order, it's out of my hands.* Which made her feel better. Enough so that she and her team successfully diverted the frantically attacking Fibians.

Finally a call came through from below.

"We're locked and loaded, Lieutenant."

A very evil smile came over her face at the news. "Well, then," she said, "let's rock and roll."

❖   ❖   ❖

Squadron Leader "Rotten Ronnie" Sutton held his fire. If he hit the low-flying Fibian its crash would damage the base more than the bugs' bombs were doing. He waited, infinitely patient, or as patient as you could be while moving at interplanetary speeds this close to cold, *very hard* rock. Very soon now the bug would pull out of his run and then Sutton would have him. He hovered like a hawk; his shadow lay on the tail of the Fibian craft like a warning of doom. The enemy hared off, still low to the surface.

All the better to deny you room to dodge, Sutton thought grimly. His fingertips moved in the couch gloves, and a squeal sounded in his ears as the idiot-savant brain of the seeker missile locked on and launched. The Speed lurched under him; this close, there was a barely perceptible instant before a globe of magenta fire exploded before him. The expanding ball of gases shook the Commonwealth fighter like transit through the outer envelope of an atmosphere. He flipped the Speed end-for-end and spent fuel to kill velocity, then arrowed upward. A giant slow-motion avalanche rolled down the dead canyons of Marjorie as the Fibian craft's huge kinetic energy was converted into vapor and heat and motion.

They fight as if their lives don't matter, he thought, with a tinge of disgust. Any species capable of building star-spanning craft should care if they lived or died. *The Mollies are fanatics, but they're* human, *at least. These Fibians fight like they're units in a machine. Fungible units, at that, like ammunition.* He didn't think they hated humans so much that killing them was a mania for them. He didn't believe they were capable of any sort of passion.

So why die doing it?

He fired his coil gun, recoil helping to bring the nose of his Speed on target; he watched a Mollie

Speed disintegrate, flaming pieces spinning off like some supersonic fireworks display. *That* one had at least been trying to dodge. . . .

There were crisply adjusted plans and wry jokes exchanged between pilots on the com. And it seemed that every second a Mollie or a Fibian died in flames. But there were more of them than there were Welters and large sections of the base were damaged. Balls of flame repeatedly shot up to be quickly extinguished in an area where broken pipes mixed volatile gases. The exposed dome of the main station appeared mostly intact, a vast relief.

His own battle computers shouted warning. Something huge was crawling downward, a fog of energetic particles hiding the details. Then the passionless soprano of the AI spoke: *Vessel is carrier.*

Shouts of triumph echoed through his headset. The enemy was breaking off. . . . It had been a raid, not an invasion.

"Go get 'em!" he shouted. "Let's give them a going-away party they'll remember!"

Pushing his Speed to redline, Sutton pursued a Fibian. It stayed just far enough in front that he sensed the bug had calculated the range of his weapons to a nicety. The squadron leader gritted his teeth and pressed on furiously.

"Warning," the Speed's computer said calmly. "Distance from base is about to exceed the amount of fuel available for return to base."

"Damn!" Sutton bellowed. A disciplined warrior, he peeled off from his chase, his heart bitter at being cheated of his prey.

The mother ship must be lurking out there waiting to pick them up. Though with these creatures, both Fib and Mollie, there could be no certainty of that.

"Damn," he said again, quietly. Then, "Let's return to the *Invincible,* ladies and gentlemen. Nice piece of work."

He didn't wax poetic over their victory, for it didn't feel like one. Most of the damage, and it looked extensive, had been done in the first few moments of the surprise attack. No help for it, but he felt failure in the destruction below.

How had they done it? The squadron leader sighed. *Another traitor,* he thought wearily. Well, that was Come By Chance Base's problem. At least *Invincible* hadn't taken more damage. *That would have been a shame. Poor old girl's barely gotten her bandages off.*

Paddy looked around for someplace to put the new bag full of dirt that Cynthia had passed out to him. He stood with his big feet on either side of Knott's head, his shoulders brushing the dirt he'd piled up and packed in as much as he could. There was no more room, nowhere to place this new consignment.

He began to feel buried alive. Which he was, but he'd managed not to know it before now.

"My love," he said. "Ye'll have to stop, now."

"Lieutenant," came the muffled reply.

"Come out of there," Paddy said, "and look at this place, now."

"Lieutenant," she insisted, grunting as she wiggled backwards down the tunnel. "Come . . . out . . . Lieutenant."

Her feet came out first. They poked around, seeking someplace that didn't have Paddy or some other blockage in it and found none.

"Oh," Cynthia said. *What do I do now?* she wondered. She wanted to ask out loud, but Knott was injured, perhaps unconscious, and Paddy was of a lower rank. *Then again, Commander Raeder never seems to feel it's out of line to ask for advice from Chief arap Moi, or Paddy for that matter.* Of course, this was a different situation. Cynthia licked her lips, then spat out the dirt she'd gathered.

"Do you have any ideas?" she asked.

"You've found no sign of light or gettin' through?" Paddy asked, his voice tight with tension.

"No," she admitted after a long moment.

Cynthia heard him mumble something.

"What?" she called.

"D'ye hear that tappin'?" he asked. "It's been drivin' me mad, so it has."

The lieutenant listened. After a moment, muffled by the dirt around her, she did. *That can't be natural,* she thought. It was far too rhythmical.

"It sounds . . . like Morse code," she said slowly.

"D'ye know what it's sayin'?" Paddy demanded, hope rising in his voice.

Cynthia shook her head, then answered aloud, "No. I'm sorry to say I don't. The captain might."

"The captain is out of it," Paddy said, sounding more like himself.

He took a small tool out of his pocket and, snaking his hand into a small hole in the packed dirt, drummed it on the pipe that he was certain was feeding them oxygen. There was a pause, then a hammering came back and he joined in with glee.

"They've found us," he cried. "Glory be, acushla, they've found us!"

Cynthia laughed along with him.

"I'd hug you if I could," she said.

"Allow me then to help you, Lieutenant my dearling."

Paddy reached down and grabbed her slender ankles, pulling her out of the hole in a shower of dirt.

She squealed in surprise and found herself doing a handstand before him.

"Now what?" she demanded. It seemed impossible that she could turn herself right side up, or be righted by Paddy. There just wasn't room.

"Let me help ye, love." He clasped her about the middle.

"Don't," she snapped. "I'll fall on the captain."

"Sure, my darling, ye can't stay like this!" he said. "Not for the hours it might be." He started to shift her weight.

Cynthia smacked him on the ankle. "No!"

Instinctively he lifted his foot and felt himself over-balancing, which would indeed bring them both down on top of the unconscious captain. With a cry he threw himself backwards and to his shock continued falling. There was a weak wind as air rushed past him, through a hole in the tunnel ceiling. A respirator was thrust over his nose and mouth and hands hauled him backwards.

"The captain," Cynthia managed, pointing, before her voice was muffled.

"He's caught on a spike," Paddy added, removing his rig to do so.

The rescuers were already in the hole.

"Okay, we got him," a voice said.

They were directed down the tunnel to the shuttle, which sped them back to the *Invincible*'s luxury berth. The battle had been played out while they were buried and they found that all they had left to do was wait for their Speeds to come home.

CHAPTER FOUR

Raeder, Sarah and their small company of mixed military jogged to the top of a hill, every eye on the smoke boiling up to the clouds.

Most people on Come By Chance lived in the cities, which was typical of this generation of colony planets. Twillingate was set in parkland, and rose from the land without the prelude of suburbs. There were isolated farms here and there, maybe an automated mine in the distance, but no towns or hamlets. The city was essentially all there was.

That distant smoke represented the destruction of an entire planet's budding civilization.

Mile after mile they had walked after the mag-lev's batteries had given out, then run—towards the fire. Peter's lungs burned, and there was beginning to be a taste of copper in the back of his throat.

They'd encountered no moving traffic for miles,

though many a small car or truck had been pulled to the roadside, sometimes surrounded by perplexed drivers and their families. The closer they got to the city, the more abandoned cars they passed.

They topped the hill and Raeder held up his hand to halt them. Twillingate had been a symphony of garden and flowerbed and soaring pastel towers. Now it was a sea of fire and rubble, twisted girders rising above flame and smoke.

"God," someone said. "So that's what a nuke impact looks like."

"No," Raeder said, shaking his head. "There's no crater. That's airbursts—defense missiles. But some of them got almighty close."

At least we're using clean bombs, Raeder thought, shaken. Not much radiation would fall onto the city, with its attendant horrors. Still, it was a vision of hell.

"Look!" Sarah said. Her arm flashed out to point at a pair of plasma plumes burning their way towards the moon.

Raeder felt a smile of profound relief tug at his lips as he watched the twin magenta flames pierce the sky.

"The military spaceport is still functioning," he said.

"Thank God," Sarah muttered. "But how do we get on one of the shuttles?"

"One thing at a time, Lieutenant Commander," Peter advised. "First we've got to *get* to the spaceport."

He waved his arm and they continued on their way. As they jogged along Peter thought about this attack. Come By Chance was well within the Commonwealth's borders. It should have been impossible for the enemy to make this kind of strike.

Of course it's probably a suicide raid, he thought. Still, it was something that made very little sense. This planet was primarily a vacation destination; it had no heavy industries, no irreplaceable minerals.

True, there's going to be a psychological factor here. It's upsetting in the extreme that they could get this close. Maybe that was the point. If they can get this close undetected, they can get to Earth undetected. But it's not going to really hurt us.

Which didn't seem like the Mollies. Oh, they were more than willing to sacrifice themselves for their cause, but what they really liked was taking hundreds of Welters with them.

"What's your take on this, Lieutenant Commander?" Raeder asked, huffing slightly.

"They're telling us they can reach us anywhere," Sarah said. "Or they're trying to soften us up."

They came to a halt. The city street before them was blocked with burning rubble. Where the tops of buildings lay smashed the smoking heaps were spiked with daggers of glass and twisted metal.

Screams could be heard and weeping—voices calling for help, or names being shouted over and over.

"Somehow," Peter said, his face grim, "I don't feel very softened."

Sarah glanced at him sideways and growled, "Me either."

"Sir?"

Raeder turned. It was Lieutenant Shelton who had spoken. He nodded his permission to continue.

"How do we walk away from this?" She gestured to the destruction before them. "These people need all the help they can get." *Tell us what to do*, her eyes begged.

He looked around. The city services had been trashed along with everything else; probably most of the civil defense net as well. Civilian electronics would have been fried by the electromagnetic pulse of the exploding bombs, so their emergency teams and hospitals, assuming any had survived, were out of communication. Not to mention that the whole city was in ruins around them. His mouth hardened to a thin line.

"We're military," he told the people with him. "It's our duty to report in. Some of us will undoubtedly be assigned planetside to aid with the wounded, to help clean this mess up. The rest of us are probably urgently needed on Marjorie Base."

He gestured towards the moon with a jerk of his head, and there was a stir in the ranks. Damage there would be more dangerous, and much harder to deal with. That was why you put military installations on airless moons or planetoids when you could.

"Either way, to be put to most effective use, they'll need to know who we are and what skills we have to offer. Not to mention the fact that our families will be interested in whether we've survived. So our ultimate goal *must* be to reach the spaceport." He looked at the somber faces around him. "That doesn't mean we're going to totally ignore something that throws itself in front of us. It just means we can't help everyone in the city all at once."

He turned and scanned the street before him. *Impassable,* he judged.

"All right," he said, turning back. "The spaceport is outside the city to the northeast. We're going around." Peter started off at a jog, Sarah at his side and, after the briefest hesitation, the others joined them.

It was hard to keep moving towards their goal. From the distance tormented cries cut into their souls as they sped past. Peter kept his eyes resolutely ahead and behind him his followers did too.

"Mo-meee!"

Peter's head jerked around; the call seemed to have come from just beside him. Less than ten feet away and dangling twenty feet above the ground a child clung to a pipe, small legs kicking furiously.

"Stop kicking," Raeder shouted. "Hold on, we're coming."

Nobody else seemed to be around here. All the voices they heard were muted by distance.

Raeder paused and studied the structure, his eyes following a path up to the terrified child. Hands and feet followed the route his eyes had found and in moments he was beside the weeping youngster.

"Gotcha," Peter said, grabbing the child, a girl, by her waist.

Without being told she clutched him around the neck, short legs clamped around his middle. He could feel the little body gasping for air, then suddenly the kid broke out with a wail like an air-raid siren. *There goes the other ear,* he thought.

When he reached the ground Shelton took the child, softly saying "Sssh," and bouncing her soothingly.

"Another little girl," Sarah said, smiling at Peter.

"Moo-kie!" the little one said, pointing upward with a chubby hand. "I want my Mookie!"

There was a small avalanche from the building and they stepped backward, Lieutenant Shelton shielding the girl with her body. When the dust cleared the kid was still demanding, "Mookie!"

"What the heck is mookie?" Raeder mumbled to Sarah.

Sarah shrugged, put her hand up to protect her eyes and looked where the child was pointing.

"Oh! Some kind of airfish," she said.

It was a little pale purple blimp, trailing fins gracefully waving, black button eyes staring at nothing.

"Mookie!" The little girl reached out for her pet with both hands.

"I'm not going back for that thing," Peter said.

Mookie was tied to a hook by a long golden ribbon; it bounced gently in a light breeze.

"It's a bladder on a string, Sarah!"

"I didn't say anything," she spluttered.

"Mommy!" the child shouted.

Sarah and Raeder looked up to see a woman's hand dangle over the edge of what had recently been the floor of her apartment.

"Now *that* I'll go back for," Peter said.

"So would I," Sarah agreed. She handed him a coil of the thin wire rope she'd lifted from the train. "While you're up there, don't forget to bring down Mookie."

The woman was alive, but unconscious. *Just as well,* Peter had thought. One of her arms was badly broken. If she'd been awake getting her down would have been a nightmare, for all of them.

They'd rigged up a stretcher from parts of a doorframe and a blanket and they'd resumed their trek to the spaceport.

The only one among them who was at peace was the little girl. With both Mookie and Mommy beside her the world was basically complete, though it would be better if Mommy were awake. The rest was just details.

There was the flash of a plasma weapon.

"Sir!" someone called.

But Peter had caught it out of the corner of his eye. Off to his left was another blocked road, the rubble piled three meters high. Buildings on either side of the street still had several intact stories and it was obvious from the remains that this had been a very wealthy neighborhood.

Those country views, Peter thought, *they must cost the planet.*

There was a flicker of light beyond the barrier, and screams and shouts sprang up. *Okay, we're gonna have to do something about that,* he thought. He looked up and down the debris in front of him. *I guess it was too much to hope that we'd get all the way to the spaceport without something like this coming up.*

There was a flurry of shots, and the screams reached a new pitch of hysteria. Raeder turned and pointed out three soldiers; he signaled for the rest of them to continue on their way. Sarah gave him a look, but nodded. She waved the others onward, looked one last time at Raeder and moved off.

Peter and his squad climbed the barrier, finding it narrower than expected once they got to the top. Below them was a small group of men, some of them uniformed like security people, behind a barrier of rubble, weapons at the ready. They were concentrating on a building to the right of the squad. From their height Raeder and his people could look through one of the broken windows to see another group of men handling some very illegal weaponry.

"Anybody got glasses?" Raeder asked.

Somebody put a pair into his hand. So far every time they'd needed something one of them had been able to provide it. *I've seen well planned campaigns that weren't as appropriately supplied,* Peter thought. He brought the glasses to his eyes. The men in the building leapt into view. *That's Skelly Briggs!*

This put a different complexion on things. Skelly Briggs was connected to every sleazy enterprise on Come By Chance. Actually, sleazy might be far too complimentary; loathsome, or criminal, or better yet both would be a more fitting description of old Skelly's business practices.

"Skelly Briggs," he said aloud.

"You're kidding! Sir," said one of the ratings.

Raeder handed him the glasses.

"Wow." The kid lowered the glasses and looked at the commander. "What are we gonna do, sir?"

"Hmm," said Raeder. "One of the biggest thugs on the planet and his torpedoes are shooting at each other. Is this Space Command's business?" He looked thoughtful, shrugged and looked at the young rating beside him. "No." He began to back down the pile of debris. He looked up at his team, who stared back down at him, puzzled. "Well, c'mon," he said.

They looked down at the fighting, looked at each other and began backing down to follow Raeder.

"They're citizens," one of the soldiers said to Peter, his voice troubled. "Evil citizens, it's true, but citizens nonetheless."

"We're not planetary police," the commander answered him. "This isn't our affair."

"We helped the little girl and her mother," another said.

"A much less complicated situation," Peter told them. "Neither of them were shooting for one thing. For another they were not well-known scum of the worst sort. I'm not putting my life, or yours for that matter, on the line for a bunch of sociopaths and psychotics. Those guys could stop fighting any time they wanted to. The only thing our interference would accomplish is to temporarily unite them in firing on us. End of discussion."

Put your breath to better use getting us to the spaceport, he thought.

"What was happening?" Sarah asked when he caught up to her.

"Skelly Briggs and some of his boys were duking it out."

She stumbled, turning wide eyes on him.

"Are you sure?" she panted.

"Yeah, I'm sure. I've seen him before." He grinned mirthlessly.

"You ever know a station that could really get rid of cockroaches?" Raeder asked rhetorically. *Of course not. They're the Skelly Briggs of the insect world. They can take hard vacuum and radiation that would fry even a rat. That's why we've taken them with us to every planet and habitat we've settled.*

He'd seen Briggs before the war, actually. And before Briggs was a celebrity, when Space Command mainly battled pirates and smugglers. They'd all spent a lot of time studying up on these creeps and Skelly Briggs was one of the worst. Since the war started he'd become very patriotic, of course—meaning that making money off Space Command personnel on leave was more profitable than more grandiose illegalities.

"Wow," she said. "Of all the people to survive the bombing." Sarah shook her head. Why did things always seem to work out that way?

Before them a crowd of people scurried away from the city, then turned back. A building seemed to shimmy, then almost majestically, it slid towards the countryside, veiled in a plume of dust.

"Hey!" one of the women in the crowd shouted at them. "Where are you going?"

"We're headed toward the spaceport," Raeder said, jogging up to her. "We're military, we're going to report in."

"You're just going to ignore what's happening here?" the woman shouted, her broad face going red with fury. "People here need help and you're just going to breeze on by like nothing's happened?"

"Once we've reported in we'll be assigned where

we'll do the most good," Peter told her. "But we can't go where we're needed most until we know where that is."

"Bull!" she screamed. "You people are never where you're needed. Why the hell didn't you prevent this?" She thrust her hands at the ruined city, tears running down her cheeks. "Whole families are buried in there! You can't just leave us."

"You want help?" he said. "Okay, I'll help. HEY!" he shouted. "Listen up! Has anybody here got something to write with?"

One man held up a small tablet and stylus.

"Great. You start taking names here. When he's finished," Raeder told them, "I want you to break up into squads of five or six and go back into the city. First squad is to find someplace stable and safe for you all to spend the night. If possible. If not, you can camp out here for the night. Second squad is to find foodstuffs and water and bring them back here. Third squad is to find blankets and medical supplies, and bring them back here. The rest are to look for survivors and to try when possible to make contact with emergency services. Whenever you find emergency services tell them your names and the names of the people with you. You will all rendezvous back here in three hours. Any questions?"

No one answered. They all looked at him, then at each other. "You, with the stylus," Peter said. "What's your name?"

"Harry Pond." He was a small, older man who looked terrified that everyone was going to be relying on him.

"Gather round Harry, here, and tell him your name. Then form up into squads of five or six. Got that?"

People began milling around, slowly making their

way towards Harry. Peter touched the arm of the woman who'd been yelling at him.

"You're in charge, here. Can you remember what else it is you all have to do?" he asked.

She took a deep breath, wiped her eyes and nodded.

"Thanks," she muttered.

"Good luck," he said.

She nodded, and Peter waved his people on.

Sarah looked back over her shoulder and watched people breaking into groups. One of them started moving back towards the city.

"I guess people just need someone to tell them what to do," she said to Peter. "I mean, they *know* what they should be doing, but they just really need someone to take charge. Y'know?"

"Yup." He looked back once. "Finally, something's going right."

Just outside the city, near the spaceport, they came upon a massive field hospital. What looked like thousands of people, most of them wounded in some way, milled around, their faces exhausted and shocked.

Peter looked it over briefly, then turned to the people he'd led here.

"This looks like a civilian operation," he said. "We'll leave the woman and the little girl with them. The stretcher crew, Shelton and I will get them settled. Lieutenant Commander, you people carry on to the spaceport."

Sarah nodded briefly and jogged off with the remaining military personnel falling in behind her. Raeder watched them go, then turned back to his small party.

"Let's try over this way," he said, pointing to a large tent visible over the heads of the crowd.

He went ahead of them, gently breaking a path.

"Excuse me," he said over and over. "Wounded coming through."

People slowly moved aside, their faces dull with shock, their skin and clothes gray with dust. They were mostly quiet. Sometimes the children cried, which caused their little girl to whimper. It felt ominous, like a calm before a storm.

In a little while they were at the entrance to the tent, where a middle-aged man in a dusty, navy blue coverall sat at a card table, noteboard and stylus before him.

"Uh, we have a lady here that needs medical help," Peter said.

"Name?" the man asked.

"We don't know, she was unconscious when we found her."

"May I see her ID?" He held out a hand, not looking directly at Raeder.

"We don't have an ID. Her building was collapsing around her. Frankly it didn't occur to me that she'd need an ID under the circumstances." Peter was beginning to be a bit annoyed. *I must be a little in shock myself not to instantly recognize a bureaucrat.* "Look." *You jerk.* "This lady," he pointed to the figure on the stretcher with both hands, "needs help."

The man looked bored.

"Is she a citizen?"

Raeder choked for a moment, though his face didn't show it. *Is this guy for real?* he wondered.

"Of?" he said aloud.

"Of Come By Chance, of course," the man said officiously. "With our resources so strained it's citizens first."

"Well we found her on the second floor of a building on the edge of the city. So I think it's safe to presume that she is not only a citizen, but a fairly affluent citizen as well."

The official looked down his nose.

"But . . . you can't prove it," he said. His voice suggested that Peter wasn't going to put one over on *him*.

Raeder put his hands on his slim hips and took a stance.

"Is there someone else we could talk to? Someone with a normal amount of human compassion, perhaps?" he asked.

The bureaucrat narrowed his eyes, and pointed his stylus at the commander.

"You're military, aren't you?"

"I'm a citizen of the Commonwealth," Raeder said, leaning towards him. "Like this lady here. Who, as a citizen of the Commonwealth, is entitled to any and all of its public services."

"Not that we know of," the man said, rising slowly to stand nose to nose with Raeder.

Peter recoiled.

"Are you suggesting she's a *Mollie*?"

The bureaucrat smirked, straightened up and prepared to speak.

"Doctor!" Raeder shouted. He gestured his team into the tent. "We need a doctor here, this woman is unconscious." He lifted the little girl from Shelton's embrace and put her into a nurse's arms. "Doctor!" he said again, and a woman in a white coat looked up.

He went over and, taking her arm, pointed to the woman on the stretcher.

"This lady has been unconscious since we found her about an hour ago. She's also got a very badly broken arm. Would you take a look at her, please?"

The doctor nodded and headed for the stretcher.

"Where can we put her down, Doctor?" he asked.

"We don't have any more beds, I'm afraid," she said. The doctor looked around, then pointed to a row of cabinets. "Just set her down there." She started examining the woman.

Raeder went up to the nurse who was trying to force the little girl back into Shelton's unwilling custody.

"This little girl is that lady's daughter," he said pointing. "This is Mookie," he said tugging the string. "We're gone." And before she could say a word he led his team away.

"Thank you, sir," Shelton said. "I was beginning to get worried there."

"So was I, Lieutenant."

"Thank you, Lieutenant Commander," Commander Trent said. He gave a judicious nod. "A very complete report."

"Thank you, sir."

Sarah sat looking at him in silence while he read something on his monitor. It made her very uneasy that he hadn't yet made eye contact with her.

"I think the best thing I can do now," she said firmly, "is report for duty to the *Invincible*."

"Do you?" Trent murmured. His eyes slid in her direction, but in their brief glance rose no higher than her waist.

"Yes, sir," she said. She gritted her teeth. Trent had a supercilious tone that got her back up.

He tapped a few keys and frowned at the information that came up.

"It says here," he tapped a few more keys, "that you came to Come By Chance for psych evaluation." He turned and looked her full in the face for the first time. His own expression spoke of disbelief that she would imagine him foolish enough to send a lunatic back to active duty.

"It was a mandatory evaluation because I was a Mollie prisoner. Briefly," she amended as he raised his eyebrows. "Last week I was upgraded to rest leave. Since I obviously can't continue to vacation here I should go where I'll be of the most use." She gave him a chilly smile.

Trent leaned back in his chair, his hands crossed on his lap and dipped his head toward the computer.

"I don't find *anything* here that indicates an upgrade."

"You could contact my doctor at Camp Seta," Sarah told him. "Doctor Pianca. She'll . . ."

He was shaking his head at her, a pitying smile playing on his thin lips.

"I'm afraid not, Lieutenant Commander. Civilian electronics are fried, EMP you know. And I can hardly clear a psych evaluation case for duty on my own." He shrugged. "My hands are tied. Now, if you'll excuse me," he turned back to his screen, "there are people I *can* send back to duty."

Sarah rose to her feet, furious and trying not to show it.

"What do you suggest I do until you feel you can allow me to do my duty, Commander?"

His thin lips took on a curl of distaste.

"I *suggest* that you find a way to make yourself useful, Lieutenant Commander. Look around you, there's plenty that needs to be done."

She saluted him crisply, he acknowledged it with something closer to a wave. Sarah turned on her heel and marched out of his cubicle-sized office, humiliated and very angry. Was this what it was going to be like for the rest of her career? Whenever some deskbound bureaucrat saw the notation for a mandatory psych evaluation was she going to be treated like an unexploded bomb?

How am I supposed to live with it if I am? she wondered. Boy, there was a question she'd love to ask Pianca.

"Sarah!" Peter said, rushing up to her. "You're cleared to go?"

"No," she told him. "Doctor Pianca didn't upgrade me to rest leave." Her lips narrowed to a thin line. "I'm still in the computer as being under psych evaluation and so Commander Trent will not let me leave."

Raeder's dark brows rose almost to his hairline. His eyes asked her if she was kidding.

"Well, that's what he said." She threw up her hands. "And there's no way to get in touch with Pianca because civilian communications . . ." She sighed. "You know."

"Leave it to me," he told her. "Go wait for me in the concourse. At that bar, okay?"

She gave him a look. "He's not going to change his mind, Peter."

"O ye of little faith." He leaned forward and gave her a quick peck on the cheek, then tipped his head in the direction of the concourse. "Go on, find us a table if you can. I'll be right there."

Sarah's mouth twisted up at one corner and she shrugged.

"Sure," she said. "Maybe when it's commander to commander things will be different. I'd really like to be wrong, Peter."

"You are," he said cheerfully. "See you in a little bit." *And I hope I'm carrying your boarding pass.* If there was one thing you couldn't rely on in this universe it was men of the same rank being of the same mind.

Raeder had to wait, of course. It was almost an hour and a half later before he even got a look at Trent.

Raeder saluted him. "Commander Peter Ernst Raeder, reporting for duty," he said.

Trent waved a salute in his general direction.

"Ah, yes," he said, the very slightest sneer in his voice. "Commander Peter Ernst Raeder, I've heard of you. You're something of a hotshot, or so your reputation says."

"Reputations are always exaggerated," Peter answered with a smile. *Almost always,* he amended mentally. *I'll bet it would be impossible to exaggerate yours, Trent. Especially if it happens to be for mean-spirited, hidebound, rule-obsessed spite.*

"I gather you've had quite a few . . . adventures," Trent said. He said adventures as though it meant enemas.

And jealous, Peter thought, *did I mention jealous?*

"Oh, I've seen a few things, been a few places," he said with a deprecating laugh. "Don't know if I'd call them adventures." *Those of us who have actually been to the front, don't think that way, as a rule. "Adventure" is a word rear-echelon types use. "Bad luck" and "screwing up" are more appropriate.*

Commander Trent studied him for a few cold moments, then sat forward and struck a few keys. He frowned, pursing his lips.

"You are to return to the *Invincible* immediately, emergency status. That means you jump to the head of the line, Commander." He plugged a red disc into the computer, tapped a key, pulled the disc out and handed it to Raeder.

"I'd like to be sure to get all of my crew who might be down here," Peter said, accepting it. "Any that are actually at the spaceport that is."

"Of course, Commander. As they come forward we'll send them up. Orders are, of course, for crew as well as officers."

"Lieutenant Commander Sarah James is here," Peter said. "I want her with me when I go up."

From Trent's expression Raeder had just proclaimed himself admiral of the fleet.

"Oh! I'm so sorry," Trent said, looking positively grateful for the opportunity to throw a hurdle in Peter's way. "That won't be possible, I'm afraid. The lieutenant commander is here for, um, a mandatory psych evaluation," he said, making air quotes around the word mandatory. "She hasn't been cleared for duty, I'm afraid."

"I, personally, have spoken with the lieutenant commander's doctor, Commander Trent. She told me that Lieutenant Commander James was fine, just tired. She's been on simple rest leave since last week."

Trent was shaking his head, trying, and failing, to suppress his smile.

"I'm sorry, but that's not in her records. My hands are tied."

Raeder leaned forward. "This is an emergency situation."

"*I* know that, Commander," Trent said, a trifle testily. "All the more reason why I can't send a woman of unknown mental health back to duty. *I'm* not qualified to make that decision, and I'm not going to."

"Perhaps you misunderstood," Peter said. "Her doctor told me she was fine."

"But it's not in the records," Trent insisted, gesturing at his computer.

"I need her," Raeder said through clenched teeth. "She's one of our best pilots."

"I can't help you." Trent offered his empty hands with a smug expression.

"It's an emergency," Raeder said tightly.

"It's against regs," Trent returned sharply.

Raeder gave him a hard look. "I guess that says everything, doesn't it?" He stood and snapped off a salute that looked like he was flicking something nasty from his fingers.

"Look," Trent said, standing, "without the regs it's just chaos."

Raeder gave him one last look of disgust, turned and walked away.

Peter entered the bar feeling like a thundercloud. He'd cursed that idiot Trent in as many languages as he knew and a few he really wasn't sure of.

I hate officers *like him,* he grumbled to himself. He gave himself a mental shake. *Okay, moving on.*

Looking around the crowded, noisy room he didn't spot Sarah but he did spot, "Sam!"

A balding, broad-shouldered pilot turned, a look of surprise on his homely face.

"Hey! Bad Boy!" He held out his hand. "Let me buy you a drink. C'mon over here, I don't want to lose my place. Hey," he called to the bartender, "a beer for my friend here."

"What are you doing here?" Raeder asked.

"Oh, down for a little R and R. You know." Sam Kazinski shrugged, a rueful expression on his face. "I've only been here about forty-eight hours. Then the roof fell in."

"Thanks," Peter said as the bartender handed over a beer. "You're on the . . . *Orion*, right?" he asked Kazinski.

"Yup." Sam patted his pocket. "Got my ticket back to work right here. I'm going up on the next shuttle."

They chatted for awhile about their ships, what they'd been doing since last they'd seen each other.

"Oh, my," Sam said and leaned close to Raeder. "Who's that lady over there?"

Peter glanced over to where Kazinski was pointing. It was Sarah, looking very pensive, eyes on the table before her. He grinned.

"That's no lady, that's a lieutenant commander."

His buddy gave him a look, then he shook his head.

"She looks to be just the type I like," Sam muttered. "And here I am being blasted off planet."

Raeder watched his friend watching Sarah. *Hmm,* he thought.

"I'll make you a deal, buddy. I'll introduce you."

Sam turned to him, eyes wide.

"You know her?"

"Yep, she's part of our squadron."

"A pilot," Kazinski said yearningly. "So introduce me." He looked at Raeder, who was wearing a wolfish grin. "What?"

"Trent won't let her leave with me, but I think *Invincible* is going to haul out as soon as I get there." He held up a hand to forestall questions. "Just a gut feeling. She's one of our best, I want her with us."

Sam straightened, looking askance at Peter.

"Oh, no. You *can't* be asking for what I think you're asking . . . for."

"Actually, I am." Peter gave him a challenging look.

The PA announced the departure of the next shuttle and called for red boarding passes.

Sam looked over at Sarah, then back at Raeder.

"It'd have to be more than an introduction," he said. "I mean, it's a *red* pass. And all she'd have is a chance to shake my hand and then she'd be gone."

Raeder nodded, looked thoughtful, then shrugged.

"That's a reasonable observation. So what are you asking for?"

"At the very least, a date."

Peter gave him a look of mock sternness. "Well,

buddy, all I'm prepared to offer is the least. I mean, anything else would be up to the lieutenant commander."

Sam looked at him, then at Sarah, then back at Raeder.

"You got a deal," he said, thrusting out his hand. Peter gripped it. "So let's get this show on the road."

"Sarah."

She looked up and at Raeder's expression offered a tentative smile.

"This is my very good friend, Pilot Officer Sam Kazinski."

Sarah blinked, then smiled warmly and offered Sam her hand.

"Any friend of the commander's is a friend of mine," she said.

Sam clung to her fingers, a boyish smile on his broad, friendly face.

"It is a pleasure to meet you, Lieutenant Commander," he said. "I only regret that it's under such trying circumstances."

"Trying," she murmured. "Yes, indeed." Sarah gave Raeder an oblique look, trying to determine the outcome of his interview with Trent from his too broad smile.

"Perhaps, ma'am," Kazinski went on, placing his hand over her still captive one, "in some future time you'll permit me the honor of furthering our acquaintance."

Astonished, Sarah looked into his earnest blue eyes and couldn't help but be flattered by the admiration she saw there.

With genuine pleasure she said, "I hope so too, Pilot Officer."

"Sam, please," he said. Raising her hand to his lips,

never taking his eyes from hers, he kissed it. "Until we meet again."

She grinned, she couldn't help it. A woman didn't meet with this degree of courtliness every day. She gave his hand a gentle squeeze and nodded.

The PA made a second call for red boarding passes.

With a sigh, and rueful look, Kazinski took his pass from his breast pocket and handed it over to Raeder. Sarah looked from one to the other, then reached out and gave Sam a hug and a kiss on the cheek.

"Thank you," she said.

He blushed, all the way up to the balding crown of his head.

"You have a good trip, ma'am," he said.

"Sarah."

"Sarah," he said with a grin.

"Don't let Trent give you too hard a time," Peter said, gripping his hand.

"Never!" Sam assured him. He leaned in and whispered, "Worth it." Then, with a wink at both of them, he turned and walked away, his short, sturdy form vanishing in the crowd.

Peter turned to find Sarah's inquiring eyes upon him. He ignored the question he knew she was asking him and took her arm.

"We'd better hurry," he said.

Sarah frowned, but held her peace, allowing Peter to rush her to the gate without further ado. Once they were aloft, though, she turned to him.

"Why did Sam give up his pass for me?" she asked.

Raeder looked at her innocently, and she could almost feel her hackles rise.

"I explained the situation to him and he wanted to help," he said.

"Really?" she said in a flat voice that should have warned him she was suspicious.

"He's a great guy," Peter said. Then he launched into an anecdote about an Academy prank they'd been involved with.

She listened without cracking a smile. Now Raeder began to get worried. That was one of his best stories; it always got at least a chuckle, and he knew he'd never told it to her.

"Do you think I'm stupid?" she asked mildly.

Oh, boy, he thought, *I'm in for it now.*

He shook his head, wide-eyed.

"Oh, good." Sarah leaned her chin on her upraised hand. "Then we have a choice of options here. Either you misunderstood the question." She stopped and looked at him. Raeder stared back blankly. "Or, we're talking about two different people." She paused, then continued, "Or you're trying to hold something back from me." She shifted in her seat so that she faced him more squarely. "Now, you're not so stupid that you would misunderstand such a direct and simple question. And I know we're not talking about two different people." Sarah leaned towards him. "Which means you're holding out on me."

He blinked and opened his mouth to speak.

"The next words out of your mouth had better be the full story, Commander," Sarah warned. "I will not settle for anything less."

He looked at her for a full minute, weighing his options. *She means it,* he thought. *Might as well come clean. If she ever meets Sam again the truth will come out anyway.* He took a very deep breath and then he told her.

"You promised him a date with me?" Sarah asked, her voice chocked with disbelief.

"Nnn-no," he said. "I *implied* that he might have a date with you."

She sat staring at him, seeming to actually swell with rage.

"What are you, a pimp?"

"Hey!" he said, genuinely wounded.

"How dare you make such a bargain about me in the first place?" she demanded. Sarah drew in a deep breath and closed her eyes. "But after . . ." She looked at him and in her eyes was a world of hurt. "I've misjudged things," she said firmly, her voice belying her eyes. "I must have, or you wouldn't have offered me up in a bargain like that."

"Sarah . . ." Raeder began.

She held up her hand.

"Let's forget it," she said. "We have bigger issues to think of right now." Then she settled back and closed her eyes, a good soldier, getting rest while it was available.

Peter looked at her and groaned inwardly. *Man, I've got a lot of ground to make up here,* he thought. *Raeder, that was a major mistake.* Then, like Sarah, he settled back to rest. *I'm not giving you up without a fight,* he thought at Sarah. *You just wait and see.*

Sarah opened one eye, saw Raeder wasn't looking, and smiled.

CHAPTER FIVE

"He's looking much better," Sarah said. It came out sounding more like a question.

"He does, he really does," Raeder agreed. *He looks like death warmed over,* he thought. Clearly the *Invincible* wasn't going anywhere soon. "Ms. Ju was looking better too, I thought."

"Oh, much," Sarah agreed.

In fact the XO had looked dreadful lying in her container of pink goo.

Maybe it's the gel; pink isn't Ju's color, Sarah mused, then her lips tightened. *Get real,* she thought. *It was the humongous radiation burns.*

The gel anesthetized as it cured, so the XO was feeling no pain, but it was still a trial seeing her like that.

"It's disconcerting," Raeder said as though reading her mind. "She's always so pulled together, so serene."

Ju's eyes hadn't been able to focus on them, and what was left of her black hair stuck to her scalp in clumps. It was probably all going to fall out.

They ought to just shave it off, he thought. *Spare her the inconvenience.*

He couldn't help but feel a little angry seeing both the captain and the XO so wan and helpless. As though things would have been different if he'd been on the *Invincible* when the missiles started flying.

The good news was that the ship was fine. The crew also, including the flight crew, had all come through the action pretty much unscathed. But it was cold comfort under the circumstances and he worried that a new captain would be appointed before Knott could take the helm again. It would be well-nigh unbearable if they had a commander thrust upon them who was to captaining what William Booth was to security officers.

At least Knott and Ju were being treated in the *Invincible*'s own sick bay. The reason given by the ship's senior officers was that they didn't wish to overburden the base or CBC's hospitals. Especially when those institutions had a surfeit of their own badly injured to care for. Indeed they'd opened the ship's facilities to the base's overflow of wounded.

Actually they'd reasoned that it would be harder to replace a captain while he was resident on his own ship. Not that Star Command wasn't perfectly capable of it, but they hoped to make it difficult at least.

Peter and Sarah walked on silently, each lost in their own thoughts, until they came to a break in the corridor. Sarah would be going back to Main Deck; Raeder, over Booth's spluttered objections that *he* was the security officer, was required to attend a debriefing regarding the recent attack. They looked into one another's eyes and smiled. He gave her arm an encouraging squeeze that he'd rather was an embrace and they parted.

As Peter left the shuttle's austere compartment to emerge into the hastily repaired tunnel leading to Marjorie Base, he thought about the meeting to come.

How the attack could have happened was the question of the day in Star Command, and an Admiral Smallwood had been sent to head the investigation. Smallwood was short and slight in build, with a big nose and quick, abrupt movements. He was famous throughout the service for grandiose schemes that *sometimes* worked.

Kind of a strange choice for an investigator, Raeder mused. Though to be fair, he himself was a strange choice for this meeting. *Much as I hate to admit it, Booth might have been the more logical choice.* As the man himself had insisted. *That is, if the criteria for attendance was assigned duties.* The activities on Main Deck didn't seem directly connected to the problem at any rate.

Then again, there was his role in uncovering Senior Lieutenant John Larkin as a Mollie infiltrator. *Of which I am justifiably proud.*

Not that it seemed to have accrued him much good karma. What it probably had done was win him the notice of the mysterious and powerful Marine General Scaragoglu. *That and my somewhat over-the-top rescue of Paddy. Which I would do again for anyone who needed a hand.*

Which he suspected Scaragoglu knew and would exploit at need. Not a good feeling if you valued your peace of mind.

As he approached the meeting room an aide came up to him and handed him a message chip, then spun on his heel and marched off before Raeder could question him. With a shrug he fitted it into his reader.

Commander Raeder, it read, *please join me in my quarters after the meeting.* It was signed by Admiral Smallwood. A sudden chill of excitement raced down his spine.

Something's up, he thought with a secret smile.

The room was dimly lit to accommodate any holo displays the admiral might want the system to throw before them. The people who sat at the round table were all commander or higher in rank, and universally solemn.

Smallwood had begun his discourse with the information that the Mollie/Fibian raiders had leapt safely from jump point to jump point by broadcasting either legitimate Commonwealth trader's signals or, worse, valid Star Command military codes.

"Stolen, or bought," Smallwood said, his small, dark eyes darting from face to face. "Or we have a Mollie agent in a sensitive place." His glance flicked to Raeder and away. "Been known to happen before. They followed the signal out guns blazing, so to speak, and annihilated three picket corvettes that we know of. Going out, there's no telling how much damage they'll be pleased to accomplish." He folded his hands in front of himself. "This is because we essentially did them no damage. They jumped in at high velocity, hit the moonbase and planet as they passed and did a slingshot maneuver around the sun to jump out again. So I must concede that the speed and unlikelihood of the attack here, of all places, made a response in force . . . problematic, at best." He glared around the table. "Regrettably we were not at our best that day."

Some of the officers around the table met that glare

with stone faces, others glanced at fellow officers, or at the notescreens before them.

"What most disappoints me, of course, is that we did not capture one Mollie or Fibian."

"Sir," said Captain Miyashi, who could not let that pass, "it is their policy not to allow themselves to be captured."

"Don't I know it," Smallwood said glumly. "Only extreme diligence has prevented those Mollie prisoners we do have from committing suicide. Still, it's *our* policy to capture valuable intelligence assets—and I would prefer that our policy be the one implemented."

"They've filed suit," Miyashi said. "They claim that by denying them the right to kill themselves we're forbidding them to practice their religion."

"I don't like those people," Smallwood said. "The Mollies would rather die for their cause than live for it. As for the Fibians, for all we know they're some kind of group mind and losing an individual might be as unimportant to them as trimming our fingernails is to us."

A gloomy silence descended briefly.

"Well," the admiral said, "I guess it's impossible to stop someone in a Speed from killing themselves if they really want to. Our pilots are to be congratulated for keeping them from crashing into the main dome of this station. And will be, officially," he went on with a glance around the table. "If there's nothing else you ladies and gentlemen have to contribute," he said, "then I'll close this meeting. Thank you for coming." He rose and left the room, his aides falling in behind him.

"Come in, Commander," the young ensign said.

She swept her arm out to encompass the small room behind her. Admiral Smallwood was sitting on the couch, reader in hand, one leg crossed over the other. Without looking up the admiral gestured to a chair.

"Please take a seat, Commander. I'll be with you in a moment." He glanced at his aide. "You're excused, Ensign. See that no one disturbs us."

"Yes, sir."

"Thank you, sir," Raeder said. He took a chair opposite the couch and looked around the room. *Odd that the admiral isn't seated at the desk,* he thought. He imagined that a short man like Smallwood would usually take advantage of such a prop.

The desk itself was not large, true, but the chair behind it was enormous. He wondered what the front of it looked like. The back appeared to be covered with genuine leather of some sort. Quite an extravagance for a little base like this one.

Smallwood tapped off his reader and put it down, then leaned back to study the commander, one arm thrown along the back of the couch, his legs crossed.

"How are things going on the *Invincible*, Commander?"

"Very well, sir," Raeder said. He paused to see how this would be received. Then, with a smile, he continued, "Captain Knott is looking better every day."

"Captain Knott looks like hell," Smallwood asserted. "And his XO looks worse. But neither of them is seriously incapacitated, so you needn't think Star Command is going to replace them with whatever's left in the barrel."

Raeder couldn't help but grin at that. Not that he was pleased to be so easily read, but the captain's status was good news.

"Your loyalty does you credit, Commander."

"If it does, sir, then the credit goes to Captain Knott. He's an outstanding officer."

Smallwood raised one brow, but smiled. He shifted his posture so that he faced Raeder more directly, his hands folded in his lap.

"As you know, Commander, the Commonwealth isn't doing very well in this war. Despite the exceptional efforts of the *Invincible* and ships like her, too much antihydrogen is being used up. As you've just experienced, the Fibian fleet is raiding deeper and deeper into the Commonwealth, and defensive deployments and convoy duty are eating deeper and deeper into our scant fuel reserves. We're making some headway against the pirates, at least. The fact that we can handle them differently during wartime is a great help there."

I couldn't agree more, Raeder thought. In peacetime pirates were to be treated as innocent until proven guilty, even when caught red-handed. Being allowed to treat them as the enemies of the Commonwealth that they were greatly simplified things.

"However," the admiral continued, "hard as it is to believe considering the number of planets that stand against them, the Mollies are slowly, but definitely winning this war."

Raeder struggled not to gape at the admiral. *To hear someone in his position put it so unequivocally . . .*

"You seem very definite, sir," he said.

"Setting aside the virtually insurmountable difficulty of our enemies having all the fuel resources at their command. Indeed," Smallwood interrupted himself, "the fact that we didn't win the war in the first few weeks pretty much nailed the outcome in their favor. But setting that aside, as I said, they also have an ally with what seem to be unlimited numbers of ships and personnel to throw behind the Mollie cause. Did you ever wonder why they would do that, Commander?"

With a shrug Peter said, "Antihydrogen. Has to

be. It wouldn't surprise me to find that after the war the Fibians simply take the antihydrogen fields from the Mollies. In fact the Mollies may well have promised to give them up in return for Fibian aid. The Interpreters have been railing about its corrupting influence for awhile now. It might well be to prepare their flocks for that eventuality."

A deep chuckle rose from behind the desk.

"Give the boy a drink, Ralph. I told you he was smart." General Kemal Scaragoglu slowly spun the chair around to regard a stunned Raeder with a pleased smile. "Close your mouth, Commander; you'll catch flies, and that's not a mission you've been tasked with."

Peter closed his mouth and tried to look respectful. *Since not even my acting talents would make* pleased *look convincing at this point.*

"I'd no idea you were on the base, sir," he hazarded.

"Well, that's good," the general said, raising his brows. "It's nice to know that something's still working." He looked pointedly at the admiral. "C'mon, Smallwood, I know you have a cache of the good stuff."

Smallwood threw him a sour look, then rose and left the room.

"As for you, Commander," Scaragoglu said, "there's no need for you to look like you just bit down on something sour and smelly. You didn't come off too badly in our last joint venture."

No, but Sarah did and Aia Wisnewski and . . . the list is probably endless where Scaragoglu is concerned. In all truth it was Sarah's suffering that mattered to him most, his resentment was on her behalf. And it was no thanks to Scaragoglu that any of them had made it back.

"And what's the reward for good work?" the general asked quietly, almost tauntingly.

Smallwood reentered carrying a tray with three glasses on it, each bearing an amber-colored tot. Scaragoglu gave him an amused glance, as if to say the pointed absence of the bottle wouldn't keep him for asking for more if he wanted it.

"Why don't you continue outlining our plan for the commander," the general said expansively. "This is not for repetition," he said to Raeder, his eyes hard.

"Of course, sir." *It goes without saying,* Raeder thought. Though with Scaragoglu, nothing did; he left nothing to chance.

The admiral settled himself on the couch and took an appreciative sip of his whisky.

"Maker's Mark," he said, smacking his lips. "Wonderful stuff. To the Commonwealth, gentlemen."

They raised their glasses, Scaragoglu's eyes sparkling with pleasure.

"An excellent drink for toasting," he agreed. "Now, if you would, Admiral." He gestured at Raeder with his glass. "Then, perhaps we can make another."

Raeder felt excitement grab him by the back of the neck, his heart rate rose and he waited for Smallwood to begin.

"In the priority of outcomes to this war that we'd prefer," Smallwood began, "first would be, we win: all the antihydrogen is ours and the Mollies are moved to another quadrant of space altogether never to be heard from again. Second: it's a draw, the Mollies remain where they are, but we have at least some access to the antihydrogen, the Fibians aren't a factor. These are the least likely outcomes, unfortunately."

"Don't be negative, Ralph, go on," Scaragoglu said quietly.

"Very well," Smallwood said, throwing the general a sour look. "Third: we lose, the Mollies hand over the antihydrogen to the Fibians as payment for their aid and we come to some sort of trade agreement with the Fibians regarding the antihydrogen. Of course the most likely scenario at this point is four: we lose, the Commonwealth falls apart and the Fibians annihilate us planet by planet."

Scaragoglu sat and blinked at the admiral, his expression unreadable. The memory of his remark about negativity hung in the air like a bad smell.

With a sigh, the general said, "Well, we aren't quite at that point yet, fortunately. And it behooves us to avoid such a fate by any means possible." He turned to Raeder with a smile. "Don't you agree, Commander?"

Peter felt a thrill of fear, so mixed with excitement he couldn't tell one from the other. He sat forward, his eyes on the general, and nodded slowly.

"In the short term," Scaragoglu said, "our goals are twofold. And first we must stop this type of deep raiding. I concede it's something of a compliment to us that they're copying our tactics so assiduously. But if the worst comes to pass," he gave a dark-eyed glance at Smallwood, "I want them to sincerely believe us too tough a nut to crack. I want them so frightened of us that the last thing they would conceive of in their worst nightmares is attacking a human world. We must find and stop this raiding party cold."

Raeder nodded. *Hard to do,* he thought. *They've been gone two days.* Hard, but not impossible.

The general leaned back, like a big cat settling in contentment.

"You will pursue them as part of a deep-penetration raid into Fibian space. Intelligence keeps spotting more and more new fleet units of Fibians. It's time we knew more about this ally of the Mollies."

"Me, sir?" Raeder asked intently.

"You, Commander." Scaragoglu gave him a lazy smile. "Who better?"

Me? Raeder thought. *Certainly not by my lonesome.*

"Is this meant to be a reconnaissance in force?" he asked.

"One of the things I like about you, Commander, is that you get right to the heart of the matter." The General nodded. "Yes, it will be a reconnaissance in force."

I'd need at least a corvette, Peter thought. *But that wouldn't be sufficient to destroy the Fibian raiding party. For that I'd need . . .*

"The *Invincible?*" he said in a near whisper.

Scaragoglu nodded. "The very same," he said.

"But the captain . . ."

The general shook his head. "Modern medicine can work miracles, and does, every day. But it's not *that* good yet. Captain Knott and Ms. Ju will remain behind to heal. Your assignment to the captain's chair is purely temporary, Commander." He grinned. "At least for now. Knott and Ju will be returned to their current berths upon your return." He turned to Smallwood. "The admiral will continue this briefing," he said. "I'm afraid I must go."

"You mean you aren't here to brief me on this mission?" Raeder asked. Scaragoglu gave him a pitying look, and he could have kicked himself for speaking out.

"You don't need to know why I'm here," the general said. Then he gave Raeder a truly evil smile. "But you might consider me your guardian angel." He stood and raised his glass on high. "Gentlemen," he said, "I give you the success of the mission."

Raeder and the admiral rose to join him. "The mission!" they said in unison, then tossed off the whisky.

"Ah!" Scaragoglu said, moving from behind the desk. "That is one fine whisky."

"Better sipped," Smallwood said.

"As is life," the general said. "When we reach a certain age." He shook the admiral's hand, then Raeder's. "May we all soon have such leisure."

After he'd left Raeder and Smallwood remained standing, Smallwood staring into his empty glass as though looking for something.

"I've ordered your sick bay cleared of patients," he said at last. "Over your Doctor Goldberg's, and the base hospital's, objections. The *Invincible* is fueled up and resupplied, all personnel not wounded are aboard. Therefore, as soon as the last patient is removed I think you should begin your mission." He handed Peter the reader he'd been perusing when Raeder had first entered. "This contains what intelligence we have on the Fibian raiders, along with the most up-to-date projections on their next target. We've also got a linguistics expert who can read and speak the principal Fibian language."

Smallwood's eyes suddenly shifted and Raeder said, "Sir?"

The admiral's mouth tightened and he shifted his shoulders as though to better settle his uniform jacket.

"The man is the best we could come up with on short notice," he said. "In fact he's one of the best linguists in the Commonwealth. The only reason you were able to get him at all was the general's influence."

Peter found the note of defensiveness in Smallwood's voice somewhat alarming.

"I'm grateful, sir," he said aloud, trying to project enthusiasm.

"Unfortunately, the man is an intense arachnophobe," the admiral said in a rush.

"Ah," Raeder said calmly. *Oh, shit,* he thought. "How did he manage to become so expert in a language spoken by beings who so closely resemble spiders?" he asked. *Because frankly there's something so kinky there that it worries me more than the arachnophobia.*

"I'm afraid I don't have that information," Smallwood said, stiffly. He reached out and took Peter's glass from his hand. "Well, Commander, you should be going. You've a million things to do, I don't doubt."

What no handshake? No, "Go forth my boy and make us proud," speech?

Smallwood hastily put down the glasses and shook Peter's hand.

"Come back," the admiral said. "Good luck."

"Thank you, sir. I will."

He stood back and saluted, Smallwood returned it crisply and, with a precise spin, Raeder was on his way.

CHAPTER SIX

Despite the admiral's assertion that the *Invincible* was ready to go, Raeder knew, and suspected that Smallwood did too, that you couldn't be too prepared for a mission like this one.

He strode along the dock, his mind racing with plans.

"These!" he shouted out, slapping a pile of boxes and moving rapidly towards the first cargo specialist to look up. Pointing he said, "These go to the *Invincible*."

"No, sir," the young woman said consulting her manifest. "These missiles are for the *Amity*."

"Not anymore," he said. He took the manifest from her hands. "I'll sign off for it. *Invincible*'s got priority. Admiral Smallwood will confirm it. Meanwhile, please get your crew started with loading these. Now."

He marched off ignoring her cry of "Sir!"

As soon as he walked onto the *Invincible* he hit the com.

"Chief Casey, Chief arap Moi, Lieutenant Robbins, please meet me in the quartermaster's office." He couldn't remember the kid's name at the moment, but his office was closer, so this would save time.

"P—Commander," Sarah said, bustling up to him. "They're taking the captain and Ms. Ju off the ship. Have you heard anything? Doctor Goldberg's done everything he could but he says the order came from pretty high up."

"You'd better come with me," he said, taking her by the upper arm and leaning close. "I'm meeting Paddy and Robbins in the quartermaster's office. We don't have much time."

She looked at him questioningly; after a beat she whispered, "We're shipping out."

He nodded. "Wait," he said, "I'll explain."

They walked on in silence until they came to the quartermaster's office. Peter found the door open and the young temporary quartermaster seated behind his desk, his usual eager expression on his face.

"Welcome, Commander, won't you come in?"

"Bryany," Raeder said, relieved to finally remember the kid's name.

The young petty officer half rose. "Would you like my seat, Commander?"

"Thank you, no," Peter answered. "I'll stand, I think."

It was a tiny office, about the size of a broom closet. Were it not for the fact that the *Invincible* was a new ship and one of the best designed he'd ever served on Raeder would have assumed that it had been converted from just such a purpose. He wasn't entirely sure he could fit behind the desk. The young, temporary quartermaster was a very small, slender man.

How did Larkin ever manage it? he wondered. Then again, Larkin was a Mollie, he probably reveled in discomfort for the cause.

They waited a moment in silence, Bryany fairly thrumming with suppressed energy. *Who needs anti-hydrogen?* Peter thought wryly. *When we run out we'll just hook up the engines to Bryany here and probably break speed records.*

"Paddy and Cynthia are on board, aren't they?" Raeder said to Sarah. "Have you seen them?"

"I saw them earlier on Main Deck with their heads together over Givens' engine, not since."

"We're still having trouble with Givens' engine?" Just as they had been when he'd first met the lieutenant. "Wait a minute, that was a different Speed."

"He caught some flack while he was chasing Fibians," Sarah said. She gave a wry smile. "But it does give one pause."

"Sorry to be so long, Commander," Paddy said from the doorway. "But we had ourselves fairly slathered with lubricants and all and had to clean up, so we did."

Raeder and Sarah looked at him blankly and Cynthia blinked.

Raeder cleared his throat. "You're hardly late, Chief. I'm just grateful you were both on board. Take a seat, won't you?" He turned to Bryany. "Could you close the door, please, Petty Officer?"

Bryany struck a key and the door snicked shut.

"O-kay," Peter said, seating himself on the edge of the quartermaster's desk. "We're shipping out in less than three hours, and I'll be in command for this mission," he told them. "We're down two Speeds and I am not leaving Come By Chance without filling those slots. So I'm going to need your help. Yours too, Lieutenant Commander James. Bryany," he said, turning to him. "I've commandeered a shipment of standard defensive and antiship missiles; they should be coming in any moment. Will you be able to handle it?"

"You bet, sir. We've got the room. The quartermaster here only allotted half the number we requested. But I did score some more mines." He sat back with a huge grin.

"Good for you," Raeder said, giving him a slap on the arm.

Paddy, Cynthia and Sarah grinned their approval. Since Knott's successful deployment of mines during *Invincible*'s last mission the obsolete weapons had developed a certain popularity with fighting ships.

"Is there anything else we're in sore need of?" Raeder asked.

"Laser crystals, sir. You can never have enough," Bryany said seriously.

"Paddy?"

"I'm on it, Commander." The big New Hibernian grabbed the arms of his chair as if to rise.

"Get anything else you think we'll need while you're at it, Chief. Lieutenant," Peter said to Cynthia, "batten down the hatches on Main Deck, prepare room for two more Speeds. S—Lieutenant Commander, find me a pilot whose discretion we can trust absolutely. Meet me at the door of the hangar for Marjorie Base, suited up and ready to fly. Let's go people, time's a-wasting."

They rose and hurried to their tasks without another word being said. Raeder thought about that as he strode down the corridor. He was proud to have the trust of such exceptional people.

Marjorie Base's hangar was at the top of the base complex just beneath the dome of the station. The whole massive structure could be retracted in segments to allow Speeds to fly out like a swarm of angry wasps. There were over a hundred Speeds serving this small base, and the place was awesome.

Though not an active post these pilots and their machines had responded like veterans to the Fibian attack. Now they licked their wounds. Easily thirty of the sleek machines had been severely damaged and were in various stages of being stripped down.

The pilots could be proud that they'd only lost eight of their Speeds in the conflict. They could be spending their time in bars, boasting of their prowess and impressing the opposite sex. Instead they hit the simulators and strove to put a finer edge on their already razor-sharp skills.

Good, Raeder thought, *there isn't a pilot in sight.* Not that the techs would be easy to fool, but they'd be a bit less fanatic about it. *Unless Marjorie Base has somebody like Robbins on it.* A thought to make a strong man shudder, especially under the circumstances.

The commander marched along, looking like someone who knew where he was going and who didn't have time for questions. His eyes took stock of his surroundings and he was relieved to see that there was a small door in the side of the dome for standard patrols to come and go. He'd been worried about that.

No way would they let me open the dome, he thought. He could put one over on small groups, but an operation like that would involve the permission of a superior officer. *Who would tell me to go back to bed or stop dreaming.*

Then he saw them. Two perfect specimens, perhaps new, for their gleaming surfaces seemed unmarked. They sat sparkling in the overhead lights, nose to tail, like two shy colts in an unfamiliar pasture.

Raeder felt the lift in his chest that the prospect of flying always brought. *Down, boy,* he thought. *Maybe someday.* For now, taking them home with him would have to do. *What I really like about them,* he thought, *is that they're adjacent to the doors.*

He turned and trotted back to the main entrance of the hangar, arriving just as Sarah and Givens came in. *Givens?* he thought dubiously. The pilot officer was a bit young, in Raeder's opinion, and one of those people who always would be.

Then again, he had been with them on the asteroid and had acquitted himself well. *Perhaps I've gotten into a habit of thought about Givens that doesn't match the real man anymore,* Peter thought. That wouldn't do. *And heaven knows I've reason to trust Sarah's judgement. Just look at our relationship.* There was a touch of smugness in the thought.

"What I need for you to do," he said as he came up to them, "is to get into the Speeds I'm going to point out to you and fly them to—" he rattled off coordinates near one of Marjorie's Lagrange points. "Wait there for the *Invincible.*"

Sarah raised one brow and Givens blinked, but otherwise there was no comment from either but, "Yes, sir."

"Follow me," Raeder said.

He led them to the two Speeds he'd selected and directed them to board and power them up. At the sound four techs came running.

"Hey!" a burly older man shouted, a chief petty officer. "What's going on here?"

Raeder turned and intercepted him smoothly.

"Sir?" the man said.

"I'm Commander Raeder," he said. "This is a surprise inspection. These pilots will be taking those two

Speeds out for a run to evaluate the level of service the techs here are providing."

"What inspection?" one of the techs, a woman, demanded.

"Yeah," said the chief. "We haven't heard nothin' about any inspection."

Peter leaned in close to the chief. "Well, then it wouldn't be a surprise. Now would it?"

The chief and his techs didn't have an answer for that one. They looked at each other helplessly, eyes blinking slowly. Meanwhile Sarah and Givens were maneuvering their Speeds into position before the crash doors.

"Who authorized this?" the chief asked as he watched them go.

"Admiral Smallwood," Raeder answered. "Look," he said, taking the chief's arm and leading him away from the two Speeds, "I can sign off for them if this is making you nervous."

"Yes, sir, if you would," the chief said. "This isn't . . ."

"I know," Peter said sympathetically. "But you know the admiral, he gets these ideas. Personally, I think that after the way the squadron performed a few days ago any questions anyone *might* have had about your operation here should have been answered."

"Thank you, sir," the chief said. He handed Raeder a notecomp and Peter signed off with a flourish. "I appreciate this, sir."

"Not a problem," Raeder said. "Uh, except that those doors aren't open." He turned and grinned at the techs around him. "Can you do something about that?"

For a moment the chief's face fell, as though he now understood that he'd been conned. Raeder stepped into the gap before he could become angry.

"That's the other downside of surprise inspections," he said with a grin, "you're not always a hundred percent prepared yourself."

The chief nodded slowly. He couldn't help but be suspicious. At the moment he wasn't sure if this was a security check or the inspection test the commander said it was.

"Chief," Raeder said, letting a snap of command slip into his voice. "The lieutenant commander, the pilot officer and I are waiting."

The chief went to his console and tapped in a sequence. Warning lights flashed and klaxons sounded, while around the door blue lights showed the implementation of a force curtain that prevented the escape of atmosphere as the crash door rose.

Sarah and Givens rolled the Speeds forward and made a vertical takeoff as soon as they were outside.

There was a chirp from the console and an irritated voice with a strong Hindi accent demanded: "Chief Powers, what the hell is going on? We have two Speeds, not cleared for takeoff, who haven't submitted a flight plan, who aren't listed on our schedule, haring off into the wild unknown at this moment. Could you explain that to me, please?"

"Let me," Peter said and leaned into range of the pickup. "Who is this?" he asked.

"Who am I? This is base flight control, Ensign Rao Singh speaking," the man answered. "Who are you? Where is Chief Powers?"

"I'm right here, Ensign," Powers said.

There was a pause. "So, what's going on?" the ensign asked, his voice betraying puzzled caution.

"I'm Commander Raeder; this is a surprise inspection authorized by Admiral Smallwood."

"Sir . . ." Again there was a pause and when his voice returned it was tight with controlled anger.

"This un . . ." He couldn't say *unauthorized* because a commander had just told him that it was, and by an admiral no less. Nor could he call it *unbelievably stupid* for the same reason.

"Someone, such as those two pilots, might have been hurt," he said finally. "They have yet to check in with flight control and their trajectory has caused us to do several very hasty emergency reroutings. *Besides* overriding automatic defense batteries which are still on red alert. Sir."

"I understand," Raeder said, his voice managing to be both crisp and sympathetic. "But as I was saying to the chief, if surprise inspections were expected we wouldn't learn much from them. Good work, all of you," he said.

He saluted the chief, who saluted back, still obviously uncertain he'd done the right thing. Peter walked off without looking back. He checked his watch once, then picked up his pace.

There are eyes boring into my back, he thought. *I can feel them. But if I turn around I'll turn into a pillar of salt. Feet, keep moving.*

He kept expecting a senior officer to call him to a halt, to demand an explanation, followed by a call to the admiral's office, followed by something close to a flogging by the admiral's notoriously acid tongue.

Then he was through the hangar doors and he moved out at a jog.

God, I hope Paddy is back with those crystals. He also hoped flight control had been warned of *Invincible*'s departure. He didn't think two surprises like that in one shift would pass unnoticed. *Once we've got those two Speeds aboard and are headed for the jump point calling us back is unlikely.* But he knew Admiral Smallwood would have a few choice words to say to him when, if, he got back.

As he approached the *Invincible*'s docking tube he saw a tall, slender, but broad-shouldered man with a shock of curly dark hair arguing with the guard.

"What's going on?" Peter asked.

"Sir, this man wants to come aboard."

"I'm . . ." the man began to say.

"What is your profession?" Raeder said.

"I am a linguist," he answered. He held out his hand. "My name is . . ."

Before he could continue Raeder tapped at his noteboard and called up a picture of a Fibian. He handed it to the linguist, saying, "What do you think of this?"

The man recoiled, visibly paler.

"He's expected," Raeder said, withdrawing his noteboard.

"Don't do that to me!" the man snapped, hand over his heart.

"I'll vouch for him," Raeder said to the guard.

"Yes, sir," the guard said and stood aside.

"I have this baggage." The linguist gestured to a pile of belongings.

Raeder picked up one of the bags. "Pick out the ones you most need to have with you. I'll have someone deliver the rest to your quarters."

"Thank you. I'm Sirgay Ticknor, incidently—LL.A., Victoria City University department of xenolinguistics." He held out his hand again and waited while Peter tucked his noteboard under one arm to take it.

"Commander Peter Ernst Raeder. I'll be in charge of this expedition. Follow me, please." Raeder led him onto the *Invincible*, away from the interested eyes and ears of the guard on duty. "Have you ever traveled on a Star Command vessel?" he asked.

"No, I haven't had that privilege," Ticknor said. "I suppose there'll be restrictions and bad food and so forth?"

Peter laughed. "Some restrictions, yes. But they'll be for your own safety most likely." He led him into the elevator. *No sense in making the civilian walk,* he excused himself. *I need to get him settled, then I've got a million things to do.* That was what *real* ship's captains had XOs to do.

"Well, most likely I'll be in my quarters working on my translations. I don't know if the admiral mentioned this to you," he said in the manner of a man who is certain that this important fact *must* have been mentioned, "but there's something of a cutthroat competition under way to see who will be first to crack the Fibian language." Ticknor looked around him happily. "And with this . . . opportunity I'm certain to be the one! You have no idea how delighted I am to be coming with you."

"Excuse me?" Raeder said. "You're telling me that you do not, in fact, speak Fibian." There was an edge to his voice and he was feeling far less guilty about using the admiral's name as he had.

The elevator halted and he led Ticknor down the corridor at a fast clip, forcing the linguist to jog a few paces to catch up.

"No one does," the linguist explained. "Humans can only approximate the language; the vocal apparatus is entirely different. It's amazing they can speak ours as well as they do. But from my studies I've deduced that human language, by comparison, is quite crude."

Raeder halted and turned to face the man beside him.

"I'm asking you," he said with exaggerated patience, "do—you—*understand*—Fibian?"

Ticknor avoided Raeder's eyes, looking down at their shoes, or off to the side.

"Well, as well as anyone in the Commonwealth does," he admitted with a little laugh.

"I'm from the Commonwealth," Peter said tightly. "I don't understand Fibian at all. Can you do better than that?"

"Oh, yes! Now I see what you mean. Yes. In a brute sort of way, certainly I can understand Fibian. But the subtleties of the language . . ."

"So," Raeder said, moving off rapidly, "if we run into a Fibian patrol you'd be able to say, 'We come in peace'?"

"Er, yes." Ticknor trotted to catch up to him, his eyes on Raeder's profile. "Is that what we're going to say to them?" the linguist asked.

"Apparently not," Raeder said. "Since you don't speak their language."

"I have a device which I am programming to speak their language." Ticknor's voice was tart, his manner offended.

"Here we are," Raeder said.

He showed the linguist into Larkin's quarters. The traitor's cabin had yet to be reassigned and Peter knew Ticknor would require room and privacy in which to work.

"*This?*" the linguist asked, allowing his bags to drop from his hands in his astonishment. He stood openmouthed, incredulous. "This is a closet! How can you possibly expect me to work in there?"

"Mr. Ticknor, this is an officer's cabin. I am right next door to you and these are the best accommodations on the ship. It's tight, I grant you, but perfectly adequate." He gave the linguist a sidelong look. "You're not claustrophobic, are you?"

"No! Having one phobia does not mean that I have

all of them! I can't believe you live in a hole like this."
He rubbed the back of his neck and shook his head,
giving Raeder a dark-eyed glare.

Raeder stepped to the door next to Ticknor's and
keyed entry. He stepped aside and gestured welcome
to the man beside him.

"Hmmph," was all Ticknor said.

"The food is really quite good, and there's plenty
of it. But space is at a premium. You'll get used to
it," Raeder said reassuringly.

Ticknor frowned. "You're having the rest of my
baggage sent to me here?"

"Yes."

"Well," the linguist gestured helplessly, "it won't
fit! What am I supposed to do about that?"

"Is everything you've brought directly related to
your work?" Raeder asked. *Because I've got to get
going, buddy, I've got things to do.*

"Yes! The translation device, the special equipment
needed to construct it, my library," he said holding
up one of the cases.

"Then I'll assign you some lab space, Mr. Ticknor.
For now, however, if you don't mind we'll just store
your baggage in here. When we've left the station and
passed the jump point we'll get you settled."

Before Ticknor could raise the objections Raeder
was certain he was marshalling Peter spun on his heel
and walked off.

Command is playing merry hell with my manners,
he thought. *Mom would be very disappointed in me.*
But then, he'd been *under* command for years now,
and he'd yet to run into someone at the top who
wasn't preemptory and rude.

The paint locker was cramped, but not nearly as
small as Paddy's cabin. Which was why he'd brought

the three techs he'd smuggled aboard for this high-stakes game here. It came with a table already installed. True, he'd had to snatch some stools from the labs to make it comfortable to play at that table, but he felt that the effort would be worth it. Music played softly in the background from a player at the chief's elbow.

"Two," said Simba. She was a slender, tawny woman with tightly braided rows of jet-black hair. Had there been no Cynthia Robbins then Paddy might have enjoyed a closer association with the weapons specialist.

Colvin dealt her the cards and sat back, his eyes hooded. He was the oldest of the four of them. A quiet man, with the solidity of a heavy-worlder. He was one of the best engine techs Paddy had ever met.

Tony Wu said nothing, just arranged and then rearranged his cards. His specialty was battle computers. Poker was not. For though he loved to play he consistently lost.

"It's a bit dry in here, innut?" Paddy asked. He brought out his flask and four glasses and poured them all a shot. "To the Commonwealth," he said, lifting his glass. "Long may she wave."

The others picked up their glasses in answer to his toast and only Simba gave him a slightly questioning look.

"And here," Paddy said. He took a packet of crisps—they never did tell you anymore just what it was they were crisping—down from a shelf and tore it open. "Help yourselves," he said with an expansive gesture.

Even Colvin and Wu looked surprised at that.

"My sweetheart gave 'em to me," Paddy explained. "She said it would make things nice."

"You thinking of getting married, Chief?" Simba asked.

He gave them a lopsided grin. "Time'll tell," he said. "If I ever do get married, me wife will have to understand that a serious game doesn't come with treats."

"I think it's nice," Simba said. She bit into one of the crisps in a way that seemed almost an invitation. "Everybody needs a wife." She winked.

They laughed and through it Paddy heard the beginning of a tone. A sound he'd been listening for.

"I love this bit," he said and turned the music to its highest volume. The sound boomed off the walls and his companions held their ears, or bellowed for him to turn it down or threw chips at him, depending on their pain tolerance. "What?" Paddy shouted back, laughing. "I can't hear you."

Finally he acquiesced and turned it down.

"That wasn't funny," Colvin said, frowning.

Wu said nothing. He picked out a card in his hand and placed it two cards further down.

Simba simply glared. "Call," she said. She had a feeling it was time to get going.

Paddy frowned. He'd rather they'd played a bit longer to take their minds off what might be going on around them. But the choice was no longer his. The worst of it was, there was nothing in his hand.

Ah, well, he thought. *The game doesn't matter.* Nor did it. The game was just an excuse to get them aboard the *Invincible*. The truth was he'd brought them all here with the full intention of kidnapping them.

Three of the *Invincible*'s techs had been on liberty on the surface of CBC. They had all been severely burned and would be hospitalized for another two weeks at least. And Paddy had no intention of seeing Main Deck face the Fibians with less than a full compliment of technicians.

He paid his debt with bad grace and demanded another hand of them.

They're going to hear the ship decoupling, he thought. *Maybe they won't kill me if they think I was caught as flat-footed as they were.* After all, how would a lowly engineering chief know when the ship was about to leave port with emergency speed?

The ship lurched and *clo-onged* with the release of the grapples and air lock.

"What was that?" Simba demanded, looking up at the ceiling.

"I don't know," Paddy said, rising. "But I'm going to go find out." He rushed out, closing the hatch behind him. *I'll just leave 'em to simmer for an hour or so,* he thought as he walked, whistling, down the corridor. It was already too late, anyway. *But if I tell them I was caught by an officer and didn't want to get them in trouble for gambling, then they might not kill me.*

Raeder sat in the captain's place in the briefing room, feeling somewhat uncomfortable beneath the startled and, in Booth's case, hostile, stares of his fellow officers. They had pulled away from the moon without a hitch but with some few of their people still on the base and one or two of the base's personnel still on the *Invincible.* Now, at last, he was about to tell them of their mission.

"The first part of the mission Admiral Smallwood has assigned us is fairly straightforward," Peter said. "We're to find the Fibian raiders that struck Come By Chance."

"If that's the straightforward part of our mission," Squadron Leader Sutton chimed in, "then I shudder to think what a blow to our collective sanity the *less* straightforward portion of our mission will be."

"One thing at a time, Squadron Leader," Raeder said with a smile. "After we've captured the Fibians then we'll discuss the rest of it."

"They . . . they want us to *capture* the Fibians?" Truon Le, the tactical officer said. The expression on his face said, *I didn't hear that correctly, right?*

Every face at the table showed astonishment and general agreement with that sentiment.

"Get a grip, people. We've done the impossible before." They continued staring. *Oh, all right,* he thought. "It's what *I* want. I'd at least like to take *one* of their ships. There's no telling what Star Command could learn from one of them. So I want our people to operate under the principle of capture if possible."

They looked at one another. After a moment William Booth, the security officer, and not one of Raeder's favorite people, spoke up.

"Are you aware, Commander, that no one has ever successfully captured any Fibians? As for Mollies," he waved his thick hands, "once you get one they're impossible to keep around. At least without a twenty-four-hour guard on 'em, which is more trouble than they deserve."

It was obvious from their faces that though it made them uncomfortable to be agreeing with the incompetent and bilious Booth, they did.

"Have you any ideas on how we should go about it?" Sutton asked. You could almost hear a drawled "dear boy" in the subtext.

"They're sure to destroy all their records," the communications officer, Havash Hartkopf said lugubriously. "I know we would."

"So what's the point?" Ashly Lurhman, the astrogator

asked. "Probably no prisoners, definitely no records. Why bother?"

"I vote we just blast the suckers," Booth said, sitting back in his chair, a slight, contemptuous smile on his broad face.

"I am in command of this ship and this mission," Raeder said firmly. "That is a *fact*. When I give an order, you will obey it because I am your acting captain." He looked directly at Booth as he spoke. "You do *not* get a vote on whether you will follow those orders or not. How you feel about these *facts* is not an issue, because this is not a democracy. And if you don't like that," his cold blue gaze raked the table, "then you have no business being an officer in Star Command."

He paused and looked into the eyes of each of his fellow officers in turn.

"What we would gain," he said at last, addressing Lurhman, "even if there are no prisoners, even if their records are wiped beyond any hope of recall, is a concrete idea of their level of technology. And from their bodies, invaluable forensic information; from their living arrangements some idea, perhaps, of how their society works. All of that would be a gold mine to Intelligence. I would like to get that information for the Commonwealth. I am requiring you to help me do it. So stop thinking we're going to automatically do this the easy way and start planning *how* we're going to do this." His gaze flicked around the table. "As of now the carnival of negativity is over."

They looked at one another silently. Booth with continuing hostility, the rest with blank or thoughtful faces.

"Fair enough," Sutton said, tapping his stylus on the table before him. "If we think we can't do it, we certainly won't be able to. My question now, and please don't think I'm being negative, is how do we find them?"

"We're going to guess," Peter said, calling up a star map. "Based on the best intelligence we have."

He told them what the admiral had said about the bought or stolen identification signals and the destroyed pickets. They looked grimly back at him.

"They've been finding their way deeper and deeper into Commonwealth territory, it's true," he said. "But Come By Chance is hardly on the beaten path. So, there's a psychological effect in these attacks, and the media will have a field day talking about deep penetration, enemy infiltration, yadda yadda yadda. But they're picking their targets carefully, no doubt with safety in mind."

Nodding, Truon Le said, "The safer they stay the more damage they can do in the long term."

His fellow officers nodded and Raeder grinned.

"Exactly!" he said.

He turned his attention to the console before him and a star map floated into existence in the center of the table. He highlighted three solar systems. The computer brought them forward, and their vital statistics appeared below their names and on the notepads before each officer.

"My guess is that they'll continue to choose similar targets for maximum safety for them, maximum psychological damage to us. Then they'll fade away into the night."

He tapped his console and one of the three planets came to the fore.

"This one's my bet. It's close, it's underpopulated, sparely protected and it has a fissile-metals refinery. Warhead triggers—not crucial, but losing it would hurt us." He raised his hands and shook them once in invitation. "Discussion?"

❖   ❖   ❖

Bella Vista was well named—the planet was lovely. It appeared to have much in common with Earth, displaying a limpid blue atmosphere and great, colorful land masses touched with green. It was a lie. The atmosphere was mostly methane and hydrogen, and the green was ammonia; the atmosphere was thick and crushing, and composed of complex volatiles which were mined by ramscoop and refined for shipment to manufacturing complexes throughout the system.

The permanent residents were those who had been brought here by the Consortium. In fact their residence was really anything but permanent. They'd been awarded the planet by the Commonwealth in reparation for their sufferings. Since that time they'd grown rich on minerals and now hired others to mine for them. They usually spent their time enjoying planets with more amenities, but maintained the fiction of a Bella Vista address.

"I hope we haven't guessed wrong," Truon Le said at Peter's side. He was acting executive officer.

Raeder grunted in reply, chin resting on his fist as he viewed the planet and its orbiting habitats, rings, and almost-moons from the captain's screen. *I do like that we, though,* he thought with gallows humor. And he hoped they hadn't guessed wrong, too. *Not that I'm ill-wishing the Bella Vistans. But we can't be in three places at once and I feel in my bones that I'm right.*

His bones, unfortunately, were as fallible as the next person's. Which frankly worried him.

"Perhaps this isn't a good time to mention it," Truon said, "but those three techs that Chief Casey shanghaied . . ."

"Shanghaied!" Peter exclaimed. "That's pretty strong, Executive Officer."

"How about pressed, sir?"

Raeder pursed his lips. "Pressed is good. But it's inaccurate. They came aboard under their own power; nobody drugged them or forced them to stay."

Truon leaned close. "Sir, they came aboard to play a hand of poker with the chief. They didn't plan to stay."

"It's not our fault that they didn't make it back to the station. What are we supposed to do, stop the war so they can shuffle to the exit?"

The XO grinned. "I guess not, sir. But they're claiming they intend to make a complaint."

Raeder leaned back with a smug grin. *Assuming any of us live to get back to Commonwealth space.* "I don't know why, but there's something about optimists that I find really admirable. Don't you?"

"Sir," Hartkopf, the communication officer, said. "The base commander has invited the officers to dinner."

Peter could understand that. There were only about four thousand people in the whole of the Bella Vista system at any time, and those were scattered. A new face showing up during your two-year contract had to be something of a treat.

"Let's invite him up to see us," Raeder countered. "Offer a change of scene."

"Mrs. Hong says she'd be delighted, Commander," Hartkopf came back. "She'd like to bring her family, if she may. She has two husbands and three teenage sons."

"Wow," Raeder said, sotto voce. You didn't meet that many polygamists. Most people thought it too much trouble. *But in an empty place like this I guess the more the merrier.* "By all means," he said. "I'm looking forward to meeting them." *Actually I'm a little unnerved by the two husbands thing. What if they're really peculiar?*

Well, then he supposed he could take refuge in

being the remote, aloof captain figure. Assuming they weren't the type of social limpets who attached themselves unshakably to the highest-ranking individual in the room.

"Sir," Ensign Gunderson said from tactical. "We have some activity from the jump point."

They'd sent the picket away and replaced it with some whiz-bang spy devices. They'd also deployed a very obvious buoy, lest the absence of the picket warn their prey away.

"They're sending a commercial signal," Gunderson said.

"Feed to my screen," Raeder said. "And cancel dinner. Ask them not to send further communication to us until we tell them it's all right."

"Aye, sir."

Raeder's view was from behind the buoy and at the moment showed nothing but a rather boring view of space. He heard the buoy respond to the commercial hail with a set piece welcoming the unscheduled ship to Bella Vista. As he watched the jump point expressed an eye-hurting moment of dissonance and a ship began to come through.

"That is certainly not a Commonwealth commercial vessel of any kind," Raeder said with satisfaction.

It was a flattened swelling disc, like a Mechanist version of a tortoise shell, with two spiky structures curving forward as if it were an insect with mandibles. Eight heavy pods on fairings ringed its stern, and the surface bristled with sensor arrays, launch tubes, focusing mirrors and beam guides for plasma weapons. Heavy missiles nestled against it.

"Destroyer class," Gunderson said, communing with the instruments. "A little more mass than ours or the Mollies. Pretty heavy neutrino flux—impressive power plant. That sucker can probably shift damned fast."

They waited; nothing else came through.

"They had friends with them at Come By Chance," Truon said over Raeder's shoulder.

"Yeah, they did," he agreed. "But there was somebody there to meet them. Here . . ." He raised his hands and let them drop.

"True," the temporary XO said.

After a moment, Raeder said, "I don't think anyone else is coming through. We'll let them get a little further in, then we'll power up and go after them. Our people are in position?"

"Yes, sir," Gunderson answered.

They waited as the Fibian cautiously shaped its vector down into the blue sun's gravity well, aiming for Bella Vista's space.

CHAPTER SEVEN

"Huntmaster, there is no picket here. It has been replaced by an automatic buoy." There was a hint of anxiety in the microtremors of the technician's voice.

Huntmaster Thek-ist paused in his reading and considered this news. Their informants had told them there would be a picket at this jump point. It was the only military craft in the entire area, they'd been told.

Now, suddenly, it was gone.

"Let me hear its message," he commanded.

A human's voice burbled unintelligibly over his com.

Holding his pedipalps in the position of the first degree of irritation with an inefficient inferior he hissed: "The translation of the message!"

The message was a very simple welcome to this quadrant of space, giving the names of the humans in charge of Bella Vista's mining community. No mention was made of the missing picket.

"What do you make of this, Shust?" Thek-ist asked his second.

For a moment Shust held a position that acknowledged the honor of having a superior seek his opinion. Then he said: "Could it be that our first attack has panicked these humans so that they withdrew their forces to guard their most important systems?"

Thek-ist acknowledged the possibility with a gesture, another encouraged his subordinate to continue.

Shust froze once again into a position of indebted respect while he thought.

The huntmaster contained his amusement. He made a habit of encouraging his subordinates to think and to speak, in part because he truly enjoyed educating the young. But the greater part was because he enjoyed having his thinking and his work done for him. Their supple young minds, for example, were superior to his in fathoming the motivations of the human enemy.

Yet so skillfully did he weave his traps that he'd heard the pouchlings refer to his command as a superior one for learning the art of war. Therefore the very best vied to stand beside him on his deck, their brilliance adding to the luster of his reputation.

Most never suspected how he used them. Those that did learned his methods and tended to rise quickly in service to the queen. Shust, he thought, would be one of them.

"Could they have detangled our plan?" Shust asked, with a gesture that denoted keen-edged thought breaking through a trap web. "They might have surmised that we are attacking the least-defended of their outposts."

"Then they would hardly leave this planet unguarded, would they?" the huntmaster asked.

"We should see what we can detangle from any neutrino signatures that have passed this way recently," Shust suggested.

Thek-ist allowed his chelicerae to show his pleasure and Shust proceeded to do just as he himself had suggested. As yet the youngster was unaware that his huntmaster sucked knowledge from him. But he was a thinker, and he would soon know. Thek-ist would have to arrange a transfer ere long. A pity, the ones you wanted to keep were always the ones you had to send away.

"The most recent craft through has the signature of an ore freighter," Shust announced. He permitted himself to show disappointment by the position of his pedipalps. "There has been some limited small craft activity in the area. Perhaps someone programming the buoy," he suggested.

"So we have several possibilities," the huntmaster said. "And we have our mission, which is to destroy the industrial facilities in this system. We shall test the web as we go."

Sutton in his Speed watched the Fibian creep cautiously forward. "Steady," he said aloud. Only he could hear his voice as they were running silent, but Sutton had needed to say it.

His instrument panel had passively registered the Fibs' scan of the area. But then they had come forward. *So their sensors aren't as highly developed as we'd feared,* the squadron commander thought.

Seventeen of the *Invincible*'s full quota of thirty-five Speeds had been deployed to await the Fibians, as well as two WACCIs. The squadron was under orders to lie silent until the enemy was far enough from the jump point to make escape impossible. Much had depended on what came through. Sutton was delighted to find it was a mere destroyer; he and his few squadron mates should be quite well able to deal with it.

Of course he'd hoped they would charge in without thinking, weapons primed and mischief on their little minds. Then the bugs could have been dealt with in a sensible manner.

The squadron commander tightened his lips. Capture was going to be very difficult. *Still, that's all right,* Sutton thought, *as long as it's not too expensive.* If it was he'd have Raeder's hide for a seat cover. *The man has no right to change orders for his own aggrandizement.*

Deep down inside, he wished it had been his own idea. The first unit to capture a Fibian ship would swim in glory.

The Fibians continued to sweep the area, but after the second time he didn't worry. He'd feared that they might refine their instruments with every pass. Now he was confident that they would or could not.

So there was nothing for them to find. The materials that made up a Speed cooled quickly and they'd hung here waiting for hours, so a thermal scan would register only cold metal. Easily mistaken for meteoroids. They'd run three ore freighters over the *Invincible*'s tracks, and the Speeds had been delivered to their positions by grappling onto the freighter's heavy skins, then dropping off, using only the most minimal power to get into position. So there would be neutrino signatures, but they would be low enough that they wouldn't seem dangerous.

Only something looking for a Speed's distinctive shape would have found what it was looking for. But they were small and easily slipped unseen through the sensory net the Fibs had deployed.

Sutton grinned. The enemy's refusal to consider small to be dangerous was going to cause them a lot of pain in the near future.

"Huntmaster . . ."

Huntmaster Thek-ist stirred on his couch. A little venom trickled from his mandibles and he groomed them irritably with his pedipalps.

"Yes, Shust?"

Shust's eyes and chelicerae indicated doubt combined with doggedness.

"Huntmaster, I think I have detected the signature of another vessel. See."

He called up data. Thek-ist knotted his chelicerae into a complex pattern that betokened the sentient mind's capacity for seeing patterns that weren't there.

"You are massaging that data with both your pedipalps and a few anterior limbs as well," he said.

"Yes, Huntmaster. But I am convinced that another ship was through before the ore carriers. One with a power plant and normal-space drive of the following characteristics.

Tik-tik-tik. Thek-ist's footclaws drummed on the deck covering. "A ship of war?"

"That is my hypothesis. A major unit—battlecruiser or carrier—and one which arrived here . . ."

" . . . in the minimal transit time necessary from our previous strike target!"

His pedipalps writhed in indecision, then firmed. "Decelerate. Kill our velocity and reverse vectors."

There was no disgrace in running from a superior foe. If there *was* a superior foe, it would show itself when he fled. If there wasn't, all he'd lost was a little fuel . . .

. . . and Shust would bear the blame for that.

❖   ❖   ❖

Raeder watched the Speeds move at Sutton's direction and said: "No!" aloud as they left a gap before the jump point. The Fibian captain saw his chance and leapt for it with astonishing speed.

Too late the squadron reacted, trying to block the Fibian's retreat. The bugs fired relentlessly, expending energy recklessly in their race for freedom. One, two Speeds were struck, to vanish in brief puffs of magenta flame.

I should have been closer, Peter thought. Even now they weren't close enough to be of any help. Raeder watched the enemy slip away, its image fracturing and fading through the jump point.

"Synchronize engine fluctuations with the Fibians," Raeder snapped. "And follow them through. Let's see where that takes us."

"We're leaving the squadron behind?" Truon Le asked.

"If we stop to pick them up there's no hope of following where the Fibs are going." Sutton would be all right; the Speeds were well able to reach Bella Vista. "Brace for jump," Raeder called.

"Bracing for jump, aye," the helmsman answered.

There was a sense of disorientation and for most of the crew the beginning of a lasting nausea that signaled the shift to jump.

Raeder sat at Captain Knott's place at the conference table and felt like a fraud. Had they followed their original orders the Fibians would still be leading them to their base and they'd have thirty-five Speeds on hand. *I'd be breaking my arm patting myself on the back right now.* Instead they had lost two pilots.

He couldn't believe how fast it had all fallen apart. There had been nothing, absolutely nothing to warn them of a Space Command presence. Yet, for no discernable reason, they had stopped and begun to leave.

The door opened and Sarah entered. She looked around and finding no one but Peter there she moved over to take the seat next to him.

"Where are we headed?" she asked.

"I *hope* wherever the Fibs have gone," he said. He reached out one finger to touch her wrist, then let his hand drop. "I only wish we had a full squadron."

"You left them *behind*?" Sarah said. She put her hand over her mouth as if to hide her grin. "Sutton will kill you."

"What could I do, Sarah? If we stopped to pick them up we'd have lost the Fibians. We may *still* have lost them, but at least by following on their heels we have a shot."

"You're still just making a stab in the dark," Sarah said.

"An educated stab," Peter said, raising one finger.

She began to laugh. "He'll kill you, Peter. He'll insist you deserted them."

"For crying out loud, Sarah, they're safe on Bella Vista by now—probably having dinner with Manager Hong and her two husbands. We didn't leave them in deep space, nor would we. He really hasn't got anything to complain about."

"Oh, yeah," she said with a sly grin. "You spend a few weeks on Bella Vista and you might feel differently."

He cocked a questioning eyebrow at her.

"Not Bella Vista, but someplace very similar. I was fifteen and my mother and father had a freelance engineering job. I had a few weeks before school began so I went with them. I swear, I could feel my blood congealing with boredom." She shook her head at the memory. "You have no idea."

"Well, he better not complain too much," Raeder said. "His job was to hold them. Did he hold them?"

"No-o." She shook her head.

"Well, this is the penalty for being just a little too slow." Peter was smiling as he said it, but there was a trace of annoyance as well.

In his secret opinion, which might end up in his report after he'd reflected on it, Raeder suspected his instruction to try to capture the Fibs might have made Sutton more cautious than he needed to be.

In the greater sense I'm responsible, Peter thought. *Considering that the orders I gave weren't exactly the orders I got.* Raeder pursed his lips. *On the other hand, if I'd been in Sutton's position I'd have made my own call and let the chips fall where they would. So he was still right. Which means Sutton is wrong and deserves whatever he gets.*

The bridge officers started filing in, Booth a distant and glowering last.

"Since we were forced to leave Squadron Leader Sutton behind I'm appointing Lieutenant Commander James to take his place."

All but Booth nodded amiably; Sarah and her capabilities were well known to them from her days commanding the WACCIs.

"I think I know what's going on here," Booth muttered.

"Mr. Booth?" Raeder said, leaning forward.

The security chief looked like he'd swallowed his tongue.

"You were saying . . ." Peter invited.

Booth looked around the table to find blank, yet unwelcoming, faces staring back at him. "Uh . . . well, we—we're going to get that final debriefing you mentioned," the security chief stammered.

Nice save, Raeder thought. He wouldn't have expected Booth to be that quick on his feet. *Then again, he must have some native cunning on his side. You don't get to be an officer without at least enough sense to come in out of the rain.*

The commander leaned forward, folding his hands on the table before him.

At last he said, "Our mission is to pursue the Fibian raiding party. This is part of a deep-penetration raid into their space. The Commonwealth feels it's time we got a look beyond the Mollie worlds and into the Fibian empire. Assuming they *are* an empire. We're to be a reconnaissance in force."

Ashly Lurhman, the astrogator, indicated that she wished to speak and Raeder acknowledged her with a nod.

"Sir, isn't *reconnaissance in force* sort of another way of saying *we have no objective*?"

"Not while I'm leading it," the commander replied. "I know that my desire to capture the Fibians seemed pure hubris on my part, but now that you know the parameters of our mission . . ."

He spread his hands and around the table heads nodded. Capturing the Fibs would have made their mission much, much easier.

"By synchronizing our engine fluctuations with the Fibians'," Lurhman said, "we should, *theoretically,* be following them to their destination. The problem is . . ." she paused, looking directly at Raeder, "that no one who has ever gone near Fibian space has returned."

Actually, not true, Peter thought. Scaragoglu had arranged for him to view a recording of a crewman who had been taken from an otherwise abandoned

ship. The man was raving, despite all that modern
medicine could do for him. Raeder would never forget
the sight of that tortured face, while the words and
phrases he'd mumbled over and over about "swing-
ers," followed by a despairing cry of, "The females,
the females," had kept Peter awake half the night.

*Not that I think the mission would be greatly
helped by telling them this. There are already enough
factual descriptions of Fibian behavior to keep us all
in nightmares for the rest of our lives. May they be
longer than the next couple of days.*

"Which," he said, answering Lurhman's unwaver-
ing stare with one of his own, "is why we need to
go there and gather information."

There were nods around the table at that.

Raeder tapped a key and a still holo of the Fibian
destroyer they were in pursuit of came up. It had
been taken in the last moments before it entered
the jump gate and the special filters used to photo-
graph it showed energy beams blasting from every
surface.

"I expect this to be a short transit," the commander
said. "They wouldn't expend energy this extravagantly
to escape if they were just going to run out of fuel
on the way back to their base. So I want the crew
on high alert. As far as I'm concerned we could be
breaking through to real-space any time now."

He tapped the key again and four ships came up:
their destroyer with two companions and a carrier.
That was the best estimate of the full raiding force
that had hit Come By Chance and the base on
Marjorie.

"This," Raeder said, and with another tap the carrier alone replaced the view of all four craft, "is the
one we have to take out."

Not that the *Invincible* could take on three destroyers

without risk. But the presence of a carrier brought their potential for success down to zero.

"When we come out of jump I want this critter gone. Find it, destroy it before they can react. As we've seen, these people react *very* quickly. Someone is to be on weapons duty every hour of every day. Understood?"

Once again, nods around the table. Snorri Gunderson, the ensign who was sitting in for Truon Le at tactical, raised his big hand.

At Raeder's nod he asked, "Did intel have any idea at all of what we would be facing?"

Peter shook his head. "What you see is what we've got. As for where these guys are going," he shrugged, "that's what we're here to find out." He looked around the table. "Any further discussion, questions?" They all looked at one another, but no one spoke. "That's it then," Peter said, rising. "Let's get back to work. If anybody has any questions or ideas, please feel free to contact me."

He put a hand on Sarah's arm as she turned to go. She looked up at him questioningly.

"I just realized," he explained, "our WACCI commander was left behind in Bella Vista's space. His second is good, but much less experienced. I was going to go over these recordings with her to see if there was anything useful we could find. I'd appreciate it if you would join us."

Sarah frowned slightly. She needed to brief her people and prepare her Speed for action. True to WACCI tradition, where she'd spent so many years, she still checked out her own craft.

"We're meeting in," he checked his watch, "two hours."

"Oh," she said, relieved. "Here?"

He nodded.

"See you then." She smiled at him and with a nod turned and walked away.

Raeder watched her until the hatch slid closed. Maybe he was soliciting her expertise. Maybe he just wanted to spend as much time with her as possible, because he didn't know what the immediate future would bring. *But the possibilities are grim.* And with that cheerful thought he returned to his office and his own work.

Peter was on his feet and running before he was fully conscious. The klaxon warned that they were coming out of jump momentarily. He swung himself into the captain's chair just barely more awake than he had been.

"How long?" he asked Lurhman.

"Minutes, sir," Lurhman snapped back. "Computer estimates four."

"Full gun crews," Raeder said to Gunderson. "Weapons hot."

"Full gun crews, aye, sir. Weapons hot, aye."

Then there was nothing to do but wait, the seconds counting down with a dreamlike slowness while their bodies sped up as they prepared to fight.

They broke through to real-space with a last stomach-turning lurch. The enemy was immediately before them.

"Kill that destroyer!" Raeder snapped.

The forward laser array struck out and caught the Fibians amidships as they made a turn to fight their larger foe. It was a spectacularly lucky shot, cutting all the way through to the center of the ship and its dangerous containment vessels. The ship blew apart with a white flare, blinding even with the computer's almost instant dampening of its glare.

"Well, that was a little less subtle than I'd hoped for," Raeder muttered.

"They managed to get off a partial communication, sir," Hartkopf said from his communications console.

Raeder sighed to himself. *Then I suppose sending up a flare like this doesn't matter.*

"Please send a copy of that communique to our resident linguist with my compliments, Mr. Hartkopf. And ask Mr. Ticknor to provide me with a translation if possible."

"Aye, sir."

"What am I looking at?" Raeder asked.

What he was seeing was a small red sun off in the distance.

Lurhman brought it in closer for him.

"Red dwarf," she said, unnecessarily. "No planets, an asteroid belt."

"That belt has a big buckle," Peter said. He tapped his stylus on the screen and the computer brought the object he'd selected into focus. "That's a station," he said, his voice slow with awe.

It was huge and would easily have made three of Ontario Station. Like the Fibians' ships it had a mechano-organic look to it. And just now it was imitating something organic all too well.

"Looks like somebody kicked over a hive," Truon Le said over the commander's shoulder.

It did at that. Ships and the Fibian equivalent of Speeds swarmed out of the station in appalling numbers.

"Sensors report the neutrino footprints of a large task force," Gunderson said. "Almost a fleet in itself."

Peter felt a distinct sinking feeling as the data flashed by; monstrous power plants surging up from standby to full operational mode, one after the other, coming up on the screen like constellations of minor suns. This was a great deal more adventure than he'd planned on.

Here I thought I was daring for wanting to take out a carrier. Sheesh!

Suddenly in the center of his screen was the face of Sirgay Ticknor.

"Commander," Ticknor said, "I can certainly translate this message but it will take time. I hope you're not waiting for it right now."

"How did you get through to this console?" Raeder snapped.

"If there's one thing I know about," Sirgay said smugly, "it's communications equipment."

"Well, Mr. Ticknor," Peter said, "we're about to have a great big battle with the Fibians, so I don't have time for this right now."

"Fibians! I thought we were supposed to try and talk to them?" Ticknor's face crumpled into a perplexed frown.

"I don't think they're inclined to conversation just now," the commander said. "And, truth to tell, neither am I. Don't attempt to speak to me again unless I've given you express permission, Mr. Ticknor. Or you'll be doing your work in the brig. Do you understand?"

Looking only slightly abashed the linguist agreed that, "Yes, of course I understand, Commander."

"Then would you please get off my screen so that I can see what's going on?"

"Oop!"

Ticknor's face disappeared, to be replaced by the sight of the Fibian horde alarmingly closer. Raeder assessed the situation for just a moment longer.

"I think discretion would be the better part of valor, here. Ms. Lurhman, direct us out of here, if you would."

"Sir!" Gunderson shouted. "There's a carrier and two destroyers exiting the jump point behind us!"

Raeder thought a vile word.

"Launch! Enemy carrier is launching Speeds!" A second later another voice chimed in:

"Missile lock-on! Enemy ship killers inbound—three minutes forty-seven seconds to intersection!"

Well, what do I say now? Raeder thought. *"Oh, shit!" is definitely out, I think. How did Knott always look so Goddamn calm at times like this?*

It occurred to him that Knott might have felt as terrified of screwing up as he did. That was both comforting and alarming.

"Ms. Lurhman? Does this place have a back door?"

An agonizing pause, then, "Yes, sir. Information is at helm."

"Helm," Raeder said tightly, "get us out of here."

"Getting us out of here, aye," helm responded.

"And in the meantime, Tactical, I suggest we stay alive."

He sat silent, eyes flicking from screen to screen. The *energy output* bar was red-lining, and he saw the little flashing beacon that showed the crew in the engineering spaces was going into their hardsuits. The weapons officers hunched over their consoles, like birds mantling over their prey—not that merely human reflexes could do much at these distances. At most, they made decisions for the machines to implement. It was a matter of whose machines did better, that and pure luck. . . .

"Interception," someone said tonelessly.

Globes of magenta fire bloomed in vacuum, geometrically perfect in the absence of air. Countermissiles lashed out, and were met by the counter-counter-batteries of automatic energy weapons on the big ship killers.

"One . . . two . . . three . . . four are through. Activating point-defense batteries."

Vibration growled through the hull as tubes spat plasma and coherent light. *Popularly known as the OH GOD batteries,* Raeder throught mordantly. Meanwhile he watched the overlapping cones on the viewtank, the possible normal-space trajectories of the various actors—the hideously numerous Fibian ships, and the lone yellow path that the *Invincible* could thread among them to the weakness in the fabric of space-time that would let them jump out. Jumping blind . . .

"Navigation, don't forget to get a good fix while we're here," he said calmly. "It'll give the computers something to work with at our next stop."

Navigation answered with a jerk of the chin. Everyone's eyes were pinned to the defense battery screens. The last of the big enemy missiles went up—not a sympathetic explosion, but the idiot-savant kamikaze mind of its guidance system trying for some damage on target after a beam killed its drive. That one was close enough that the *Invincible's* kilotonnes of mass toned and shook. And that meant *close*, in vacuum.

"Rad dosage below critical parameters," a tech announced. And: "Prepare for—"

Reality twisted, and if Raeder's stomach hadn't already been knotted with tension he would have lost all interest in food. They found themselves spat out of jumpspace into the vicinity of a small yellow sun.

"No planets," Lurhman said almost at once.

"Lots of traffic, though," Gunderson observed. "Too much to distinguish any one craft type. It's *busy* out there."

"Station," the astrogator said.

"Two of them," Gunderson's voice followed Lurhman's with no pause. "Small ones. But well armed."

Raeder's screen showed a small fleet of destroyers, backed up by three cruisers.

"That's a little too large a mouthful, even for the *Invincible*," Peter said. "Plot us out of here, Ms. Lurhman."

"Aye, sir," the astrogator said.

She had them jumping almost as soon as they made their turn.

"We weren't as closely followed as I'd feared," Raeder said to the XO.

"No, sir." Truon licked his lips.

"And I wonder why?" Raeder said thoughtfully. "They were plenty determined before—and even if we were jumping blind, it was to somewhere they had the plot for. They should have been able to tag us." He shook his head. "Well, at least we've got—" he looked at the view "—a couple of hours' grace."

"Where to now, sir?"

Peter rubbed a finger across his upper lip and frowned. Going on seemed absurd under the circumstances. The enemy, the well-prepared enemy in its overwhelming numbers, was somehow sending word in advance that a Welter had blundered into their territory. *Which kinda means we've lost the element of surprise,* Raeder thought dryly.

"I think we should try this when they're not lined up at the door with clubs," he said aloud. "Ms. Lurhman, can you get us back to Bella Vista?"

"Not directly, sir. We'll have to go back to our last jump point and skip across to the one that leads to Bella Vista."

Raeder thought for a moment. "Maybe that's something they won't expect us to do," he said. "So let's do it, Ms. Lurhman. Plot us a course for Bella Vista." *We'll just have to hope for the best.*

❖   ❖   ❖

Huntmaster Sek-Thh signified his approval of final repairs to his ship and settled down on his couch. He fixed his eyes upon the jump point with a frozen patience, half watching, half planning.

"Surely, Huntmaster," his second said, "the humans wouldn't come back this way."

"Who can tell what these creatures will do?" Sek-Thh answered. "My thought is that this might have been a sacrifice intended to relay information to a larger raiding party."

"No outgoing signal or message-pod was detected," the second reminded him.

"No," the huntmaster mused. "That is true. But, if our human allies are typical of the breed, there's no telling what insanity will appeal to these beings."

His subordinate adopted a position indicative of complete agreement.

"And so we wait, and we watch," the huntmaster said.

"The jump point is becoming active," a subordinate called out.

The huntmaster's attention achieved a sharper focus. As he watched a human vessel came through.

"Fire on my call," the Huntmaster said.

"Whoops!" Raeder said.

Some of the other cries on the bridge were considerably more profane, but a captain—even an acting one, recently promoted—had to keep a certain dignity. In a flat tone he continued: "Fire forward batteries on acquisition!"

"Target acquired," Gunderson said. "Firing forward batteries, aye."

These were weapons usually used for close-in defense against missiles or Speeds, not intra-ship fighting. *I wonder who was more surprised.*

The Fibian destroyer swelled in the screens, the

distance scales on either side blurring as the vessels approached. Raeder felt his hands clenching on either arm of the combat couch; you *never* got this close to another vessel in open space—the only time he'd seen data like that on an approach screen was when they were docking with a friendly.

The organo-mechanical shape of the Fibian would have been visible to the naked eye by now. Foamed ablative armor blasted off in chunks, and then the energy weapons began to gnaw deeper into its vitals. They were launching missiles—insane, at this distance, where the chances of damage from their own warheads were so great. Then—

The screens went blank for a second; when they cleared there was nothing but an expanding mini-nebula of gas and dust where thousands of tonnes of fighting vessel and scores of sentient beings had been.

"That's got her," someone whispered.

That's got us, *too,* Raeder knew. Their path to Bella Vista was well and truly blocked. If they hadn't had their weapons hot they might be the ones currently enriching the interplanetary medium.

"Mr. Goldberg," Raeder said to the helmsman, "turn us around, if you please."

"Aye, sir," Goldberg answered. *Invincible* began to swap ends.

"Ms. Lurhman, plot us into that jump point."

"Aye, sir."

"Sir," Gunderson said. "We have incoming. That destroyer launched everything and some of it was lying doggo—programmed, or knocked out for a second, I can't tell. But it's coming in fast."

Raeder swallowed and looked at the interception cones. The missiles were accelerating straight in; the *Invincible* was killing her forward vector and going straight back the way it had come . . . rather slowly.

"Time to intercept?"

"Right when we jump, sir. Can't say closer." Hands skipped over boards. "Launching counter-missiles . . . sir, we're going to be awful short on munitions if this keeps up."

"Better an empty magazine than a warhead sunk in our middles," Raeder said.

Time slid away. The carrier was a fast boat with a high power-to-mass ratio, but you still couldn't throw a capital ship around the way you did a Speed. Seconds to jump, one second—

Invincible shuddered, the alarms crying out like a human in pain. Gunderson looked up from the console, pale and face dripping with sweat.

"That one got through," he said. "It was *big*. . . . We'd be fragments if we hadn't been transiting to jumpspace. Just caught the fringe of the energy release."

Damage Control was going into what looked like a Mututhu ritual dance. "Sir, we've got a problem. We're losing containment on one of the main antihydrogen lines—we're going to have to vent it."

"Let me see—" He looked, the instinctive reluctance to waste fuel the war had bred fighting with the figures . . . and losing. "Vent," he said.

Raeder let out a pent breath. *Well, going back is out.* They were using antihydrogen at twice the designed rate—you *couldn't* shut down a line while you were in jumpspace.

"Ms. Lurhman, please find us the next untried exit point," he said. *I sounded admirably calm, just then, didn't I?*

"Aye, sir. It looks like it will be some distance away, sir. I don't have precise data."

"Don't worry, Ms. Lurhman, we can keep occupied." Raeder looked around the bridge at his busy crew. *God, I love these guys,* he thought. *I sure hope we get a chance for rest before the next foray.* "Have the crew stand down, Mr. Truon," Raeder said. He stood up. "I'll be in my office if you need me. You have the bridge."

"I have the bridge, aye, sir."

CHAPTER EIGHT

Deshes tickled the tummy fur of her male partner and whinnied happily when he did the same to her. She felt deliciously wicked, enjoying the pleasures of mating without *actually* mating. But then, even the queen was said to so indulge herself. *Of course,* Deshes thought, *her majesty is* very *wicked.* Could a sub-queen do less?

The male positioned himself, so lost in ecstasy he'd completely forgotten the rules of this game.

They never learn, the young sub-queen thought, disappointed. That was the only real problem with this delightful pastime. The males tended to get overexcited. *And if you like them aggressive, as I do* . . . Well, then there was some attrition since they sometimes refused to take no for an answer.

With blinding speed Deshes grasped him by the neck and flung him. Carefully, so that he skidded across the floor to bump against the wall rather than splatter. The last time had been such a mess.

"No," she said aloud. Quietly spoken, without emphasis.

Deshes hoped the tone of her voice would soothe the overwrought male. However, the way he leapt back onto his feet and stood pulsating, eyes fixed, was not reassuring. He was a good soldier and she would rather not have to kill him.

He did not speak but scuttled towards her, instinctively keeping a respectful distance, but obviously not deterred from his ultimate goal.

Her chelicerae flattened in extreme displeasure. She could hardly call in more soldiers to cart him off as they would instantly fall under the spell of her pheromones as well.

Perhaps a strategic retreat, she thought. Leave him alone in here until her pheromones had dissipated and he came back to his senses. Her taskmistress, second to the queen, would never accept three such deaths in less than a month.

"Lady?" It was the voice of Sheek, her youngest daughter. "I regret the intrusion."

Sheek, being young and terribly staid, did not approve of her mother's pleasures and so, very likely, didn't regret the intrusion at all. But the sound of a second female voice had caused the soldier to flatten himself submissively to the floor, panting now in terror rather than passion.

A very welcome intrusion indeed, my daughter.

Aloud she said, "No doubt you had good cause, child. What is it?"

As she spoke Deshes moved backward towards the door of her chamber, every eye on the panting male.

"The fleet commander at Isasef Station sends word

that they harry a Commonwealth vessel towards us. A light carrier he said."

Deshes perked up. "Ah, delightful!" she said. Fibian females loved to hunt as much as the males and had a stronger territorial instinct to drive them on. The intrusion of these humans aroused and pleased her very much. "I shall come to the command center directly."

"Understood, Lady. Second, out."

Deshes turned to the male, who seemed utterly cowed now.

"Stay!" she hissed, and left her quarters.

As she moved towards the command center she thought about Sheek. Her daughter never missed an opportunity to flaunt her rank. And she was indeed, despite her youth, second in command of this outpost. It was an accomplishment to be proud of, to be sure. But her obsession with it displeased her mother.

Sheek was not her first daughter. The ladies were, as custom demanded, from other clans. Only Nrgun had not sent a lady to Syaris. Deshes had given life to four; none of the others had finished their sulky, ambitious, disapproving adolescence in her presence. Fostering them out had put Deshes in debt to three of her contemporaries, and she was determined not to have to do it again.

The queen herself, only four cycles older than Deshes, had yet to birth a daughter. Though, of course, aside from personality conflicts a royal daughter would bring her own special burden of difficulties.

But her majesty was young, there was time enough for a princess.

There must be a trick to it, Deshes thought sourly. Some correct mixture of pheromones that allowed one to play safely with males and to bring a daughter to maturity. *Perhaps I'm too young to have daughters,* she mused. *Perhaps to Sheek I seem more a peer than a parent.* That might explain the child's aggressiveness. If she saw her mother as a rival . . .

Deshes made an unconscious gesture of flicking away a line of thought. She entered the command center quickly and found her couch.

"Replay the message," she commanded. She watched and listened to the communiqué and when it was over she made a little toss of her head. "Easy prey," she mocked. "So small—barely a mouthful. Create a web before the jump point and try to capture them. We'll have them for dinner."

Deshes turned to Sheek and gestured invitation to join her at the feast.

Sheek made her mother a very pretty gesture of delighted acceptance, then spoiled it by saying, "But we must remember, Lady, that these have proven a thorny mouthful before now."

It was quiet on the *Invincible*'s bridge. The tension of never knowing when the jump exit would come up was exhausting and people hoarded their energy. Which kept talking to a minimum.

Raeder sat in the captain's chair, brooding and, like the rest of the crew, waiting. It was to be hoped that they'd lost the Fibians and that they'd come out in an unexplored and unpopulated area of space. Then they could creep back to the Commonwealth carrying their precious information. And just incidentally save their own bacon.

"Sir," Lurhman said, her voice leaden with weariness. "Computer detects a jump point. Ten minutes."

An unknown one then; Lurhman would have told him if she knew where it led.

"Sound first warning," he said.

"First warning, aye."

A muted tone sounded throughout the ship. Some would sleep right through it, but for others it would provide a friendlier waking than the subsequent klaxon. Throughout the ship crewmen and women made their way to their battle stations and tried to be alert.

On the bridge Raeder took the time to sign off on a few documents and to update his log. It was better than just waiting.

The five-minute warning sounded and any who hadn't yet found their stations now ran to them. People looked forward to not being nauseated any more, yet dreaded what they might find.

Raeder counted down the last seconds to himself, then closed his eyes and gripped the arms of his chair as they jumped back to real-space.

He opened his eyes. *Oh, shit!*

Before them in space was a small armada of Fibians in a globe formation. And Raeder knew, as certainly as if one of them had his neck gripped in its pincers, that there were more coming through behind him.

"Can we—?" he began to ask.

"No, sir," Lurhman answered, anticipating him. "The jump point is already active. We can't go back."

"What's forward?" The commander stared fixedly at the Fibians.

"Searching," she said.

With a gesture Peter called over Truon Le.

"Classic global formation," he said to his acting XO.

"Soon to be a complete globe," Truon observed.

Raeder gave him a look and the XO cocked an eyebrow as if to say, "Yeah, I know, but I had to say it."

With a hand to his upper lip Raeder thought for a moment.

"We'll use electronic countermeasures to delude them into thinking we're flying in all directions. Then we'll move the actual ship away from wherever the other jump point is." *There'd better* be *another jump point.* "Ms. Lurhman?" he said aloud. "How's that search coming?"

"I'm just beginning to get some readings, sir."

"Good work, Lurhman." And it was good work. The woman could practically pull information out of the ether, despite the fact that there wasn't any such thing.

"They'll be firing at everything we send out, sir. Ourselves included," Truon said.

"Yes, but we'll be sending out a *lot* of misinformation. Once Ms. Lurhman has that jump point nailed for us I want them to see us, just for a millisecond."

The XO's face paled for a moment and his eyes widened.

"Then we leave a final countermeasure in our place and bolt for the jump point," Raeder continued.

Truon Le looked dubious, but he knew there really weren't many options.

"Obviously, we can't surrender," Peter said. "If it looks like we can't make it, we're going to have to blow this vessel wide open. We can't let them get ahold of our technology. Or us."

The XO nodded.

"I suppose," Truon said, "that they would have done the same thing if we'd gotten them into a position where capture seemed inevitable."

"Not necessarily," Peter objected. "Even though their only real contact with human beings has been with Mollies, they know damn well we won't eat them."

✧   ✧   ✧

"Fools!" Deshes screamed. With her pedipalps she shredded the tapestries that decorated her quarters. "Pouchlings and fools!" The furious sub-queen dug her claws into the plush surface of her couch and tore it apart, flinging the stuffing around her with abandon. "You lost the prey? From an inescapable trap? Where is my ship that you should be bringing to me? Where is my FOOOD?"

"As far as we can tell, Lady, they have moved on to Sesares Sector."

Sheek conveyed this obviously unwelcome information in a carefully blank manner. Her mother had immediately raced to her own quarters and locked herself in lest she murder indiscriminately while in a rage. But Sheek was aware that her mother held the key to that door and that her voluntary imprisonment might well be abandoned in the face of any ill-timed disrespect.

Deshes froze, her fury so great that she could hardly move to draw breath. The urge to kill was almost overwhelming, but that way led to greater disgrace than she already endured.

Sesares was the domain of the sub-queen who fostered her second daughter. Deshes was duty bound to inform her of the humans' incursion. Doubly so in the face of her indebtedness for that fostering.

I don't want to! she thought fiercely. *They are* mine*! They will be mine!*

"Follow them. Find them. Bring them," Deshes commanded, her voice flat and hard. "Or do not come back to me."

"Your will, Lady." Sheek cut the transmission and froze, considering her mother's words. At last she decided that it was not necessary for her to personally attend to the matter. Though it would be wise on her part to stay out of the sub-queen's way for a few days.

"Put me through to Huntmaster Sah Mahex," she said to a communications tech. "And bring me something to eat." It would be necessary to impress upon the huntmaster the painful nature of failure. Dining as she spoke would subtly underscore her mother's commands.

"Sir?"

Peter looked up to see Paddy looking in the door uncertainly.

"C'mon in, Chief," he said with a welcoming gesture. "How are those repairs going?"

"As well as can be expected, Commander. Considerin' that we've got emergency seam repairs on a tenth of the plating and two seriously distorted hull frames. She needs a shipyard's attentions to be fully recovered. But she'll do."

"Barring another fight like the last one?" Raeder said.

Paddy gave him a pained smile and shrugged.

"D'ye mind if I shut the door, now?" Paddy asked and closed it without waiting for the commander's answer.

The big New Hibernian came over to the desk, withdrew two small glasses from one of his pockets and placed them on the desk. Then from another he withdrew a polished flask. He looked up at Peter, his tongue caught between his teeth and gave the acting captain a mischievous wink.

"'To settle the nerves, ye might say, after a harrowing escape." He poured a tot. "Or perhaps, and this is my preference, to celebrate that very escape." He lifted his glass. "The Commonwealth!" he said and tossed it back.

Raeder picked up the glass warily and took a cautious sniff. Tears sprang to his eyes.

"What kind of a creature *sniffs* fine liquor like that?" Paddy asked with a grin.

"The kind that has to play captain."

"But I've toasted the Commonwealth," said Paddy, blue eyes wide, as though he couldn't believe the commander would so slight their beloved homeworlds.

"The Commonwealth," Raeder said, and took the most minuscule sip possible. Even so he felt his sinuses clearing. "What are you trying to do to me, Chief, drink me under the table?"

"No. But you might could use the rest, y'know. We need you functioning in all your parts, sir, if ye don't mind me saying so. Have ye slept at all these last two days?"

"Some," Raeder admitted.

"Aye, it is hard to sleep with your mind full of those Fibians, isn't it?" Paddy gave him a sidelong look. "Is there no end to them, sir? They're swarmin' like . . . like . . ."

"Bugs?" Peter suggested helpfully.

There was a chime at the door and Raeder called, "Come."

Sarah looked in with a smile. Then she spotted Paddy.

"Your card partners are looking for you," she said to him.

He turned his blocky shoulder away.

"Ahhr, aren't they always, so? No peace have they given me since we left the dock. Ten years in the service and they don't know a signal to disembark from a ship about to leave its moorings. And for this they blame me! Tcha! It's a wonder the great armathons know what the spots on the cards mean."

"I hope they're worth the trouble," Peter said, taking another cautious sip.

"Oh, they are, at their work they're grand. They don't seem to see this as the great adventure it is, though." Paddy looked aggrieved.

"Well, you know what they say about adventure, Chief." Raeder put his feet up on the desk. "Adventure is someone *else* in deep shit—"

"Far, far away," Sarah finished for him. "Does that mean this isn't an adventure?"

"Oh, by any standards *this* is an adventure," Raeder told her.

"Perhaps you should go and tell your friends that," Sarah advised Paddy. "So that they'll understand just how fortunate they are to be along."

The New Hibernian gave her a look from the corner of his eye.

"It's a hard day when a quiet drink must be interrupted for the benefit of those spalpeens," he said. But Paddy took up his glass and flask and with an informal salute and a regretful smile he left them.

Sarah closed the door behind him and took his seat before the desk. She and Peter looked at the glass Paddy had left behind.

"What's that?" she asked.

"I don't know, but I expect it to melt the glass momentarily." He grinned and looking up waggled his brows. "Want a sip?"

She picked up the glass and sniffed, squeezed her eyes shut and blinked a few times as she put it back.

"No thanks, I'd like to keep the enamel on my teeth for now. Besides, if Stores knew we were drinking the fluid they need to clean metallic film from plasma tubes, they might get upset."

They sat for awhile in companionable silence, then both looked up and smiled.

"So," Sarah said at last. "What do you make of all this Fibian activity?"

"Nothing good," Peter answered. "To me it looks like the Fibs are massing for a major offensive."

Sarah nodded, her face thoughtful. Of course she'd know what the mass of ships meant. She'd been trained in intelligence.

"Unfortunately we're too far from the nearest Commonwealth system to send warning. And it's deadly to go back. . . ."

"It could be just as deadly to go on," Sarah said, picking up Paddy's libation. She dipped a fingertip in it and touched it to her tongue. Her face convulsed into a hideous grimace.

"Paddy would have loved to have seen that," he said with a grin. Then more seriously, "You're right. It's deadly to go back, it might be deadly to go on. So I've decided to go on."

"Did you pick heads or tails for go on?" Sarah asked, carefully putting the drink back.

"Tai—I mean, that's what analysis indicates is the optimum course. After all, we *know* what's behind us."

"*And* they're chasing us."

"There is that."

The com chimed and Raeder touched a key.

"Sir," Truon Le said, "Ms. Lurhman reports another jump exit coming up."

"How long?" Peter asked.

"Five minutes, sir."

"Sound warning," Raeder ordered. "I'm on my way."

Peter and Sarah rushed from his office.

"Uh, I was wondering when you'd have need of some Speeds," she said.

His jaw dropped and he turned to goggle at her as they strode along.

"You fighter jocks are crazy, you know that?" he answered. "We'll need you when we don't have to make a high-speed transit through whatever Fibian minefield we find ourselves in. Remember Sutton back at Bella Vista having his boring dinners with Mrs. Hong? Only here you'd *be* dinner and you wouldn't live long enough to get bored."

"I agree," she said. "But I agreed to ask. Thanks for saying what I thought you would." Sarah gave him a mock frown. "All except that crazy jocks thing."

He flashed her a grin as they parted ways, he to the bridge, she back to Main Deck.

Peter swung himself into the captain's chair and brought his screen online.

"Report," he said.

Truon Le handed him a noteboard and gave him the highlights verbally.

"All battle stations are active, all weapons are hot," he finished.

"Thirty seconds to exit," Lurhman said.

Raeder focused on his screen. "Give me feed," he said after a pause.

"Sir, I can detect no naval units. If there's anything here, it's far away or powered down so far it's leaving no footprint."

That's a change, Raeder thought, nodding. *For . . . what, four jumps now? Four. Each system more heavily fortified and each one with still more in the way of major Fibian units. Another two systems like the last and they'd out-mass the whole Commonwealth fleet by themselves, never mind the Mollies.*

"But there's a lot of traffic through here, sir." The ghost-traces of ships' drives came up on the screen. "I'm highlighting those the system and I think were warships. Either that or they have a *lot* of luxury liners."

A disconcerting number of the trails glowed green. Liners, couriers and perishable-freight carriers were the only civilian ships that had footprints anything like a war vessel's. Most of a military ship's drive capacity was useful only when you had to maneuver very violently very quickly.

"And I'm getting a hail from those buoys," Lurhman went on. "Let's see . . ."

Infraray and radar probed; passive sensors drank down every particle and computers extrapolated.

"Sir, those aren't just beacons. They're automated forts. Not much maneuverability, but they're heavily shielded and they're armed for bear. They're repeating the hailing pattern, at higher intensity—I think that's an identification-friend-or-foe-or-we-open-fire."

"Trusting lot, if that's their notion of a navigation bouy," Raeder said. "Get Ticknor."

"Ms. Lurhman, I think we should withdraw if that's possible."

"They're not coming through behind us yet, sir," the astrogator said calmly. "We'll end up back in the frying pan, though."

"That may depend on how many of their ships they sent after us," Peter said.

"The buoys have locked onto us, their weapons are hot," Gunderson said from tactical.

"Take us back, Ms. Lurhman."

"Yes, sir. Taking us back, aye."

"What if we meet them in transit?" Truon asked the astrogator.

"Theoretically we should be able to see one another. Parts of the ship, or even individuals, might pass right through one another. Theoretically," she emphasized. "No telling what will really happen."

Eeeuuw, Peter thought. *What if this happens while*

we're leaving jump? Does that mean I might end up with six legs or claws? He shook his head. *Concentrate on the matter at hand,* he told himself sternly, and tried not to see himself with a tailwhip.

"Is there any possible way that we can use that?" Raeder asked. He looked at Truon, then over to Lurhman at her console. "Maybe plant a worm in their software, or something?"

Truon looked thoughtful; to a tactical officer this was an appealing idea.

"We have no idea if our computers are in any way compatible," Ashly mused.

"There might be something we could use though," the XO said. "Physics is universal, whether you've got eight legs, two, or none."

Raeder nodded. "They must have some stuff they've gotten from the Mollies, even if it's only translation programs . . ."

"I think I've got something that will answer," Gunderson interrupted. He looked embarrassed. "Something my sweetheart sent to me. It's a worm with a learning curve. It can teach itself any software code on a machine once it's established itself. Then it can destroy whatever it's learned." He shrugged at their astonished expressions. "She's very clever."

"Give her a kiss for me when you get home," Peter said. "As long as she doesn't come near any of our systems. And get ready to transmit that sucker. Attach it to anything Mollie, or . . ." He keyed up Sirgay Ticknor's lab.

"Yes," the linguist answered.

"Mr. Ticknor, do you have anything in your recordings of Fibian interactions that might be straight computer code? No . . ." he wanted to say human, but couldn't, "individual interaction, but straight machine language."

"Yes, I do," Ticknor replied looking surprised. "Most of my resources are composed of such inter-actions, in fact. That's what's been making a straight translation so difficult."

Before the linguist could launch into a lecture on the differences between spoken and machine languages and their relationship with human processes, Raeder cut him off.

"Please upload a sample to me now," he said. "Preferably something that's very common, as though it was the first thing any machine would think of saying to another."

"Certainly," Ticknor agreed.

He fiddled with his console and Peter relayed the information to Gunderson as it came up. He glanced over at the tactical officer, who nodded to indicate that he was getting it.

"That should suffice," Gunderson said after a few moments.

"Thank you, Mr. Ticknor," Raeder said.

"May I ask why you needed it?" Ticknor looked as though he was willing to chat all day.

"I'll let you know later," Raeder said. "Right now we've got to see if we can use it. We'll be making a jump in—" he checked his clock "—two minutes. You'll want to brace youself."

"Again? We just jumped back to real-space! I just can't take this, Commander Raeder. It's very upsetting to my system. I work best if I have regular meals and minimal stress."

"I know exactly how you feel, Mr. Ticknor." *I've heard about it often enough.* "But there's no help for it." He cut the connection before the linguist could mount another protest. *I guess talking a lot goes with being a linguist.* But you'd think the man would realize they were just a little *busy* here.

The truth was Raeder knew the linguist was hoping to bend his ear about the size of his lab. It actually was the largest lab space on the ship, but that didn't mean it was big. Ticknor just couldn't get the notion of "compactness" into his headspace. He flatly refused to believe that they were alloting him luxurious, by their standards, amounts of space.

"I'll have this ready for transmission, sir," Gunderson said. "Should the opportunity arise."

"Thank you, Ensign," Peter said. He didn't know if he should hope for that opportunity or not.

CHAPTER NINE

Sirgay turned back to his machinery, brow furrowed with annoyance at the commander's bruskness. *I don't think that he likes me.*

Maybe it was because he had a phobia. A lot of these gnarly, ultra-macho military types probably couldn't even spell arachnophobia, let alone tolerate it in someone else. Certainly they would never suffer such a flaw in themselves. *They don't even know the* meaning *of the word fear.* He sighed. *I wish the general hadn't shot his mouth off about it.* It wasn't like it was something he could help. He'd tried all sorts of therapies; sometimes they worked for a while, but it always came back. So did the dreadful fascination. . . .

"And it's not like it's important," he said aloud.

It was so frustrating the way people made such a big deal about it. *I mean, if the Fibians looked like bears or cats or even house flies there wouldn't be a problem at all.* At least no more of a problem than anyone else would have.

Maybe Scaragoglu's mention of his arachnophobia was military code for, "Kick this jerk around as much as you like, he hasn't got the guts to stand up for himself."

Well, at the first opportunity, assuming the commander gives me one, I'm going to show him just what I'm made of.

Ticknor sighed and his shoulders drooped. *That sounds* so *pathetic.*

"Work," he urged himself.

He connected his new translator machine to his computer and began downloading the adjusted program into it. While it ran he went over to the coffeemaker and began to pour himself a cup.

Then they hit jump.

Thoughtlessly, instinctively, Sirgay's hands jerked and hot coffee flew everywhere. It splashed across his console and shorted out the translation device; electricity arced and spluttered, smoke began spiraling up from the device.

"I'm getting some very strange readings," Gunderson announced.

"Upload to my screen," Raeder instructed the tactical officer. Peter studied the information for a moment. "What does this stuff mean?" he asked.

He'd stood a watch at tactical early in his career and could identify just about anything that might show up on its computer. But this . . . this stuff was weird.

It was energy, and it had patterns, but they didn't seem to correspond directly to anything he'd ever seen before. Was this the backwash of their own passage or . . .

"It's them," he guessed. Ships didn't interpentrate

in jumpspace often enough for the phenomenon to be familiar. "Gunderson, get that program ready to transmit. See if you can detect anything that you can hook it onto."

"Readying program, aye," the ensign said.

"Ms. Lurhman," Raeder said, "I don't understand how this sort of thing could still be theoretical. We've been using jump points for travel for a very long time now."

"Before the war all transits were scheduled," she said. "And the only time you'd need to worry is when one ship is jumping in as another is jumping out. The timing would have to be perfect for them to intersect even slightly." The astrogator watched her board avidly. "My guess is that this is more of a bow wave than our backwash. I don't think we've met them yet."

Raeder's fingers dug into the armrest of his couch, into the padded covering that sheltered the combat gloves when they weren't on code red. He started guiltily as the fingers of his right hand poked through the fabric. Leaning over he examined the damage.

You can hardly see it, he thought, brushing at the tears. But the old man would find it tout suite, he had no doubt. *I'll have someone fix it when we get back to base.* The difficulty would be in keeping Knott away from his chair until it was fixed. *Could have been worse. I might have broken it clean off.* He had yet to get his own chair fixed.

Raeder frowned impatiently. He was trying to avoid the main issue; what was going to happen in the next few minutes?

He tapped his com for general address and began to speak.

"Attention all crew. This is your acting captain speaking. In the next few moments we may be experiencing what has up until now been a purely theoretical scenario. We may be actually passing through a Fibian vessel. We will be able to see them. They will see us. But we will not be able to interact anymore than you can with your own shadow. Only information may be exchanged in that state. But since we will be able to see one another I want all sensitive material covered from view. Where possible and where it won't endanger the crew, make it dark. Starting immediately. Use your uniforms if you have to, lie on your consoles, but cover up. Raeder out."

He took off his own jacket and covered his screen and console. "Turn down the lights," he said. "And turn off all unnecessary consoles. Buddy up where possible. Those whose consoles are shut down, crowd around active positions."

Truon Le pulled a drop cloth out of a cabinet and draped it over the holo display unit.

"It got left behind by the workers when we rushed them off the ship," he explained.

Raeder nodded approval. With luck such drapes were available all over the ship.

This is going to be interesting, he thought nervously. He was worried, but he was also excited. It would be the first time that humans had gained a look at the inside of a Fibian ship.

"I want every recording device we have running when and if we merge," he said.

"Yes, sir," the XO said. He called on the *Invincible's* tiny military history unit to get to the bridge on the double with their equipment.

Then they waited.

Ticknor put down the coffee pot and raced for the fire extinguisher. He fumbled with the locking mechanism with panic-clumsy fingers. Suddenly, an odd sensation came over him, as if his skin was being

pricked with ten thousand tiny pinpoints, and he
paused. It was reminiscent of the sensations he'd felt
just before the violent thunderstorms that plagued
the prairie town where he'd grown up. The hair on
his arms rose as a tide of energy bathed him and
he shuddered in reaction.

Then, a table flowed towards him. He backed off;
the sparking of his translation device became unimportant as this apparently solid object came through
the wall. Too soon his back struck the bulkhead
behind him and he squawked and sucked in his gut
as the table's edge came on like a guillotine in slow
motion. Ticknor screamed when it reached him,
putting out his hands to stop its awful progress.

He gasped as the tabletop slid through him without
a hitch. He could see his legs and feet through its
semitranslucent surface, and felt its passage as a warm,
vaguely tickling sensation.

"What's happening?" he said out loud.

A Fibian voice attracted his attention and he looked
up. Through the wall came a Fibian, an actual, living, breathing, eight-legged, eight-eyed, whip-tailed
monster. And it was watching him.

Ticknor froze, feeling as though a band of iron was
tightening around his chest. Lightning seemed to
flicker at the corners of his vision and his heart began
to race.

The Fibian moved, so fast it seemed impossible.
Ticknor screamed, a full-bodied howl of honest terror and he snatched up the coffee pot, flinging it at
the Fib. The Fibian ducked, seeming to flatten in an
impossible maneuver, then it raced forward, its tail
poised over its back, dripping acid.

Screaming, "No! No! No!" at the top of his lungs,
Sirgay plunged towards the other side of the table.

Man and Fibian raced around the tiny room, both

of them making a great deal of noise. Ticknor grabbed the still-sputtering translation device and flung it at the Fib. Instinctively the Fibian put out his clawed hands to ward it off.

Ticknor bolted for the door, then through it as the device gave off a blinding flare of energy. The linguist locked the door behind him, then raced down the corridor on tiptoe, trying to stifle the desperate little sounds he was making. Where the corridor branched he slowed down, then plastered himself to the bulkhead and crept forward. Sweat dripped into his eyes and he wiped it away with the sleeve of his lab coat.

At last he came to the corner. He didn't want to look. Ticknor's heart pounded and his stomach felt pinched, his mouth was dry and he *really* needed to pee. But the ship's people needed to know. Someone had to tell them that somehow the Fibians had managed to penetrate the ship. *And I guess that's me.* He took a deep shuddering breath and leaned forward to look out into the next corridor.

Three Fibians were staring back at him. They leapt forward and Ticknor fainted dead away.

The Fibians hissed and growled as the human slipped right through their chitinous fingers, then they drifted away helplessly and slid through the wall opposite, still chittering their disappointment.

"Mr. Ticknor?"

He felt a light tapping on his cheek and moaned softly.

"Mr. Ticknor!"

The tapping turned to a shaking as a hand gripped his shoulder and jiggled it briskly.

With an effort he opened his eyes to find a young woman leaning over him, a frown on her pretty face. She was wearing a uniform.

"Mr. Ticknor, what happened?" she asked impatiently.

He blinked. A uniform? Why . . . ? Then he remembered. He tried to sit up and only succeeded in jerking his head and giving himself a charley horse in his neck.

She pushed him down with embarrassing ease.

"What happened?" she repeated. "Should I call a doctor?"

"I'm fine!" he snapped, humiliation making him rude. He managed to sit up, clumsily, on his second try. Rubbing his neck he said, "There's a Fibian in my lab. I don't know how it got there, it came through the wall. I swear it did."

The woman looked relieved and he could see that she was fighting a smile.

"You didn't hear the announcement then," she stated with certainty. "What you've experienced is something that was only theoretical before now. Two ships meeting in jumpspace. We passed through one another. We've all been seeing Fibians. But they're gone now. We couldn't touch each other either. Do you think you can stand now?"

She stood and offered him a hand up.

He was going to ignore it, but then decided he was still too woozy to gain anything by being surly.

"It looked so solid!" he said. "I would have sworn he was real."

The woman blinked. Her lips tightened for a moment, as though she was impatient.

"You must have missed the announcement," she repeated. "They were real, they just weren't solid."

Ticknor rubbed his neck again, and winced.

"So it won't really be there . . . in my lab?"

The woman shook her head. "Shouldn't be." She looked at him for a moment then seemed to come to a decision. "Let's go take a look." She took his elbow and gently steered him down the hall.

"I'm all right," he said weakly. But he let her take charge. Women liked that sometimes. As long as deferring to them didn't get to be a habit. "This is it," he said, indicating the closed door.

He tapped in his entry code and the door slid open. Stepping inside, he tripped and looked down. When he saw what lay on the floor Ticknor leapt backwards with a scream. He knocked the woman down and they sprawled on the floor in a brief but frantic collision of knees and elbows. Ticknor managed to crawl over her to the keypad and with a few taps the door closed and locked.

The linguist collapsed panting against the wall and glared at the puzzled and resentful woman just fighting her way free of his long legs.

"You said it wouldn't be there!" he accused. "You said it wasn't solid! Well, it seemed pretty damn solid to me!"

Peter tapped in a private line to Ashly Lurhman, the astrogator. Her face appeared in a small square on his screen.

"Yes, sir?" she asked.

"I suppose they'll be after us any second now," Raeder said.

"No, sir. They'll have to return to realspace, then reenter the jump point. You can't turn around in jumpspace."

Raeder nodded. "Good," he said. "Ms. Lurhman," he added after a pause, "where are we going?"

"Um. I've directed us back to our last jump," she said. "It was the quickest thing I could do, sir."

"Good," he said again. "I'm sure I read somewhere that it's possible to change your exit point while in jumpspace. Is that correct?"

"Yes, sir. I've read that, too. It's theoretical, though." She looked at him suspiciously.

"What do you say we crack another theory?" Peter asked. He offered the astrogator an encouraging smile.

She licked her lips nervously.

"What can you locate in the way of alternate jump exits?" he asked.

Lurhman glanced down at her board and tapped a few keys.

"The one I've directed us to," she said at last. "Which was our last port of call. The one just before it." That had been a small but *very* active outpost. "The one before that." She looked up at him. "That would be the Fibian space station, sir." She tapped again, licked her lips and looked up, almost unwillingly. "I've got another, sir. It doesn't show any traffic at all."

"Take it," Peter said.

"Sir . . . the fact that it's unused may indicate that it leads to some dangerous destination. Too close to a sun, or a neutron star. The fact that they don't use it could be construed as a warning."

Raeder frowned. "It's a chance we'll have to take, Ms. Lurhman." He nodded. "Do it."

"Aye, sir."

He watched her intent face as she made the change.

"How long until we exit?" he asked her.

"Not less than forty-eight hours, sir."

"Good," he said. He'd hoped for more. The crew were tired, and so was he. But this would give them some time to rest, as far as you could in jumpspace. "Stand down," he said to Truon and the XO passed the order.

Raeder was suddenly exhausted and he rotated his neck in a futile attempt to loosen the kinks. He'd seen to it that the rest of his people got sufficient rest, primarily by ignoring his own needs. Now it was catching up with him at last.

"Mr. Truon," he said and rose from the captain's chair, "I'm going to get some rest. The bridge is yours."

The XO saluted him. "The bridge is mine, sir. Good rest."

"I'll have a meeting with the senior staff tomorrow morning," Peter said. "0800."

"0800, sir. I'll pass the word."

"Thank you Mr. Truon." Peter started to move off.

"Sir?" It was the unwelcome voice of William Booth, the security officer. His face appeared on Raeder's screen in a little square marked SECURITY OVERRIDE.

Peter sat down again. *What could this possibly be about?* he wondered.

"Report," he said.

Booth licked his lips and looked very nervous.

"I'm with Mr. Ticknor down in the labs," he said. "We've got a situation here that you need to look at, Commander."

The man's eyes fairly begged, *Please, take this out of my hands.*

"Is Mr. Ticknor there, Mr. Booth?" *He hasn't hung himself or anything over the prospect of seeing that many spiders, has he?* That was all this mission needed.

"Commander," Ticknor said, shoving Booth aside, "we need you down here immediately! This is," he swallowed visibly, "t-terrifying, but it's huge. You've got to come!"

"I'm on my way," Raeder said, more convinced by Booth's willingly giving up center stage than by the linguist's demands.

"Sir?" Truon Le said, his dark eyes bright. He looked like a pup straining at his leash.

"Ms. Lurhman," Raeder said, "you have the bridge."

"I have the bridge, aye, sir," she agreed and went back to her board.

Peter and the XO entered the people mover and took it all the way to the lab area. Raeder didn't feel like wasting time; he was too damned tired and besides, according to Ticknor, this was huge.

He and Truon rounded the corner to see Booth, Ticknor and a female security person grouped outside a lab's closed door.

"What's going on?" Peter asked.

Ticknor started towards him, his hands held before him.

"We've got a Fibian!" he said.

Peter stopped and looked at the linguist, then over his head in an unspoken demand at Booth.

"It's true, sir," the security officer said. "Petty Officer Lewis called it in, and I've seen it too."

"Lewis?" Raeder said, looking at the young woman.

"Excuse me?" Ticknor said before she could do more than open her mouth. "This is *my* Fibian. I mean, it's by my doing that we *have* a Fibian at all."

Raeder looked at him for a long moment, then at the two Space Command personnel.

"May I see it?" he asked Ticknor.

The linguist blinked at him, then looked at the door, then back at the commander. Slowly he seemed to sink, shoulders hunching, knees bending.

"You want me to . . . open the door?" he asked at last.

"Yes," Raeder said crisply. "How else am I going to get a look at it?" He waited a moment, while Ticknor straightened up. "It is in there?"

"Oh, yes. It's in there."

The linguist shuddered, squeezed his eyes shut and

shook his head, breathing as though preparing himself for a deep dive. Then, with a trembling hand, he reached forward and punched in a code. The door slid sideways and he flung himself aside, his back to the wall.

Booth and Lewis took out their side arms. They were only meant to stun, but it impressed the commander that they did so. He moved cautiously into the tiny room. And stopped. Truon slid in beside him and gaped at the twisted figure on the floor.

It was still breathing. A rhythm that caught Peter's eye and wouldn't let go. Probably because everything else looked so impossible; he could almost *feel* his brain holding desperately to something familiar. *And ain't nothing more common than breathing,* Peter thought.

Unconscious, the Fibian looked much smaller than any pictures he'd ever seen of them. And, though completely helpless, it also looked like one of the most dangerous creatures he'd ever seen. It lay in a tangle of claw-tipped limbs, the acid from its tailwhip slowly eating its way through the floor covering. And the front of its face had more sharp edges than a butcher shop. The chitin on its thorax was blackened as though burned.

Raeder backed away.

"We're going to have to move it," he said. "I want it in the brig. Restrain that stinger. Now, while it's unconscious."

Booth didn't look too happy at the orders, but he pulled out a radio and called up some more of his people. Then he looked at Lewis.

"Do you have any cuffs?" he asked.

"Yes, sir." She pulled out a half dozen of the flimsy-looking plastic rings. Her eyes were huge. Lewis obviously expected to be ordered to truss up the alien.

Booth pulled out a few of his own cuffs and stood considering the Fibian. Then he took off his belt and, with his teeth gritted, leaned over the Fib to clasp it around the creature's "waist." That done he clipped and locked one pair of cuffs to the belt, then another around the tail about a quarter of the way down from the acid-dripping tip. He tightened it until it was firmly clasped, then locked the other end to the pair attached to his belt.

Booth sat back, white-faced, and wiped sweat from his brow. He glanced over his shoulder at Peter.

"Should I restrain its claws, sir?"

Raeder was frankly impressed. He didn't like Booth and he didn't want to, but he gave the man credit for doing a good job in bad circumstances.

"Yes," he said. Then he put out his hand. "I'll help."

The other security crew showed up just as they'd locked the last chitinous limb in a restraint.

"There should be a stretcher around here someplace," Peter said to Booth. "Get him to the brig. I'll send Doctor Goldberg down to take a look at him. Her. It. Whatever." Heaven only knew if the good doctor could help the critter, xenobiology being largely theoretical. *But then, what isn't today?* Raeder asked himself.

He left the lab to find Ticknor had slid down and was sitting against the wall clasping his long legs in trembling arms. The commander squatted down beside him.

"Quite a coup," he said to the trembling linguist. "You've done something none of us has: captured a living Fibian."

The linguist shuddered violently.

Leaning close, Peter said, "They're not really spiders, Mr. Ticknor. You've got to make yourself understand that. They're intelligent beings. They have spacefaring capabilities, for crying out loud. They're way above bugs, at least as far above them as we are."

Ticknor looked at him and raised an expressive brow. *All right. They're intelligent, spacefaring beings with eight limbs, tails like a scorpion, claws, chitin and mandibles. And they probably really do eat people. But they're not bugs. Any more than we're monkeys.*

At that moment the stretcher bearers went by and Ticknor buried his face in his knees with a moan.

"Don't you understand?" he said to Raeder. "It's not something I can jolly myself out of. It's totally without reason or common sense. Terror is like that." Ticknor looked up at the commander and his dark eyes blazed. "I doubt you'd know anything about that."

"If you mean I've never been frightened, you're wrong. When I had my Speed shot out from under me I didn't know if I was going to die out there in the black or not." He looked Ticknor in the eye. "But I've been lucky. I've never had to contend with anything like this."

The linguist looked away, a bit embarrassed.

"Can you study it via a screen?" Peter asked.

"Yes," Sirgay answered, looking a bit more contained. "I won't like it, but I can do that."

"Good. Then I'll have them install a two-way communications screen. The controls will be at your end." Raeder gave him a thin smile. "I'll even give you a second lab to work in."

Ticknor brightened. "Thank you," he said. "That would help immensely." He stood up. "Excuse me, please. I've got to see if I can repair the damage to my translation device. I'll need it more than ever now."

He offered his hand and Raeder shook it firmly.
"Good work," Peter said.

With a faint smile and a nod Sirgay returned to
his lab. As the door slid closed, Peter jerked his head
towards the people mover and he and Truon moved
off.

As they marched down the corridor together the
XO said quietly, "There's a guy who needs an ego
massage."

"If he breaks the Fibian language, and right now
he has a better than even chance, he'll get mas-
saged until he melts. Assuming he can get around
the way they look." Raeder shook his head ruefully.
"And assuming we ever make it back."

Raeder folded his hands before him on the conference table and looked at his fellow officers.

"Well," he said. "I hope you're all well rested and
fed?"

There were nods and smiles at that.

"This morning we have some good news and some
bad news," Peter continued. "You've probably already
heard our good news."

He missed dining in the camaraderie of the officers'
mess. Part of that camaraderie was the gossip, so he
knew without being there that they'd have already
heard about the Fibian. Solitary splendor lost some
of its charm at times like these.

"Doctor Goldberg, do you have a report for us
regarding our . . . guest?"

"Beyond the fact that its chitin wasn't breached and
it's conscious, I'm afraid I can't tell you much. While
it was out I did as full a scan as I could on its vitals
and that's important information. Eventually I'm sure
I'll be able to come up with something regarding this
particular Fibian. But this is the first healthy one we've

ever caught. It seems listless and disinclined to communicate. For now, I recommend keeping it restrained. I've put some acid-resistant material around its stinger, and I hope that the critter won't be able to work it off too soon.

"We've also put together a sort of protein pap for it to eat." The doctor shook his head. "Everything we've heard about them indicates that they eat live food, but we don't have anything like that except for hydroponics. And I doubt it's a vegetarian."

There were grins around the table at that.

"I wish I had more to offer, but for now that's all I've got. But I can't guarantee that we can keep this creature alive. It may be under orders to commit suicide at its earliest opportunity."

Raeder grimaced. He'd had orders that *were* suicide, in his time, but never orders *to* suicide. Still, it wouldn't do to assume that because they *looked* like bugs they had an antlike lack of individuality.

"We'll have to hope for the best," he said. "I'm fully aware that you're playing it by ear, here. Maybe our linguist can help you."

Goldberg nodded dubiously.

"At least you might be able to speak to it."

"That could only help," Goldberg said.

"Anyway, that's the least of our problems," Raeder said.

Around the table officers glanced at one another, then returned their gaze to Raeder.

The commander tapped several keys.

"What you're seeing on your screen is a projection of how far our fuel will take us at our current rate of consumption." Peter sat back and watched them read, watched their faces change as one by one they looked up at him. He nodded. "I've double checked this. We're nearing the point where even optimum jumps on a least-effort course will leave us dry before we can return to Commonwealth territory. We're hundreds of light-years beyond any human exploration. And at the moment, unless Ms. Lurhman has good news for us . . ."

The young astrogator looked down and shook her head.

"We have no idea where we're headed," he continued.

Augie Skinner—the engineering officer—looked pained.

"It's the damage those engines took during that last battle," he explained. "We're burning fuel at an incredible rate. To be precise, we're venting about twenty-five percent as much as we're burning. Do you have any idea how dangerous it is to vent monatomic antimatter? I'm all ready to close the shunt and redirect, but I need normal space to do it in."

Raeder nodded and held up his hand. "I'm aware that you've worked miracles on those engines, Mr. Skinner. Nevertheless, unless we find some antihydrogen soon we're going to be in deep trouble. So I want each of you to try to find some way we can cut back on our fuel consumption." *Not that it will probably make a big difference in the long run, but at least it's a productive way to spend our time.* Then he reminded himself that negativity was a luxury they couldn't afford right now.

"And let's not forget we're under pursuit," Booth said.

There ya go, Peter thought. *That didn't help a bit, now did it?*

"Thank you, Mr. Booth, that almost escaped us."

CHAPTER TEN

The shift into real-space seemed almost easy.

Maybe the more you do this the easier it gets, Peter thought. Then he looked around at the too thin, too pale faces on the bridge. *Maybe I'd better not say that out loud. Someone might throw up yet.*

He had his screen do a global scan of the area. But there was nothing to see, nothing but distant stars, that is. At least on visual. Raeder switched his screen and gave a slow whistle. *Wow!* he thought. *You don't see that every day.*

Before them were no less than three jump points side by side.

Their energy fields roiled in glowing colors the computer had chosen. The patterns those colors made were almost painful to look at—light seemed to bend at strange angles that the eyes wanted to reject. It took him real effort to keep watching. Across the three jump points the computer showed electric blue tracks, representing ships' neutrino signals, running everywhere between them.

Raeder knew that they weren't looking at human traffic. A cluster of jump points like this one would be famous if it belonged to the Commonwealth. He'd been taught in the Academy that the juxtaposition of more than two jump points was possible, but merely— the word of the month—theoretical.

So this is definitely not ours. Most likely it's Fibian. It could belong to some heretofore unknown alien species. But Raeder hoped not. *My dance card is already too full for comfort.* So he'd go with the easy and obvious. It was Fibian. Peter folded his hands and tapped his two index fingers on his upper lip. *I feel like I'm playing a shell game here and we're the pea. Round and round we go and where we end up . . .* Unfortunately this game was rigged, since the Fibs would be waiting with daggers drawn wherever that happened to be.

"Let's just brush by each one of these jump points," Peter said to the helmsman. "Let our tracks get lost in the general noise. Then we'll pick one of them at random and dive through."

Not that it would make much difference in the long run. *I'm just feeling ornery enough that inconveniencing the clowns following us is going to amuse me.*

"Ms. Lurhman," he said, "I'm going to allow you to choose our route. Surprise me."

"Looks like our pursuers are going to make that choice for us, sir," Lurhman said. "Something's coming through behind us."

Huntmaster Shh-Feth endured the jump back to normal space without allowing it to interfere with his examination of the information before him. The emissions of the prey ship indicated a vast consumption of fuel. It should only be necessary to keep them on the run until they ran out of antihydrogen and then they would have to surrender.

That, at least, will please Lady Deshes, he thought.

Little else about this mission would. Shh-Feth winced at the memory of blundering into the territory of the sub-queen, Lady Sysek; unannounced—and obviously in pursuit of Commonwealth prey. Questions . . . would be asked. Even now Lady Sysek might be asking them.

Why return home? he asked himself. *Why not engage in battle with the prey and perhaps die an easy death?*

Why? Because his lady had issued an order and everything from his culture to his genes felt the compulsion to obey. Despite the undoubted outcome for himself, and perhaps even his crew.

No! he thought. *Deshes is strange—wicked, even.* He shivered deliciously as he thought of the rumors about his lady. *But she is not a fool. She will not dispose of a trained crew for no better reason than pique.* Besides, Mesoo, the queen's second, would have her head for such waste.

But his own life was certainly forfeit. *Therefore, I must do my last duty as perfectly as I can.* For the next time he saw his lady might be as food.

"Huntmaster?" the steersman said, his voice quavering with trepidation.

Shh-Feth looked at him, and disliked the color of his crewman. The dull red of his scales had turned almost brown.

"You may speak," Shh-Feth commanded him.

"The prey has diverted, Huntmaster. They run towards the Three Fledrook."

The huntmaster lurched up from his couch, then

slowly sank down again. His own scales were the same
dull brown as his underling's from the shock of such
disastrous news.

"At all costs," he said slowly, "they must be captured
or destroyed."

Failure to do so would be an offense to the
queen herself, and undoubted death for all of
them . . . perhaps even for Lady Deshes.

They were on their way through jumpspace to . . .
somewhere. Ashly Lurhman had told him that there
was no sign of an exit for the next thirty-six hours
at least.

At this point, the longer the better, Raeder thought.

He had made his way to engineering to have a little
one on one with Augie Skinner, the engineering officer.
As he walked, the commander looked around the
unfamiliar territory with approval. Engineering was
perfectly shipshape, the people alert and busy. But
then, this was the *Invincible*; he'd expected no less.

How quickly we become spoiled, Raeder thought
with a rueful smile. *As the old saying goes, one day
on the bridge and you're drunk with power. Two days
and you stop realizing you're a powerful drunk.*

"Mr. Skinner," he said as he came up behind that
worthy. "I wonder if I might trouble you for a word."

Skinner turned from the screen he'd been leaning over, an expression of extreme concentration on
his face. For a moment he seemed almost puzzled.
Slowly the clouds cleared as he mentally shifted gears.

"Sir!" the engineer said at last, straightening up.
"How can I help you?" He leaned closer to Raeder.
"Would have come to you, Commander."

"Frankly, Mr. Skinner, I was feeling restless. And
I've never been down here before. I was on the flight
deck, working with the Speeds."

Raeder looked around with an approving air. Then he turned back to find Skinner looking at him, and he blushed and grinned.

"Well," Raeder said, "everyone is treating me differently. I guess it's only natural that I start acting . . . acting like I'm channeling Captain Knott."

Skinner's lips lifted slightly in what would be a grin in someone else. "Thought I recognized something familiar there."

"Okay," Peter said, "let's start over. I came down to talk to you about the engines. Thought maybe you could show me what you're doing."

The engineer nodded and with a jerk of his head he led the commander towards the engine room. They slipped into the special coveralls that would shed any loose particles that might be clinging to them. Anywhere that antihydrogen might be in use an effort was made to keep stray particles out. If something as small as a skin cell came into contact with the stuff the explosion would be formidable.

Raeder shifted uncomfortably. The suit he was wearing was a little short in the body for him; if he straightened up, he might well be singing soprano until they got him to a regeneration tank.

Just a very quick inspection, he promised himself. *At least the feet are big enough.* The two officers then moved through a series of specially designed rooms that burnt off, then washed, then blew off anything that might still cling to them.

Skinner led the way into a complex of conduits and massive, self-contained engines, their exteriors boxy and blank except for screens on their surfaces that showed flow patterns, heat, fuel consumption, and so on. The fusion engines were quiet, cooling down from their brief use in real-space. Just now the transit engines were engaged and their soft hum pervaded the massive room.

There were indications everywhere of the hit they'd taken. One of the walls had temporary bulkheads pressed in place, bubbly lesions marking where metal and plastic had melted in the blast. Beside the breach one of the transit engines was down completely. Very likely it would remain so, given that its shielding was mostly gone. It was a miracle that it hadn't exploded and taken the ship with it.

Fortunately the superior engineering that had gone into the *Invincible* had once again showed its quality during the emergency. The automatic shutdown had worked perfectly, reversing the flow of antihydrogen already in the engine and storing it in its safe.

The other damaged engine was in permanent overdrive. Raeder could see where they'd fitted a feed shunt to the partially melted conduit. The worst of it here was that the control baffle had been destroyed, thus antihydrogen roared through the engine full throttle, so to speak, and out into the carrier's wake.

"There's nothing salvageable left of seven at all," the commander commented.

Skinner shook his head. "Gonna need a whole new engine," he said. "Modular unit. Simple enough in a shipyard, although they'd have to take hull plating off. Even if we could fix seven we'd have to shut down the engines to do repairs. As for eight, we just haven't had time for anything more than the patch job she's running on now."

"If we just shut it down . . ." Raeder began.

Skinner shook his head again.

"M'not sure we could get out of jump with six engines, sir."

The commander raised his brows.

"Theory is that you need three engines worth of power to get into, through and out of jump. We can do it with one engine down, theoretically we could do it with two out. But no one's ever tested that."

"What if we stopped?" Raeder asked. "Just shut down, then repaired eight while we're drifting. Couldn't we just start up again and continue our journey? We'd be safe from attack here in jump."

"Shut the engines down completely?" Skinner said. Raeder nodded. The engineer scowled and rubbed the back of his neck. "Don't know. M'not sure we could get enough power up to get back out."

"Theoretically," Peter said.

"Theoretically," Skinner agreed. He looked at his wounded engine with worry in his eyes. "Don't think it would make any difference now, anyway, sir, given how much fuel we've consumed so far. Maybe we should leave this theory untested."

Peter grimaced, then tried to rub his face with both hands, only to have them stopped by his faceplate. *Now I see why Captain Knott rubs his neck when he's worried,* Raeder thought. He took a deep breath. *The man's right,* he admitted. Somehow, getting out of jump and fighting seemed to favor them more than testing an obscure theory. *Despite the luck we've been having with that lately.*

"Do we have enough fuel to get us out of jump?" he asked.

"Yes, sir," Skinner said. "Would've told you if we hadn't, sir."

Peter thought he looked a little pained. *I guess I would too if someone came down to Main Deck and reminded me to fuel the Speeds.*

"Um . . . I suppose you've adjusted the fuel consumption on the other engines to compensate for eight's massive appetite?"

The engineer looked around them before he answered.

"They're not running at the same high level of consumption, sir. Have to take their baffles offline for 'em to do that. All the operating transit engines need to be running at pretty much the same rate." Skinner looked thoughtful. "Guess it's a design flaw they'll need to work on."

"Mmm," Peter agreed. *Jeeze, I'd never realized what an optimist Augie was. Here we are running out of fuel, running towards and from an angry, well-armed, well-fueled enemy, and he's thinking of making a complaint to the manufacturers.*

"Would you like to take advantage of Chief Casey?" Raeder offered.

A look came over Skinner's face and Peter suddenly remembered that Augie and Casey frequently played poker together. As Peter himself had once or twice. *Yeah, I guess if someone came along with a straight line like that I'd get a funny look on my face, too.*

"I mean . . ." he began.

"I know, Sir." Skinner waved a hand to forestall further explanation. His face looked mildly pleasant, so Raeder knew that inside he must be howling with laughter.

"Talented as Paddy is, Sir," Skinner gave a one shouldered shrug, "there's nothing he could do here until the engines are down." He looked around them, his eyes slightly unfocused as he listened to his engines. "When there'd still be the problem of all the antihydrogen already used up."

Peter nodded. "Well, off the top of my head I can't think of anything else to do. I guess we'll just have to take our chances."

"We've been doing all right so far," Skinner said.

There he goes again. I must look pretty hopeless if Augie Skinner is trying to cheer me up. In all the time Peter had known the engineering officer he'd only seen the man break down and smile twice.

"That's true," Raeder said. "We are doing all right." And to his own surprise, he felt better for saying it.

Ticknor made another adjustment and tried his translation device again. The Fibian on the screen ignored him. It appeared to be building itself a web. The sight made the linguist's throat tighten, but he persevered. Eventually though he just stopped talking and watched.

"What do you think you're going to do?" he mumbled sarcastically. "Catch flies?"

The translation device murmured and bleated and at last the Fibian's head came up. The alien said something, waving its pedipalps and clicking its mandibles as its chelicerae subtly changed positions.

"Foolish . . . stupid . . . food-prey . . . leather back," the translator spit out. "I cannot . . . rest . . ." The remainder was untranslatable.

Ticknor sat back with a gasp. The translation device worked, sort of. *Perhaps my tone of voice will reach him.*

"We mean you no harm," he said.

The translation device bleated once. The Fibian ignored him.

Ticknor rubbed his face then snorted. *My tone of voice. As if it were a dog. Hey!* He had a sudden revelation as he watched the alien. With a flurry of tapping he called up the recording of the Fibian and listened carefully. The creature's voice was somewhat high-pitched with a warble to it. The linguist's eyes widened. *But without much variation in inflection!* It's delivery was fairly monotone. *Thus the movements of its hands . . . I think those are hands, and mouthparts.*

In fact . . . He ran the recording through very slowly. The Fibian's whole body had adopted a stance that seemed, even to a non-Fibian, to speak of contempt and loathing.

Body language! he thought. *The subtleties of body language are very important to them.* Of course they were important in human interaction, too. But to most people they were invisible; perceived and acted upon, but unconsciously. He suspected that to the Fibians they were a much more obvious part of any conversation. *They add the inflections that are missing from the spoken word.* And he had it on record!

Unfortunately we have very little use for insulting language. The commander was sure to remind him of that.

The linguist attempted to get the Fibian's attention once more, but the alien continued to ignore him, working relentlessly on its web. Eventually it was finished, for which Ticknor was grateful. The sight of its posterior waving around like that was disquieting. The Fibian settled itself into the center of its construct and froze.

I've got to get it to talk, Sirgay thought desperately. *Without a larger sample of words to work from we'll have nothing when we need the translator.* Like now, for instance.

He leaned back in his chair and looked at the ceiling. He'd been watching that bug for hours now and had only one, rather obnoxious, remark. Ticknor sat forward and began to play a recording of Mozart. The spiders at home seemed to like it. Or so he'd read.

The Fibian sat frozen in its web. Silent.

I wonder why it hasn't killed itself. I was under the impression that they did that sort of thing. Or was that the Mollies?

Of course it still might commit suicide. Fibians

were supposed to prefer their food live, weren't they? Well it wouldn't find that here. They didn't even have lab rats. So all their captive had to do was refuse to eat whatever they came up with and it would die soon enough. Sirgay considered that. *I don't think they'd even try to give it anything intravenously.* For one thing they had no real idea how its circulatory system worked. For another, and more importantly, they wouldn't dare to breach its shell.

Ticknor shuddered as he imagined the crew trying to force-feed the thing. It would be a battle royal.

Maybe that's a way to approach it, he thought.

"Are you hungry?" he asked.

The Fibian sat unmoving in its web.

I hate the way it doesn't blink. Perhaps it was performing some sort of buggy zen thing wherein it would just quietly will itself to death. *That would be a lot less messy for everybody.* But, dammit! he didn't want the thing to die.

"Do you want to live?" he asked.

Its chelicerae moved very slightly.

I'm going to assume that's a defiant sneer. If I were a captive warrior I'd like to think I'd sneer at my captors.

"Water?" Ticknor offered.

He hit a key and water flowed from a spigot on the wall. The linguist watched his subject as the liquid flowed into a basin.

At first there was no reaction; the Fibian stared forward just as it had been doing since settling in. Then, Ticknor would have sworn he saw a quiver shake the creature.

He'd forced himself to read about Terran spiders, which the Fibians closely resembled, and now remembered that many of them preferred a moist environment and were easily dehydrated.

With a tap of his keys he slowed the flow of water to a trickle and watched the creature. Its mouthparts moved. He replayed the last few seconds of the recording of the Fibian that was constantly running. They most definitely moved.

"The water is pure," he said. "Uncontaminated, no drugs, safe."

The translator was silent, but Ticknor hoped that one of these words would reach their prisoner. *I guess at some level I'm still pushing for that tone of voice thing.*

But the Fibian held firm.

Ticknor considered, then tapped a few more keys, raising the humidity in the Fibian's cell.

"Is that more comfortable?" he asked.

He felt a strange sense of pity for the captive and raised the humidity again, and again, until the air in the cell was visible from the vapor. As he watched the Fibian's chelicerae worked. Tightening the focus of one of his cameras he saw that the Fib was drinking the dew that had condensed on its shell.

Maybe this could be a first step, he thought.

Ticknor watched the creature. It angled its head so that drops flowed down the diamond-shaped face to where it was gathered by its mouthparts. It drank for a long time. Then went back to its inscrutable stillness.

"Now that you have taken sustenance from us perhaps you would be willing to talk to me."

The translator spoke a few words and the Fibian jerked as though he'd been touched with a live cattle prod. It lifted its head and seemed to stare directly into the screen before it.

It spoke, slowly, as though it wanted him to understand. After a moment the translator said, " . . . gave me nothing. I gathered . . . myself."

"There would have been nothing to gather had I not increased the humidity in your cell," Ticknor said.

The Fibian continued to stare silently at the screen, but its whole body quivered.

"All I want is to learn your language!" Ticknor said. "To speak, to communicate, to talk!"

"Talk," the Fib said flatly. It cocked its head to the side in a quizzical manner.

"Just talk," Sirgay agreed.

The Fibian spoke again, still with that inquiring cast to its body. The translator finally spat out, "Not betray?"

"No!" the linguist said, leaning forward eagerly. "Not betray. Just talk." He waited a moment. The Fibian remained motionless. Finally Ticknor said, "You have accepted sustenance from us. But all we want is to talk."

The Fibian settled back again. It spoke and gestured, and then went still.

The translator said only, "Think."

"I will leave you in peace, then," the linguist said and darkened the Fibian's screen.

He could still see it, of course. In order for it to be kept from killing itself a twenty-four-hour watch was in progress. So its privacy was already hopelessly compromised. *Which might not mean a thing to it*, Sirgay thought, somewhat defensively. And which also meant that it would be foolish not to watch it, in case it did something revealing and important.

It sat in its web and stared at nothing.

My translation device works! Ticknor thought giddily. *If the Fibian agrees to talk to me we'll soon be able to hold real conversations with them. God, I'm good!*

Ticknor busied himself with watching the recordings of the Fibian's brief exchanges with him and making copious notes about the creature's body and hand positions. It greatly helped the linguist to be so involved with watching parts of the creature. It prevented him from having to endure the hideous impact of the whole.

Two hours later he looked up at the live screen. The Fibian had not moved.

Maybe he's waiting for me to get in touch with him? Well, of course he was! As far as the Fibian knew no one was watching him. Therefore why waste energy trying to communicate.

Ticknor brightened the creature's screen and returned its audio.

"Have you come to a decision?" he asked.

"Will talk," the Fibian said.

CHAPTER ELEVEN

Waves rushed to the shore, receding with a hiss. Peter lay in the warm, soft sand; comfortable, relaxed, enjoying a blissful lassitude. Slowly he became aware. But he resisted, lying still when his body urged him to move. The sound of the waves slowly changed from a gentle susuration to a soft chime. Raeder turned his head lazily to look at the chiming waves. He wondered idly why they were doing that.

BBBRRRAAANNNGGG!

Raeder rolled out of his bunk and onto his feet still expecting to brush off sand. He patted his hands down his body and found himself still dressed except for his shoes.

He groaned aloud. *I bet Captain Knott never groaned when he got out of bed,* he scolded himself. He was glad the crew couldn't see him now. *I doubt it would do much for their faith in my leadership.*

Peter staggered the two steps to his desk and flopped down. He checked the time. *We should be in jumpspace for eight hours yet.* Of course, that was Ashly's best estimate. *And few estimates come out right on the numbers.*

He keyed up the bridge and Ms. Lurhman's face appeared. She looked embarrassed.

"Report," he said, managing to sound crisp and alert. He'd been afraid it was going to come out something like, *"Unnhh?"*

"Sir, we're coming up on the jump point. I estimate thirty minutes."

"On my way," he said, before she could say anything else. *There's coffee on the bridge,* he reminded himself by way of a bribe.

He rubbed his face vigorously, glad for antibeard enzyme. *Wish I had time for a shower.* He got up and left his quarters, making a brief stop to wash his face and brush his teeth. *Maybe that will convince my body I'm officially awake whether it likes it or not.* Usually he woke up right away. This lurching through molasses feeling was very strange. Peter made himself walk to the bridge, hoping the exercise would wake him up. *No point in getting there in a hurry if I'm a zombie when I arrive.*

Truon Le put a cup of coffee in Raeder's hand as he stepped off the elevator.

"God bless you, Mr. Truon." Raeder sipped cautiously at the steaming brew. "Report," he said.

"Ms. Lurhman found us an exit point much sooner than she'd expected. She says it's possible that it was hidden by some other ship preparing to exit. That's what the energy readings seemed to indicate."

"How long ago was that?" the commander asked, seating himself in the captain's chair.

"Six hours, sir."

Raeder cocked an eyebrow at him.

"We woke you and told you, sir, as soon as Ms. Lurhman made her discovery and you said to carry on."

"I *did?*" *Wow, I haven't done that since I was at the Academy,* Peter thought. Of course, when that happened at the Academy his eyelashes had also fallen out from sleep deprivation. *Moving on. Do we go through here, or keep on?* He tapped his fingers on the arm of his chair.

"Bad news now, or bad news later," he said aloud. "We'll go through here and take a look. Ms. Lurhman, Mr. Goldberg, take us through."

"Aye, sir," they said in unison.

Raeder scrolled swiftly through the log to see how the hours he'd been resting had passed. His exact words to the XO had been, "Thank you, Mr. Truon. Carry on." *Jeeze, I sounded so ... so ... conscious, there.*

He felt the transfer from jump begin and changed his screen to external view.

"No enemy ships," Gunderson said, his voice showing his astonishment. "There's your basic traffic buoy, evidence of considerable traffic, nothing overtly hostile going on, sir. It's really a buoy this time, not an orbital fort masquerading as one."

Raeder switched screens and looked at the neutrino tracks the computer sketched out. All very straight-forward; no skulking, no lurking, no recognizable patrol patterns.

"Don't these folks know there's a war on?" Truon asked quietly from over Raeder's shoulder.

"Maybe we're so far behind the lines that we've hit civilian territory," Peter said.

"Even so, sir, with all the military craft we've been

seeing, why wouldn't they spare a picket for what looks, going by the traffic, like a major commercial center?"

"Good question," Peter said. "Let's get a little ways from here," he said to Goldberg. "See if we can get lost. Because the guys coming in after us know very well there's a war on." *And they're looking to bring it on home to us.*

"Moving out, aye, sir," the helmsman answered.

He moved them forward, looking for the heaviest patch of neutrino signatures he could find.

"I'm seeing some activity, Commander," Gunderson said. "There's a squadron of ships headed our way. They're broadcasting a message."

"Send a recording to Mr. Ticknor with my compliments," Peter said. "Tell him I need a translation ASAP."

"Aye, sir."

Raeder tapped his fingers and considered their situation. If these were peaceable non-Fibian folk the *Invincible* roaring into their territory with weapons hot couldn't look good. On the other hand, if they were blood-sucking Fibians—and Fibians *literally* sucked—then who cared? What was the likelihood of finding *two* space-faring sentient species in the same war? Conversely, these could be some peaceful breed of Fibian. . . .

By the same token, there's no evidence whatsoever that Fibians understand the meaning of the word peaceable.

"Sir," Rivera, the com-tech said, "Mr. Ticknor would like a word with you."

"Put him through." Raeder nodded to the linguist when his image came on the screen, pleased that Ticknor had taken his warning seriously. "You have something for me?" he said.

"Yes, Commander. They're asking us to identify ourselves. Specifically they want to know what clan we are."

Clan? "Can you make me up a message that tells them we are being pursued by hostiles?" Raeder asked.

"Yes . . . but what about this question about clans?" Ticknor looked anxiously out of the screen at him. "That could be important."

"I have no doubt that it is, Mr. Ticknor. But we have to survive to find out more. Get me that message so that we can broadcast it. If we don't they'll fire on us, Mr. Ticknor. And that would be bad."

Especially since I think that's two battlecruisers and their destroyer screen, or Fibian equivalent. The *Invincible* could outrun most things it couldn't fight. It couldn't outrun a battlecruiser for long, not with the state their engines were in, nor fight two of them. Or even one, with the carrier's depleted Speed squadrons.

"Yes, it would," Sirgay answered through clenched teeth. "Should I ask them not to shoot, or perhaps ask them for help?"

"Asking them not to shoot sounds good," the commander said. "Asking for help could get us into trouble further down the line."

Ticknor turned to his console and carefully spoke the words they'd agreed on.

"I'll just run this by my associate," he said.

Peter's brows shot up. "Who?"

"It was one of those serendipitous things," the linguist said. He waved a hand. "It's complicated. But he's willing to work with me on this translation stuff." Sirgay turned away for a moment, then came back. "He says it's fine if we send it out blind, by which he means audio only. There are complex gestures that should go along with the message, but if they can't see you they'll read them as given."

"I have the message at com, sir," Rivera called out.

"Thank you, Mr. Ticknor." Raeder took a real look at him for the first time since they'd started talking. The circles under his eyes were so deep the man looked like a raccoon. "I'm probably going to be calling on you a great deal in the next few hours. Are you going to be all right?"

Ticknor grimaced. "I guess I should have slept some while we were in jump," he said. "But the work had to get done . . . and I was feeling sort of, not exactly nauseated . . ." Half a dozen people nodded unconsciously. He shrugged. "I'll do my best, Commander."

"Thank you, Mr. Ticknor. But at the first opportunity I think you'd better get some rest."

"That's very kind of you, sir. But, I'm—"

"I want to keep a line open with you, Mr. Ticknor, in case we get any further messages. So I'm going to hand you over to Tech Rivera. Raeder out." *I hated to do that,* Peter thought, *but he'd go on for hours if I let him.* "Send out that message," he said to Rivera. "But give a little static to make it seem our com has been damaged. Keep us on this course, Mr. Goldberg."

"Maintain heading, aye, sir."

Raeder's screen split. Part of it showed the oncoming Fibian patrol, mere computer-generated dots at this distance. The other half showed the jump point behind them. His mind was split, too. Part of him wondered if Skinner and his people were taking advantage of this downtime to fit a new baffle onto transit engine eight. He wondered when the oncoming Fibs were going to question the *Invincible* keeping her weapons hot. He wondered when their pursuers would break through into real-space. He wondered if continuing to run forward was going to be a huge mistake.

"Sir," Gunderson said, "estimate that the advancing Fibians will reach us in three minutes."

"Sir," Rivera said. "A new message from the Fibians. I've relayed it to Mr. Ticknor."

Raeder tapped a key, "Ticknor," he said, "what have you got for me?"

"Damp your weapons, or we will be forced to assume you are hostile," Ticknor said. There was sweat on his brow and his dark eyes were anxious.

"Thank you, Mr. Ticknor, Raeder out." He switched the linguist back to Rivera.

Now what? If we don't shut down our weapons the Fibs in front will fire on us. If we do we might be sitting ducks for the Fibs coming in behind who I know damn well will fire on us. He was about to make a decision about a civilization which he knew absolutely nothing about. On the third hand it wouldn't be good to have *both* sides firing on them.

"Mr. Gunderson, stand down on weapons, but remain on high alert, keep our ECM ready."

"Stand down on weapons, aye, sir, maintain high alert and ECM. Here they come," Gunderson said.

Their pursuers came out of jump so fast they seemed to appear by magic. The oncoming Fibs increased their speed and raced through the *Invincible's* neighborhood as though she wasn't there. Firing commenced almost immediately from both sides, with those that had been pursuing the *Invincible* trying desperately to get around the new aggressors and at her.

The crew on the bridge broke into relieved cheers, pumping their fists and slapping each other on the back.

"Wow," Peter said. *Is that "Hey, that's my pork*

chop!" or *"Get off my turf!"* we're watching? He tapped a key. "Mr. Ticknor, the home team is attacking our pursuers. Can your . . . associate give us a reason why?"

Without saying a word Ticknor turned away from the screen and spoke. Raeder could hear muted sounds, like conversation, but in an unknown language. In fact, it sounded a lot like gargling, mixed with hissing and popping sounds. Finally the linguist turned back.

"Sna-Fe tells me that if we've blundered into another clan's territory then they will attack the more aggressive ships, particularly if they are Fibians of another clan. No out-clan Fibian ship may enter the territory of another without permission or it will be assumed that they are raiders."

Really! Peter thought. "If we survive the next hour or so I can see we're going to have a whole bunch of interesting questions for your little buddy, Mr. Ticknor. I'll let you go now, but please stand by."

The commander watched the two Fibian squadrons duke it out. They were much too close to the jump point for the *Invincible* to slip by unnoticed. *From the way they're behaving it looks like our old friends would really like to blow us out of the sky.* A definite change in attitude; he'd gotten the distinct impression before that they wanted to cripple the Commonwealth raider for capture. *And who's to say that our new friends wouldn't take umbrage at our attempting to leave the party so soon.* In fact, he'd be willing to bet that they would. *I need more information.*

"Mr. Ticknor," Raeder said. "What can you tell me about this clan structure thing?"

"I'll see what I can find out, Commander." Ticknor turned from the screen and spoke for some time.

Finally he turned back to the screen, looking a bit embarrassed. "He says that he can't give us any information that might betray his people. He doesn't want to talk about anything classified."

"This isn't classified," Peter said. "He's known about it all his life, hasn't he?"

Ticknor gave a nod and turned to the Fibian. After a moment he came back.

"He says you're right. He has known about this all of his life, and soon you'll know about it too."

Raeder waited, then when nothing was forthcoming he spread his hands and said, "So?"

Ticknor blinked, then held up one finger. "Uh, I'll ask."

After a moment Ticknor said, "Sna-Fe says he is of Clan Snargx, the red clan. The clans are distinguished on first sight by color. There should have been something about their ships that indicated this."

Raeder turned to Truon. "Could you look into that for me, please, Mr. Truon?"

A moment later the XO's image popped up on a square of Raeder's screen.

"The ships' markings were predominantly blue, sir."

Raeder relayed that to Ticknor, who came back with, "The blue clan is Clan Nrgun, their queen is Tewsee; an older queen with a passion for learning."

"Too-see?" Raeder said. *There's a nice old-fashioned-sounding name. I've always had a way with old ladies myself. . . . What am I thinking of, we're talking about a gigantic carnivorous bug here.*

"Close enough, Commander," the linguist said. "The translator will remove any mispronunciation."

"How many of those things do you have available?" Peter asked.

"Four." Ticknor looked a little nervous. "I haven't programmed them all yet."

"I'd like to have one of them on the bridge, if you have one ready. I'll send someone down to pick it up," Raeder told him, his tone of voice making it clear that this wasn't a request.

The linguist looked downright alarmed, and made little plucking gestures as he spoke. "Commander, I can't stress enough that a lot of the subtleties of meaning in the Fibian language are conveyed with body language. In other words, the full message will not be audible." He looked at Raeder for a moment. "Do you understand?"

Raeder rubbed his upper lip.

"Do the blues know about humanity?" he asked Ticknor.

Ticknor blinked, then asked Sna-Fe.

"He says he doesn't know." Ticknor looked worried; he shrugged. "He says he's just a . . . I think that shift of the legs mimics someone carrying a heavy load."

A grunt, Raeder thought. *Well, maybe some things are universal. At least universal among species with hierarchies.*

"Ah . . . lower-status unit. How would he know what a queen knows?"

"Good point," Raeder agreed. "Are they likely to be hostile to us? That he might know."

"Sna-Fe says they're an old, established clan, confident, but careful. And he says that given their queen's proclivities they might welcome you as a source of new knowledge."

That could be good, that could be bad. "Knowledge" could be acquired through "vivisection," for example. Or it could be *culinary* knowledge. Fibian behavior to date wasn't encouraging; on the other claw, it was now clear they had their own divisions, just as humanity did. Raeder glanced at the soundless explosions growing and fading in the space between the ships of the two Fibian clans. *I think that until we've spoken for a little bit I'm not going to let them see us.* It seemed safer that way.

"Thank you, Mr. Ticknor. Please stand by."

He sent out the signal for a video conference and his screen soon filled with the faces of his senior officers. One square of the screen still held the ongoing battle, and Raeder kept a weather eye on it. Briefly he outlined their situation.

"I must admit," he finished, "I'm not too sanguine about becoming an object of study for this new clan of Fibians. I'm interested in your opinions."

"I think this critter is tryin' to pull the wool over your eyes," Booth said. "Red is probably the color for warriors, blue most likely just means civilians."

"Then why are they fighting, Mr. Booth?" Ashly Lurhman asked, her voice carefully neutral.

"Sir," Truon Le said, "I think we should go with the blue Fibians and see how that turns out." His eyes strayed to his screen. "Assuming they win. It could be a priceless opportunity to study them and perhaps to gain allies. That was one of the purposes of this deep-penetration raid, to find out how the Fibian species is organized."

I.e., we're losing the war and ready to try any desperate, crazy idea, Raeder translated mentally.

Skinner said, "Set charges throughout the ship, something low-tech and undetectable. If things look bad we can blow 'em."

The rest of the officers nodded agreement. The rest save for Booth.

"What is this, a class trip?" he demanded angrily. "You're talking about learning from them? Hey, people, the Fibians are the Commonwealth's enemies! They *eat* people for God's sake! Here we are with a God-given opportunity to hit 'em where they live and you want to set charges and just blow the *Invincible* up? What's wrong with you guys? This is a quantum opportunity to trash a lightly defended Fibian system and grab some antihydrogen. Without which we are dead ducks, people."

Raeder was proud of his fellow officers; not one of them rolled their eyes.

"At the moment, Mr. Booth, the blues are kicking the tar out of the reds. I sincerely doubt they'd be doing that if they were in league with them. It would be too expensive, *and* it would be stupid. They've eliminated two destroyers and they're keeping the reds from reaching *us*. Which the reds are giving every indication of really wanting to do. Why would they do that? What could they possibly gain by fooling us like that?"

Booth held up a hand. "A look at Commonwealth technology." He bent back one finger. "An understanding of Star Command tactics and capabilities." He bent back another. "A possible Trojan horse." He bent back a third. "And a large number of experimental subjects." He looked out of the screen belligerently. "I say we hit 'em now, hit 'em hard while they're preoccupied and—"

"Get our butts fried, no questions asked," Raeder said, cutting him off. "Haven't you ever heard the expression 'the enemy of my enemy is my friend,' Mr. Booth?" From the confused look on his face Peter guessed not. *I bet he still hasn't figured out "that man's father is my father's son."* "I'd rather risk making the Commonwealth a new ally than a new enemy."

"In that case, Commander," Sarah James said, "I'd like to suggest that the squadron go to the aid of the Blues."

"What!" Booth shouted. "Are you crazy?"

Raeder leaned back in his chair and considered Sarah's proposal. On the one hand it might put them in good standing with the Blues. Lending them a hand would also make the *Invincible* less beholden to them. It would give his fighters the chance to strike back at the Reds. They'd been denied a chance at them so far and were chafing at the bit. *The more I think about it the better I like it. I really don't appreciate being chased . . . especially when I suspect the chaser has a saltshaker in one hand and a fork in the other.*

Also, there didn't seem to *be* an other hand.

The commander interrupted Booth's tirade to say, "Get the squadron together, Lieutenant Commander. I'll get on to our tame linguist to see if he can come up with something that will allow us to warn the Blues that we're coming in on their side."

"*No!*" Booth pounded on his desk until his hair flew. "Commander, no!" he insisted.

"Yes, Mr. Booth. The decision is made. Pending any objection from Mr. Ticknor regarding Fibian courtesy in these matters. I'll be in touch, Ms. James. Thank you all, Raeder out."

Next time I call a general meeting maybe I'll just leave Booth out of it. It would be a deadly insult, but it might keep the man from either giving himself a stroke or destroying his career completely. It really wasn't good form to shout "NO! NO!" at a superior officer, even given the looser attitudes of wartime.

Besides, matters like these don't really relate to his field of expertise.

They should, but this was Booth.

"Mr. Ticknor," Raeder said, when the linguist's exhausted face appeared on his screen. "We'd like to send the squadron out to help the Blues help us. Could you find a way to ask your friend how to do that without causing either alarm or offense?"

"He's really not *my* anything, Commander," Ticknor said, sounding aggrieved. "And he specifically said that he wouldn't help us against his own crew members."

"Are you refusing to help us, Mr. Ticknor?" Raeder said, so calmly menacing that Truon turned around to look at him.

"No, no, *I'll* help. But I can't compromise Sna-Fe. It wouldn't be right."

"Do you want the *Invincible* and all who are on her to be considered booty to be taken by the winner of this battle that we are watching?"

"No, Commander, of course not, but . . ."

"Would you like to be a lab specimen, with a Fibian leaning over you, drooling acid and warming up a laser scalpel?"

A complex shudder.

"Then find out, Mr. Ticknor. But before you do, make up a message to the effect that we are sending out fighters to help them defeat our enemy. Then send it to me and Tech Rivera. Thank you, Mr. Ticknor."

Why am I wasting my time explaining things to this guy? Peter wondered. He was supposed to be making the commander's life easier, not throwing ethics class jargon at him. *Probably it's because I can see that he's working incredibly hard and I do have to maintain some sort of working relationship with the man.* And partly it was because Peter kept having to be rude to Ticknor and Raeder's beloved mother had gifted him with an automatic guilt response.

"Paddy, Lieutenant Robbins," Sarah said as she strode up to them. "Get ready, the commander might be giving the order to scramble any minute."

The two blinked once, looked at one another, then with broadening grins they began issuing orders.

Sarah watched the spread of those orders by the movement of techs across Main Deck. With a grin she turned to the com.

"All pilots report to briefing," she said, then repeated it.

Soon they'd be rushing from their bunks, their Speeds, their simulators. *I'd better get there before them.* Sarah rushed from Main Deck to the small theater used for debriefings and called up images of the Blues rushing to the *Invincible*'s defense. She was highlighting the blue designs on their ships as the first pilots began to filter in.

When every seat was filled she looked up, then slowly let an almost feral smile spread across her face. In the audience every face matched hers.

"I'm sure you've guessed by now that I haven't called you hear for a revival meeting," the lieutenant commander said. "Heavy as your souls undoubtedly are with sin."

The pilots chuckled at that; they'd seen the activity on Main Deck and knew exactly what it meant.

"I've got some vital information for you, though."

Sarah struck a few keys, then turned to the large screen behind her. For the first time the pilots watched Fibians fighting Fibians in defense of human beings. There could be no mistaking that crablike configuration, any more than they could fail to distinguish the Commonwealth's preferred double-hammerhead shape. Jaws dropped around the room.

Sarah tapped a few more keys and one of the craft was frozen by the computer, then drawn forward for a close up view. The lieutenant commander highlighted some markings on the front and sides of the craft.

"You will note that these markings are blue," she said. "These are the identifying symbols of Clan Nrgun. They are also known as blue clan, hence the blue identifying marks. These," Sarah tapped a key and another craft came into sharp focus, "are red clan ships. Note the red markings. They are of Clan Snargx."

The pilots liked that and she could hear a soft chorus of *snar . . . snr . . . gx* throughout the theater. Suppressing a smile she tapped on her console and they quieted.

"The Reds have gone near kamikaze on us out there. They now seem dedicated to getting to us, with, I'm sure, no friendly intent. We also have seen no reinforcements coming to aid the blue squadron fighting on our behalf. So the commander—"

"Lieutenant Commander?" It was Raeder's voice.

"Here, sir," James said eagerly.

"The Blues have accepted our offer of assistance. Please deploy your Speeds."

"Yes, sir," Sarah said. Her face wore a determined smile.

"Good luck people," Raeder said.

The pilots leaped up cheering. Sarah allowed it for a moment, then tapped her console again. It took a moment but they were soon seated again, bright eyes focused on her like a pack of wolves on a tray of raw meat.

"Thank you, Commander," she said.

"You're welcome, Lieutenant Commander. Raeder out."

Sarah held up her hand when they would have become airborne again, and the pilots settled down. She let them stay that way for a long minute while she looked them over.

"All right," she said. "We will keep discipline. I want each one of you mindful of the markings I've shown to you. Do not fire on any target if you cannot see these markings. Take *no* chances that you might be firing on a friendly. I want these Blues to be so impressed by our flying and our shooting that they come away with the idea that they don't know squat about either of those things." Sarah gave them another long look. "Am I understood?"

"Yes, sir!" the squadron shouted.

"Then let's get moving ladies and gentlemen, we've got a battle to fight."

"I hardly know what I shall report to our lady," Sum-sef admitted. He clicked his mandibles uncertainly, while his body took a position that denoted astonished awe. "Never have I seen fiercer fighters."

"They did terrible damage to the Red clan ships," Feh-soo agreed. His own posture indicated that he wished permission to speak more freely.

With a slashing, inviting gesture his huntmaster gave it.

"What *are* these beings?" His pedipalps indicated burgeoning fear. "Why was the clan Snargx in pursuit of them? Is it possible that we have aided criminals?"

"No to your last question," Sum-sef said with a gesture of polite rejection. "I say this because not once did Snargx attempt to justify their pursuit of this ship. Instead they fought their way towards the aliens as though to keep them from telling us anything of the matter."

His second positioned his pedipalps in the first degree of tentative agreement.

"As to your other questions," Sum-sef said, "we will know the answers in time. And I am sure that they will be to Snargx's detriment."

Feh-soo snapped his tailwhip in agreement.

After a moment's thought the huntmaster said, "We shall invite them to accompany us to Nrgun."

His second froze in a neutral stance until Sum-sef indicated that he desired his officer's opinion.

"What will we tell our lady?" he asked, still neutral.

"We will tell her that we bring her the greatest mystery of this or any other age, and its solution. We bring her knowledge in the form of an unknown and intelligent species."

"But Huntmaster, what if this is some Snargx plot to penetrate our defenses? That ship could be filled with assassins, or plagues. I would put nothing past the Reds; they have no conscience—warm-blooded."

Sum-sef looked thoughtful upon hearing his second's thoughts on the matter. After a moment he said, "We will invite them to follow us. We will make it clear that if their weapons show active on our screens we will assume they intend to use them against us and will react accordingly." He looked directly at his second. "And so we will."

"What if they choose not to accept this invitation?" Feh-soo asked.

"Then we must let them go." He made a gesture like a shrug. "They are intelligent creatures, they have shown us no hostility—quite the contrary—we must respect their choice. But," here he made a pinching gesture with his pedipalp and his chelicerae showed amusement, "where would they go?"

"Back where they came from, Huntmaster."

"To do so they must go through Snargx territory. And the Reds do not seem too friendly towards these aliens. To go forward is to find themselves in the territory of Clan Lince, and subject to an unknown welcome." Sum-sef lifted his pedipalps in an expansive gesture. "So why not come with us?"

"As you say, Huntmaster." Feh-soo looked uneasily around the command center, at the techs busy at their machines. "But everything will change now, won't it?"

"Yes," Sum-sef said, and settled himself lower in his couch. "It will."

CHAPTER TWELVE

"Aliens?" Lady Sisree asked. "What do you mean, aliens?"

One of the lady's charms was her ability to hide negative reactions. To one and all, unless she specifically wished otherwise, Sisree projected serenity and interest. And so she did now, though internally she was mightily perplexed.

"We have not seen them ourselves, Lady. So far we have only the strange configuration of their ships to go by. But as you can see, those ships are very strange."

Sisree examined the images that Sum-sef had sent to her and found the ships themselves and the movements the fliers·made with them were indeed very strange. She had never seen the like. Certainly they were formidable fighters.

A little thrill of fear went through her at the

thought. Until now Clan Nrgun had been invincible, with nothing at all to threaten its tranquility. But these . . . *aliens*? Were they in fact another life-form, or was this some bizarre yet sophisticated plot to destroy Nrgun? Either possiblility could cause indigestion and, regrettably, Clan Snargx was all too capable of dreaming up such a mad scheme of conquest.

"You may bring them to the clan home," she said at last. "But they may not leave their ship until we have considered this matter. Also, close watch will be kept on them at all times."

"Yes, Lady. I was wondering if any might be permitted to visit their ship?" His posture indicated great respect blended with intense curiosity.

Sisree wore a considering look for a moment. "Has such an invitation been extended?" she asked.

Would the huntmaster presume to withhold such information?

"No, Lady. I spoke hypothetically." Sum-sef lowered his fore-body respectfully.

In general the lady did not require such abasement; it was an instinctive reaction to something subtle in her manner. It was always wise for a male to keep his place.

"I will take your interest into consideration, Huntmaster, should such an invitation be forthcoming." The lady's pedipalps rippled in a way that indicated that it was time to close this interview. "I will have my assistant schedule a personal interview for you as soon can be managed upon your return," she said. "Please stay on until Has-sre can arrange an appointment."

With a click, Sisree was on her own again. She rose from her couch and paced her room, climbing the silk-lined walls over and over again. At last, with a resigned click of her mandibles, she returned to her console. There was no escaping her duty. She must inform the queen. With a few taps she found herself looking at Hoo-seh, Queen Tewsee's first assistant.

With a graceful gesture Sisree conceded his position as a near equal in status. Hoo-seh instantly responded with a respectful gesture that acknowledged the inherent superiority of the queen's second.

"It is excellent to see you looking so well," Sisree said.

"And a great joy to be able to say the same to you, my lady."

Hoo-seh positioned his pedipalps in the first degree of respect. Not mere flattery, either. He did indeed respect the lady for her political acumen as well as her general attractivness. Also he was well aware of the esteem in which the queen held her second. Consummate politician that he was, Hoo-seh cultivated the second's good will.

"I find I must request an audience with her majesty," Sisree told him. "It is a matter of some urgency, and also some secrecy." She indicated a subtle apology for not saying more with the tilt of her head.

Hoo-seh froze momentarily in a position of intense and respectful curiosity.

"If it is her will, you must, of course, listen to what I have to tell her majesty. I will tell her of your intense interest, First Assistant. But I must, given the sensitive nature of my news, tell her majesty in privacy first."

Hoo-seh bowed. "You have made contact at an opportune moment, Lady Sisree. The queen is just finishing with her last appointment and has nothing scheduled for another stansis."

"I will await contact," Sisree said, giving him a nod of thanks. With a click she was once again alone with her thoughts. After a moment the lady began to gather together all of the information the huntmaster had sent to her, as well as her brief interview with him, and arranged it in some order, so that the queen's questions might be answered expeditiously. Although there wasn't, at present, any answer to the most pressing question of all.

Were these indeed aliens?

"Well, ladies and gentlemen," Raeder said to his senior officers, "we find ourselves in a most interesting situation." He tapped his stylus on the table before him. "I'd like to say it's unique, but unfortunately the Mollies beat us to that."

"Sir?" Booth raised his hand.

"Yes, Mr. Booth?" Raeder supressed a grimace. *I knew what I was in for when I invited him to this meeting,* he thought. *So I'll just have to bite the bullet and put up with him.*

"Exactly what sort of threat are we operating under?" The security officer looked subdued and very serious.

"Well . . ." Peter looked around the table. Everyone wore much the same expression as the security officer. The commander cleared his throat. "We are in fact operating under threat. But they are very reasonable threats," he said, lifting his hands as though to stave off objections.

"I might have known," Booth muttered.

"Mr. Booth," Raeder said, looking hard at him. "I'm answering your question." Peter waited a moment longer, until Booth's eyes reluctantly fell.

"They are escorting us to their clan home," the commander continued. "We've been warned that if our weapons go hot, they will assume that we intend to fire them and we will be fired upon." He gave Sarah a grin. "I think you seriously impressed them out there."

The lieutenant commander smiled and blushed; around the table officers tapped their Academy rings in approbation. All but Booth, who didn't take his eyes from Raeder.

"Sir," he said, "what do the Fibians intend to do with us, once they've taken us to their planet?"

Raeder just looked at him for a moment. "Fair question," he said at last. "Especially if one assumes that we are being *taken* somewhere. In fact, we're not. We've been invited to accompany them. Had we wanted to we would have been permitted to leave after the battle."

"Hunh! That's what they tell us now. Sir. Now that we're doing what they want us to do. How do you think they'd react if we just stopped right now and said we'd changed our mind?"

"I honestly think they'd let us go, Mr. Booth. I also think they'd consider us boors and that they might not be so welcoming next time someone from the Commonwealth dropped in."

Peter tapped his stylus in a steady beat. He took the quiet way his officers allowed this conversation to go on without their input to be an indication that they, too, had reservations.

"Here's the situation, people," he said leaning forward. "We have one transit engine down, we have one in desperate need of repair. Not to mention the repairs needed to the hull. And we have wounded to tend." Peter looked around the table. "Moreover, we do not have enough fuel to get us home."

There was an almost invisible ripple around the table at that; tiny shifts in position, or glances crossing.

Some of them had known it for a fact, the rest seemed to have had a sense of the situation. Even so, they'd have to be stone not to show some reaction.

"Even if we did have that much antihydrogen," Raeder continued, "we would still need to travel through Clan Snargx's territory. With one engine out, one in need of repair. This craft was built as a *fast* raider. With one ankle broken, we'd have to try and smash our way through. Do any of you really want to try a slugging match with major capital units . . . with the other side right next to their supply bases?"

He leaned back and idly rolled his stylus to and fro. Then he looked up, his gaze finding each face for a long moment.

"So you see, our options are to take a chance here, or die for certain, out there."

He watched his officers weigh what he'd said. Waited quietly until each one looked him in the eye and nodded. And then there was Booth.

"Then we have to establish our superiority," the security officer insisted.

"Lest the natives get uppity, Mr. Booth?" Truon Le asked with a crooked smile.

The security officer bristled, but before he could answer Raeder stepped in.

"I think we've established ourselves as, if not superior, certainly equal to themselves, thanks to the squadron. We've also treated them with all the courtesy we can."

Peter rubbed his forhead. "Mr. Ticknor, our linguist, tells me that the Fibian language includes a lot of body language which is necessary to be really understood, and to indicate subtleties of meaning and courtesy and so forth. Which brings us to another point that's been worrying me. How are they going to react to the way we look?"

It was as though the whole group of them took a deep breath.

"I suppose we look every bit as bad to them as they do to us," Ashly Lurhman said, wrinkling her nose.

Doctor Goldberg looked thoughtful. "If they're as xenophobic as humans are we'll have to reveal ourselves slowly and carefully. I can put together some text and pictures that might prepare them somewhat."

"Perhaps some entertainment recordings," Sarah said. "Dance, for instance."

Goldberg nodded slowly. "That might be a good idea. I certainly wouldn't recommend showing them war stories."

"Especially the kind where one or two humans defeat legions of Fibians," Truon Le commented dryly.

They all chuckled at that. The Commonwealth Office of Information had been putting out plenty of *those* ever since the Mollie–Fibian alliance had become known. In fact, they'd reached as far back as the twentieth century for models.

"If we have any of those on board," Peter said, "it might be a good idea to pull them from the computer. I wouldn't want them to think we're guilty of xenophobia, or hostile intentions, either."

"But we're guilty of both," Sarah said with a sly grin.

"But I don't want *them* to know that," Peter said. He leaned forward again. "Mr. Hartkopf, I want you to monitor transmissions out there and to relay them to Mr. Ticknor for study. If they *have* entertainment transmissions of their own we might find those especially revealing."

Sarah gave him an old-fashioned look and Peter turned to the doctor for support.

"Well," he asked, "wouldn't they?"

Goldberg chuckled. "They might very well be unintentionally revealing, sir, but we have no context. It might take years for us to define those traits that are meaningful to Fibians, as opposed to humans."

"Well," Raeder said, "they would at least provide Mr. Ticknor with a library of gestures and so forth that he isn't getting from voice transmissions." *Not that I think he's sleeping any easier for not seeing them. He already knows what they look like. Still, he's been holding up very well in observing our prisoner.*

"I want it understood now," the commander said, "that no one is to reveal themselves to the Fibians until further notice. There will be no outside repairs done, no visual transmissions, internally or otherwise, until we've tested the waters with these people. I firmly believe that they are civilized and at least disposed to be peaceable. But there's really no telling how something as traumatic as a shipload of totally alien beings will impact them . . . or their culture."

"Let's hope they think we're adorable," Lurhman said.

"Let's hope they don't think we look tasty," Booth muttered.

"On that happy note," Raeder said, "let's move on to engineering's report on their repairs."

Her majesty's chamber was an enormous bower of pure white silk, the walls woven in such a way that subtle patterns formed, changing with one's angle of view. Soft light penetrated from some undisclosed source, keeping the whole room uniformly and pleasantly bright. An occasional sculpture or plant hung suspended, adding a touch of color here and there.

The queen's couch was made of fresh webbing every day and swung from the high ceiling, comfortably supporting her under her abdomen and thorax.

Before her swing was a single couch of a more ordinary sort. More of them could be added at need but in this, less formal, room she preferred to keep things simple and uncrowded.

Hoo-seh advanced respectfully, enjoying the give beneath his clawed feet from a depth of silk one only found in the palace. He lowered his fore-body submissively and Tewsee acknowledged his obeisance with a gracious gesture.

"Seat yourself, First Assistant," the queen said. "I would have you present as my second tells us more of her tale. Begin," Tewsee said.

At her command a projection of Lady Sisree flared into existance between them. Hoo-seh could see the queen through its translucence, yet the second's image was clear.

A few sentences later the first assistant looked through the projection to the queen. He was terribly shaken. The voices that the huntmaster claimed came from the strange ships sounded like none he'd ever heard. What sort of faces must these beings have to produce such sounds? Hoo-seh shivered. But he could see that the queen was excited and eager to meet these creatures.

"We are faced with two possiblities," Tewsee said. "They are genuinely alien, or they are a fraud. This leads to four possibilities. Either Snargx knew of these aliens and did not want us to find out about them, or they did not know of them but for one reason or another found it necessary to chase them into Nrgun territory in order to destroy them. I doubt that would be to protect their good friends in Clan Nrgun," she said dryly. "Or, they are a fraud perpetrated by another clan on Snargx for the purpose of raiding their territory. In which case, I expect them to reveal themselves shortly and invite us to

share in the joke. Or they are a fraud being perpetrated on Ngrun by Snargx as the means to effect
a raid of some subtle kind."

"Five possibilities, Majesty," the Lady Sisree
reminded her gently.

Tewsee cocked her head questioningly.

"If they are genuine, they may wish to establish
diplomatic contact."

The queen lifted her head, her chelicerae shifting
to show genuine pleasure.

"Wouldn't that be wonderful?" she said.

"Calm down," Raeder said, finding it hard to take
his own advice. "Just take deep breaths." He inhaled
in instruction.

"I'm trying!" Sirgay snapped. "I'm just not
succeeding."

The doctor handed him a bag and told him to
breathe into it. Which he did, and it slowed his
breathing, without having any noticeable effect on the
panic that made the linguist want to scream.

"Try walking," Doctor Goldberg urged him. "Get
up and move around, do something with all that
adrenaline."

Ticknor bounced to his feet and began marching
back and forth, swinging his arms. Raeder and
Goldberg ducked and did their best to move out of
his way, but the room was too small for three men
and a panic attack.

"Let's go into the corridor," Raeder finally suggested.

Ticknor was there before them. He marched away,
he marched back. Goldberg and Raeder stood in the
sick bay's hatch and watched him.

"How long has he been like this?" Peter asked the
doctor.

"Not that long, about forty minutes. I called you

as soon as he came in because he was saying he couldn't do it. I thought you needed to know."

"Isn't there some sort of medication for this?" The commander gestured down the hall at Ticknor. "I mean, *look* at the poor guy."

"He's on medication," Goldberg said. "He's been taking it regularly and, frankly, I don't have anything better in stock than what he's taking. I also wouldn't recommend upping his dosage. Not if you want him as a translator; as a lawn ornament, possibly." He shook his head. "With a fear this deep-seated drugs can only do so much. I think it's pretty remarkable and a tribute to his character that he's been able to keep going this long by himself."

"So what should we do?" Peter asked. "Medication isn't the answer, what is?"

"Frankly, Commander, I think part of the problem is isolation." The doctor held up his hand when Raeder would have protested. "I *know* we've been busy, crisis after crisis. I know that. He knows that," Goldberg said, pointing to his patient. "But things have slowed down now and he's more vital than ever. So if we want him to be able to function, we've got to open up and make him part of the group."

"What are you saying?" Raeder asked, his brow furrowed.

"I want him to mess with us. I think he should be included in any meetings about how we're going to deal with the Fibians. I think that we should at least *try* to socialize with him."

"You mean, like, invite him to Paddy's poker games?"

"Yes! Especially if we can get them to treat him with a little respect. The man is our resident Fibian expert, and he's damn near killing himself to do his job. If it takes a little nurturing, if we have to hold

his hand a little bit, then yes, by all means invite him
to poker night."

"Doctor, when it comes to poker Paddy doesn't
even respect me." Raeder put his hands on his slim
hips and watched Ticknor pace. He shrugged. "If what
you're talking about is distraction . . ."

"That's exactly what I'm talking about. Something
to get his mind off the way Fibians look. Distraction
will do very well. In fact, at the moment, it's the only
game in town."

Raeder shook his head.

"It seems cruel, but you're the doctor." He leaned
closer to Goldberg. "Should I let him walk a little
bit more?"

The doctor gave his patient an appraising look.

"Yeah," he said. "Give him a couple of minutes.
Meanwhile, you can be setting up a game."

"Still seems pretty cold," Peter said, doubtfully.

"Yeah, well, sometimes the cure can seem worse
than the disease. But we have to do something.
Maybe you can keep Paddy from making this game
too high stakes."

Raeder snorted and turned away.

"Yeah, and maybe I can convince him to wear a
tutu."

Ticknor sat at the table fairly thrumming with nervous energy. He looked around at his fellow players,
who looked back at him like a tank full of sharks, long
after feeding time at the aquarium was due.

They were a mixed lot: officers, some chiefs, some
enlisted. But they all had chips on the table and the
ease of familiarity about them.

"Now," Paddy began, "you bein' new here we're
gonna let you be the dealer for this first hand." He
took a sip of his drink and gave the linguist a toothy

smile. "'Tis a tradition with us. No rank in the mess, as the sayin' goes . . . and this is as messy a place as the good ship *Invincible* affords."

The others all chuckled. Ticknor shrugged gamely.

"Sure," he said, and offered them a nervous smile. "Cards?" he said and reached out for the deck Paddy offered him.

He shook the deck from its protective package and his hands began to dance. Cards began to flow back and forth in fans and riffs that Raeder had only seen in vids. And their ultranervous, high-strung, totally intellectual linguist began a litany of rules that told one and all at the table that this pigeon had teeth.

"That was an *excellent* game," Sirgay told Raeder as they moved down the corridor to officer country.

The linguist shuffled the pack of credit chits with the same enthusiastic skill he used on cards.

Raeder offered a pained, polite smile and nodded.

"I worked as a pit dealer when I was in college," Ticknor confided. "I *love* poker. I thought I might go into it professionally for a little while there." He tapped Raeder on the arm. "James Scott offered to teach me, to be my manager when I got a little experience on me."

Raeder's eyes bugged. Even he'd heard of James "Scotty" Scott. *Well, that explains why I am now totally broke. If this guy could impress James Scott, for God's sake! We never had a chance.*

"Well, I think we all learned a little something from playing with you tonight," Raeder assured him. "I hope it helped."

Ticknor stopped.

"Yes. Yes, it did. Thank you, Commander." He looked embarrassed. "Sometimes, it just catches up with me and I freak," he said. Sirgay shrugged and laughed nervously. "I guess I needed a little less bug time."

"They're not bugs," Peter said firmly.

Ticknor looked down and waved his hands as though to erase what he'd just said.

"I know, I know. I don't mean to disparage them, I'm just trying to make this more manageable some way."

"They are not bugs," Raeder said again. He looked hard at the linguist. "They are *not* bugs. They are not spiders. They are a sentient species, the first we've ever encountered. Now, you are going to have to convince yourself that they are *not* bugs."

Ticknor wouldn't meet the commander's eyes. He held his hands up, palms out, and kept pushing them towards Raeder's chest in a calming motion.

"I know, you're right. But they look . . ."

"Maybe you could think of them as being more like a lobster," Peter suggested. "That might help your perspective."

"No, I don't eat lobster. Lobsters are just big bugs."

"Lobsters are not bugs," Raeder said and started walking again. "*I* eat lobsters." He took a few more steps. "They are not bugs."

Ticknor was shuffling his chits again.

"Actually they are," he said as they walked along.

I didn't need to know that, Peter thought.

Goldberg had a lot to answer for.

Peter sat quietly, in deep thought, after watching Doctor Goldberg's proposed instructional recording to familiarize the Fibians with the human shape.

"You don't like it," Goldberg said.

"No, no," Raeder said, straightening in his chair. "It's not that at all. In fact I think it shows a great deal of talent. Maybe you should get into movies after the war," he suggested with a smile.

"But . . ." the doctor said. He cupped his hands palms up and wiggled his fingers in a *c'mon, give* gesture.

"Well," Ticknor said, "maybe it should be more technical-medical and less—and on our menu today."

Goldberg frowned at him.

"I thought we should make it clear that we're omnivorous. They're sure to wonder about it," he said.

Peter was nodding though.

"I think Mr. Ticknor has a point, Doctor. We can cover the eating stuff in a later vid. This is just an introduction to our general appearance. Besides, we cook our food, they . . . don't," Raeder said with a grimace. "It's quite possible that they might find our method of preparing food for eating as disgusting as we find theirs."

Goldberg looked thoughtful; at last he nodded.

"Yes, they might well consider us to be carrion eaters . . ." He grinned at them. "I'm pretty sure I wouldn't want to sit down to dinner with a genuine carrion eater myself."

"Fewer pictures of other Earth life," Sirgay interjected. He had a distant look about him, as though he hadn't heard most of the conversation. "Right now it looks like you're saying—'Earth, you never saw so many things to eat.' "

Raeder and Goldberg just looked at him.

"Well," the linguist shrugged, "I'm trying to see it from their perspective."

"Maybe he has a point there, too," the commander said. "Just strip it down to an introduction of what we look like. Maybe you could work up to it easy. Show them our clothes first, or something. Then build up slowly from the skeleton to the flesh."

"I'll bet they like our skeleton," Sirgay muttered. He looked up. "It's the only thing about us that looks remotely like them."

Goldberg nodded and made a note.

"Okay, I'll go with that," he said. He looked up. "Anything else, gentlemen?"

"Not at the moment," Raeder said, rising. "If I think of anything, I'll get back to you. Hey!" He snapped his fingers and pointed at Ticknor. "Maybe we should show it to your associate."

Ticknor nodded. "That's a very good idea. I know he's bored, I'm sure he'd enjoy it. I don't know how far we can trust his opinion, though."

"Understood," Raeder agreed. "We have to take everything he tells us with a grain of salt, but so far he's come through for us."

"I get a feeling he's very young," the linguist said. He stood and turned to go. "Nothing definite, just a sense that he's very naive."

"Ask him how old he is," Raeder said. "When we've established contact with the Nrguns we can check his age against their life expectancy and find out if you're correct."

"That could be important," Goldberg said and made another note. "By the way, how does he seem to you, Mr. Ticknor? Is he eating and drinking? Does he seem depressed?"

"I—I'm really the wrong person to ask about that stuff," Ticknor demurred. "I just can't say."

"Maybe it's time you interviewed him yourself, Doctor," the commander said. "We don't want our guest to fail just when we need him most. But I wouldn't mention anything about Clan Nrgun to him."

"I think you're probably right there, sir," Goldberg said. "I wouldn't want to add to his anxieties. But he must suspect that we're still in Nrgun territory. Where else would we go?" He held up a hand to ward off a repeat of any warnings from Raeder and Sirgay. "Don't worry though, I won't bring it up. May I use your equipment, Mr. Ticknor? Perhaps interview him from your lab?"

"Sure," the linguist said. "I've got to catch up on some stuff in my other lab."

Goldberg rubbed his hands in glee.

"I'm looking forward to meeting the young fellow."

Truon, Hartkopf and Gunderson seated themselves at the conference table. They'd been the last to arrive, perhaps because it was their report that the senior officers had gathered to hear.

"The planet, or clan home Nrgun, is very densely populated," Truon began. "There are also a great many orbital habitats and factories around the planet. From what we've seen of Nrgun's surface it wouldn't be unreasonable to assume that some of these habitats are farms, since the surface shows no sign of any such places. Or," he cocked his head, "nothing that *we* would recognize as such."

"Are there green areas at all?" Doctor Goldberg asked. "Parks, untenanted lands?"

"There are a substantial number of greenlands, Doctor," Gunderson said. "Certainly enough to keep the atmosphere healthy. Indications are that their atmosphere is very close to Earth normal."

"We'll still need a sample to determine if it's safe," Goldberg cut in.

They all nodded at that; it didn't pay to get cocky.

"As you can see," Truon said, calling up a holo of the Nrgun system, "there's a narrow asteroid belt here." A red arrow appeared on the holo and pointed to a belt that wasn't very wide but consisted of much larger pieces than the one in Earth's system. "We've found evidence of mining going on here. And, as we noticed when we first exited the jump point, there's substantial merchant traffic. Much of it from outside this system. We've noted ships of Fibian configuration marked with four different colors so far: green, orange, yellow and purple."

"Six clans that we know of," Raeder said slowly. "And we thought tangling with *one* of them meant we were fighting above our weight." *Boy, if we screw up here, we could pretty much be resposible for the end of the human race. No pressure, no pressure, just truckin' along.* . . . "Anything else, Mr. Truon?"

"We have yet to see any ships with the specifically military shape that have anything but blue markings. From that we conclude that either Clan Nrgun is the premiere power among Fibians or that all of the clans are equally powerful and none has warships in the others' home space."

Raeder nodded. *Two very different things there.* But they had no way of knowing which conjecture would prove accurate at this point.

"Anything else?" he asked.

"Well, sir, this is only speculation," the XO said. "But," he tightened the focus until a space station midway between the asteroid belt and Nrgun came into view. "based on the emissions that we've detected coming from this station, I'd say it's an antihydrogen factory."

Around the table officers leaned forward to study the holo. It didn't look too different from the factories the Commonwealth had started up again at the beginning of the war.

"And based on the amount of exports they seem to be making," Gunderson said, "I think we can assume that their process is far more efficient than ours."

Now that, Raeder thought, *is good news.* It meant that they might be able to purchase some for the trip home. *It also gives us something to negotiate for once we've opened formal relations. Scaragoglu screwed up.* The notion warmed him a little. *The old devil should have sent a diplomat along with us.*

"Apparently," Peter said aloud, "it's still not as efficient as mining the stuff. Otherwise Snargx wouldn't be cuddling up to the Mollies." Raeder suddenly slapped his forehead. "Nrgun didn't know about humans before we showed up here. Therefore it follows that Nrgun doesn't *know* about naturally occurring antihydrogen!"

"The question now is," Sarah said into the silence that followed, "do we want them to know about it?"

Raeder shook his head.

"We'll need to know more about them before we decide. I suspect that we'll have to come clean before we're finished here. I mean, it's not too much of a stretch to assume that once the Mollies and Snargx have flattened the Commonwealth the Mollies will find themselves being rolled over. So Snargx's ultimate goal might well be to upset the balance among the clans and nominate themselves as first among equals."

"That certainly gives us something in common," Truon said quietly.

"At the very least it gives us something to think about," Peter agreed.

"Sir," Skinner said raising his hand slightly from the table.

"Yes, Mr. Skinner?"

"The Nrguns might be able to supply us with parts to repair our engines. There's the chance that theirs will be too different," the engineering officer allowed. "But we should find out."

Raeder nodded. *Pure Skinner,* he thought. *Focused, incredibly focused.*

"Thank you, Mr. Skinner," the commander said. "That will definitely go on my list of things to discuss."

Sarah looked across the table at Ashly Lurhman, then turned to Peter.

"Ms. Lurhman and I would like to suggest that as the two highest ranking females aboard that we go with you to the planet when you go down to negotiate."

"It appears, from things Mr. Ticknor has been telling us, to be a matriarchal society," Lurhman put in quickly.

Raeder looked over at the linguist, who stared back like a nocturnal animal caught by a bright light.

"It's . . . I . . . Sna-Fe told me that red clan is ruled by a queen, and that his huntmaster is under the comand of a female." He shrugged and looked around the table nervously. "I didn't think it was classified, or anything."

"No," Raeder said, trying to look pleasant so that he wouldn't scare him. "It's not classified, don't worry about that. It's just that it's something *I* should know." He gave the linguist a friendly nod. "Just keep me informed. Anything you think might be useful when we're talking to these people, please, just share it with me."

"You told me not to call you," Ticknor pointed out.

Raeder threw his head back.

"Ah," he said. "Well, I meant during a crisis. You can tell when those are going on by the crew running to battle stations and announcements over the com and warning chimes and so forth. *Then* it is a bad thing to just call me up. But otherwise, while I'm on duty, if you feel it's something I need to know, certainly, feel free to call me."

"Thank you," Sirgay said. He opened his mouth as if to say something else.

"Ms. Lurhman, Ms. James, thank you for offering your services. I agree, it would probably be diplomatic to include you both in any landing party we send down."

The two women grinned at the commander, then at each other.

"Is there any other business?" Raeder asked.

Ticknor said, "Yes!"

Peter turned to him in some surprise at the violence of that "yes."

"Sorry," Ticknor said, grimacing with embarrassment. "Didn't mean to be so vehement. I was going to suggest that the next time you speak to our escort you request an expert in protocol to coach us and guide us so that we don't risk offending anybody."

"Excellent suggestion, Mr. Ticknor," Raeder said, and meant it. "Thank you, I'll do that. Now, if there's no other business." He put his hands on the arms of his chair as if to rise. There were no takers. "Then we'll adjourn. Thank you everyone."

CHAPTER THIRTEEN

Queen Tewsee and her second settled down onto their couches in their separate chambers to watch the recording the aliens had provided. They shared a linked com, which allowed them to watch and comment in concert.

The two females were genuinely devoted to one another, friends as well as mother and daughter. But the biology of their species would not allow two mature females to peacefully occupy the same space. They had not truly been together since Sisree reached her adult phase, twenty years ago.

It could be done, of course. For the space of a ceremony, for example, in a time and place large enough, populated by enough males to dilute their powerful pheromones, under circumstances so rigorously plotted out that no individual quirk could cause offense. Then two or even more mature

Fibian females could come together. But such occasions were rare, occurring once a century, if that.

In a sense Fibian females were also rare. Once this hadn't been so—when the species was young and the world was wide there were many. Each female was a queen in her own territory, a law unto herself. Now, in Clan Nrgun there were two hundred females for every hundred million males, but only one queen.

Each of these would lay approximately five hundred thousand eggs, only one of which would be a daughter. Males were raised in groups of one hundred by a cluster of ten adult males. But adult females would be responsible for raising their daughters to maturity. Then the youngster would be given her own quarters removed from her mother; they would thereafter communicate only through vid while she was instructed in her duties.

It was fortunate that Fibians could choose the gender of their offspring, so that the birth of every female could be planned as needed. It made for a very simple method of birth control; fewer queens, fewer Fibians. But it was galling, it went against instinct.

Then, as they gained spaceflight, the Fibian people rejoiced that they could send their daughters exploring again, seeking out new territories to claim as their own.

It had taken centuries to accomplish, but Clan Nrgun had filled every available niche in its own system and they'd had to curb their birthrate again.

Then with the discovery of jump Nrgun sent colonists to other systems where they became autonomous clans. This was the occasion of one of those rare meetings between queens. A time of ceremony, of passing power from the original clan home to the new. There were six clans now, each becoming distinct, each developing its own ceremonies, traditions, outlook.

They still sent out explorers, but it had been less than thirty years since a new colony, that of Clan Snargx, had been turned over to its young queen. So the urgency, and therefore the interest, was less among the older clans.

There was also a loose association of clan queens who arbitrated issues of trade and exploration. But it would take a unanimous vote to actively, that is militarily, interfere with the running of another queen's clan. In all their history such a vote had never been needed.

Tewsee, despite her excitement about them, feared that the appearance of these mysterious, and very well armed, aliens might give rise to such an occasion. Their appearance from the territory of Clan Snargx, the aggressive behavior of Snargx's huntmasters in pursuit and the lack of communication from Snargx's queen disturbed her. At the very least an apology for an armed intrusion into Nrgun space was in order.

Though they had yet to broach the subject to one another, her daughter, Sisree, concurred. They'd worked together long enough for each to have a feeling for the other's reaction to any given event. By no means did this mean that they agreed on every issue, it merely meant that they could anticipate one another's reactions and concerns with uncanny accuracy.

As the alien's presentation unfolded such concerns temporarily faded into the background.

"Unlike Fibians," it began, and it displayed a still picture of a warrior with blue chitin, the figure rotating to show all sides, "humans do not have a natural hard protective covering."

Next were displayed a pair of objects that appeared

to be shed skins, though far neater than the product of molting.

"What you see here is called clothing," the narrator intoned. "Specifically the clothing, or uniform, of Commonwealth Space Command personnel."

"Are they trying to be confusing?" Sisree grumbled, halting the recording.

"Mmm," her mother answered absently. "Coverings for special purposes are uniforms," she suggested. "Commonwealth is where they come from. I'd like to know what the purpose is of this Space Command, though. They seem awfully well armed for a scientific expedition."

"Or even for prospective colonists," Sisree agreed.

"You'll notice there is only room for four limbs in that *uniform*," Tewsee pointed out.

"I did," the lady said flatly. Her chelicerae spread in an expression of extreme revulsion. "What can they mean by 'do not have a natural protective covering'?"

"Yes, that gave me pause as well. Surely they can't mean that their organs are exposed. Can they?" Sisree felt an unpleasant stirring in her digestive sac. "Let us continue and find out," she suggested.

"This is a human skeleton," the voice continued.

An ethereally delicate figure appeared on the screen. Tewsee stopped it in order to examine it more closely. Four limbs, she noted with satisfaction, not even vestigial evidence that there had ever been more. She rotated the figure slowly. Ah, there was evidence of a tail there. A stinger whip perhaps? The queen rotated her head in a negative gesture. Surely there would be no chance of something so useful degenerating into this silly little appendage.

"The head is interesting," Sisree observed.

Tewsee gave the head her attention. The face was

narrow and curvy, with a strangely determined look about it.

"I only see space for two eyes," she said at last.

"Ugh," said Sisree. Then, "Oh, dear. I've always thought of myself as being so very sophisticated, so ready for new ideas. But . . . oh, Mother, they're just completely awful!"

Tewsee clicked her mandibles in wry amusement. "Can one ever truly be prepared for the unimaginable?" she asked. "I admit to having always dreamed of finding another intelligent species out there somewhere. But I've always seen them as being very much like us. This is going to be quite a challenge to adjust to. Shall we continue?"

"Yes, Mother."

Now there were two of the revolving skeletons side by side, one smaller than the other.

"The female of our species," the voice said, and a golden glow flashed around the smaller skeleton, "is generally smaller than the male."

The display layered on internal organs, without explaining their purpose, then musculature, and finally a soft outer layer. At last the human faces could be seen.

"The human species has several distinct subgroups called races."

The faces morphed from one race to another, changing color, changing features and hair while the voice described the environmental factors which might explain the differences.

They stopped the recording again and quietly studied the faces on their screens. They'd been stopped at Asian.

"I don't think that they realize that they do indeed have clan colors," Tewsee said thoughtfully.

"Well, they also said that they didn't have a

protective outer layer either," Sisree muttered acerbically.

Tewsee clicked her mandibles and snapped her tailwhip in amusement.

"I believe they said it wasn't hard like ours, not that they had none at all." She looked at the faces before her. "This *hair* is interesting," she said. "What do you suppose it's for?"

"It's mostly black," the lady commented. "Perhaps it's for embellishment."

Tewsee waved her tailwhip. "As good a reason as any other. I wonder what happened to their tails?" she said as the motion reminded her. "I also find it strange that their females are smaller. But then, they're so completely different." She restarted the recording.

"This is a smile," the voice told them. "A smile is a display of friendliness or mild pleasure."

On the screen the two faces altered their configuration. Under the skin, muscles contracted and bunched, the mouthparts pulled back to reveal the chewing plates called teeth, slick with moisture, the eyes narrowed.

"This is laughter," the voice said.

Immediately the faces changed completely, their mouths convulsed, pulling further back from the teeth, the teeth opened—revealing the wet pink flesh within. The eyes disappeared almost completely behind folds of skin and the hairy markings above them lifted and arched. From their throats came a rather shrill barking sound repeated rapidly with strange howling changes of inflection.

"This denotes amusement or pleasure," the narrator continued. "Humans find many things to be an occasion for laughter. It might even be a natural reaction to a mild surprise."

"I'm sorry to hear that," Sisree said. "I think it looks repulsive."

"We can tell them that," her mother replied. "Though we'll probably get used to it in time."

The recording went through a variety of facial expressions, each one denoting some strong emotion.

"Please, Mother, stop it for a moment," Sisree begged. "I can't take anymore."

Tewsee stopped the recording and waited for a moment before she asked, "Are you all right?"

"Yes. It's just . . ." Her pedipalps quivered. " . . . seeing *faces* writhing like that and changing all the time . . . it's horrible! How are we supposed to deal with these creatures when we can barely stand to look at them?"

The queen was silent a moment. "I think they are sensitive to that," she said at last. "That's why they've taken such pains with this recording. This motility in their faces *is* disturbing, I can't deny it. But I like their sensitivity. So, you and I shall watch this recording until we are used to their features and their voices." She paused. "Or at least we'll finish it in one sitting. I think they deserve that much attention at least."

"You are right, mother," Sisree conceded. "They are trying to be sensitive; it's obvious from the way they worked their way so gradually up to showing us their appearance." She thought for a moment. "Mother, does it occur to you that they seem to know what *we* look like?"

"Yes. Which leads me to believe that they do indeed have some sort of history with Clan Snargx, and not a happy one either."

"All the more remarkable, then, that they would be so conscious of our feelings." Sisree clicked her mandibles thoughtfully. "Let us see what else they have for us to look at."

Tewsee restarted the recording, well pleased with her daughter's common sense.

The faces on the screen morphed into the faces of two different individuals, though still male and female. Their clothing changed from the Commonwealth Star Command uniform to another type of uniform altogether. These were in one piece and very close to the body; they might as well not have been wearing anything at all.

"These humans are professional dancers," the voice said. "They will enact for you an art form known to our people as dancing."

The two individuals joined appendages and flowed toward one another. The male lifted the female, who positioned her lower appendages rigidly. Then, when he placed her back on the ground, they both began to move their upper and lower appendages together in time with a rhythmic and not unpleasing sound.

"How are they making those noises?" Sisree asked, fascinated.

"I'm not sure that they are," the queen answered. She watched the humans hop and join and separate with increasing delight. "This is pleasant!" she exclaimed.

"I like it too," Sisree said, rather surprised at herself.

They watched the dancing until the end and then they replayed it.

"I wonder if they have more?" Sisree asked her mother.

"Let's hope so," Tewsee said enthusiastically. "It's such a charming idea . . . Just imagine how it would look if Fibians were doing it!"

"Oh! Yes! That could be very exciting."

Sisree considered the notion, imagining lines of males moving together in the same way at the same

time, guided by pleasing sounds. One of the types
of dancing they'd been shown had the dancers bang-
ing their feet on the floor so that their tapping made
an exciting counterpoint to what their bodies were
doing. With more legs to use surely Fibians could
excel at such an art.

"Yes," she said again. "But that's for another day.
Right now we need to decide what to do about these
visitors."

"We'll see them, of course," Queen Tewsee said.

"Then let me be the one to see them in person,"
Sisree requested. "That way if there is something
unfortunate in their biology which causes a violent
reaction you won't be directly involved."

"Prudent," the queen said. Something in her voice
implied that prudence was very overrated. "I agree.
I will be present by vid, of course."

"I actually think they'll understand," Sisree said,
and there was a trace of wonder in her voice.

"It should be interesting to discover what they have
to tell us," the queen mused.

Sarah ferried them down to the planet guided by
Fibian ground control. There were significant lapses
by Ticknor's little gadget, but with good will and
patience she managed to get them all landed safely.
Not to mention the aid of Ticknor himself, who was
listening in and tapping Sna-Fe for advice on terms
not yet covered in their conversations.

The linguist would be accompanying them by com
and would see and hear everything that they did. This
was for the obvious reason that Sirgay would have
been catatonic in five minutes if directly confronted
by a Fibian.

Doctor Goldberg and his team had determined
from samples provided by the Fibians that nothing

in the Fibian atmosphere, water or earth appeared to be damaging to humans. It was the usual thing; even biologies similar enough to be mutually compatible always lacked *something*, which made infection by alien microbes vanishingly unlikely. Bacteria died of some unicellular equivalent of scurvy if they tried to invade, and the Fibian version of DNA was nothing a Terran virus would find possible to hijack, or vice versa.

So it was without the encumbrance of suits that Raeder, Sarah, Ashly Lurhman, the ship's lawyer, Marion Trudeau, and the ship's historian, Mark Hu, disembarked to meet Sun-hes, their escort and instructor in protocol.

They stepped out of their shuttle directly onto the tarmac. They'd been told that they would immediately be taken to the palace and so would not enter the terminal. It was visible from where they'd landed, and looked like a gigantic tent, tinted a pale blue.

A Fibian awaited them, standing before a small craft that doubtless would take them where they were bound. The Fibian stepped forward to introduce himself and they recognized Sun-hes from their conversations on vid.

Raeder saw that Sun-hes held his pedipalps in the second degree of respect. This represented high regard towards one whom the Fibian considered his student and therefore automatically of lower status; the commander was suitably honored. He returned the greeting with the same degree of respect, which was proper for a student to a teacher. But he was very conscious of Sun-hes' courtesy in treating him as an equal.

"I know that I should leave this to our good queen," Sun-hes told them, "but I cannot resist welcoming you to our beautiful planet and the lovely city of Quesh."

"Thank you, teacher," Peter said. "I am certain her majesty would expect no less of you. We're looking forward to seeing your city and your world."

"With respect," Sun-hes said cautiously, "it is the custom to bow the head slightly when speaking of the queen." And their instructor demonstrated by bowing his head at the word queen.

"Thank you," Raeder said. "We will remember."

"You will not object to our scientists examining you briefly to determine whether you might present some danger to her majesty?" Sun-hes gestured with both pedipalps to a contained vehicle nearby.

"Uh . . ." Raeder looked at his cohorts for guidance.

"Reasonable," Trudeau said. "It certainly conforms with Earth's customs and immigration regulations."

"I have no objection," Sarah said, carefully holding her hands in the second degree of respect.

The others nodded agreeably.

"Of course," Raeder said cheerfully. "You will accompany us, teacher?"

"Yes," Sun-hes replied. Something in his manner implied that he was a fussy individual faced with people he knew would be a trial to his sensibilities. "We will need all the time together we can manage to prepare you for your interview."

As they entered the vehicle Raeder looked around in puzzlement. There was a row of rather tall, narrow, curved padded benches lined up against one wall. The others entered behind him and crowded up, wondering how the furniture worked.

Sun-hes tapped Raeder on the shoulder and the commander moved aside for him. The Fibian positioned his body over one of the benches and settled down, looking as comfortable as someone could with that many limbs to consider.

Peter moved forward and cautiously mounted the

bench as though getting on a horse, then he leaned
forward until his chest met the upper curving end.
Sarah and the others followed suit, grinning at how
awkward they looked and felt.

"There you are," Sun-hes, said. "Everyone
comfortable?"

No, Raeder thought. "As comfortable as we can
be," he said aloud.

Their instructor told the pilot that they were ready.
The doors slid shut and they felt themselves moving.

Peter looked around and frowned at the absence
of windows.

"We were hoping to get a look at your beautiful
city," he complained.

"There will be much time for that later," Sun-hes
assured him. "For now we must concentrate on protocol. You know absolutely nothing, and that will not
do."

"Surely her majesty," Raeder said, carefully bowing his head at the mention of her, "will understand
that and cut us some slack?"

"She will cut off your head if you offend her!" Sun-
hes adjusted his position to communicate earnestness.
"That is her right, the right of all our great ladies."

"Life and death?" Peter murmured.

"Absolutely!" Sun-hes leaned forward. "What does
'cut us some slack' mean?" he asked.

"It means that given our complete, if understand-
able, ignorance of your culture and the forms of
proper Fibian behavior, but also given our willing-
ness to learn and our, hopefully obvious, desire not
to give offense, her majesty might give us a little
leeway . . ." Peter began to flounder, "Er, room to
maneuver . . ."

"We're hoping her majesty will be tolerant of our
mistakes," the lawyer interjected. "To cut someone

some slack means to be tolerant or patient with them."

The Fibian cocked his head questioningly. "I understood that from context," he allowed. "But what precisely do these words mean? Slack means to loosen. But how does one cut looseness?"

The humans looked at one another in confusion. In Peter's ear Ticknor was nattering on in a long dissertation on the origin of the phrase.

"Uh, it's such an old saying," the commander said at last, "that its true meaning has been lost. Like you, teacher, we take its meaning from context."

"Ah," Sun-hes said, clicking his mandibles and snapping his tailwhip in amusement, "we have sayings like that ourselves."

He'd noticed the humans jump when he snapped his tailwhip, and also the winces and widened eyes.

"This," he said and snapped his tailwhip again, "denotes amusement. As when you bare the bony protuberances inside your mouths."

The humans nodded.

"Our apologies, teacher," Raeder said. "We know you would not intentionally harm us. But we are wary of those." He pointed at Sun-hes' tailwhip. "We're not well protected against inadvertent damage from them."

Sun-hes pulled it around and held the tip out to them.

"It is dry, as you can see. Only when threatened or driven by some strong anger does it exude acid. Our own carapaces are subject to damage from it, so we must be careful. It is considered the height of vulgarity to be out of control of this organ. And carelessly damaging another's carapace is a criminal offense."

Peter reached out cautiously but Sun-hes let it drop back behind him.

"However, it is probably best to avoid contact. Your outer covering does look delicate.

"Now, as I said," he continued briskly, "this," he snapped his tailwhip, "denotes amusement. It would appear that your species changes the shape of your face to do the same. I hope you will not take offense when I tell you that the bunching and stretching of your faces is . . ." He made a gesture that denoted suffering. " . . . difficult to watch," he finished. "I suspect that her gracious majesty, who is exquisite in all ways, would be much too polite to mention this. And so, I take upon myself the necessity of asking you this. Please do not move your faces any more than you absolutely have to. As you see, ours do not move at all."

Raeder and his people nodded.

"That means agreement to our people," he said. "Though it can also indicate reverence." He shook his head. "This is a negative."

"Ah!" Sun-hes said, pleased. "Then you also augment your speech by body movements. I am pleased. This means that you are much further ahead than I'd dared to hope."

Their instructor then began teaching them in earnest, continuing until they landed and the scientists came to escort the humans away to be examined.

The pilot interrupted Sun-hes' lecture to announce that their escorts were waiting without.

"Please stay with us," Peter asked him. "Correct our behavior where necessary to avoid misunderstandings. And continue your instruction as we go along."

"As you wish," the teacher said with a little inclination of his head. "That means yes?" he asked.

Raeder nodded and the Fibian snapped his tailwhip.

They were met at the door by a small welcoming

committee of five Fibians, each holding his pedipalps in the second degree of provisional respect.

"They are all senior scientists," Sun-hes told them. "You should offer them the second degree of respect in return."

Peter and his companions did so, then debarked from their craft.

"To whom is it appropriate to offer the third degree?" Raeder asked.

"One's students, the pouchlings of persons of the same status as yourself, or generally anyone you don't know and are dealing with in a trading capacity."

They exchanged greetings with the scientists, whose behavior expressed a particular reverence for the females in the party, then each of them took one of the humans in tow and led them towards the laboratory building.

The lab building was, no doubt, utilitarian, but it was unlike anything the humans had ever seen. Several stories high, it seemed to consist of a framework that resembled a hive, the whole wrapped in heavy white webbing, like a haunted house with the cobwebs on the outside.

As soon as the humans entered the building there was a minor kerfuffle as the visitors' blunt feet instantly damaged the webbing.

"You must be heavier than you appear," one of the scientists commented.

"Well, all of our weight is on our two feet," Sarah said. "Where yours is more evenly distributed."

"This could be a problem at the palace," Raeder observed. "We wouldn't want to damage her majesty's home. Perhaps you could call ahead, teacher, and ask them to put down some sort of shielding?"

Sun-hes was clearly torn; the humans recognized this because he froze for almost a full minute as he made up his mind what to do. At last he moved his pedipalps.

"That—" he rolled his pedipalps one over the other again, "is a gesture of acquiescence. Could one of you," Sun-hes said to the scientists, "direct me to a com?"

Raeder watched him move off, then turned to his crew.

"I think it would be a good idea to take a page from the Fibian's book and freeze to immobility whenever we're uncertain about something."

"Good idea," Lurhman said, deadpan. "I'd hate to rub my nose and discover I'd declared war."

They told the scientists that they were willing to answer questions as well as they were able, and they would allow an examination that did not require them to contribute bodily fluids. They breathed into containers after being cautioned by their lawyer that some of their DNA would be trapped, along with a fair sampling of the germs of at least four worlds. They refused to give samples of the hair that fascinated the scientists, at least until some sort of treaty was worked out.

They managed to prove to the scientists that their mere presence would not be poisonous to her majesty, and left them eagerly anticipating future donations of blood and tissue.

At last they were free to go and they were piloted to their interview in the palace.

Even to human eyes the palace was a world away from the plainness of the laboratories. The roof resembled the draped, tentlike effect of the terminal they'd seen at the spaceport, but it glowed pure white in the sunshine. It was almost the same height as the lab, but very clearly had fewer stories. There were windows all along the front, framed in webbing that pleased the eye with its precise geometric arrangement. The main doorway was very tall, at least five meters and wide enough for ten Fibians to walk abreast.

"Aren't there any doors?" Hu, the historian, asked.

"No," Sun-hes said. "We use force fields. After all, the only things we need to keep out are vermin and bad weather."

"What sort of vermin trouble you?" Sarah asked.

"Oh, little omnivorous animals, small insects, that sort of thing. You don't have problems with these?"

"Well, yes, we do," Raeder said. "But we prefer to use impenetrable materials to keep them out and conserve power."

"But these 'impenetrable materials' would be useless when you push them aside to leave the building yourselves. Isn't it so?"

"That is a defect," Peter admitted.

"As for conserving power, we don't find power to be a problem. Is your power source so weak?" Sun-hes' head was tilted forward, with the chin tucked in. "This head position indicates skepticism," he said.

"We have excellent power sources," Raeder said carefully. "But many of our citizens feel that they are dangerous and should be kept away from population centers and that limits us."

"We haven't had an accident with a power source since shortly after we discovered jump," the instructor said. "Perhaps that is something you will want to discuss when our people talk about trade."

Peter nodded, and Sun-hes echoed the motion with his own head.

"We have a few moments before the lady can see us," Sun-hes said. "Let us go to the balcony and look out over the city. If you have any questions I will be delighted to answer them."

Without waiting for an answer he turned and led them along the front of the building to its even longer side. The palace was built on the edge of a precipice and the land dropped away in a sheer thousand-foot cliff. Below lay the city of Quesh, a series of interconnected tunnels and buildings made of an often opaque drapery of webbing that lay in humps and spikes, mostly tinted blue. There were gardens between the buildings, dressed with a brilliant array of flowers and rather spiky-looking trees, like saguaro cactus with leaves.

In short, thoroughly . . . alien, Raeder thought. *Well, it would be surprising if it was all done in Neo-Victorian, wouldn't it?*

Fibians moved about below in their thousands, creeping along the bridges, sometimes upside down, moving across roofs and down streets. Raeder heard Ticknor's voice choke, and he hoped the linguist wouldn't lose it completely.

Just then a young Fibian appeared from somewhere above them, leaping into space with a hissing yodel and missing them by centimeters. Even Sun-hes started. Ticknor actually screamed.

Raeder turned his head aside and muttered, "Listen, Mr. Ticknor, you've got to get hold of yourself. We *need* you right now, and deafening us is not helping!"

He turned back to find Sun-hes watching him with an inquisitive tilt to his head.

"Our linguist," the commander explained, "with whom you've spoken, was startled by the appearance of . . ." Raeder waved below where the Fibian had disappeared.

"I was startled myself," the teacher admitted. "But I would not begrudge the young their exuberance. I once made that leap myself." He snapped his tailwhip.

Raeder nodded and restrained his smile.

"I was hoping," Sun-hes continued, "to meet Sirgay Ticknor. Why did he not come down?"

Talk about a loaded question, Peter thought. *How do I answer that one honestly without causing offense?*

"Mr. Ticknor felt that he could be of more aid to us on the ship, where he has access to all of his notes on your language," Sarah said. "He would automatically know what might be confusing to us and can speak directly into our ears. He also wanted to be there to supervise the collection of data on Fibian customs and body language that you are providing, teacher."

"Well, perhaps I will be privileged to meet him later," Sun-hes said amiably. "I was wondering," he continued, "why does Sirgay Ticknor have such a long name? Is one of these an honorific of some kind?"

"'Mr.' is an honorific for a civilian male," Raeder said, "'Ms.' for a female. Actually we all have two or more names. One portion is a family name, the others are personal names."

"How interesting!" Sun-hes said. "I look forward to learning more about your culture."

"Your pardon, gentle people."

They turned to find a rather tall male standing behind them.

"My name is Has-sre. I am first assistant to Lady Sisree, who wishes to see you now."

"I was told that we were being introduced to her majesty," the commander said with a little bob of his head.

"The lady Sisree is her majesty's daughter," Has-sre explained. "Her majesty will attend by vid for this first meeting."

"Of course," Peter said. *Probably a good idea. I bet*

we'd do the same thing. "We understand completely. Please, lead and we will follow."

Has-sre moved his pedipalps from a neutral position into that of the second degree of respect.

"This way," he said and moved off.

CHAPTER FOURTEEN

The Fibians had laid down some sort of hard plasticlike sheeting over the webbing on the floor and their feet rebounded from it with a *whoompa whoompa* sound, the Fibian's footsteps . . . or clawsteps . . . *tac-tacing* in counterpoint.

We sound like a tap-dancing tuba player, Raeder thought.

He felt a brief pang for the dignified entrance he'd imagined making into the presence of the leaders of the single nonhuman sentient species yet discovered. But the only other solutions that had come to him were some sort of snowshoe arrangement, an image he'd instantly dismissed, or crawling in like a snake.

Has-sre turned to them as they approached the door of Lady Sisree's private audience chamber. A heavy veil of webbing shrouded the entrance, so that nothing could be seen of the room beyond.

"I will go before you to announce your presence to the lady," he said. "Please wait here."

Peter and his group nodded. Has-sre turned to Sun-hes uncertainly and their teacher responded with an affirmative gesture.

After the first assistant had gone behind the curtain, Raeder turned to Sun-hes. He imitated the gesture the Fibian had made to Has-sre.

"This means yes?" he asked.

Sun-hes nodded and a nervous Peter struggled not to laugh.

"If I had a tailwhip," he said, "I'd have just snapped it."

Sun-hes snapped his. "It seems we share a sense of humor," he said. "Surely with a basis like that for friendship all should go well between our people."

Peter made the gesture for yes.

"The lady will see you now," Has-sre said. He pulled aside the curtain.

Raeder and his party moved forward, walking on tiptoe as they tried, unsuccessfully, to keep the plastic from rebounding quite so noisily.

So much for a decorous entrance, the commander thought. *We look like we're trying to sneak up on her ladyship. And it was my idea, too.*

Then he lifted his head and saw her. Through his ear link he heard Ticknor building up to a scream, saying, "Ah—ah—ah—ah," over and over. *You screech in my ear, Ticknor, and I'll give you something to be really scared of.*

She was enormous, huge, gigantic, easily twice as large as the males who accompanied them. The males were around five feet tall, give or take three inches, which made the lady who towered over them at least ten feet in height.

And I thought the front door was just for show,
Raeder thought.

The lady was slung in a huge web hammock that
hung from the ceiling high above them; it creaked
slightly with her every move. Gems that looked like
emerald, diamond, and tourmaline were woven into
the fabric of it and glittered in the soft, omnidirectional light. Behind her was a large screen from which
the queen appeared to be looking the humans over.

Raeder wondered if the queen was really that
much larger than the lady Sisree, or if it was merely
an illusion caused by her appearing on vid—some
sort of holographic protocol.

He and his crew held their hands in the position
of the first degree of respect and bowed their heads
courteously. Sun-hes had told them that bowing from
the waist was simply too ghastly looking, for in that
Fibian-like position it suddenly appeared to him as
though they had been cut in half, with three sets of
legs and most of their thorax missing.

Lady Sisree extended her pedipalps to her guests.
This gracious gesture was usually only offered to
Fibians in the highest favor. Sisree offered it in this case
because she wanted to know more about these aliens.
The type of information that could easily be gathered
simply by touching and smelling them, as well as getting
a really close look at them. Their skin, for example, and
hair were very intriguing to her, and her mother was
most interested in their simple-looking eyes.

Sun-hes froze in astonishment at the magnitude
of the lady's condescension, so Raeder knew it was
an exceptional moment. He went to stand by her
couch and reaching forward gently touched the lady's
armored fingers.

"What is this?" she exclaimed in her sweet, wavering
voice.

Her great head rushed forward and Peter had all he could do not to jump backwards at the suddenness of the movement. He could almost feel his heart bump up against the top of his skull from the shock. From Ticknor he heard nothing and surmised that the linguist had fainted.

Sisree inhaled and he could feel the rush of air flow from him towards her as she did so.

"Where did you meet with a Fibian child?" Sisree demanded. "You," she gestured towards Sarah, "come forward."

Sarah did so, bowing her head as she reached the lady's couch. Strands of her hair lifted and flowed towards the lady's giant face as the Fibian examined her.

"It is not of our clan," the lady said. "But it is most definitely the scent of a Fibian child."

"Answer," said Queen Tewsee. "Where did you meet with this child?"

"We thought he might be young," Raeder said, "but we had no idea he was still a child. He's easily as tall as our teacher, here."

"An older child, by the scent," Sisree confirmed. "But not yet at his maturity. I smell fear as well and perhaps . . ." She sniffed again. "Hunger?"

"We've done our best with protein paste and fluids," the commander told them. "But we've nothing on board that ordinarily would be part of a Fibian diet."

"Hungry, alone and frightened. You will bring him to me," the queen said.

"He is a child of Clan Snargx," Raeder told her, "and seemed frightened at the idea of contact with Nrgun."

"He is a child. I will make him one with our clan," Tewsee answered.

"He has been helping us to learn your language," Sarah said.

"Sun-hes will help you with that," the queen told her. "You will bring the child to me immediately," she said firmly. "When I have spoken to him I will see you again. This audience is now ended."

The screen went blank, as did the lady Sisree, who sat motionless in her hammock. Raeder and Sarah looked at one another.

Peter opened his mouth to speak and Sisree interrupted him. "This audience is over," she said. "You will go and get the child, then you will return here. When the queen and I have finished speaking with the child the audience will resume."

"I was wondering," Raeder said quickly, "if we might have clearance for another shuttle to bring him down? It would save time."

"Agreed," Sisree said. "Has-sre, see that it is done. You and your party may wait without," she said in dismissal. "We will call for you when we are through."

The humans bowed their heads, backing away with one eye on Sun-hes until he turned his back on the giant female, then they followed suit and left the audience chamber.

"Truon?" Raeder said.

"Here, sir," the XO answered.

Here indeed: along with most of the other senior officers Truon Le had been listening and watching through the same link that Ticknor was using.

"I'm on it," Truon said.

"My executive officer is taking care of it," Raeder said to Sun-hes. "Sna-Fe should be on his way in a few minutes."

"How is it that no one else seemed to notice the scent of this youngster?" Trudeau asked with a lawerly squint at their protocol expert.

"Our ladies have an enhanced sense of smell," Sun-hes answered. "Our scientists have instruments that can also detect odors such as the scent of a child or of another clan: but we had no idea that we would find them lingering about your persons." He changed the positioning of his body, until he looked more foursquare somehow. "Why is it that you never mentioned the prescence of a Fibian on board your ship? Let alone a child."

"It was a matter between Clan Snargx and ourselves," Raeder said after a moment's thought. "We didn't want to involve Clan Nrgun in our troubles."

"A good answer," Sun-hes replied. "In any case I will ask no more; it is not my place to do so. Shall we continue our lessons in the interim?"

"Sir!" Truon said through their link.

Raeder held up his hand. "What is it, Truon?"

"Please wait a moment," Sarah said quietly to their teacher. "The commander has an incoming message."

"We have a problem. When we went to the Fibian's cell and told him that the queen wanted to see him, he went nuts. He's throwing himself against the walls. We've retracted the sink and toilet into the walls and inflated the wall covering to minimize any damage he can do himself, but he's just wild, sir."

Raeder looked at Sun-hes a moment, then came to a decision.

"When my people informed the youngster that he was being taken down to the planet to meet your queen he . . . panicked," the commander said. "We're worried that he might do himself an injury. Is there some gentle way that we can render him unconcious until he's here? Maybe even after he gets here. We don't want to risk his doing her majesty an injury."

"That would never happen!" Sun-hes said instantly. "No Fibian of whatever clan would offer harm to a queen." He snapped his tailwhip weakly. "For one thing, you've seen the difference in size between us. What harm could the child do?"

"I have no idea," the commander said. "But I wouldn't like to see it happen. Nor do I want this child to do himself an injury. How can we calm him down?"

Sun-hes froze for a moment, then said, "Project this sound to him." The protocol expert then began to emit a low and rather pleasing hum interspersed with short sharp clicks of his mandibles.

"Are you getting this?" Raeder asked.

"Yes, sir. Transmitting." After a moment Truon said, "This is amazing! The Fibian is slowing down, he's falling, he's on the floor. I think he's asleep, sir!"

"Keep playing that sound to him as you transport him," Peter said. "We don't want him waking up in transit."

There were a lot of ways an angry, frightened person could hurt themselves, and everybody else, while in a shuttle.

"Aye, sir," Truon said. "He's on his way."

"He's asleep and on his way," Raeder told the group. "Thank you, Sun-hes, you may have saved that kid's life."

"It is nothing," the Fibian said with a negating gesture. "I have fostered many children in my time. Sometimes they become overwrought."

"Does that always work?" Lurhman asked.

"Oh, yes," Sun-hes said. "With a hundred children in care at any given time, we need something that is one hundred percent effective. One would have to overuse it terribly for it to even begin to lose effect. The hum loses its power entirely in adulthood, of course. Which is probably just as well."

"Wow," Lurhman said softly. "A lullaby that really

works. We sure could have used that at my house when my baby sister was born. That kid never shut up."

"You have nothing like the hum?" Sun-hes asked. "How do you manage all your children?"

"Well, we're wired differently," Sarah said. "And we have fewer children at a time."

"I am most upset," Tewsee said as she paced her chamber. She had renewed contact with her daughter as soon as she saw the aliens leave the room. "Why would they withhold such information from us?"

"The child is hungry and frightened," Sisree reminded her mother. "That is nothing to boast about." She waved her pedipalps in a graceful gesture that denoted confusion. "I wonder how they obtained custody of him?"

"The child himself will tell us that," Tewsee answered. "I only hope that I have achieved some degree of calm before he arrives. I would hate to frighten the poor little thing more."

"He will be on the cusp of adulthood, Mother," Sisree reminded her. "Not so small."

"But a delicate time of life, my dear. Or have you forgotten so soon?"

Sisree rotated her head and snapped her tailwhip. No, she hadn't forgotten, nor was she likely to with her mother to remind her.

"I wish I knew of some of your escapades, Mother. I'd rather enjoy having something to throw at you at moments like these."

"What escapades?" the queen asked. "I was always a perfect model of decorum. I knew my place and honored my mother with my flawless behavior."

"Oh, dear!" Sisree said dramatically. "Something is stirring in my digestive sac."

Tewsee clicked her mandibles. "I've told you often enough to chew the proper number of times, daughter."

Tewsee snapped her tailwhip, and clicked her mandibles heartily. Then she grew quiet.

"What will we do if the humans kidnapped the child?" she asked.

"We will find out why. We will find out all that we can." The queen paused. "Their ship is wounded and will probably need extensive repairs before they can return to their own system. We could refuse to help them with those repairs, refuse to let them come to the surface of the clan home. If they then decided to leave, the problem would be out of our hands. If they decided to stay . . . well, I suppose we'd have to feed them."

"And if they stay and then start to have young of their own?"

Tewsee shuddered. "Not a pretty thought, daughter. If that should happen then the children would be treated differently. If we are going to punish them for abusing a child how could we justify abusing theirs?" The queen flicked her pedipalps as though disposing of something nasty. "This unpleasantness has given me an appetite," she said. "I shall have something to eat before the child comes."

"Should I have the child fed before he sees you, Mother?" Lady Sisree asked.

"No. I shall feed him myself. It will help him to imprint on me. Have the child brought to me directly from the spaceport. Don't stop to clean him or speak to him or anything else. I want him here immediately."

"I understand, your majesty," Sisree answered, accepting the order with formality.

Has-sre came in and with a bow to his lady said,

"The aliens have released a shuttle, your majesty. It should be at the spaceport within fifty stansis."

"Excellent," Tewsee said.

"The aliens have also asked for permission to greet their shuttle when it lands," Has-sre said.

"Why?" the queen asked suspiciously.

"They said that they wished to assure themselves that the child arrived safely."

Sisree sat forward on her couch. "Do they actually mean to imply that they imagine *we* would do the child harm?" she demanded.

"I could not say, Lady. I suspect that they wish the reassurance of meeting with their own kind."

"That is a generous thought, First Assistant," Tewsee said. "It does you credit, and it might well be so. Quesh can be a bit overwhelming, I suppose."

Sisree clicked her mandibles. "Visitors from other clans have said so," she allowed.

The queen was silent a moment. Then she said, "I want to think well of our visitors, daughter. But at this moment I don't see how I can."

"You should eat something, as you suggested, Mother." Sisree rose from her couch. "As will I. Let the aliens go to greet their fellows at the spaceport, I can see no harm in it." The lady looked hard at her first assistant. "They will be watched to determine that there is no exchange of weapons or some such. Won't they, Has-sre?"

The first assistant bowed. "Of course, my lady."

"Until later, then," the queen said after a thoughtful pause.

"Until then, Mother."

"Couldn't resist, eh, Mr. Truon?" Raeder said to his XO. *Well, I wouldn't have been able to either in his position.* No indeed, he'd have found any means necessary to hit the planet's surface at the earliest opportunity.

Truon smiled a bit sheepishly, but nodded in agreement.

"We've brought some extra food and water with us as well," he told the commander. "Since we didn't know how much longer you'd be here."

"How's Sna-Fe holding up?" Peter asked as he watched some ratings guide a float-pallet down the shuttle's ramp.

"Sound asleep, sir. At least as far as we can tell. He's breathing and he's quiet." Truon shrugged. "For all we know he could be in a coma."

"That would be bad," Raeder said. *Bad for him and bad for us.*

It had been a while since he'd seen the young Fibian, and he didn't look good. Not just because he was unconscious and sprawled in an ungainly heap upon a piece of furniture not designed to accomodate his shape. His shell was dull; it even seemed to be flaking apart in places and that couldn't be good.

"Poor kid," Sarah said. She looked at Raeder almost apologetically. "I know it's not our fault. His being with us was the merest fluke. But knowing he's just a boy . . ." She gestured helplessly. "It's just too bad."

"My impression from things our instructor has said leads me to believe that someone Sna-Fe's age on a fighting ship is highly unusual," the ship's lawyer said. "Do we know whether *that* was a fluke, someone bringing a favorite son along, or is it Clan Snargx company policy?"

Raeder frowned in thought.

"Mr. Ticknor?" he said. "Are you listening?"

"Yes, Commander."

"Well? Did you ask Sna-Fe about this? Is it unusual

for someone as young as he is to be on a Snargx warship?"

"I never thought to ask that question specifically, Commander. You'll recall that I told you I *suspected* he was rather young. But he steadfastly refused to answer any personal questions or questions about his ship, or his friends. He was a clam. I'm sorry."

"That's all right, Mr. Ticknor, not your fault. I'm glad that you asked some questions, though. If her majesty asks if we even tried to find out anything about this kid, we'll be able to say yes. How are you holding up?"

"Better than I thought I would," Sirgay answered. "I, uh, lost it there for a few minutes," he said, sounding embarrassed.

"I noticed." Raeder grinned. "Can't say I blame you. I hadn't expected her to be so big."

"No," Ticknor said in a falling-away voice.

"Okay," Raeder said, not without some sympathy, "catch you later. Keep up the good work."

A crew of Fibians came up to the small party of humans. One of them stepped forward, holding his pedipalps in a very sloppy third degree of respect, almost the fourth.

"We have been sent to gather up the young one and bring him to our queen," he said.

Sun-hes went rigid at the implied disrespect inherent in the soldier's attitude. Raeder noticed it also, and simply dispensed with Fibian courtesies, pointing at the floating pallet.

The soldier gestured his companions forward and they trotted into position around the unconscious figure. The humans kept hold of the pallet and looked to Raeder questioningly. He nodded and the humans stood back, letting the Fibians take charge.

"You should go back to your ship now," the Fibian

leader said. "You," he said to Raeder, "should return to the palace to wait on her majesty's pleasure."

"You must give me your name," Raeder answered, "so that I can tell her majesty of your courtesy in the performance of your duties."

The Fibian froze and a full thirty seconds later said, "Sim-has is my name. I am a huntmaster of the queen's guard. She will know me."

"Excellent," the commander said, awarding the Fibian an exaggerated grin. He waggled his eyebrows. "I will be sure to tell her."

The huntmaster spread his chelicerae in unconscious revulsion and backed away a few steps, then quickly spun about and hurried after his soldiers.

"I think you may have grossed him out a bit there, sir," Lurhman said cheerfully.

"Gosh I hope so," Raeder said. He frowned. "Though that's probably unfair of me. From all he knows we're kidnappers and child abusers."

Sarah sighed, then with a shake of her head turned to Truon Le.

"Did you say you brought food?" she asked the XO.

"Yes, I did." He gestured to one of the ratings and the young woman rushed into the shuttle, returning with a large container.

"I didn't know how long you'd be here," Truon said, "so I had them pack enough for this evening and for breakfast."

"Good!" Hu said and took possession of the bin. "I'm starving."

"You'd better get going," Raeder said to the shuttle crew. "Thank you, Truon."

The XO saluted and Raeder returned it.

"Good luck, sir."

"Thank you, Truon. Same to you." *After all, my luck is your luck.*

On the way back to the palace Sun-hes eyed the food box curiously.

"If I do not overstep by asking, Commander, what is it that humans eat?"

"Well," Peter said. *How do I answer without giving offense?* "We humans are omnivorous. Unlike Fibians we make fruits and vegetables a regular part of our meals."

"Some of us," Trudeau said, "eat only vegetables and fruits."

The humans watched their Fibian teacher closely to see if they could discern how this was affecting him.

"You do eat meat, then?" Sun-hes asked.

"Ye-es," Raeder said. "But . . . we cook it."

"We have to," Sarah put in. "Our mouthparts don't handle raw meat very well. Neither do our digestive systems."

"What we're trying to say," said Hu, "is that we don't eat *live* prey."

"Oh," the Fibian said and became quiet for a time.

Oh? Peter thought. *Oh, as in uh-oh, or oh, as in oh, yeah, that's what I thought?*

"You know that we eat our food live?" the teacher said.

The humans nodded.

"Yes," Raeder said. "May I be frank?"

Sun-hes invited him to continue with a gesture.

"We find that terribly disturbing. So we assumed that you might find our eating habits equally disturbing. It would probably be best if we didn't eat in front of each other, don't you think?"

The Fibian made a noncommital gesture. "I'm not a diplomat," he said. "And neither are you, I suspect." Raeder and the others clapped their hands in what they'd agreed would substitute for smiles and laughter and struggled not to change expression. "I will try to find some delicate way to convey this information to her majesty and Lady Sisree. It is definitely something they should know."

"Sun-hes," Raeder said. "I must tell you that Clan Snargx has been making war on us, in alliance with some of Star Command's human enemies. What will happen if this child of Clan Snargx tells the queen something untrue about us? What if he says we deliberately harmed him?"

"He will not lie to the queen," Sun-hes assured them.

"How can you know that?" Lurhman asked. "He might well consider it his duty to Clan Snargx."

"He might if a huntmaster, or a soldier, or I were to question him. But he cannot lie to the queen. She has said that she will make him one with Clan Nrgun. He will not be able to lie to her."

The humans looked at one another.

"How does that work, exactly?" Raeder asked.

"Exactly?" Sun-hes said. "I do not know. This is hardly my area of expertise. But our females can release hormones that cause emotional changes in us males that can change our behavior."

"Even against your better judgement?" Lurhman asked.

"Judgement is the first thing to go," Sun-hes assured them with a click. "Have you humans no equivalent?"

"Well . . . yes, I guess so," Raeder said. "But it's kind of mutual, and not under anybody's control." His glance flicked over to Sarah and he found her looking at him, a fond smile in her eyes.

"You should allow Has-sre to examine the contents of that box," their teacher said. "He will want to, I'm sure. If you offer it would be courteous."

I think I'll just take that as an order from the queen, Raeder thought. *However courteously expressed.*

"We'll do that," Peter said.

"It won't take long, will it?" Hu asked. "I'm really hungry."

The child ate the last bloody slice of meat and Tewsee crooned him to sleep. She sat on her couch and just watched him breathe. After a solid meal and a great deal of reassurance the child was already looking better. His color was slowly changing from red to blue and just now was caught in a violet hue. Rather pretty in its way.

After a few minutes she rose and quietly left the room. Little Sna-Fe had given her much to think about. And all of it was terrible. She was reluctant to even speak about it but knew that soon it would be all that she spoke of, and all that she heard spoken of. So now she retired to her rooms for a last hour of peace. On the way she told Hoo-seh, her first assistant, to see to the child, so that he wouldn't wake up alone in a strange place. The poor little warrior had done that too often of late.

Alone in her room Tewsee huddled miserably, trying to remember what the world had felt like before she'd spoken to a child of Clan Snargx.

"And, of course, it is considered courteous to praise the goods one has purchased once the bargaining is done. But only with street vendors should one be offering to bargain."

"Surely," Trudeau said politely, "when hammering out a trade agreement a great deal of bargaining goes on."

"Yes," Sun-hes agreed with a click of his mandibles.

"But then it is called negotiation."

The humans clapped their hands to show amusement.

After this many hours of practice, Raeder thought, *we're all getting pretty good at this no-facial-expressions-show-your-feelings-with-your-hands thing.* And it had been a good many hours.

Raeder stood. "Aren't you tired?" he asked the Fibian.

Stopped in full spate of explaining the Nrgun ettiquette of negotiation, Sun-hes stared at the commander for a moment, confused.

"Tired?" he said at last. "I have been enjoying your company." He made an encompassing gesture. "Do I seem . . . ?"

"Actually, you seem as though you could go straight through to tomorrow morning without pausing for so much as a sip of water, teacher. Do Fibians ever get tired?" Raeder stood up from where he'd been sitting against the wall and folded his arms across his chest.

Sun-hes looked around at the humans, then looked at Raeder.

"Yes, I am tired, not bored by any means, but a bit weary."

"Hungry?" the commander asked.

"That, too, Commander."

"Perhaps you should go and get something to eat, then," Peter said.

"I would not feel comfortable leaving you alone and hungry while I ate," Sun-hes said. He looked around at them again. "I will go and inquire what sort of accommodation might have been made for you. Obviously you can't be expected to sleep in the hallway." He moved down the hallway towards the reception area. "I will be right back," he said over his shoulder.

"Thank you, Commander," Mark Hu said. "I'm starving."

"I suspect Sun-hes liked the way you handled that, sir," Trudeau said. "Nothing direct, all very polite, if pointed. I feel like we've learned a lot today."

"Thank you, Trudeau," Peter said. "What I'd really like to learn is what's going on.

"Well," Sarah said, "if what Sun-hes told us is true and the child can't lie to the queen—"

"That's a big if," the commander said.

"Granted. But if it is true, then the queen knows that we didn't kidnap Sna-Fe, nor did we deliberately mistreat him. They probably cleared that up pretty fast," she said. "The way the two females acted I'm sure it was the first thing they asked him."

"What's your point, Lieutenant Commander?" Trudeau asked.

"Her point is," Raeder said, leaning against the wall next to Sarah, "that over the last few hours Sna-Fe must have filled their ears with Clan Snargx's doings for the last few years. And I don't think it made very soothing listening." He resumed his pacing. "It all depends, of course, on the character of Clan Nrgun."

"They seem really nice," Lurhman said hopefully. "Even when that huntmaster was rude to us the reason he was rude is a kind of a respectable one. Don't you think?" she asked Sarah.

"We've been to the spaceport and here," Sarah said. "We've mostly talked to Sun-hes, and a little bit to the huntmaster of the ship that escorted us here." She shook her head. "That's too small a sample to determine the character of a people."

"But we're asking them to do that based on an equally small number of people," Raeder said. "It's unfair, and probably unrealistic, but I'm hoping they decide to trust us."

Sun-hes came hurrying down the hallway towards them.

"You are to be escorted into the presence of the queen herself," he said, visibly nervous.

"Can we eat first?" Hu asked plaintively.

"No time," the teacher said. "Your escort is on its way and the queen's chambers are across the palace from here. It will take a while to reach her."

A small group of six guards appeared and came to a standstill before the humans.

"The queen commands your presence," their leader proclaimed.

Raeder wasn't sure, but he thought he recognized their aquaintance from the spaceport. *More respectful this time, though.* The Fibian held his pedipalps in a crisp third degree of definitive respect. *Or maybe he's just more careful within the palace walls.*

"Okay, people," Raeder said, "let's go."

Despite Sun-hes' instruction not to bow because of the way it looked, Peter found himself bowing to Queen Tewsee. It was that or fall down. She *was* bigger than the lady Sisree, unbelievable as that seemed. He found himself fighting down an atavistic terror that wouldn't have been out of place in Ticknor's worst nightmares.

Suddenly he felt Sarah's hand in his and he pulled himself upright and looked the queen right in the eyes. *Don't speak,* he reminded himself. *Royalty speaks first or everyone remains silent.*

"From what Sna-Fe tells me his capture and subsequent imprisonment on your ship was the merest accident."

"That is true, your majesty," Raeder said. His heart still beat fast enough that he imagined it was visible through his uniform shirt.

"He also informs me that your people have cared for him as well as you can. You humans do not eat live food, he tells me."

"No, your majesty."

"What do you know of the affairs of Clan Snargx?" the queen asked.

"Very little, your majesty. They are allied with our human enemies, and we have no idea ourselves how that alliance was formed. Nor do we know why they have made it."

"Why do you *think* they have made this alliance?" Tewsee asked with a bitter emphasis in her flat and wavering voice.

The humans glanced at one another. *I think they're doing it for the antihydrogen,* Peter thought. *What I don't know is whether I should share that with you.*

Trudeau leaned forward and whispered in his ear, "She knows. Or she wouldn't ask so directly."

True, Peter thought, remembering his success in sending Sun-hes off to inquire about their food and lodging. *I'm definitely no diplomat or I'd have realized that.*

"Your majesty, our enemies are in possession of a rare and wonderful natural resource that the Commonwealth requires in order to survive. The Mollies, our enemies, do not want to make use of this substance themselves, and they do not wish to share it with us. Their hope is that if they deny us the use of it most of humanity will die, or fall back into barbarism."

The queen froze as she thought that over.

"It seems," she said at last, "that Snargx has found the perfect ally. Beings as mad and cruel and perverted as themselves. I will not ask you why these humans wish all of humanity to die. It is none of Clan Nrgun's affair. Snargx never told you humans that there were other clans out here, did they?"

"I cannot answer that, your majesty," Raeder said. "They may have told our enemies. Though that seems unlikely, given the nature of the Mollies."

The queen leaned forward, putting her face on a level with Peter's.

"Is it true," she asked, "that some of Clan Snargx's representatives have executed human prisoners by eating them?"

Raeder found himself holding his breath. Strangely, though her appearance frightened him still on a visceral level, he didn't feel threatened by her.

"Yes, your majesty, it is true. I have seen vids of such executions."

With a sound like a gasp, she turned and fled the room. Peter stood there and blinked in astonishment. *Now what?* he wondered. *Do the guards come in and make mincemeat out of us?*

Sun-hes collapsed slowly into a little pile of legs and joints.

"Are you all right?" Sarah asked him. She approached the Fibian cautiously and knelt by his head. "Sun-hes?"

"Intelligent beings," he said weakly, his voice sounding like a squeaking hinge. "How could they?"

The humans, used to centuries of man's inhumanity to man, exchanged glances but said nothing.

"Are you going to be all right?" Raeder asked, kneeling beside Sarah. "Should we call for help?"

A shudder wracked the Fibian's armored body and he struggled weakly to his clawed feet.

"There is no help for such a monstrous thing," the teacher said. "I wish the knowlege of it was not in my head." He shook his head as though to dislodge the unwelcome images it conveyed.

Hoo-seh entered and spoke to them. "Her majesty is too overwrought to continue this audience tonight. She requests that you accept our hospitality for the night, that you may continue your discussion in the morning."

"Thank you," Raeder said. "We would be honored to accept her majesty's hospitality."

"I will leave you then," Sun-hes said. His body still shook with spasms. "I wish to be alone."

"They're very upset," Hu said when they were alone together in the room that had been prepared for them.

Raeder looked at the heaps of webbing, looked around for some sort of washroom, then looked around for a certain box.

"Anybody see the food?" he asked.

"Here it is," Sarah said.

She bent down behind one of the fluffy heaps of webbing and hoisted it up with a smile. Raeder went over and took it from her.

"Who's hungry?" he asked.

"Sir," Hu said, putting his hand on the commander's arm.

Raeder looked into the younger man's earnest face.

"What is it, Hu?"

"They're *very* upset about this eating of prisoners, sir," the historian said. "Isn't it possible that they'd like to, maybe, erase that knowledge?"

Raeder closed his eyes for a moment. When he opened them he considered Hu.

"I understand what you're asking, Hu," Raeder said. "And I know that in human societies there's certainly evidence of attempts to eliminate bad news by eliminating anyone who knows about it. But, somehow, given their behavior so far, I don't think we have anything to worry about." *At least not yet.*

"What happens, happens," Trudeau said. "To be blunt, they've got us whenever they want us, and there's nothing we can do about it. We couldn't even if we were back on *Invincible*, not with damaged engines and short of fuel."

"So, given that fact," Lurhman said, reaching into the box and pulling out a sandwich, "we might as well eat. I'm—"

"Hungry," Hu said and snatched the sandwich out of her hands. He took a big bite and said through a very full mouth, "If I gotta go, at least it will be with a full stomach."

"Should we watch him to see what happens?" Sarah asked, arching a brow.

"Heck with that," Peter said reaching into the box. "I'm starved."

CHAPTER FIFTEEN

Sisree reluctantly wakened to the persistant chime of her com.

"Light," she said and slowly the light in her room rose. "Stop," she commanded when it was bright enough to see, dim enough that it would make her desire to be still asleep apparent to her caller. She tapped a key on the console beside her couch. "Yes," she said sharply.

"We need to speak, Sisree," her mother said. "Get yourself awake and call me back."

The screen went dark.

Sisree's head came up and all the cobwebs of sleep were instantly gone. Never had her mother sounded so upset, not for earthquake, fire, raid or pestilence.

"Light," she said again, this time allowing it to rise to daytime brightness.

Then she tapped her mother's code into her com.

"Sisree," her mother said as though she'd never interrupted herself, "we have a problem."

"The aliens?" the lady asked.

"No. Or at least they're part of the problem, but probably not the cause of it."

"Then it must be the fact that Snargx was pursuing them," Sisree said. She'd been expecting daily to hear complaints from a Snargx representative about the short, ugly battle that had brought the humans into Nrgun's orbit.

Tewsee froze at the mention of the clan name; then, very slowly, her chelicerae spread in an expression of extreme revulsion.

Great unease stirred in Sisree's mind as she watched. Of all the reasons her mother should call in the dead of night, a loathing for Clan Snargx would have been the last she'd have guessed.

"Why?" she demanded.

"I don't want to tell you," her mother said. "I don't want to know this myself." The queen shook her head dismally. "We must convene the council of queens," she said. "Immediately!" She emphasized the urgency with a grasping gesture.

"What explanation shall I give?" Sisree asked reasonably.

"A reason so terrible I only want to say it once, before all. I have a witness to crimes so evil that I cannot call them anything else. Snargx must be stopped." The queen looked at her daughter for a moment, fairly vibrating with emotion. "You will see to this for me, daughter?"

It was a request, plain and simple, and not an order. Her mother's state was alarming to Sisree, as the queen quite obviously couldn't hide her feelings. Clearly Tewsee couldn't contact other queens looking like this; shaking and with her chitin almost gray with shock. The loss of prestige would be too great.

"Of course I will, Mother. How urgent shall I say this is?"

"Very. Lives may depend on it, Fibian lives, *children's* lives. I will take care of the preparations on this end if you will speak to the other queens, Sisree. Begin now, there's no time to be lost." Then she disconnected.

The lady stared at the blank screen and let out her breath until she wheezed. Then she straightened and called Has-sre. She hated to break his rest but she could hardly do this all by herself.

Raeder and his people entered the presence of Queen Tewsee in an undeniably scruffy state. Their clothes, while not actually wrinkled, were less than fresh. Their hair was unbrushed and the men sported unshaven faces.

"Did you rest well?" Tewsee asked them.

Even in her upset state she could see that they looked very different. It would disturb her greatly if she were responsible for a permanent decline in their health. They knew absolutely nothing about these creatures and, after only one night on Nrgun, they appeared to have changed and not for the better.

"Quite well, your majesty," Raeder said with a little head bob. "Thank you for asking."

Actually they'd slept very badly. If the queen's obvious distress weren't enough to keep them awake all night, the utter failure of their beds was. The humans had become stuck to the inviting bundles of webbing piled up in an obvious attempt by their hosts to cushion the floor.

Poor Hu had become so enwrapped that it had taken a good half hour to release him. Then it had taken a while to pick the pieces out of their own hair and off their clothes. The stuff had left a vaugely sticky feeling where it had touched flesh. They'd ended up sleeping on top of the plastic their hosts had laid down.

Trudeau had slept the most: they knew that because the rest of them had drifted in and out of a doze as they listened to her recite bits of legal code in her dreams. Her claim that morning to have slept poorly had met with, to her, a puzzling lack of sympathy.

Peter felt as though he ought to ask if the queen had slept well, but Sun-hes had warned them not to ask personal questions. So Raeder stood before her trying to look pleasant without moving a facial muscle. *We probably all look like hell,* he thought. Certainly her majesty did. Even as a novice at picking out individual Fibians he could see a change in her. She looked older somehow, duller.

"Young Sna-Fe has given us much to think about," the queen said at last. "Though his report of your people and their treatment of him leads me to believe that you are . . . a decent people."

"Thank you, your majesty," Raeder said, and bowed his head again.

"I understand that your ship has been extensively damaged, Commander. We will send workers and engineers to aid you in your repairs," Tewsee said. "This work will be done in thanks for your aid to one of our clan. Perhaps, later, when the work is well under way and you have leisure, we can talk of trade and other matters."

"Thank you, your majesty." Head bob. *I'm begining to feel like I'm on an endless loop,* he thought. *Pleasant and agreeable. Is this the way diplomats have to behave all the time? How do they do it?*

"You will wish to return to your ship now to prepare," the queen told him. "My second assistant, Fuj-if, will assist you. If you have any questions or problems please call upon him for his aid."

Here we go. "Thank you, your majesty."

In response to a final wave of her pedipalps Raeder and his people backed away. When they'd gone ten paces he turned and led them from the room, trusting that some Fibian fart catcher would direct them where to go.

I'm feeling like a bit player in my own life, he thought, frustration making him grumpy. *But I'm no diplomat and I know it. Thank you, at least, seems like a safe thing to say.*

Whether he should have accepted the queen's offer of help was, as far as Raeder was concerned, a moot point. They needed her help or they'd never see the Commonwealth again. *So if that's a faux pas we'll just let the real diplomats find some way around it.*

Outside the audience chamber Sun-hes awaited them.

"I am sorry not to have been at your disposal this morning," he said, obviously looking them over. "It is most unusual for her majesty to hold an audience at this hour."

I can believe it, Raeder thought. The sun had only been up for an hour. *The dew is still on the web, as it were.*

"Will you still be coming up to the ship with us to help with our language lessons?" Raeder asked him.

"Yes, if you will still permit," the Fibian said with a gracious gesture.

By now Peter fully suspected that in addition to being a protocol expert, Sun-hes was also a secret service agent.

Nevertheless, better the spook you know and all that.

"You'll be very welcome," the commander said. "I should warn you right now though . . ." Peter took a deep breath. *I don't want to have to say this.* "Our linguist, Mr. Sirgay Ticknor . . ." He bit his lower lip as he wondered how to phrase this.

"Finds the Fibian body shape very, very disconcerting," Sarah put in. "It's an irrational reaction, which he admits himself, but he can't seem to help it. I think he's improving somewhat, though."

You do? Based on what? Peter wondered. *Wishful thinking?*

"That must make his work somewhat difficult," Sun-hes said diplomatically. "Given that much of the context of our remarks is in our body language."

"He noticed that right away," Raeder assured the Fibian. "He's one of the Commonwealth's best linguists."

Sun-hes clicked his mandibles.

"But . . ." he said.

"But he won't want to actually be in the same room with you," Sarah said regretfully.

"Thank you, Commander," Ticknor said in his ear.

"Moving along," Raeder said, rubbing his hands together. "Do you need to bring anything with you? Reference texts, a reader, personal belongings, that sort of thing?"

"I have all the belongings I will need packed and on their way to the spaceport," Sun-hes said.

Spy, Raeder confirmed to himself. "What about food?" he said aloud.

"Ah. That I did not pack." The Fibian looked around. "But here is the queen's second assistant."

Fuj-if was rather narrower in his body than their teacher and slightly bluer in color. He greeted them with his pedipalps in the second degree of respect.

"I have arranged a transport for you and your party

to the spaceport, Commander," the Fibian said. He handed over a small device. "This will alert me that you are in need of my aid, if you press the blue square."

"Thank you, you are most kind," Raeder said. "In fact I am in need of some assistance. Our instructor here will be coming with us, so we'll need Fibian foodstuffs, and perhaps someone to prepare them." *Although how much preparation is involved in eating your food raw and with the fur or feathers still on, I've no idea.*

"Of course, Commander. It has already been seen to."

Fuj-if raised a pedipalp and from out of the walls, it seemed, their escort appeared.

"You have only to call on me if anything is needed," he said. "Farewell."

"Thank you," Peter said. *Endless loop!* "Good-bye."

Once they were alone with Sun-hes in their transport Raeder said, "Mr. Truon?"

"Here, sir."

"We're going to need private accomodation for two," the commander said. "And one of the sealed labs for the storage of our Fibian guest's food supply."

"Yes, sir."

"And I'd like to call a staff meeting at 0900 to discuss needed repairs."

"I'm on it, sir."

"Thank you, Mr. Truon." *That's it. I'm not saying thank you for the rest of the day. I'd like to call a meeting? That seems to imply there's an option. That's way too conciliatory for a military officer. When I get back to the* Invincible *I'm gonna start issuing orders and* not *thank people for following them.* That ought to put the world back into its proper perspective.

❖   ❖   ❖

"Mother?"

"Yes, Sisree?" Tewsee tapped on her com so that she could look at her daughter. "What news?"

"The queens are coming. You didn't say, but I assumed that you didn't want me to invite Clan Snargx's queen."

"No!" Tewsee said. "It is about Syaris that I need to speak to them. We'll give her a chance to speak when the time comes." The queen stroked her digestive sac as though to calm it. "Thank you, Sisree, you have done well." She clicked her mandibles. "And well I know it. Getting our sisters together is a prodigious undertaking."

Sisree snapped her tailwhip. "It will keep our assistants hopping for days," she agreed. There was a pause and Sisree watched her mother move restlessly around her chamber. "Won't you tell me what this is all about?" she asked. "It will help you to organize your thoughts. I can ask questions that the other queens might and help to prepare you."

"I honestly don't know if I can bear to do that, daughter," Tewsee answered. "I feel it would be like . . . like deliberately scarring you."

"Then at least let me interview Sna-Fe. I feel it's only fair that I be somewhat prepared, Mother. Never have this many queens gathered in one place together. They asked, quite reasonably, why this couldn't be done by vid, and I had to tell them I didn't know. It made me feel as though you didn't trust me."

"You know that I trust you," Tewsee said, turning away. "This isn't an issue of trust."

"That's probably not how your sister queens feel, Mother." Sisree began pacing her own chamber. "They're showing a great deal of trust by coming here at your urgent request, sent through me, but which

I cannot explain. One might almost say they are show-ing an unprecedented degree of trust."

Tewsee flicked her pedipalps impatiently. She tossed her head and said, "Very well, Sisree. I will send the child to you. Interview him, find out what I know and I wish you joy of it!"

The screen went dark and Sisree was brought up short by her mother's angry and most unwilling cap-itualation. But she would not refuse the concession.

"Has-sre," she said into her com.

"My lady?"

"Send for the child Sna-Fe. I invite him to dine with me."

"Yes, my lady."

Sisree wondered for a moment if the senior assistants knew what Sna-Fe had told her mother. Then with an impatient sound she rejected the idea. If he had known anything of value Has-sre would have told her. The first lady of Nrgun settled back to her work and tried to put Snargx's lost child and his secrets out of her mind.

The Fibians seem to like working with Augie Skin-ner, Peter thought. *I'll bet it's because he never changes expression.* Funny how an attribute that drove most of his human companions round the bend made him popular with the aliens. Maybe Augie was one of those star-lost souls Peter's crazy Aunt Kelly used to talk about. *That's it,* he thought with an inner smile, *Skinner should have been a Fibian but something went wrong with the delivery order.*

You could see the Fibian technicians change in attitude when some more gregarious crew member came up to them. The Fibs sort of stiffened. Kind of like a lot of humans did after they'd been speak-ing to Augie for awhile.

Sun-hes had told him frankly that it was very, very hard for the Fibians, "To watch your faces squeezing and bunching and writhing the way that they do. To us, faces aren't supposed to do that."

Raeder approached the knot of alien and human engineers.

"Are you gentlemen ready for our meeting?" he asked, holding his hands in the third degree of respect due to those of inferior military rank.

"Yes, sir," Skinner said, with a typically distracted salute.

"We are, Commander," the leading Fibian engineer answered.

They were holding the meeting in the engine room at the request of both groups of engineers, basically so that they could point to what they meant. Skinner knew that Raeder was an engineer, but he felt the commander was a highly specialized type of engineer who had only the most rudimentary knowledge of the engines. As far as Raeder was concerned, compared to Augie himself, that was a not unreasonable assessment.

"You will notice," the head Fibian engineer began, and launched into a lengthy and complex explanation of the problems of engine numbers seven and eight. "We therefore recommend completely replacing the worst damaged of the two," he concluded.

"The whole engine?" Raeder said.

He felt his face react to the surprise and tried to damp it down. *That's extremely generous of them,* he thought, not a little awed. Suspicion pricked him, but the scrounger in him tamped it down ruthlessly. *Never look a gift horse in the mouth.* At least not right in front of the giver. There was always time later to count the teeth.

"Her majesty is most generous," Raeder said.

"She is first among queens," the first engineer said in a little burst of patriotism.

With a glance at the hatch they'd come through, Raeder said,"But how could such a large item be brought in here?"

Skinner pointed to the still jury-rigged patching on the wall beside the defunct engine.

"Shut off the grav in here," he said, "open the wall and float it into position. We can take the old engine apart easy since we don't need to repair it, just cut it up so all that remains are the connections. We can fix the wall afterwards."

The commander nodded. "Very good. Do it."

There were mandible clicks from the Fibians and smiles from the *Invincible*'s engineers at that. Really all that they needed Raeder for was permission. Now they could get things under way.

"I'll leave you gentlemen to it, then," Peter said as the engineers were drawn almost irresistibly into a planning circle that now excluded him.

"Thank you, sir," Skinner said, looking at him vaguely and once more offering a salute that had much more in common with a wave.

Raeder returned it to the back of the engineering officer's head and shook his as he walked away. *I bet Augie always saluted the Old Man.*

Maybe someday he'd have acquired the force of personality that demanded crisp salutes. *Maybe not. Maybe my style is to have people do superior work even if they don't salute according to the manual.* He knew Skinner respected him and, after all, with types like the engineering officer some leeway was a good policy. He wasn't lax; his people were a good crew, knew their jobs, did them well and responded to emergencies as if they were daily occurrences. *Of course, on the* Invincible *they are.*

There were more ways than one to be a good skipper.

A whole new engine! A Fibian engine with all the insight that would lend into their technology. And all the Fibs got in exchange was a look at their tech and the burnt lumps of the wrecked engine.

Clearly the queen's desire to thank them extended a little deeper than he'd suspected.

Is this an apology? he wondered. Obviously Sna-Fe had told her about his superiors killing and eating humans, which is why she'd asked for confirmation. Equally obvious was her upset over the issue. If it was an apology it was a brave one, offering far more than words, leaving her people potentially vulnerable. *It also says, "we're not like them." I can respect that.*

His mental and physical wanderings had brought him to sick bay and the tiny office of Doctor Ira Goldberg.

"Doctor?" Raeder said, tapping on the hatch frame.

Goldberg looked up, his brows raised in inquiry. "Ah, Commander. Come in, come in. To what do I owe the honor of this visit?"

Peter noted that Goldberg's eyes became busy the moment he'd locked them onto his visitor. They took in Raeder's eyes, his skin, his body, resting briefly on his artificial hand as they searched out the reason for this call.

"I'm fine, in case you're wondering," the commander said, taking a chair. "The reason I dropped down is that I've had an idea and I wondered if you might have something that would make it possible."

Goldberg spread his hands in invitation and looked with interest at Raeder.

"Our facial expressions and gestures to the face visibly bother our Fibian friends," Peter explained. "I was wondering if there was some way we could

freeze certain muscles to make our faces less mobile."
He looked expectantly at the doctor. "Something
reversible, of course."

"Absolutely," Goldberg said. "I can even do it without giving you a numb sensation. You'd probably want
to freeze the eyebrows and limit the function of the
cheek muscles. Leave you enough to talk, but not to
grin or grimace."

"Exactly what I was hoping for," Peter said. "Uh,
how long will it last?"

"How long do you need it to last? Up to ten
hours? No problem. If you're going to be doing it
daily I'd recommend doing it only for a few hours
at a time, though. The immediate, but fairly rare,
side effects of this stuff can be headache, slight
nausea and, if you've overused it, an unfortunate
tendency to develope muscle tics for a few weeks.
If you're going to be in constant communication with
them and don't want to be caught by surprise I can
do something surgical—also reversible—that might be
better. But of course, that would also be more
painful." Goldberg studied the commander as though
wondering where he'd make the first cut.

"Chemicals will be fine," Peter said hastily. "For
me, at least. I'll have the crew who are going to be
working closely with the Fibs call and discuss it with
you directly." He rose. "Thanks, Ira, that will make
things easier for everybody."

As he turned to leave Goldberg asked, "Any chance
I might get a look at the planet?"

Raeder turned back, looking thoughtful.

"Yes," he said at last. "I think I should take at least
the senior staff down to have a look. Next time I go
down I'll bring you and Truon." He grinned. "I don't
think I have to worry about Augie. I think for him
the world ends at engineering's door."

✧   ✧   ✧

Raeder answered his com to find himself looking at . . . Lady Sisree, he decided.

"Your Ladyship!" he exclaimed in surprise. Then was surprised that he'd come up with such an anachronistic title so instinctively.

She clicked her mandibles delicately in response to his astonishment.

"We have invited the queens of the other clans to clan home Nrgun to meet you humans," she said. "Two will be in our system by this evening and I've already sent them a copy of the presentation that you gave to my mother and me."

"Oh?" Raeder said and he felt the hair raise on his scalp. *But I'm not a diplomat!* he screamed mentally. *I shouldn't be the one doing the meet and greet thing!*

This could be a disaster for the Commonwealth, to have someone untrained in diplomacy, of his relatively low rank, making this kind of contact with the most influential people of a whole species.

"They were most pleased by the section on dancing," Sisree went on, oblivious to the panic boiling in Raeder's mind. "My mother and I were wondering if we might impose upon you for a live demonstration."

I'm doomed. Raeder could find his way around a dance floor reasonably well. He liked his social life, and women liked to dance, so he'd learned. But he was no performance artist. *Still, sometimes people can surprise you with their hobbies.*

"I'm not certain that we have anyone aboard who could competently perform for you," he said honestly. "As I said earlier, those people on the recording were professional dancers. But with your permission, I'll check my crew for skills and get back to you as soon as possible. We're most flattered by this request, Lady, and will try to answer it."

Sisree clicked her mandibles daintily. "I will await your call then, Commander. If I am not available, then Has-sre, my first assistant, will be able to discuss it with you. Until then, Commander."

"Until then, Lady."

As the screen went blank Raeder pictured the blundering dance recitals his sister had been in. Glittery costumes on seeming hundreds of lurching little girls. His mind supplied a bevy of female crew members in similar garb, trying to fuddle their way through something jazzy. After a moment he wanted to cry.

Get a grip, Raeder, he told himself. *When in doubt, delegate.*

With a tap of his finger he was in touch with the captain's secretary, an individual he'd hardly used as yet.

"I need you to go through the crew's records," Raeder told him. "Find me those crew members who have some experience in dance."

The secretary blinked. "Yes, Commander."

"This is top priority," Raeder said. "Get back to me on this as soon as you can."

"Yes, Commander."

Raeder cut contact and smiled. It tickled him to imagine the secretary wondering why *dancing* of all things should become such a top priority item. Once again the image of his formidable crew grimly, clumsily tap-dancing their way through his sister's old routine darkened his thoughts.

Work, he told himself sternly, and manfully struggled to make repair reports more interesting than what his mind's eye insisted on seeing.

Forty minutes later, when he'd finally settled down and was accomplishing something, his com chimed.

"Yes," Raeder said distractedly.

"Sir, I'm afraid that we don't have any dancers listed in the crew's records," the secretary said. "The closest thing we have is Technican Hunding, who was captain of her drill team in high school."

"A drill team?" Raeder said thoughtfully. He tried to think of the kind of thing a high school drill team might do. "No dancers at all?" he asked.

"None listed, sir. But then people might not think of it as something important enough to put in their military records. I could put out a call for volunteers."

Raeder's heart shrank at the thought.

"Have Hunding report to my office," he said. "I'll talk to her first."

Peter knew Terry Hunding; she'd been working on Main Deck since he'd been aboard. He knew that she was a hard worker, competent, but shy. *Drill?* he thought. He could picture a Marine Corps drill team going through manuevers involving plasma rifles. Rifles were clearly out of the question in this case. *Rifles would probably lead to a political disaster.* But the crisp, fancy marching had possiblilities. He'd have to see.

"Ooh! Sir! I could train Fibians to do it!" Hunding said with alarming confidence and enthusiasm. "I'll bet they'd really take to it."

It turned out that hers had been a flag team, four-time champion of the blah blah blah flag wave-off, or something. She'd rattled the name off so quickly Peter hadn't caught it. Her blithe assumption that it would be familiar to him was a clue to how completely she'd been immersed in the world of decorative drill.

But she'd managed to paint a word picture brilliant

enough to penetrate the clouds of memory and he recalled once having seen a very impressive demonstration of her specialty. Heck, it might have been her team for all he knew.

"They'd look wonderful!" she continued. Her bright eyes looking inward at some scene of ranks of Fibians waving flags in coordinated formations. "Do you think they'd like that?" she asked, shy once again, but still eager.

You really loved doing this, didn't you? Peter thought, looking at her in some amazement.

"Do you think you could do it?" he asked. A foolish question, he knew that as soon as the words were out of his mouth.

"Oh, yes, sir," Hunding said with an airy wave. "I was captain of my squad and we never lost one meet. I can't believe adult Fibians could be harder to manage than a bunch of teenage girls."

Raeder smiled. *Good point. With credentials like that you ought to be sitting on my side of the desk.*

"Keep your face absolutely blank," he instructed her. He held up one finger to her in admonition, then tapped in a call number. Lady Sisree's face appeared on his screen instantly.

"Ah, Commander. Have you been able to find dancers for us?"

"Not dancers, Lady, but something that I think you will enjoy very much. May I present Technician Hunding, who is a championship drill instructor. She has a proposal to make to you."

Hunding blinked, but managed not to smile or frown or change expression in any way. Her voice, however, managed to convey cartwheels and back flips of joy when she spoke. She talked of Fibians marching in unison, waving flags.

"We could take representatives from each clan,"

she said enthusiastically. "Do the clans have some symbol to identify themselves?" she asked.

"The colors of our clans differentiate us," Sisree answered, somewhat bemused.

"Then the flags can be the colors of the clans! I can have your volunteers managing a simple drill by the end of the week," Hunding finished.

"I have seen no demonstration of this," Sisree said, troubled.

"I once saw one," Raeder told her. "It was very impressive, all those people moving together, tossing their flags and spinning them. Very entertaining."

"By the end of the week," Hunding insisted, "I can have something for you to look at. Then, if you don't think it will do, you've only to tell us and nothing is really lost but a little time." She smiled and then visibly forced the smile right off her mouth.

"A good proposal," the lady answered. "I will call for volunteers."

"I would like to have twenty-four in the team," Hunding said definitely. "But some people just don't have the coordination. So it's usually best to set up an audition so that people can try it out and see if they're made for it. To get twenty-four we should have a pool of no less than fifty."

The lady clicked mandibles, obviously enjoying Hunding's enthusiasm.

"I shall see to it, and I will have my second assistant find a place spacious enough for you to have your . . . audition. Thank you, Commander," she said. "I am most appreciative of your efforts."

"It was no trouble at all," Raeder assured her. *Nor was it,* he thought as the screen went dark. He glanced at the bright-eyed young tech. *And here's hoping that it won't be.*

"You go and work out some routines for this,

Hunding," he said. "I'll clear it with your officers. Um . . ." he said as she rose to depart. "Before you go down I want you to report to Doctor Goldberg. He's found a way to freeze our facial muscles so that we don't gross out the Fibians."

"Oh, thank goodness, sir," Hunding said. "I don't know if I could be expressionless all the time."

I know you couldn't, Peter thought. *Not without rupturing yourself some way.*

"If there's anything you need . . ." he began to say.

"Oh, pictures of Fibians, sir, so that I can make computer representations of my routines."

"See my secretary," Raeder said magnanimously. "Perhaps we could send one of your mock-ups to Lady Sisree so that she could see what you have in mind."

Hunding looked stricken.

What, there's some unwritten rule of fancy drilling that you never give previews? Peter thought.

"That might not be such a good idea, sir," the young tech said. "I don't know if any of them *can* do it and I'd hate to get her expectations roused and then let her down."

"Good point, Hunding," Raeder said, impressed. *You* are *going to end up on this side of the desk one day.* He gave her a salute. "You'd better get started."

"Thank you, sir." She gave a very smart salute and spun on her heel in a perfect military turn.

Showing off? Peter wondered. When she was gone, he grinned and shook his head. It was nice to see that kind of enthusiasm at his disposal. He tapped his com and the secretary's face appeared.

"Clear Technician Hunding's posting to a special project for the next two weeks," he said.

❖   ❖   ❖

Hunding looked out over the multicolored horde of Fibians and clasped her hands nervously. She'd run the volunteers through some simple tests and had rejected out of hand any who failed. There were now thirty volunteers milling about the room. The colors tended to group together, which she supposed was only natural, but she couldn't allow cliquishness. She clapped her hands.

"Attention," she called. The hard, blank faces turned her way and she swallowed. "I'd like you all to line up in rows of ten across."

She waited patiently while the translation device made the same request even more politely. With a professional eye she watched them move. She liked the flowing smoothness of their gait, but she thought she'd like it more when four legs moved forward in unison instead of one after the other. But *could* they do that?

She frowned, or tried to, when she saw them bunching up by color again. Not so much in rows as in batches, with a slight but definite break between the colors. They began to talk again and the noise level soon grew. Hunding waited until she was certain they were as lined up as they were going to be.

"Silence in the ranks!" she bellowed and the Fibians shut up and looked forward. "Those are not *lines*," she shouted. Shouted and sneered simultaneously, a skill she'd learned early and used often.

The Fibians looked around and a few shuffled nervously forward or back until they were more in line with their neighbors.

"Why are you here?" she asked them.

The aliens looked at one another, even crossing color lines in hope of finding someone with the answer.

"You!" Hunding's finger stabbed out and caught an

Orange just as he looked forward again. "Why are you here?"

The Orange froze, thinking it over, pondering the hostile, commanding tone of the human female.

"I was asked to volunteer. For the pleasure of my queen," he said at last.

"You are here to please your queen!" Hunding bellowed.

There was a shifting in the ranks, such as they were, at that.

"Faces forward!" Hunding ordered.

They all looked at her.

"Are you all here to please your queen?" she asked.

They looked at her, their pedipalps almost unconciously held in the second degree of respect and in some cases aiming slightly higher, but none of them spoke.

"You will answer!" Hunding said. "Are you here to please your queen?"

"Yes!" the Fibians shouted, somewhat raggedly, but with a pleasing enthusiasm.

"Then you will follow my orders and you will learn!" Hunding informed them. "Form lines of five."

The Fibians scrambled, trying to stay with their fellows.

"Stop!" Hunding shouted. "Form up behind one another."

They shuffled into position, one behind the other.

"This rank," she pointed to the far left row, "stay where you are. All other ranks move one step to the right."

They did so. Hunding looked at their arms and wondered exactly how far apart that would make them. Far enough, she decided and ordered them to reach out to the right with their right pedipalp.

"With your arm stretched out like that you should

be in line with the shoulder of the person next to you. If you are not, take a step forward or back until you are."

The Fibians moved until they were in neat rows.

Hunding counted out the rows, starting with the right and skipping the ones between.

"This row, this row, this row, take one step forward." The rows moved, raggedly, but that would improve. "This row, blend into this row, this row, get into this row. Form lines of ten across," she ordered them just as they finished, not allowing them time to think, or color coordinate again.

Hunding broke them into lines, moved them forward and back again and again until no one was standing next to a male of the same color. As much as that pleased her, it pleased her more that the lines they ended up in were perfectly straight, every face was looking forward and their backs were straight, their heads lifted and their pedipalps in the exact same degree of respect. She didn't know which degree it was, and didn't greatly care. In fact, it was a nuanced degree below the first and represented a great deal of fear and respect.

"Look at the person next to you," she ordered them.

Hunding watched the Fibians turn their heads left and right, then blinked as they turned them almost all the way around. She thought there was an almost subliminal freezing when they realized that they were isolated from their clan mates.

"The person beside you is very important. The person beside you is your *teammate*! It is your duty and responsibility to make certain that your teammate looks good, does his job, knows the routines and executes them perfectly. Just as it is *your* job to look good, do your job, know the routines and execute them perfectly. Do I make myself clear?"

The rows of Fibians looked back at her, then turned their heads very slightly towards their teammates. Some gave an afirmative gesture with their pedipalps. They settled down and stared blankly ahead, as though hoping she couldn't see them.

Hunding put her hands on her hips and let out an exasperated breath.

"When I *ask* you a question," she bellowed, "you will *answer* that question by shouting *yes*! All of you will shout *yes* in unison. Do you understand me?"

"Yes!" the Fibians shouted. It sounded far softer and less aggressive than a group of shouting humans would have, but then Fibs didn't yell as a rule.

Hunding nodded approval.

"If I ask you if you understand, and you have answered yes, I will then ask if there are any questions. You may then put up your ha—pedipalp and I will acknowledge you and you may ask your question. Do you understand?"

"Yes," the Fibians shouted.

"Are there any questions?" Hunding roared.

Thirty pedipalps hit the air.

Hunding's shoulders dropped and she looked down. Looking up again she said, "I will answer questions from the front row, going from left to right. You—" she pointed at a blue "—what is your question?"

It turned out that most of them had the same questions. Mostly, "Can't I stand beside Sem-sne?" etc. Or, "How can I make sure a male from another clan is doing his job? I'll be at home doing my own job."

"No, you may not stand next to your clan mates unless I tell you to. The only importance of clan color while you are working with this team is in determining how to use that color to make the ranks look interesting while marching. When you are with the team you are responsible to your other teammates and they are responsible to you. When you are not with the team, then obviously that need not necessarily apply—beyond the normal behavior of civilized people." She thought that ought to cover things fairly well.

Hunding reminded herself that these people had never done anything remotely like this before and that she had to be patient. She regretted that she wouldn't be able to scowl and sneer as spectacularly as she would have liked. Her old teammates had told her that half the stuff they broke their necks to do was in fear of one of her ferocious scowls.

"The first thing we are going to learn is the basic marching step," she said. "I will demonstrate. Left, right, left, right, left!" Hunding marched in step, calling out the cadence for a full thirty seconds. "Did you see that?"

"Yes!" the Fibians shouted.

"Any questions?"

Thirty pedipalps shot up.

She waved them down and fought the sinking feeling in her stomach.

"It will take some practice and it will take some balance. Yes, I want all of your left feet to lift, then I want *all* of your right feet to lift *at the same time*! When you lift your left foot," she demonstrated, "throw your weight onto your right foot. Do you understand?"

Their "Yes" was more than a little doubtful.

"Get into rows five across!" she ordered. "Far left rank, take two steps to the left!"

The Fibians in that rank looked confused; heads turned, shoulders twitched, but they soon established that they were in fact the rank she was speaking to and took two steps to the left. Hunding ordered the other rows to spread out until she was certain that if anyone fell over they wouldn't fall on a teammate and start a war.

"All right, let's begin," she said, looking them over. "Left!" Hunding lifted her left leg.

The Fibians tried to imitate her and, as though the whole room had suddenly tilted forty-five degrees, the whole group lurched left, helplessly off-balance and ended up in a pile against the right wall.

Hunding stared at them, blinking. Then as she noticed them getting rather unfriendly while disengaging themselves she began barking orders. When they were once again in neat rows she gave them a significant glare.

"That was no one's fault," she said. "So there's no point in taking it out on another clan, now is there?" Silence greeted her remark. "That was a question!"

"Yes," the Fibians said flatly. It was the first time they'd answered in perfect unison.

Hunding decided it was a start. She had them put their pedipalps on the shoulders of the males next to them as they practiced lifting their feet. That worked out very well and, she told herself, it gave them a basis for trusting and relying on their teammates regardless of clan.

By the end of the afternoon they could march in place. They were still a little wobbly, but they could do it without actually falling over.

"I'm very proud of you," Hunding told them. "I wasn't sure you could even do this. There was a chance that your nervous systems wouldn't allow it. But you've passed a major hurdle." She applauded them, they stared blankly at her. "Please be seated."

Thirty Fibians dropped as if they'd been shot. Hunding looked at them uncertainly. She wondered if she should have them get water or something. Then she decided that she'd better keep going while she had them in hand. She could always ask advice later.

"I wanted to show you this."

She aimed an instrument behind her and clicked it on. A holo-vid of her old team came to life, showing their triumphant victory over their nearest rivals, a Texas team of ferocious competitors. She watched the vid with pride for a few moments, then turned to her students.

The Fibians were riveted; they leaned forward, all of their eyes focused on the presentation before them, bodies frozen in position. She watched them watching until the vid was over.

"That was pretty advanced stuff," she said. "I don't expect anybody to be doing some of that stuff any time soon. But in five days I hope to have you doing this."

Hunding turned and clicked again. A computer simulation of Fibians marching began to play out. It was a simple routine, and very brief, with only one easy flag maneuver repeated several times. She'd been very pleased by the way the Fibians looked when their legs moved in their marching step. Very crisp, very precise.

"Any questions?" she asked when it was over.

"You really think that we can do that?" a Green asked.

"Based on what we accomplished today, yes, certainly," she said confidently. She held her hands in the second degree of respect. "Keep practicing if you have a spare moment, and I'll see you here tomorrow at the same time. We'll practice walking in a march cadence then." She nodded encouragingly at them, though inside she was visualizing a great many pratfalls. "You are dismissed."

Later that evening when she was making her report to the commander she told him that the team had done "Marvelously!"

At his very dubious look she said, "My evaluation is based on experience, sir. I've begun with far less promising material than I had today, believe me."

"Good," Raeder told her. "I'll take you at your word on that. Lady Sisree is looking forward to this."

"I think it's good that she's never seen drill before," Hunding said naively. "I think she'll be delighted."

Peter raised an eyebrow at that and humphed.

Maybe she's right. Maybe if we'd only shown them amateurs dancing we'd have been able to pull off a dance recital. He considered the notion. *Nah!*

CHAPTER SIXTEEN

Lady Sisree was thrilled by the preview performance Hunding's drill team put on for her. She expressed amazement and wonder at the way the team moved their feet, especially when they waved their flags while doing it.

"It's wonderful!" Sisree said. "The queens will be so proud of all of you!" she told the team, the position of her pedipalps making her delight obvious.

Hunding was certain that she could see the males preen. Of course for Fibians seeing a female in the flesh, so to speak, was an event to remember.

"Thank you, on behalf of the team, Lady Sisree," Hunding said with dignity.

The lady tilted her great head and looked at the young human in mild surprise. It was impossible to be absolutely positive without asking, but she was almost certain that Hunding's attitude wished her away.

"I probably should leave you to work," the lady hazarded. Theoretically if it didn't matter one way or the other, then Hunding would invite her to stay.

"Oh, thank you, Lady Sisree," Hunding said with an unflattering enthusiasm. She leaned closer to the Fibian giantess. "I'm afraid the team couldn't help but be distracted by your presence and there's *so* much for them to learn by the welcoming ceremony."

Which was absolutely true, but still. Sisree hesitated.

"I can't begin to tell you how much your interest means to the whole team," Hunding said confidentially as she moved towards the door. "This is such a new thing here, and of course they're *in* it, and they really don't know how it looks. So your obvious enjoyment of their new skills is a tremendous boost." She tapped the control that opened the two massive doors. "I hope you'll be pleased with their complete performance."

Unseen by the human, Sisree's tail tip quivered with amusement at young Hunding's boldness. She was pleased that someone of such single-minded obsessiveness was involved in this project. It made her certain that it would be a notable event.

"Carry on," Sisree said with a gracious gesture. She cast one last, long look at the worshipful would-be drill team and withdrew.

"So," Hunding said, switching off the recording, "as you can all see you've got that routine down cold. Congratulations!" She clapped her hands and aimed her applause to encompass all of them.

There were more than a few tailwhip snaps and the room clattered to the gentle clicking of mandibles. The males weren't even divided up by color anymore; orange sat by green, by blue, by yellow, enjoying one another's company, their chitin clashing terribly.

"Now, there's one last thing you have to learn," Hunding told them. "And that's marching into the hall."

She clicked her handheld control and the lights dimmed, and a holo appeared showing a computer simulation of what Hunding had in mind.

"We'll keep it simple," she said. "You'll march in ranks of five, by color." On the screen yellow led orange, followed by green, blue and purple. "I've organized you to resemble a rainbow," Hunding explained.

She turned to her team with what now had to pass for a big grin since her surgery. Her face actually held a mildly pleasant expression. It faded as she saw that every Fibian had raised a pedipalp; some of them held both up.

"It's about the way the colors are organized, isn't it?" she said. Hunding felt a little discouraged, but she'd half expected it. "All right, what should we do?"

They told her, and they told her why. Blue had to be first because blue was the first clan. Green was the second clan, orange the third and so on.

"Okay," Hunding said reluctantly. "We'll do it your way."

Inside she was rather annoyed. Once she'd conceived a routine she rarely had to change it and she felt the ire of a thwarted artist. She froze the recording and reorganized the colors as they'd requested.

"But let's not have any more changes, okay?"

"Yes!" the Fibians shouted, as ordered.

"O-kay," Hunding said, "I've got a question. Can Fibians whistle?"

"Yes," the team said. There was a certain reserve in their answer, but Hunding didn't notice.

"Great!" she said. "I've got a piece of music I'd like you to hear."

She hit her control and the images on the screen were now moving to the "Colonel Bogey" march. She beat the time with her hand, enjoying the memory of marching and whistling herself in those golden high school days in Kansas. Hunding looked out over her new team as they stared intently at the hologram.

Boy, I am so not *in Kansas anymore.*

"Commander, Lieutenant Commander James is here to see you."

"Thank you, Semple. Would you ask her to wait a moment please."

Peter imagined Sarah's eyebrows going up at that. But he felt a need to at least *pretend* to some distance between them. It helped to keep him sane. Whenever he was in the same room with Lieutenant Commander James his instincts told him to sweep her into his arms and kiss her with mad, passionate abandon. His preference heartily agreed with his instincts. Unfortunately Space Command took a dim view of such goings-on while on duty. They hadn't been alone together for weeks.

He felt like he'd been on duty for years—long, lonely, desperately uncomfortable years. He thought of that last night at Camp Stick 'Em Together Again; the color of her hair in the moonlight, the sparkle of her eyes . . .

"You can send the lieutenant commander in now, Semple."

Peter leaned back in the Old Man's chair and smiled at the empty space that Sarah soon would fill.

"Did I come at a bad time, sir?" she asked as she bustled in and saluted.

"Not at all," he said, returning her salute. "That will be all, Semple," he said to the secretary, who hovered in the doorway. "Please be seated, Lieutenant Commander."

When the door had closed behind Knott's secretary they just sat and grinned at one another for a long, pleasant minute.

"Why do you keep calling Semple by name?" Sarah asked. "It's noticeably repetitious."

"Because I keep forgetting it. I forgot he was even out there for about three weeks; now I'm enjoying the experience of having a flunky." Raeder waggled his brows at her.

Sarah laughed.

"That *flunky* is the captain's secretary! You just keep reminding yourself of that or one day when the Old Man is back and you need to see him in a hurry you may find yourself cooling your heels in the outer office instead."

Peter flattened his hand against his heart and gazed at her wide-eyed.

"You have put the fear into me, my love. I shall remember to bring him roses on Secretary's Day, I swear I will."

She raised a brow, then grinned. He grinned back at her.

"So, why did you want to see me?" he asked.

"A leading question if ever I heard one," she snapped back. "Well, aside from the suspected reason, I've been thinking about the Fibians."

"And?" Raeder encouraged.

"And, it seems that Snargx is guilty of some very deviant behavior. I understand it's the newest of the clans and that they've only been in that quadrant of space for about fifty years. Is it possible that this behavior came about because of some brain-disturbing virus? Could Sna-Fe be a danger to Clan Nrgun?"

"It's a good enough possibility that I'll bring it up to the queen when next we speak," Peter said. "But I honestly doubt it. They're pretty astute scientifically, meaning I'm sure they gave our erstwhile passenger a good thorough going-over before they let him anywhere near their queen."

"Mmm. I'm just going from their reactions," Sarah explained, looking thoughtful. "A negative response that strong would seem to argue that this is unheard-of behavior."

Peter put his hand up and waggled it back and forth.

"It argues that they're very nice people," he said. "But we don't know anything about their history. They might react that badly at hearing this news because they thought they'd gotten away from behavior like that. I believe that some humans were just as repulsed when they heard the news. The fact is that most humans don't behave like the Mollies—and *they* most definitely don't behave the way they do because they've got a bug."

Sarah wrinkled her nose.

"No, they're sick, but they're deliberately, stubbornly, willfully sick. And there's no excuse for that." She sighed. "Do you ever worry that they won't like us once they know something about our history?"

"Yes," he said with a judicious nod. "But then, there's always Clan Snargx."

Sarah barked a laugh, then shook her head.

"I wonder if Lady Sisree and Queen Tewsee have had a conversation like this," she said.

"I wouldn't be at all surprised," Raeder agreed. "It's one of the things that makes me think human-Fibian relations have a chance. We've both got appallingly similar skeletons in the closet."

❖   ❖   ❖

The evening of the gala welcoming ceremony was glorious, at least by Fibian standards. To the humans it was pleasantly cool, but unpleasantly humid.

The entire front of the palace was decorated with floral wreaths and lanterns that emitted pleasing scents. Pleasing to the Fibians, that is. The human guests could barely make out a scent at all.

Raeder, Sarah, Truon, Hunding, Sun-hes and the doctor disembarked from their transport right on the palace's front terrace.

Sarah took a long, deep sniff. "Just the barest hint of citronella," she pronounced, sounding a bit surprised.

"Pretty name," Peter said.

"On Earth it's used as a bug repellant," Goldberg informed him.

Raeder looked back at the doctor, his medicated face very bland.

"These *people* might have bug problems, too."

Sarah couldn't help but smile at that, which meant that the corners of her mouth lifted very slightly.

"Commander," Hunding said shyly. "I'm going to go gather up my drill team now, if you'll excuse me."

"Certainly, Hunding, you go ahead." Raeder watched the shining-faced young tech hurry off. "She looks happy," he said.

"Even with most of her face frozen," Truon agreed. "Maybe it's because she's young."

"Nah," Peter said with a dismissive wave of his hand. "It's because for a change she's in complete charge. Remember what that was like?"

Sarah's hazel eyes brightened a little with humor.

"Oh, yes," she agreed. "Heady stuff, indeed."

"There's Fuj-if," Sun-hes said, and gestured towards the second assistant where he stood on the terrace before the grand front entrance.

Fuj-if spotted them at almost the same moment and bustled up to them.

You ain't seen nothing till you've seen a Fibian bustle, Raeder thought. He wondered if he'd ever get used to the flowing gait of those multiple legs of theirs.

"Welcome, welcome humans!" the second assistant said effusively. His pedipalps were held in the second degree of respect, but with a sort of energy to the position that might have been interpreted as gladness to see them. "Her majesty is so looking forward to seeing this presentation that your subordinate has been preparing for us. Lady Sisree has been telling the other queens about you humans, and has, of course, distributed copies of the presentation you made for our own queen. So they also are looking forward to this evening's . . . drill, with enthusiasm."

Wow. No pressure or anything. Thank the powers that be that Hunding has already gone off to gather her team. He'd been amazed at the difference in personality that the shy little tech had shown when commanding her Fibian squad around the practice room. *But this would be a really bad time to get hit by stage fright.*

"Thank you, Second Assistant," Raeder said, also with his hands in the second position.

Fuj-if clicked his mandibles at the sight and gestured towards the building behind him. "Allow me to lead you to your place within the gathering hall."

The second assistant turned and paced grandly away. Raeder and his crew looked at one another and, squaring their shoulders, paced grandly behind him.

The hall that Fuj-if led them to was an enormous web-wrapped cavern rapidly filling with a multicolored horde of Fibian soldiers and politicos. The conversational volume dipped for a moment when the small group of humans entered. Then it rose again to an even greater height.

Both Queen Tewsee and Lady Sisree would be here tonight, though they would stay at opposite ends of this mighty hall. Raeder figured you could stuff a corvette-sized craft in here. It would be tight, but not impossible.

The other queens would attend virtually from their spacecraft and enormous screens lined the walls so that they would be visible to their representatives and fellow queens. The webbing around the screens had been faintly tinted with their clan colors, as was the area around Tewsee and Sisree's couches.

Fuj-if led them to a place near the queen's couch.

"Her majesty has invited you to stay by her side," the second assistant said. His manner and his posture told them that this was a signal honor. "If you will excuse me, I have other guests to attend to."

Raeder and Sarah both graciously allowed that they would be able to entertain themselves in that spot as well as any other.

"Sim-ne, we must tell her!" Fan-le insisted. His distress was obvious and it was mirrored by the postures and pedipalp positions of the soldiers around him. "I really think that she suspects something is wrong, but she doesn't know what. We have to tell her."

Sim-ne looked at his second and indicated agreement with a flick of his gloved fingers.

"Very well," he said. "I will go out to the front gates and wait for her."

He wasn't terribly worried about the presentation; Hunding had run them through several pieces of alternate music choices in case they hadn't been able to master the whistling. Once she'd been satisfied that they were getting the "Colonel Bogey" march, however, she'd concentrated their energies there. What worried him was how he was going to tell her.

He'd kept expecting her to pick up on their dissatisfaction and humiliation as they tromped through the music. They all had. When they'd all stopped dead in shock as she'd whistled with them the first time he'd been certain she'd understand that one just didn't *do* that. But Fan-le was right, she couldn't see it. It must be a human failing.

He walked out the nearest door to avoid the crowded hallway and marched along the nearly deserted terrace towards the front of the palace. He turned the corner just as Hunding entered the grand portal.

He saw the other humans arriving, but didn't see Hunding with them. They were of higher rank than she was, though, so he assumed that she would be coming later. He set himself to wait.

Hunding stunned them all to immobility when she walked in without Sim-ne. They looked at one another. Where was Sim-ne, they silently asked. Had he told her the awful truth? More important, should someone else tell her? The answer to that was yes, of course. But no one wanted to be the one to do it. The task had been delegated, let the delegate come forth.

They shuffled into their places at Hunding's direction, casting furtive, desperate glances at each other.

"Where's Sim-ne?" Hunding asked.

"He went looking for you," said Fan-le.

"Oh?" She was surprised, and not pleased, but she couldn't allow herself to be distracted at this point. "Well, we'll just hope he gets here before we have to start," she said.

Abdomens curled under in nervous reaction to that. They'd all so hoped that she would ask *why* he'd gone looking for her. That would have given them an opening to tell her. As it was, they now felt compelled to keep silent, as they always did when faced with Hunding's forceful personality.

Lady Sisree came into the hall and took her place on her couch, a padded apparatus like the ones on the transport that had brought the humans from the spaceport. One by one the screens around the room brightened and showed the faces of the visiting queens. Those in the hall responded by performing a Fibian bow to each new appearance, pedipalps held in that one exquisite degree below the full first degree of respect. That honor was reserved for their hostess, Queen Tewsee.

Tewsee appeared from behind Raeder and his group of officers, taking her couch so quietly that if the Fibians in the hall had not begun to bow they'd never have known she was there.

"Welcome," the queen said. "Welcome my sister queens and all of your followers. Welcome to my daughter, Lady Sisree, and a special welcome for our human friends." She gestured towards Raeder and his people and they bowed.

At this point all eyes were upon the Welters. Until the queen had pointed them out, Sun-hes quickly informed them, it was impolite to actually stare at the humans.

The humans returned the stares, stone-faced.

Interesting, Raeder thought. *Being stared at by people with eight eyes is much worse than being stared at by people with two.* About eight times worse, in fact. He also noticed that they seemed disinclined to *stop* staring.

At last Tewsee began her welcoming speech again and let the humans off the hook. For it would be rude to look elsewhere while a queen was speaking.

"That was intense," Sarah said out of the corner of her mouth.

"Yeah," Peter agreed.

"When do we get to see Hunding's little performance?" Goldberg asked.

The doctor was clearly enjoying himself. He'd spent years involved in discussion groups about theoretical aliens and he couldn't get enough of looking at them. Raeder was afraid that he was going to start asking them embarrassing questions at the first opportunity.

Truon whispered, "As soon as the queen has finished speaking."

Which we should not be doing right now. Raeder turned and gave the doctor a significant look. *Boy, I'm so nervous you'd think I was going to be tossing a flag around.*

Hunding ran around, arranging her little squadron of Fibians to suit her aesthetic sense. Adjusting lines, reminding them to straighten up. She could *feel* nervous tension coming off of them in waves.

"Just relax," she said to them. "You have no reason to be nervous, you're going to be fantastic! Head up, Ame-ce!"

"We've got to tell her!" Ses-teh muttered.

"All right," Fan-le said, "I'll do it."

"No talking in the ranks," Hunding snapped. "Now remember, you don't start whistling until the doors begin to open, then you continue whistling until you've all marched into the hall and have taken five marching steps in place. Got it?"

"Yes!" they shouted.

"Lady Hunding!" Sim-ne hustled up to her. "I was waiting for you outside."

"Never mind that," Hunding said, "just get in line. And it's just Hunding. Not lady anything."

"I have something I must tell you," Sim-ne said, following her instead of seeking his place as ordered.

Hunding turned and frowned at him. Nothing happened to her face, of course, but she projected frown at him and his pedipalps automatically found what the team had come to feel was the proper degree of respect for this human powerhouse.

"There'll be time for that later, Sim-ne," she said. Hunding pointed ruthlessly to his place with the blues. "Get in line, now!"

Her strange eyes glittered at him in a threatening way and the Fibian soldier was very much inclined to obey. But from behind him came a wave of desperate encouragement from his teammates.

"It's about the whi . . ."

The great doors began to swing open and Hunding pushed Sim-ne into his place.

"Later," she said. Then she hurried to stand in her place by the doors. She put her silver whistle to her lips and when the doors were fully opened she blew on it.

Immediately the ranks began to march in, whistling the jaunty tune for all they were worth.

An audible gasp went up around the room as the whistling marchers filed in. Raeder smiled, sort of, because he'd always enjoyed this tune. He assumed that the collective intake of breath was in awe of the drill team's achievement. They way they were moving was incredible, and the rhythmic sound of their feet was most impressive.

Beside him the queen began to rise from her

couch. Slowly, grandly, like some strange hot-air balloon she came to her feet. Across the hall, the Lady Sisree began to rise also.

Wow! Just like the king during Handel's "Hallelujah Chorus," Raeder thought. Raeder turned to Sun-hes and thought he looked rather gray.

"Are you all right?" he asked.

"They're whistling!" Sun-hes said. The coarse hairs sprinkled over his chitin were standing out in horror.

"So?" Peter said.

"Whistling is . . . is . . . it's a vigorous invitation to sex!" the Fibian said.

"Oh God!" Raeder raced across the floor trying to attract Hunding's attention. "Hunding!" he half shouted.

Hunding looked up at the sound of her name and saw the commander heading towards her. His face was calm, but his lips were pursed as though to whistle and his index finger sawed frantically across his throat. Instantly she put her whistle to her lips and blew the changes. A tap on the control mechanism she held brought forth a rousing John Philip Sousa march.

A glance over his shoulder showed Raeder that the queen and Lady Sisree were sinking back onto their couches, looking strangely transfixed. The Fibians around the hall, including the other clan's queens on their screens, wore a similar look.

Oh, God, he thought. He moved up to Hunding. "No more whistling," he said. "That's an order."

"No, sir," she whispered.

He gave her a doubtful look.

"There's no more whistling."

With a curt nod Raeder made his way back to his place by Queen Tewsee. After an embarrassed moment he looked up at her without moving his head. She was looking down at him. He sidled a little closer to her.

"We had no idea, your majesty," he said quietly. "Whistling carries no such connotation among humans." *Well, wolf whistling, but that's another story.* "We're terribly embarrassed and deeply sorry to have caused you or the other queens any distress whatsoever."

He instinctively cast her his most appealing look, knowing that it would mean nothing to a Fibian.

After a moment Tewsee's mandibles began to click, very softly, but very rapidly. She put her pedipalps up to hold them still and her tailwhip began to vibrate. The queen forced her eyes away from the little human and she concentrated on the drill being performed for her benefit. For the most part she was successful, but every now and again she would be overcome by an almost irresistible trembling.

Raeder watched her for a moment with some apprehension. Then he turned to Sarah.

"Please go down and tell Lady Sisree what happened," he whispered. "She's looking a little shell-shocked." *And well she might. Our hostess arranges for and looks forward to this event only to have the performers strut in making lewd suggestions. What must she think of us?* He started to snicker and had to cover his mouth before he lost control. *Oh, God. This has to be one for the books.*

He glanced up at the queen. She glanced down at the same moment and they both had to look away, both trembling with barely controlled mirth. Both solved their dilemma by staring fiercely forward, watching the drill team as though maintaining a heartbeat depended upon it.

Throughout the evening all of the principals avoided looking at one another as it tended to bring on an almost painful bout of the giggles. Most inappropriate for a serious diplomatic reception.

CHAPTER SEVENTEEN

Raeder entered the darkened room and the holograms of the various queens turned to look at him. Their mandibles began clicking almost immediately. He blushed and the clicking became louder as they noted this sign of embarrassment.

"Welcome, Commander Raeder," Queen Tewsee said. "Come and be seated by me."

They were actually alone in the room except for her first and second assistants, but Raeder felt the presence of the other queens, though they were in attendance only as color and light.

"Please forgive us our amusement, Commander," the orange queen said. "But it really was funny."

"Thank you, highness," Raeder said with a slight bow, "for being so understanding of our ignorance. I assure you I was as surprised as you were."

"Oh, I doubt that," the green queen said mildly.

There was a round of mandible clicking at that. This was an informal meeting and the tone was very light. With the exception of Tewsee who, to Raeder, seemed to radiate tension.

"Tell us about your people, Commander," Tewsee invited.

"For the most part," Raeder said, "we're a peaceful people. Our military was designed primarily to ward off and deal with raiders, something I gather the clans are familiar with." He seemed to detect a slight stiffness at that. *All right, no references to bad things happening between Fibians,* he thought. "We call ourselves the Commonwealth," he went on.

Raeder described the government as best as he could, wishing he'd paid more attention in civics class. As he'd been warned he would. *But even Ms. Prinny couldn't have imagined I'd be trying to explain this stuff to giant, sentient insects.* He told them that the Commonwealth extended to over three hundred planets scattered throughout the galaxy.

"You mean that you don't settle an entire section before moving on to the next?" the orange queen asked. "How very haphazard."

"Well," Raeder said, "it seems to work for us. For the most part." He would have been grinning sheepishly if his face hadn't been frozen. "We can and often are methodical in our methods," he explained. "But the urge to explore," *and exploit,* "and to be first is very strong in us."

"Are you saying, Commander," Tewsee asked, her head cocked at an angle that expressed astonishment, "that if a human settlement exists in a sector then . . . in some way that sector is spoiled?"

Raeder went blank for a moment. It was a good question. Now how did he answer it without making the whole human race sound completely nuts?

"Actually, for some of our people, the answer to that question would be yes. But these would be the exception, the explorers—true pioneers, and not the general run of people. Most people, when they leave their home planets, want to be going somewhere that has already been explored and settled to a certain extent."

"So there is more than one kind of human, beyond what you call racial differences?" Cembe, the orange queen, asked. Her pedipalps indicated confusion, one held palm up, one down.

"More like individuals who have preferences which they pursue. Enough people have similarities in their choices that they become a type of person, regardless of racial characteristics." *Did that make any sense at all?* Raeder wondered.

"It's so very mammalian," Lesni said with a quirk of her purple head.

"Well it would be, wouldn't it?" the green queen responded acidly.

There were mandible clicks at that and Raeder applauded politely, his hands producing a sound very like their clicks.

"Do go on, Commander," Tewsee invited.

Ah, where was I?

"Naturally, exploring one's sector is something of a luxury in a settlement's early days." *Settlement is such a wonderful word,* Raeder thought, grateful to the queen for mentioning it. *It has such a homey, nonaggressive sound. Settlement's a much better word than colony.* "Once a planet is rich enough to mount an expedition to methodically map its surroundings though, it's also populous enough to have people who want to be somewhere different, perhaps develop a new settlement. So when the explorers discover a planet that will welcome human habitation there are always people ready to follow them there, rather than waiting for a new planet to be discovered in their own sector."

The queens were silent as they contemplated this.

"Essentially," Cesat, the yellow queen, said with careful precision, "your people have claimed three hundred systems without fully settling or exploring any of them."

"Well, three hundred *planets* anyway," Raeder said. "I really don't know if the Commonwealth has a policy about this sort of thing." He shrugged and spread his hands. "In all the time we've been in space we've never encountered another sentient species before the Fibians. So there may not even be one, because it never mattered before."

Quiet astonishment met this remark.

"Well," Saras, the green queen suggested, "you should come up with something because this pell-mell race through the stars is unacceptable."

"But there are infinite systems, your majesties," Raeder said soothingly.

"No resource is inexhaustible," Tewsee said gently. "And thinking that one is can be a sure source of disappointment at least and disaster at worst. If your people have settled any planets in Fibian-claimed systems they will have to vacate them!" The green queen's body language became unmistakably aggressive with this pronouncement.

"Your majesties," Raeder said, "I'm only a humble commander in our military. I'm not a diplomat and I have no business trying to conduct discussions with you as though I were. I have no authority over such matters, none whatsoever."

"It is certainly a matter to consider when those with more authority do come to us," Tewsee said. "For now, perhaps, let us turn the discussion to lighter matters."

For the next hour they discussed such minor matters as travel and trade and the drill team. Which, despite its disgraceful entrance, had completely enthralled the queens, one and all.

"It was a disaster," a worried Raeder confided to Sarah later that day. "They learned a lot that they didn't like and I didn't learn anything but that."

"What didn't they like?" Sarah asked, taking another bite of sandwich.

"They don't like the way we colonize. What they do is inhabit the first hospitable planet they come to, then they explore and exploit the entire system before they even attempt to find another."

Sarah nodded thoughtfully.

"Yeah, that sounds like them. They're pretty methodical," she said. "They fight that way, too. Methodically. It's probably why they haven't beaten us completely. We keep pulling the rug out from under them." She smiled. "Good thing for us we're unpredictable."

"But they're learning." Peter threw down his sandwich after only one bite. "Those hit-and-run missions were something they picked up directly from us, and when I say us I mean *us!*" He rubbed his forehead and groaned.

"That was inevitable," Sarah said with a sigh. "They're an intelligent species and any successful species is adaptable." She threw up her hands and shrugged elaborately. "Not our fault."

"Have you noticed we're all using body language more?" he asked.

She grinned.

"Sure—we're adapting." She rose and tossed her lunch debris in the disposal. "Listen, you haven't blown it. You told them you couldn't answer certain questions, you told them you weren't authorized to do things. I can't see how you could alienate them by being honest." She moved to the door and turned to smile at him. "And never forget Clan Snargx. Their behavior has put all of the clans in a very poor light. One they'll want to get out of as soon as they can, you mark my words."

"Nrgun calls forth the splendor of Lince!" Hoo-seh called out. Queen Tewsee's first assistant pounded a staff on a hollowed wooden box, the sound echoing from the unshrouded chamber walls.

This great room was a sacred place to all Fibians, the ancient meeting place of their kind from the days when tools were made of bronze, at once arena and court. It had no amenities; the floor was dirt, the walls stone, the ceiling branches with mud plastered into the gaps. The only ornaments were suitably barbaric: catching-nets and spiked metal clubs, like squares of barbed bronze net on the end of long poles, weapons from the savage childhood of the race.

No changes beyond necessary repairs had been allowed for millennia. The great palace had been built around it, holding the chamber in its center like a secret. It was the very center of Fibian civilization.

As soon as the echoes died away, in the space nearest Clan Nrgun's queen, bloomed the green holo-image of Queen Saras, of Clan Lince, the second oldest of the clans.

"Nrgun calls forth the splendor of Bletnik!"

Across from Saras and to Tewsee's left appeared a holo of Queen Cembe of the orange clan, third oldest. Hoo-seh called on Clan Streth and the yellow queen, Cesat, appeared. Finally he called on Clan Vened and Lesni, the purple queen, manifested.

Each queen held a lump of fat in her pedipalps—

poverty food and quite disgusting to their refined palates. In order to speak, to question, they must take a bite of fat and chew it while they spoke. It cut down on unnecessary questions and long-winded speeches. Each queen took a tiny nibble of fat now.

"Who calls us here, and why are we called?" the queens chanted in unison.

"I call you," Tewsee said, and she moved forward to stand in a circle of light that matched their own images. She bit into the cube of fat in her pedipalp. "I call you not merely to witness the first meeting with a new species," she said, "but to tell you of an evil that works to destroy one of our clans and perhaps ultimately the peace of all our clans."

The formal beginning thus completed Tewsee draped herself over the couch her first assistant brought forward. She bit into the fat again, claiming the right to speak.

"With them the humans brought a child of Clan Snargx," Tewsee said. "He came to be on their ship through a most remarkable accident. But that is a story for another day. Naturally, when I became aware that the humans had a Fibian child on their ship I demanded that he be brought to me."

Around her the queens clicked mandibles in quiet agreement.

"Satisfied that the humans had done him no harm, I questioned him as to how one as young as he came to be in space at all." She paused, her head slightly bowed, and with a delicate swipe of her pedipalp she wiped away a crumb of fat from her chelicerae.

"Snargx makes war upon these Commonwealth humans, ostensibly in aid of their human allies, called Mollies," she said at last. "There is more to it, of course, though our human visitors are reticent. Theirs is a military ship, and thus not crewed by diplomats.

I suspect their leader is afraid of telling us too much. Fortunately my young source does know the reason for this war, or thinks he does. It seems the humans have encountered a huge field of naturally occurring antihydrogen. Sna-Fe doesn't know why the humans his clan is aiding don't want the other humans to have it, but they are willing to fight to keep it for themselves."

Saras of Lince, the green queen, took a bite from the lump of fat she carried, thus gaining herself the right to speak.

"Snargx must have known of these humans for a long time to become embroiled in a war on behalf of one human clan against another. Why have they kept them secret from the rest of us?" she asked. "Has anyone heard a word about humans before now?"

All of the queens indicated no.

"So . . . why was the child of Snargx in space?" Lesni, the purple queen, asked. She scraped the fat from her tongue with her chelicerae and pulled it off with her pedipalps, patting it back onto her lump.

Tewsee took a sizable bite, to the silent respect and wonder of her fellow queens.

"The silence of our sister clan in regard to humans might seem strange if it didn't occur simutaneously with their discovery of this unique natural resource. Then Syaris' silence becomes ominous."

The queens shifted uneasily. Several signaled disagreement.

"According to Sna-Fe," Queen Tewsee continued, "Syaris and her ladies and their daughters are having offspring at an incredible rate. They've been doing so for the last fifteen years. Children such as he are brutally trained and ruthlessly shipped off to war as soon as they are coordinated and strong enough to manage weapons. Thousands of them have been killed in battle already."

There were gasps and gestures of negation from all around the small circle of queens. The yellow queen, Cesat, took a bite.

"But we have only this child's word on this," she pointed out. "The humans might have done something to him, tortured him perhaps, into making these wild accusations."

Tewsee was still chewing and so could answer instantly.

"Nothing that my finest physicians could find in a number of examinations indicates that Sna-Fe was mistreated in any way by the humans. If anything, even according to the child himself, they went out of their way to be kind and helpful to him. Nor have I told you the worst of what Snargx has done. They have not only eaten humans . . ."

There was another collective gasp at that and Saras of the green clan chewed and spoke.

"That is an outrageous charge!" Saras made a gesture of repulsed disbelief. "To think that a civilized people such as we would eat an intelligent being is incredible! Besides, they are allied with humans. Surely such a barbaric act would destroy their relations."

"To be fair, Sna-Fe has never actually seen this with his own eyes, but only heard rumors of such," Tewsee admitted.

Around her the queens made satisfied gestures that said, *I knew it!*

"It is mere slander then," Cesat said. She turned her yellow head aside in a gesture that expressed embarrassment at Tewsee's naivete.

"However," Tewsee continued, chewing doggedly, "Sna-Fe has witnessed with his own eyes . . ." The blue queen began to pant with stress. "Punishment drills . . ."

Overcome, Tewsee turned her back to her fellow queens as she struggled to regain her composure. Behind her the others exchanged troubled glances.

"Tell us," Lesni encouraged around a tiny nibble of fat.

"He has seen officers and once a lady . . . eating Fibians."

"*No!*" Cesat sprang from her couch. As an afterthought she bit a piece of fat and spoke again. "I cannot believe that! Cannibalism?" Her whole body rejected the idea. "Why? Why would Syaris do such a thing? And why should we believe the humans when they say such things?"

"But the humans haven't said these things," Tewsee said firmly. "It is a Fibian that makes these claims. With your permission I will have him come in."

Her fellow queens exchanged glances, then one by one nodded their agreement. Hoo-seh quickly moved to the door and with a gesture and a quiet word invited the young Fibian inside.

Sna-Fe had never felt smaller in his short life as he looked around at the circle of queens. Gray with terror he threw himself onto his face before them, and lay shivering.

The queens, taken aback by this display, were silent. Fibian children were usually full of confidence and delighted to make the acquaintance of a female. Even children as old as this one.

Tewsee went to his side and stroked the child's back gently until he could be convinced to stand up and face them.

"Tell my fellow queens who you are, child," Tewsee invited. "Or rather, who you were."

"I am Sna-Fe, a third-degree weapons technician,

late of the second battle cohort of Clan Snargx, under the direct command of Lady Sysek, who is fifth lady to Queen Syaris."

"Fifth lady!" exclaimed Saras. She waved a green arm. "There should be no more than three at this point in Snargx's settlement of their sector."

"There are seven ladies, majesty," Sna-fe told her shyly.

"Seven?" Lesni exclaimed.

"That I know of," Sna-Fe added.

Purple was the youngest clan next to red and it had taken them three hundred years to need seven ladies. "Syaris has been queen for less than seventy years," she said. "She can't possibly need seven!"

"That would depend on what her plans are," Tewsee murmured.

"Are you a good tech?" Cembe asked with an encouraging dip of her orange head.

"Yes, your majesty," Sna-Fe said. "I was at the top of my class."

"What of those who do not make good techs?" the yellow queen inquired. "What happens to them?"

"They are put to work on farms or in factories," Sna-Fe told them.

"And what of those who are lazy or naughty and don't work hard on the farms or in the factories?" Tewsee asked.

Sna-Fe looked down, shifting from foot to foot as his chitin went gray again.

"You may answer, child," Tewsee said. She placed a gently encouraging pedipalp on his head. "No one will blame you for what you must say."

"They are destroyed, your majesty," Sna-Fe said quietly. "Sometimes they are made an example of and are eaten, pieces of their bodies distributed to those whose work has not been satisfactory, as a warning."

"This is a lie!" Saras stated. Her chitin had a sickly green tint to it. "It is not possible, and it makes no sense!"

Tewsee looked at Saras with sympathy. Syaris had been one of her daughters, and Clan Lince had been proud of her rise to queen of a new clan.

"I agree that it makes no sense," she said aloud. "Are there more questions you have for my child?"

There were, and though the answers were painful to hear, the queens kept asking until they were convinced.

"Still," Saras insisted, "we should also question these humans. The child knows nothing of the politics of this situation."

"Agreed," Tewsee said. "But I think we've endured enough this day. Let us retire and give thought to what we've learned and think of what we'll ask the humans."

"Agreed," the exhausted and troubled queens said in unison.

"Tomorrow then," Tewsee said. "At the same hour."

She watched the queens blink out in sequence, turning her head aside at the defeated posture of Saras. Sharing her burden hadn't lightened it, and she was ashamed of being the one who had told them. She wondered, as they all must be wondering, what had happened to the red clan to have made them such monsters.

She stroked Sna-Fe's tense back.

"Come," she said, "have dinner with me. And then we can play a game of nalls. Would you like that?"

The young Fibian nodded. Then he looked up at the queen.

"I did not lie, your majesty. Really I didn't." His pedipalps begged for belief.

"I know you did not, my son. But it is hard to hear

these things and we do not want them to be true."
She lifted his head with one claw-tipped finger. "But
they are true, and now we must think of what to do."

Sun-hes was visibly nervous. Raeder did not find
it reassuring that the protocol expert was fidgety.
The Fibian paced from side to side of the corridor, tugging at the silk on the walls with each of
his clawed feet in succession. *If he's ready to climb
the walls, how should I be feeling?* the commander
wondered.

The protocol expert came up to him, his pedipalps
in the second degree of respect.

"Did I tell you that if they wish you to join the
discussion they'd give you a lump of fat?" he asked.

Raeder nodded.

"If you wish to speak you must chew the fat,"
Sun-hes said.

"You have done a fine job of instruction," Peter
told him, making soothing motions with his hands.
"If anything goes wrong, no one will be able to blame
you. Your work has been flawless."

Sun-hes rotated his pedipalps one around the other
to indicate his distress. "I simply cannot feel that way,"
he said. "Though I thank you for your support," he
added hastily, with a respectful gesture.

Far be it for a protocol expert to cause offense, the
commander thought wryly.

"With your excellent instruction and Ms. Trudeau
to advise us we should do just fine," Sarah reasured
the Fibian.

She and Peter crossed glances. He could imagine what she was thinking. *Who would have thought
that we'd one day be comforting a Fibian.* Less than
a month ago they were an enemy that literally ate
humans alive, and would have caused nightmares

even if they didn't. Now they were people, and damn nice people, too.

"I suppose I am still unnerved from the . . . incident," Sun-hes confided.

"Anyone would be," Sarah soothed.

Especially poor Ticknor, Peter thought.

The protocol expert, convinced that good manners could overcome any obstacle, had arranged an "accidental" meeting between himself and the linguist in the corridor of the science section. Mr. Ticknor was still under sedation.

And poor Sun-hes could probably use a hit of something himself. Raeder studied the nervous alien. There was a definite hint of gray around his . . . mouth, the commander supposed.

The great barrier of wood, definitely not a door, slid aside and Hoo-seh, Queen Tewsee's first assistant, stood before them.

"Clan Nrgun calls forth the representatives of the Commonwealth," he intoned.

"Uh—" Raeder held up a finger and rushed over to him. "We are representatives of our ship, the *Invincible*," he said. "We have not come here as official representatives of the Commonwealth."

There was a pause while the first assistant digested this.

"Good going, sir," Marian Trudeau, the ship's lawyer, whispered.

"Clan Nrgun calls forth the representatives of the Commonwealth ship *Invincible*," Hoo-seh said, rather more loudly, as though to quell any other quibbles the humans might have.

The Welters and Sun-hes filed in behind Hoo-seh.

Peter was surprised by what he saw; it looked a great deal like simulations he'd seen of medieval human great halls. Between the dark soil of the floor and the smoke-blackened walls and ceiling the giant queens were the only touches of color in the place.

Hoo-seh led the humans to a circle of their own; the sixth circle of the great circle of queens, which should have held a representative of Clan Snargx. Hassocks of a sort, with bundles of silk on them to act as cushions, had been provided for their comfort. Raeder and his people held their hands in the first degree of respect and bowed their heads to Queen Tewsee.

"Please be seated," she invited them. When they had done so she said, "In the interest of saving time and energy, we feel it is time for plain speaking. You may dispense with the protocol of chewing the fat."

"As you wish, your majesty," Raeder said. "Though I may be constrained from speaking by the need to . . ."

"We will tell you what we know," Tewsee interrupted. "I think you'll find that we are quite well informed. Well informed enough that there is very little you need to keep from us for security reasons."

Peter swallowed with difficulty.

"Thank you, your majesty," he said.

"We know that you are at war with a set of humans who call themselves Mollies. My new son tells me that everyone in Clan Snargx finds these humans to be absolutely insane. Yet, for some reason Snargx has allied itself with them against the Commonwealth. My son tells me that the Commonwealth Star Command are excellent soldiers, clever and swift to battle. But then we knew that from the way you aided our own people in expelling the Snargx raiders from our territory."

Raeder silently bowed his head in acknowledgement. *Thank you, Sarah.*

"We know that what you are fighting over is a field

of naturally occurring antihydrogen which the Mollies wish to keep from you. Now, tell us more."

Raeder could feel his mouth dropping open.

"That . . . sums up the situation very well, your majesty," he said after a moment. "What sort of information can we add to what you already know that will clarify things further?"

"Why do these Mollies want to keep this resource from you?" Saras asked.

Raeder faced the green queen.

"They want to bring about the fall of our civilization," Peter admitted. He couldn't see how telling them that would hurt the Commonwealth. *Heck, it might even gain us some sympathy.*

"It would seem that insanity is not the exclusive province of Clan Snargx," the purple queen said.

Saras turned her head to glare at Lesni. She was disconcerted enough by the accusations leveled at her daughter without snide remarks being made.

"Why would they do this?" Tewsee asked.

"I don't know if you Fibians have a religion," Raeder began.

"Please explain," Cesat said. Her yellow pedipalps gestured curiosity.

"In the simplest terms possible, it is a philosophy that assumes the existence of an interested supernatural being," the commander said. "Humans have a number of these philosophies and sometimes large numbers of us grow incredibly ardent about our beliefs in those philosophies. To the extent that we will go to war over them, and suffer privation and death to defend them. The Mollies are such an obsessed group of people. They will risk everything to further their beliefs."

"But what exactly do they believe, Commander?" Cembe, the orange queen, regarded him quizzically.

"I'm really not all that well acquainted with their beliefs," Peter said. "They're very secretive about them until you've joined their ranks, and even then reveal little until you've been with them awhile and they're sure of your devotion to their cause. What we of the Commonwealth do know, because the Mollies have told us this, is that they believe we are evil and must be stopped from spreading that evil across the stars."

"I don't know if you're evil," Saras said. "But I do believe you should stop spreading across the stars as carelessly as you have been."

"That will be an issue for another day," Tewsee assured the green queen. "For now let us concentrate on Snargx and their involvements."

Saras conceded the point with a gracious gesture.

"Why do you believe Snargx is helping these strange people?" Lesni asked.

Raeder hesitated and Trudeau looked at him for permission to speak. He gave it with a nod.

"In law," she said to the queens, "it's a good rule of . . . it's a good rule to ask, who profits? If the Commonwealth didn't have the ability to leave its planets for trade then we would cease to exist as a power. The Mollies would welcome this. They've also stated that they have no intention of exploiting the antihydrogen field for themselves. This would seem to leave that resource open to claim by whoever comes along."

The queens went absolutely still at that, and remained so for several minutes.

They must have thought this too, Peter thought. *It's the only logical reason I can think of for their fighting on behalf of the Mollies.* The Mollies hated their own race, surely they must despise the aliens even more. *I'll never believe the Fibians have been converted.*

"I sincerely doubt," he said into the silence, "that they've been converted to the Mollies' beliefs."

"No," Tewsee said. After a moment she spoke again, this time directly to her fellow queens. "With such a resource at their disposal Snargx would be a very formidable force."

She left that thought alone for them to contemplate, and contemplate it they did. The humans, Tewsee noted, grew restless after only a few moments. She ignored them, concentrating her attention on the queens around her, watching their every small movement in hopes of gaining knowledge of their thoughts.

"This cannot be allowed," Saras said at last, her voice grating like the scraping of two stones. "No clan should be so much more powerful than another. It upsets the balance and invites evil."

"It must be stopped," Cembe agreed with a firm jerk of her orange head.

The others signaled their consensus.

"This resource belongs to the human Commonwealth," Tewsee declared.

She watched her sister queens narrowly to catch any sign of disagreement. There was none; each of the queens signaled her consent to this with unmistakable firmness.

"It is not that we do not desire it," Tewsee explained to the humans. "It is that it would disturb our peace, upset the balance of our civilization. Worse, it would seem to endorse the evil for which Clan Snargx has been responsible. We will stop them from aiding your enemies. Now, all that we need to do is decide how."

Hoo-seh appeared at Raeder's side.

"If you will be good enough to accompany me, Commander," he said respectfully.

The commander and his party bowed to the

queens, backed away for ten steps, then followed the first assistant from the room. Peter was almost to the barrier when the soft clicking of mandibles alerted him to the fact that his silk cushion was stuck to his butt.

"You could have told me," he said to Sarah out of the side of his mouth.

"I didn't notice," she whispered. "I was trying to unstick mine from my own tush."

Hoo-seh clicked mandibles at the sight of the humans trying to dislodge a material that only stuck to their hands.

"If you will allow me?" the Fibian asked.

"Allow you?" Raeder said. "I beg you."

In a trice, and with the assistance of Sun-hes, the Fibian had them cleaned up.

"What happens now?" Raeder asked the first assistant.

"You will be informed, Commander," Hoo-seh answered. "For now I advise you to return to your ship. Send home any Fibians who are still visiting with you. When the queens adjourn they will be ready to move and you must go with them."

CHAPTER EIGHTEEN

"When I asked Lady Deshes about the humans that had been driven into Clan Nrgun's sector the lady said, and I quote, 'They are a sick and twisted people who lie and kill without provocation.' "

Huntmaster Sum-sef spoke as calmly as though he reported directly to his queen at the end of every mission, let alone to five of the towering females. They were intimidating, as was the place of their meeting, but for the pride of his clan and his queen the huntmaster made himself behave as though it were a matter of indifference.

"I then asked the lady why Snargx had not called upon the other clans to help them in this fight. The lady replied that Snargx could take care of itself without needing to crawl back to their elder sisters for help."

"Arrogant!" Saras muttered angrily.

"Did the lady say why Snargx had not apologized for pursuing their enemy into Nrgun territory without warning us?" Tewsee asked.

Sum-sef hesitated, then answered, "The lady said that her huntmasters were in pursuit of their lawful duties and that she would not apologize for that."

The queens were stunned to silence.

"This is a very bold attitude for a lady to take," Lesni said at last. Her pedipalps indicated profound disapproval of Lady Deshes' attitude. "It would be too strong coming from Syaris herself. But from a lady . . ."

"Go on," Tewsee said to her huntmaster, wearily certain of what she would hear.

"I then asked the lady's permission to continue my journey to bring my queen's greetings to her queen. Lady Deshes told me that it would not be necessary, that she would convey my queen's message. I then asked if she was forbidding me to continue my journey and she replied that she was."

"Did she explain?" Saras demanded.

The huntmaster shifted his stance, an irrepressible indication of his nervousness.

"The lady said that as a sub-queen it was her choice and that she chose not to accommodate me. She told me that she knew her queen would stand behind her decision because Queen Syaris had no time for every little huntmaster who claimed to bear the greetings of his queen when all he really had to offer was impertinent questions."

"Sub-queen?" Saras of the green clan said, her voice low, her stance vaguely threatening. "Oh, I don't think I like the sound of that at all."

Tewsee rose from her couch and looked around at her fellow queens.

"Then I shall bring her my greetings in person," she announced.

"And so shall I," Saras instantly agreed.

Cembe, the orange queen, rose. "Bletnik will join you," she said.

"And Streth," Cesat added.

"And Vened." Lesni tilted her purple head. "Five queens come to call. That should get our young queen's notice."

"Sir!" Truon Le's voice woke Raeder from a sound sleep.

"Yes?" he answered hoarsely.

He rose and groped his way to his desk. Even half awake he'd recognized the worry in the XO's voice. The light in his quarters rose slowly, something he'd programmed, so that his eyes wouldn't be stabbed by a sudden increase in illumination. Flopping down in his desk chair Raeder hit the com button and his wall screen filled with the anxious face of his XO.

"What's happening, Mr. Truon?" the commander asked, sleep falling away rapidly.

"Fibian ground control has told us to make ready to depart the system. We've been asked to escort the queens to Clan Snargx territory."

Peter's mind froze for a beat. *As prisoners, observers or active participants?* he wondered.

"Patch me through to Lady Sisree immediately," Raeder said. He ran his fingers through his hair and regretted his ungroomed appearance. *Of course she might not even notice,* he comforted himself.

"It is Has-sre you see, Commander Raeder," the sleek-looking Fibian said when the screen cleared. "My lady is unable to attend you. However, in anticipation of your call she has left this message."

Without waiting for permission or comment Sisree's first assistant transmitted the recording.

"Commander," Lady Sisree said from the screen,

"on behalf of my mother and all of the queens we request that you not be alarmed by this turn of events. Please accompany them on their journey to confront Queen Syaris directly. It is the hope and the wish of Nrgun and her sister clans that we can make things right between your people and ours. We wish you to know that the *Invincible* and all of her people are under Nrgun's direct protection."

The recording ended and Has-sre appeared in its place.

"If there is anything which your ship requires to make its departure certain, Commander, please let me know and I will expedite matters."

"Thank you, First Assistant," Raeder said, his hands in the position of the second degree of respect. "I will confer with my officers immediately and call you if we have any such needs."

As soon as they disconnected Raeder called a teleconference, waking some of his officers from sleep.

"Ladies and gentlemen," he told them, "our Fibian friends have decided to go see Clan Snargx at close range and they have requested us to accompany them under the express protection of Clan Nrgun."

"It's a trap!"

Oh, for crying out loud! Raeder had forgotten to cut Booth out of the loop.

"Trap or not, Mr. Booth, we're going. What I need to know is if there's anything missing that we need to make us mobile. Skinner?" Raeder asked the engineering officer.

"We completed the engine tests today, more than satisfactory. We're stocked up on antihydrogen, bulkheads in engineering are shipshape. We're ready."

A virtual Shakespearean monologue coming from Augie, Raeder thought.

"Water? Food?" Peter said, turning to the quarter-master. *Toilet paper?*

"We're set, sir!" The young temporary quartermaster grinned like a demented chipmunk.

"We could probably use a good set of coordinates," Ashly Lurhman said through a yawn.

"They've sent them up," Truon Le advised her. "I can download them to you there."

"Please," she said. "The sooner I look at them the sooner I'll know if I need anything else."

"This is a mistake!" Booth said.

"Thank you for your input, Mr. Booth," Peter said. *I could buy a better closed-loop audio recording for a decicredit.* "And thank you all. I'll be on the bridge if you need me. Raeder out."

The commander tapped a few keys and found himself confronting Has-sre again.

"We seem well supplied, First Assistant," Peter said. "For which we offer our thanks to your people. But we would like to have a Fibian officer accompany us and brief us on things as we go along. We wish to make no mistakes on this mission."

"Of course, Commander," Has-sre said smoothly. "We would also like to offer you the services of Sun-hes, your instructor in protocol."

"We would be delighted to have him accompany us," Raeder assured him. "In which case we will need supplies suitable to the sustenance of two of Clan Nrgun's citizens."

"It shall be done, Commander," Has-sre assured him. "Good journey to you."

"Thank you, First Assistant."

Raeder stared at the blank screen for a moment. He couldn't help but feel uneasy at the suddenness of this departure. But he was willing to trust Queen Tewsee. For now.

❖ ❖ ❖

Two days later Queen Tewsee looked at the face of a very young lady, who claimed to be second to Lady Deshes.

"You?" the queen asked. She permitted her pedipalps to indicate her astonishment, but hinted at admiration in the tilt of her head.

Sheek bowed her head profoundly low, her pedipalps unquestionably demonstrating the first degree of respect.

"My mother wishes me to have as much experience as I can gather. She says that one can never know too much."

"Your mother is correct," Queen Tewsee said graciously. "Knowledge and experience are very valuable. But it is to your mother that I must speak. Though I mean no slight to you, young lady. Where is the lady Deshes?"

Sheek froze for a moment. Then, with an undeniable air of satisfaction, she said, "My mother is working on her experiments." A gesture of her pedipalp expressed disgust.

"What experiments are these, child?" Tewsee asked.

The young Fibian drew herself up but turned her head aside in a clear indication of embarrassment.

"She is experimenting with obtaining sexual gratification without fertilization."

Tewsee went absolutely still at that. At first she was simply numb with shock at the implications of what the child had told her. It was, quite simply, unheard of.

"You mean . . . with males?" the queen asked.

All females could easily manipulate males with their pheromones, causing them to become hypnotized into a state of mindless lust. But it was to be used strictly for the purpose of mating and it was considered, quite simply, *wrong* to do so for no justifiable reason.

"Yes, your majesty." Sheek was looking out of the screen with a distinctly eager tilt to her head. "Quite a few don't survive," she added.

Now Tewsee drew herself up to her full height, suppressing the hiss of rage that would only have frightened this child and the males who were working beside her.

"I am Queen Tewsee of Clan Nrgun," she said in a voice of command. "I am taking over Isasef Station as of this moment. Neither messages nor ships are to leave this system until I have permitted it. Do you understand?"

"Yes, your majesty."

This time Sheek bowed from the waist. She was a little frightened now at her boldness. But she was more frightened for her mother than for herself. Too late she thought of consequences and guilt assailed her. Still, there had been only good reports of this queen, which made her believe that while Deshes was in terrible trouble she would survive it. At least for now.

"You will broadcast my voice throughout the station, with the exception of your mother's quarters," Tewsee said. "We wouldn't want to disturb her, now would we?"

"She is my daughter," Cesat insisted.

The yellow queen gazed out of the screen with a determined set to her head, but her chelicerae showed her repugnance. Whether it was for the task or Deshes or both was less clear.

"She was your daughter," Tewsee agreed. The position of her body indicated sympathy, her pedipalps showed resistance and determination of the first degree. "That is why you should not involve yourself in this. Now she is a daughter of Clan Snargx and no longer your responsibility. Let another handle this unpleasant task. I put myself forward to do it: it was I, after all, who started us on this journey. Or choose another if you prefer, but spare yourself, for she was your daughter."

"What do you plan?" Lesni asked. Her own body language was carefully indeterminate, though her purple exoskeleton was far less glossy than usual from shock and stress.

"I plan to imprison her," Tewsee said. "And I plan to claim this station for Nrgun until such time as we can find a new queen for this system."

The other queens froze while they considered this. Clearly they couldn't leave the station deprived of its lady. Not least because it would be dangerous to leave so many rudderless males bound to Deshes and Syaris and the other sub-queens at their rear. The child, Sheek, was far too young to be left in charge, despite her apparent competence, so obviously one of the queens would have to claim both the station and the males.

"Should we consider now who we will ultimately place in charge of this sector?" Cembe asked. The orange queen's whole manner was elaborately disinterested, a response to the tension her fellow queens were undoubtedly feeling.

"Certainly we should be considering candidates," Tewsee said impatiently. "Though I do not think that we can allow anyone from Clan Snargx to go unclaimed or unpunished. From what we've learned most of them are very young or still children, and all of them have been raised in a most perverted fashion. I advise that we bring them home, some to each clan, thus dissipating the strength of the evil that has been done to them. Let us reseed this sector with new colonists."

"Yes," Saras said immediately. "This is a good plan. Punish the leaders, the malefactors—reeducate their victims." The green queen bowed her head. "I salute you for your wisdom, Tewsee. Go to the station, do what needs to be done."

"Let us not reseed this sector until we have determined that it is safe," Cesat spoke up. "Perhaps there is something here that has caused this insanity."

The others indicated their agreement with the yellow queen. There wasn't one of them that didn't hope that this whole mess had to do with some external factor.

"I shall have Deshes imprisoned on one of my ships," Tewsee said. "And I will leave my third assistant in charge of the station. While I am about this work, think about what we should do with Syaris and her rather too numerous ladies. I shouldn't be gone long."

With that she broke off communication and rose, suppressing a sigh. No, this shouldn't take long at all.

"No, Sheek, you may not meet me at the lock. I wish our time together to be undisturbed and when I first come aboard I will have pressing business with your mother."

"I can show you to her quarters," the young lady said eagerly.

Tewsee was both oddly charmed and disconcerted by her eagerness. Her mother was fairly young and it was possible that the budding daughter instinctively reacted to Deshes more as a rival than as a parent.

"You may send me a guide who can escort me to your mother's chambers, my dear. But I am relying on you to begin indoctrinating Suv-aus, my third assistant in the running of the station. Both you and your mother will accompany us on our journey and there will be little enough time for you to teach him."

Sheek abandoned her unnatural maturity and actually wriggled with excitement at that.

"I shall teach him very well, your majesty!" the child assured her. "I shall have one guide for you and one for him waiting to welcome you."

The screen went blank and Tewsee stared broodingly into it for a few moments.

"Poor child," Suv-aus said, watching his queen to see how she reacted.

"Yes," she agreed. "Poor child. I suspect she's been given far too many duties for one so young. But I think she is also very clever, Third Assistant. I think she shall keep you very busy indeed."

Deshes watched the slightly larger male vanquish his rival and gloried in the carnage. The males had both released their own pheromones and the rich male scent that filled the room exhilarated her to the point of intoxication. She was delighted with this experiment and couldn't wait to share the idea with the queen. Syaris would be *most* amused.

The winner of the combat staggered towards her, and Deshes toyed with the idea of letting this one succeed in depositing his seed with her. Then laughed at herself. It wouldn't do to let her excitement carry her away. Though the idea *was* tempting. She lay back, inviting the male closer, and released the scents of her own elation and desire into the air.

The door to her chamber flashed aside and the sterile air of the corridor swept in to taint the delicious atmosphere she'd created so carefully. Deshes flung herself to her feet and faced the door with murder in every line of her stance—and froze.

Before her stood a queen. Instinct tempered her stance without her knowledge; her mind was too stunned to believe what she saw. Then she was stunned again as the queen assailed her with a wash of pheromones that completely overwhelmed her.

Deshes dropped to the floor, exposing her neck, her pedipalps raised in a plea for mercy. She didn't think. She merely felt and what she felt was pure terror.

The male had likewise flung himself to the deck, but he simply lay there, too exhausted emotionally and physically to even plead for his life.

Tewsee looked at him, looked at the crumpled body at the far side of the room. She turned to the small escort Sheek had sent her.

"See to your brothers," she commanded. She turned to her own soldiers. "Take this female to the *Fledrook Hunter*, imprison her in a sealed room. No one is to speak to her or to approach her."

The males moved forward and seized Deshes, who looked up in wonder to find herself spared. There was much in the wash of scent coming from the blue queen that indicated she was extremely fortunate.

"Thanks and praise, great queen . . ." she began.

"Be silent!" Tewsee ordered. "Do not speak to my soldiers! And if you release the smallest trace of scent I will give myself the pleasure of tearing you to pieces personally."

Deshes bowed, totally quelled, and allowed herself to be led trembling away.

Tewsee stared at the bloody stain on the floor of Deshes' chamber and felt a stirring in her digestive sac, and a great loathing filled her. She and her sister queens had much grim work ahead of them.

"Come," she said to her guide, "lead me to your young lady."

❖   ❖   ❖

Sheek ran to her as though Tewsee were her own mother, gently stroking the queen's pedipalps and forelegs. The younger female trembled as she did so, babbling her gratitude all the while.

Tewsee began to stroke the child's head and back, and before many moments had passed Sheek's chitin had begun to cool from red to blue. Over the child's head Tewsee gave a nod to her third assistant and he made some adjustments to the station's atmospheric plant.

Within moments the queen's scent permeated the station, telling those who labored there that they now belonged to her and she to them. With utmost relief the males surrendered, beginning their change to Clan Nrgun without the slightest hesitation.

It was immediately apparent to the watchers on the *Invincible* that Isasef Station had undergone a sea change. For one thing the running lights switched from red to blue and many small craft began to run from Nrgun's ships to the station.

"Send a polite inquiry to her majesty's flagship," Raeder said. "I don't care who answers as long as *someone* is willing to give us some information."

"Aye, sir," communications said.

"I'll be in the office," Peter said.

He rose from the captain's chair and made his way to Knott's ready room, adjacent to the bridge. He sat at the desk and called Stuart Semple, the captain's secretary, on the com.

"Get me Sim-has, Mr. Semple, and Sun-hes as well."

"In person, sir?" Semple asked.

"On screen will be fine," Raeder said.

They tried to keep the Fibians' travel through the corridors to a minimum as a surprising number of the crew found themselves genuinely appalled by the creatures. Which naturally offended the Fibians, who were straining themselves to the utmost to endure the company of people *they* considered loathsome in appearance.

Meanwhile, Ticknor was still gratefully under heavy sedation in sick bay. Dr. Goldberg had shrugged hopelessly and said it was really up to the linguist himself how long this would last. When he was ready, he wouldn't start curling into a ball and screaming as he came awake.

"I know that seems unsympathetic," the doctor had said. "But I'm not his regular physician or therapist and this thing goes pretty deep. We just don't have time here to deal with this kind of problem."

All Raeder could do was thank his lucky stars that Ticknor had come up with a working translation device. Constant interaction had aided in programming the devices and the Fibians had found it remarkably easy to imitate Commonwealth speech. They hadn't told Ticknor. No sense in making a bad situation worse. The humans had learned and now understood a great deal of the Fibian language; they just found it impossible to speak.

"Commander?" Sun-hes asked from the screen. "How may I be of use to you?"

That was one of the things that Raeder had noticed about Fibians; they served their queens and ladies, they were of use to other males.

Peter opened his mouth to speak when his screen split and Sim-has, their Fibian military advisor, appeared.

"How may I be of use, Commander?" he asked.

"Awhile ago," Raeder told them, "a single small vessel went from Queen Tewsee's ship to Isasef Station. Very shortly thereafter the running lights turned blue . . ."

Both the Nrgun Fibians gave cries of joy.

"Our queen has conquered them!" Sun-hes exclaimed. "The station belongs now to Clan Nrgun as do all those within."

"Really?" Peter said. *And without a shot fired. Hmm.* "How did that happen so easily?"

"It is a matter of Fibian physiology, Commander," Sim-has explained. The young huntmaster paused as though to collect his thoughts. "This is an ability unique to queens. They alone can release chemicals that will change one from being a member of one clan to being a member of another. The male, or lady, must be willing to convert however; if they are not willing then the chemical will poison them."

Raeder considered this for a minute.

"What if someone only pretends to convert?" he asked.

"Impossible, Commander," Sun-hes, the protocol expert, said. "One changes. The color of one's chitin, one's scent and the scents that one responds to, all of these are changed to the signals that would make one as much a member of Clan Nrgun as though one had been born on our homeworld."

"It must be total surrender," the huntmaster said, "or it will be death. We do not claim to merely change our loyalties, we actually change what we are."

The Fibians gazed at the commander, waiting to see if he had any other questions.

"Wow," Raeder said wistfully. "I wish we could do that with the Mollies." *I'll bet there's a million of 'em that would secretly love to be Welters.* "So," he said, sitting forward in his chair, "this means that we can safely leave this station behind us."

"Yes, Commander," Sim-has agreed with a gesture that indicated he had gotten the concept completely.

Raeder looked at them for a moment before he

said, "What will happen when the queens confront the queen of Clan Snargx?"

"Her name is Syaris," Sun-hes said. "That depends largely on her. Though I am not privy to the agenda of the queens that we are accompanying," he admitted.

The huntmaster made a high-pitched sound that Raeder didn't doubt was rude.

"Their majesties will demand that she surrender herself to their judgement," he said. "If half the rumors are as true as the facts you humans and young Sna-fe related to Queen Tewsee, they will not permit her to continue ruling Clan Snargx."

"And if she is unwilling to step down?" Raeder asked.

"Then she faces war with all of the clans as well as with you humans," Sim-has said. "But she cannot resist unless her clan is behind her. And if what has happened on Isasef Station is an indication of how her people feel about her, then there should be no difficulty."

"They *change*?" Doctor Goldberg said carefully.

"Change color, change scent, change attitude and loyalties," Raeder confirmed.

He looked around the conference table at his fellow officers and a universal rueful grin spread among them. They were obviously thinking the same thing he had. Wouldn't it be great if they could do that to the Mollies?

"How long does it last?" Booth asked suspiciously.

"A lifetime unless another queen comes along and claims them," Raeder said.

"So what's to stop—" Booth began.

"Only queens can do this," Raeder interrupted him. "And we know that five of them are headed for the sixth. There is no seventh, so these guys should stay Clan Nrgun until they die or Queen Tewsee turns them over to one of her sister queens."

Booth subsided darkly.

"Mr. Gunderson," Raeder said to the tactical officer, "what have you got to report to us?"

"Major traffic through this system, sir. Military signatures for the most part. Ms. Lurhman tells me they're taking the exit point that we emerged from when we entered this system in pursuit of the Fibian attack vessel. There's some heavy metal out there, sir. The equivalent of the Home Fleet, probably more."

Towards Bella Vista, and the half of the squadron that had been left there. He could only hope that Sutton had the good sense to keep a low profile if all Clan Snargx was doing was passing through. He tried not to think about the inevitable conclusion if they'd been forced to fight. Raeder leaned back slowly.

"What sort of numbers are we talking about here, Ensign?"

Gunderson crossed glances with Truon and Lurhman.

"I think we're talking invasion force, sir," Gunderson said. "At least as much as we have that's not tied down in essential patrol or system-picket work, total. A lot of heavy ships have passed through here, military signatures as I said. An incredible number of smaller craft too."

"If they're what's coming through the back door I sure hate to think about what's coming through the front," Peter said grimly.

There was silence around the conference table at that.

"We should warn the Commonwealth," Hartkopf said after a long moment.

"They passed through days ago. And the kind of numbers we're talking about," Truon said, "they have to know by now."

"Would the queens let us go anyway?" Goldberg asked.

"Yes," Sarah said firmly. "No question about that, but I don't think that would be the best use of the *Invincible* or her people right now." She leaned forward and placed her folded hands before her on the table. "If the queens succeed in their efforts to remove Syaris from . . . office, I guess, then they will be in a prime position to call off the Fibian invasion fleet."

Raeder's eyes had flicked from one speaker to the next as his officers hashed it out. He'd felt the glow of an inner smile when Sarah's opinion coincided perfectly with his own.

"I agree with Lieutenant Commander James," he said. "Queen Tewsee has expressed the desire to, quote, 'make everything right between our peoples.' Given that it should be a simple matter to convince them to stop the invaders. Without Clan Snargx backing them, Star Command should be able to mop up the Mollies in short order. So we're going to stay with the queens and then lead them or their people back to the Commonwealth to stop the invasion."

"This could all be some elaborate hoax," Goldberg suggested. "A joke with our arrival at Queen Syaris' court trussed for dinner as the punch line."

The others looked to the commander for his response.

"It would be elaborate all right," Raeder said. "Pointlessly so since they've had us pretty much in their power since we entered Nrgun space. Besides, we've been observing these people for over a month, not an in-depth study I realize, but long enough to notice that they're very different from what we know of Clan Snargx."

There were thoughtful looks around the table at that, some nods, some lowered eyes.

"We'll do more good this way than running back to the Commonwealth to tell them what they've almost certainly found out by now."

As they entered the Snargx home system, two imprisoned sub-queens in tow, a phalanx of automated buoys swept up to demand their names and business.

"Why are there no crewed ships here to meet us?" Cesat demanded. The yellow queen seemed to take this robotic greeting as a personal insult.

"Unimportant," the buoy responded. "Identify yourselves, state your business, or be fired upon."

"Queen Tewsee of Nrgun."

"Queen Saras of Lince."

"Queen Cembe of Bletnik."

"Queen Cesat of Streth."

"Queen Lesni of Vened."

"Commander Peter Ernst Raeder of the Commonwealth Star Command ship *Invincible*."

"We send our greeting to Queen Syaris and request a meeting with her," Tewsee said.

They waited as the buoy sat silent before them. The tech boards on their ships showed that their greetings and request had been transmitted.

"Request denied," the buoy announced. "You must leave the area immediately or you will be fired upon."

"I don't think they're taking those things seriously enough," Peter Raeder said thoughtfully.

The Fibian officer waved his pedipalps. Raeder swallowed slightly; when they did that it always reminded him of a Commonwealth Arts Council nature documentary he'd seen once. One entitled *Microscopic Jungle of Death*. He'd seen it when he was seven and had nightmares about it for months.

"It is unthinkable that a robotic mechanism would be authorized to fire on a *queen's* personal ship," he said.

"I think that the red clan will find many unthinkable thoughts perfectly thinkable—even attractive," Raeder said grimly. To his own Tac board: "Do we have the specs?"

"Analysis from our last encounter, sir. They're loaded for bear, and fairly well hardened, but there are a couple of vulnerable points."

"Take them out."

Tewsee gave a startled jump as a flash of laser fire burst the robot apart. The other buoys simply sat there, inert.

"Who fired?" she demanded.

"The humans, your majesty," her huntmaster answered.

"Get them on the com for me," the queen said.

"I'm sorry if we startled you, your majesty," Commander Raeder said before she could speak. "We rather expected such an answer, so we incapacitated the other buoys and were ready to disarm the last one."

Tewsee stared at him. These beings were so small and so soft looking that it was easy to forget that they were also dangerous. His bland face didn't show it, neither did his posture, but the queen detected a lilt in his voice that spoke of satisfaction, perhaps even smugness.

After a moment she said carefully, "There are no pickets here."

"I suspect that Queen Syaris has stripped her sector

of all the military vessels she has," the commander said. "I think that they've been sent to invade the Commonwealth."

"You never spoke of this," Cembe remarked. Her orange face popped up in a square at the top of both Raeder and Tewsee's screens.

"We didn't know that you didn't know, your majesty," Raeder said. Then wished he'd phrased that better. *I hope the translator could keep up with that,* he thought with an inward wince. *If you knew that we knew that you didn't know that we knew . . .*

"Let us have our communications technicians create a secure link between our vessels, Commander," Tewsee suggested. "That way we won't be caught unprepared by your fire next time."

"Yes, your majesty," Raeder agreed. "Hartkopf, see to it," he said over his shoulder.

"Aye, sir."

"We go on," Tewsee said.

"Aye," Cembe agreed, trying out the human word. "We do."

"If you so much as attempt to land, my people will shoot you out of the sky," Syaris said.

Her stance was extremely aggressive, a battle stance designed to make her look larger and more formidable. It was not mere posturing either; the color of her chitin, a glaring scarlet, confirmed that.

Tewsee considered the young queen with regret. She was so lovely, and had been so promising. When living in Clan Lince she'd been a brilliant student and capable of exquisite diplomacy. And now? Now she had apparently run mad.

The two prisoners had confirmed that they each had four daughters, all at their queen's command. Eight young females. Maybe more! They had yet to recover one of Syaris' sub-queens, and there was no reason to assume that she would not also have been ordered to have female children.

It would be very difficult for the clans to absorb so many. But it must be done. They were children, innocent in this vast evil Syaris had visited on her people.

Tewsee drew herself up. "Syaris," she said regally.

The other queens joined her as she spoke, their words going out in a broadcast that overrode all attempts at blocking the signal. It was heard by every Fibian on the planet below.

"We, the council of queens, demand that you submit yourself to us for judgement in the matter of crimes against an intelligent new species and against your own people."

"You have no power here," Syaris shouted. "Go hide in your palaces until I send for you!" Her whole body spoke of contempt and loathing.

"People of Clan Snargx," the council of queens intoned, "we require you to submit your queen to us for judgement."

Raeder, listening to the broadcast, thought that he heard a strange undertone to the queens' united voices. He tapped a key.

"Sun-hes," he said, "I assume you're listening to this broadcast?"

"Yes, Commander," the protocol expert said.

It was unusual for a Fibian voice to convey anything but mere words, but something in the tone of Sun-hes' voice made Peter look at him more sharply.

"Am I imagining it, or is there something happening there with the queens' voices?" the commander asked.

"What you have witnessed, Commander, is something so rarely invoked as to be legendary. This undertone that you hear quivering in their voices is an irresistible command. At least to all right-thinking Fibians. It depends on how disturbed this population is, or how loyal. Though to overcome such a compulsion, they would have to be very dedicated to their queen indeed."

You mean that we'll be able to take over without a shot fired? Again? Wow! For a moment Raeder wished that humans could solve their problems so simply, then discarded the idea. *For one thing it would mean that, like, ninety-nine percent of the population never got to have sex. That's a bad plan, very bad.*

"So this could get very interesting," Peter said.

"Very," Sun-hes agreed.

Syaris froze at the sound of the queens' voices, froze in terror, froze in anger. How dare they interfere with her? She called the same compelling quaver into her own voice and backed it with her powerful pheromones.

"Attack these invaders, fire on them!" she commanded.

Those Fibians in the war room with her responded to her commands, turning to their boards and calling up their weapons. But in the depths of her new and modern palace a crew of lowly technicians shut down the air plant while others shut down the palace's communications system. They moved to cut power to the war room. In ten minutes the only members of her clan that Syaris could influence were in the room with her.

On the bridge of her flagship Tewsee waited for what would happen. At a technician's board a message came through from the planet below.

"Your majesty," the crewman said from a patch of her screen.

"What is it?" she asked.

"A citizen of Snargx reports that they have isolated Queen Syaris in the war room of her palace, but they do not dare to enter. Those with her are still attempting to fire on us."

Tewsee thought for a moment. "Stay in communication with him, and put me through to my fellow queens," she said at last.

The other queens appeared one by one on her screen and Tewsee waited until they had all gathered. Then she explained what the technician from below had said.

There was silence when she'd finished.

"Well, we cannot all go," Saras said at last.

"No," Cesat agreed. There was a grimness to her posture that was reflected in all of them.

"Tewsee," Lesni said at last, "you have been our leader in this from the beginning. Will you now go down and face Syaris?"

The others indicated agreement with this plan, reluctantly in one or two cases. But they all recognized that Tewsee had dealt fairly and well with their two imprisoned ladies. They knew that she would not lose her perspective now and kill Syaris before she could be brought to judgement.

"I will," Tewsee said. Inside she was resigned and unhappy, but she would do her duty.

On the *Invincible* they watched and listened, keeping their weapons hot and trained on military targets.

"There's not much down there in the way of defenses," Truon Le remarked quietly.

"No, there isn't," Raeder agreed. "I don't think she expected anybody to come and call her to account." *Maybe this Syaris really is just crazy.*

It was tragic that one mad individual should have

so much power over those around her. Of course it had happened in human society, but then it was pure charisma. If they'd wanted to, the many followers of the madmen of history could easily have turned on their masters. According to their Fibian advisors this was not an option for any of Syaris' people who were within a mile of her pheromones.

"Put me through to Queen Tewsee," Raeder said suddenly.

In a moment her face appeared on his screen.

"Yes, Commander," she said.

Raeder was impressed by her graciousness. Here she was preparing to do battle with the enemy queen below and she reacted to this importunate alien with no sign of impatience in her manner.

"May I suggest that you have your soldiers wear space suits when you go below," Raeder said.

There was a slight shift in her chelicerae that indicated mild amusement.

"The air is quite breathable below, Commander," Tewsee replied.

"The reason I suggest this is that Sim-has, your military advisor, has told us that a queen can send out pheromones that persuade a male to change clans. He said that if they resist they die. A suit should protect them."

There was a slight *tic* as one finger of the queen's pedipalp touched the hard surface of her cheek. Tewsee indicated that he was correct.

"An excellent suggestion," she said, "for which I thank you."

"I was listening in to the communication from below that you received awhile ago," Raeder continued. "They've isolated Queen Syaris and her pheromones in a large room?"

The queen agreed with a gesture. A slight trace

of impatience showed through in the quickness with which she moved.

"Make it easy on everyone and pump knockout gas into that room. Then have your people gather her up and put her somewhere safe where she can't influence her own clan and can't harm yours." Peter waited to see how she would react. Maybe there were inviolable rules about this sort of thing. "I mean, she's done enough damage, it would be a shame if she harmed one more person."

Tewsee stared at him, frozen, for a full minute. Then she slowly nodded, deliberately using the human gesture.

"An excellent suggestion," she said. "And I agree, she should not be allowed to harm one more person. We will do this, Commander. I thank you for your suggestions."

As she signed off, Tewsee reflected that humans were frighteningly acute in matters of war and mayhem. As flexible as their—she made herself be frank—regretfully disgusting faces. Frighteningly adaptable and inventive . . . Of course, she didn't know their history. *I must assign experts to study it in detail, as soon as possible.*

"Everything so safe, so serene, so secure!" Syaris raged. "The whole world reduced to a nursery. Nothing ever changing, no challenge, no growth possible. My role was determined years before my planned birth! *Look* at us! We were designed to be warriors!"

She stood panting before the holographic images of her fellow queens, her gaze skipping from one to the other and back again.

"You don't understand at all. Do you?" Syaris said.

"We are trying to," her mother said. "We are trying to discover how a brilliant student—"

"Did you even notice what I was studying?" the renegade asked.

"History," Saras said, a bit off-balanced by the question.

"I was studying the old queens! Their wars, their methods of ruling, their attitudes towards life and those around them. And I long ago concluded that they were alive and we were simply not dead yet. Cautiously creeping from system to system . . . ugh." She turned her back to them and was quiet for a moment. "I swore that if I ever had the chance I would lead my people as a conqueror, a warrior queen who would take what she wanted and face the consequences."

"Which is why we are all here," Tewsee said. She thought it was time to put a stop to such histrionic nonsense. "We *are* the consequences. We have spoken to your ladies and they have told us how you led them astray."

"I did not lead them," Syaris said with contempt, turning towards the blue queen. "I did as I pleased and they chose to follow my example."

"Did you or did you not command them all to have four daughters apiece? Did you or did you not command them to have far too many young and to raise and train those children with a brutality that I never read of the old queens employing?" Tewsee's whole body radiated contempt right back at the younger queen. "Did you or did you not eat the flesh of your own clan and of intelligent aliens? Do you deny doing these things?"

"I refuse to acknowledge your authority to even ask these questions of me." Syaris turned away again and adopted a pose that spoke of wronged virtue. "I have never wronged your clans. You cannot say that I have, therefore this invasion is totally unjustified. But I see what you will do, you will persecute me for my beliefs and there is nothing I can do to stop you. But one day you will see that I am right, that the old ways are best. Watch your new human friends," she said over her shoulder. "There you'll see malice and abuse. But you'll also see a people who know they're alive!"

"Let us retire," Tewsee suggested and her form winked out.

The others followed until Syaris was left alone with her mother.

"Why?" Saras asked.

"My will," Syaris answered. "What is a queen who cannot make her will manifest?"

The holo figure of Saras was the last to join their meeting in Tewsee's quarters on her flagship. The other queens greeted her with averted heads and hunched shoulders, indicative of embarrassment.

"She's mad," Tewsee said. Her posture expressed sympathy. "She's also very clever or we would have known it before turning this system over to her."

"By her own admission," Lesni said, "these ideas were in her head when she was living with Clan Lince."

"What shall we do with our criminal daughters?" Saras asked.

Cesat looked at her quickly, then showed her agreement with the question. "They must be punished," she said.

"There is no precedent for something like this," Cembe said. She shifted her orange body uneasily. "Despite Syaris' claims, the old queens didn't eat their own young. At least not within historical times . . . in the days of myth and legend, but . . ."

They all gradually turned to Tewsee, who looked back at them for a long time before she spoke.

"I am unwilling to be the one who decides what must be done," she said.

"You are the only one of us who hasn't a guilty child involved in this horror," Saras said. "We look to you for impartiality. And wisdom. You have both."

Her fellow queens pleaded with her, their stance and their pedipalps showing longing for her aid.

"Very well," Tewsee said at last. "Here is what I think. I think that these, our daughters, are insane and weak and that they have allowed themselves to commit many evil acts. I think that we made very poor decisions when we placed them in charge of this sector. Therefore, upon us I place the task of taking in these wronged and brutalized children of Snargx and using whatever resources are necessary to heal them and to make them happy and useful citizens of our clans."

"Agreed," Saras said. The other queens indicated agreement as well.

"Our errant daughters must be sterilized," Tewsee went on. "I would not have their genes continue, and they are unfit to mother another generation."

Silence greeted this.

"You do not mean to execute them?" Lesni asked.

"As I said, they are mad. Syaris is most definitely insane," the blue queen said. "I think we can all agree with that?"

The others indicated that they did.

"Somehow she convinced her ladies to go along with her insanity. Since what ensued from that was pure madness I am forced to conclude that they also are insane."

The queens looked at one another.

Cembe shrugged orange shoulders, indicating an uncomfortable agreement.

"I suppose that must be the case," she said.

"Very well," Cesat, the yellow queen, said, "they're insane. Now what do we do with them?"

"We sterilize them, then place them on a livable planet, each to her own continent or large island, and we go away." Tewsee looked each of her fellow queens in the eye. "We are each of us capable of surviving on our own, and so the old queens did. Let them emulate their admired forebears in splendid isolation. While we get on with the task of cleaning up their self-indulgent mess."

The queens stirred and hunched their shoulders.

"Yes," Saras said. "It is just and merciful. Let us do this." She gave the blue queen a sharp glance. "And their male accomplices?"

"The same," Tewsee suggested. "Find a liveable, undeveloped world and leave them there. A different one, it need hardly be said."

"What of our human . . . friends?" Lesni asked. "What if they make demands?"

"They have a right to make demands," Saras said bitterly. "Without the interference of Clan Snargx they would have defeated their enemies long since. I suggest that we find out what demands they might make from Tewsee's Commander Raeder before we make any promises, though."

"He is not—"

"I second the motion," Cesat said. She tipped her yellow head at Tewsee. "He may not belong to you, but he is most closely associated with you. I think he will be more likely to tell you what they might want than he would me, or any of the rest of us."

The others indicated their enthusiastic agreement.

"That's settled," Saras said. "Now let's get to work."

"Conquer this," Saras told her daughter, sweeping her arms out to indicate the clearing in which they stood. "And know that you are alive."

The image of the green queen winked out, leaving

Syaris alone with her stack of boxed vitamin supplements. Clan Snargx's erstwhile queen listened for sounds of life from the unfamiliar vegetation around her. Then she looked up at the darkening sky and her chelicerae shifted. Her mandibles clicked once, then again and again until her whole body shook in a paroxysm of amusement. A whole world to conquer. How delightful.

"We've left a satellite above with just one job," Fuj-if said to the gathered males. "It will detect any electrical energy over biological levels; when it does it will fire a laser cannon and obliterate the source of the reading." He looked around at Queen Syaris' accomplices. "It is my personal hope that your first job will be to build a power station. But such a quick end is undoubtedly more than you deserve."

He winked out, leaving the males standing in shock, befuddled from the sheer speed with which their world had changed.

"What will happen now?" one of them asked.

He got no answer.

"Clan Snargx had no soldiers at home, your majesties, because they'd been sent to invade the Commonwealth."

Raeder paused and tried to evaluate what effect, if any, this announcement had made on the gathered queens. They'd been strangely reluctant to allow him this interview, trying to fob him off with Clan Nrgun's queen alone. But he'd been insistent. *They'd only get together and talk about me behind my back anyway,* he thought. *At least now they'll be starting on the same page.*

"I've no idea how large an armada set forth from here," he continued, "though I can tell you they left four days ago. I also know that it might be too much for my people to handle, especially with the Mollies lending their weight to the battle. I ask you to stop Clan Snargx's ships. Is there some way that you can make them turn back?"

"There might well be," Tewsee said. "Lead us to your Commonwealth; we will follow and we will do what we can to help."

"I do not wish to be so long away from my people," Cesat protested. "Nor so far that communication is impossible."

"We've all been away from our clans for at least two weeks," Lesni noted. Her stance indicated that she found this stressful.

Tewsee looked around at her fellow queens.

"You left this to me," she said. Not technically true, but very close. "I shall go with our human friends, and so should you. We have killing to stop. Or have you forgotten that Syaris crewed her ships with children?"

Shamed, the queens indicated that they would follow Tewsee on her mission. But they were not pleased to have had this thrashed out before the human and it showed to one with the eyes to see.

"We will be extremely grateful, your majesties," Raeder said, not seeing but suspecting. "I know that our people will look forward to a long and profitable association with the clans once they have this situation explained to them."

"Profitable?" Saras asked with a suspicious tilt to her green head.

"The Commonwealth thrives on trade," Raeder explained. "And we always have more dancers than we can find performance space for." *At least I hope so.*

"Will they not hate us for the war Fibians have made on you?" Cesat asked.

"To be honest, your majesty, I think that some of our people, and some of yours as well, will have difficulty accepting our physical differences," Raeder said. "But I think that more of us will be fascinated by those very things. It's not our way, once the treaties are signed, to refuse to deal with our former enemies. And, of course, _you_ never were our enemies. I think this will all work out," he finished.

And I think I'll shut up now because I'm not a diplomat and I shouldn't be saying these things.

After a moment Queen Tewsee rose from her couch.

"Lead, Commander Raeder. We will follow you."

CHAPTER NINETEEN

I shouldn't be risking the ship, Raeder thought, as his body shook off the transit shock—or some distant, potential-staff-officer part of his mind did. A larger part leaned forward with a predator's intentness as real-space information began to flow into the assault carrier's instruments.

The rest of him knew that the *Invincible* wanted to be in on the kill; the crew certainly and, in some intangible, unprovable way, the ship herself. All the long grinding years of the Mollie war demanded it, the ghosts of lost comrades were cheering them on ... and the hand he'd lost so long ago when his Speed blew up was itching fiercely, even though the prosthesis was utterly incapable of it.

The darkened bridge of the light carrier shone blue and green with the lights of the displays. A crackling tension filled the filtered, neutral-spring-pine-scented air.

"They're turning to fight, sir," the tactical desk said. "Launching first squadron of Speeds as per instructions . . ."

Raeder nodded, hoping his face was as implacably blank as he desired. Sarah was out there, her sensors feeding in the data that became these antiseptic lines and graph-bars.

His own lips shaped a silent prayer, and then a silent whistle as the figures came in.

"Sir, there's been one hell of a fight here," a sensor analyst said with hushed reverence. "I'd estimate at least fifty, possibly as many as a hundred capital ships lost—no counting how many light units. A lot of them enemy, but at least twenty or so ours."

There was a slight shocked gasp across the bridge, at the implication of the molecular fog that drifted in the hard vacuum of space:

> How many dead drift graveless
> In the emptiness of space;
> And they died so far from Earth and home
> And the green hills' warm embrace . . .

It ran through him, a fragment of a lament as old as humanity's journey beyond Sol system . . . or as old as the habit of war that had followed the species out into the great frontier.

"Give me the status on intact units," he said with relentless calm.

"Launch," he said when the recital was through. *In the proverbial nick of time*, he continued silently to himself.

The *Invincible* began to shudder as the Speeds darted out of the launch bays. The screens showed enemy fighters coming about, part of the rear guard of the force that was englobing the Commonwealth's

navy and hammering it back towards the jump points
that led to humanity's inner worlds. A carrier and
a battlecruiser started the slow business of killing
their forward vectors and reversing to engage this
new—but tiny—threat. That made the red cones of
their possible trajectories narrow and shorten; the
Invincible's lay broad and blue across the screens.

"Oh, how surprised they're going to be," Raeder
said.

Alarms beeped discreetly as the Fibian—the
friendly Fibian—fleet started to emerge behind him.

The Commonwealth's fleet ought to be getting
their first hint that something new was on the chess-
board about now. Despite fear and tension, a slight
wry grin quirked at Raeder's mouth. He would bet
his pension that a certain acquaintance would be
watching those reports firsthand.

All the webs trail broken, General Kemal Scaragoglu thought to himself, as he watched the figures
and columns in the display tank, astonished at his
own dispassion. *All the tools fall broken from my
hands. At the end, nothing works.*

The lines on Admiral Grettirson's face were deep,
graven as if with a laser etcher in the mountain gran-
ite lining a Norwegian fjord. He drew a deep breath
and spoke: "There's one good thing about this," he
said. "The Mollie fleet is effectively defunct. They
came right at us and we annihilated them."

Scaragoglu nodded. He looked over at Adrienne
Clarkson, the Prime Minister's liaison with Space
Command. The elderly civilian looked a little lost on
the command deck of the *Chateau Laurier,* but her
blue eyes were firm.

"What's the situation, Admiral?" she asked crisply.

"Madame Minister, as I said, we've destroyed the

Mollie fleet. Always knew we could, if they came out and gave us a stand-up fight. We've also inflicted heavy damage on their Fibian allies. Our people have inflicted casualties at a two-to-one ratio."

"But?" she said sharply.

"But the Fibians outmass us by three to two; rather more, in heavy units. We have more carriers, but we've lost a lot of Speeds and it'll be the heavy metal that counts from now on."

The admiral's long fingers moved, and patterns of scarlet and green webbed over the display tank. "It's become an attritional battle, not least because we *must* hold this jump point. As our strength declines, the gap in capacities grows geometrically."

"We've lost?"

"Madam Minister, if we don't withdraw now, we will be forced away from the jump point in no more than three more days of combat—possibly half that, if they're willing to pay the butcher's bill. Then the Fibians can move units through, and *still* have enough force to englobe us. We can't retreat for long—we're running short of munitions. If there's to be anything left to defend Earth and Tau Ceti, we must retreat and attempt to hold the jump point from the Sol-system. exit."

"And the rest of the Commonwealth?" Clarkson asked quietly.

"We can hold the two central systems with what we have left. For a period of some months, at least; we've hurt them badly. If we disperse the remaining Space Command units, we will not be able to defend anything for so much as a week. The enemy will mass and smash us one system at a time."

"You're telling me that we've lost the war, Admiral?"

"We've lost this battle, ma'am. I'm giving you my

best advice, and that of my staff. It is of course your prerogative, as representative of the civil power, to accept or refuse it. We stand ready to carry out your orders." His shoulders slumped. "I . . . I don't want to lose any more of my people without a reason."

Scaragoglu gave a brief prayer of thanks to his grandfather's God that he wasn't in Clarkson's shoes, or the admiral's.

"Sir!" one of the staff aides said. "Sir, we have new footprints! Multiple units emerging from jumpspace, Fibian signatures—"

The multithousand-ton mass of the *Invincible* shuddered as it drove through a cloud of ionized gas that had been a Fibian—an *enemy* Fibian—ship not long before. Invisible fields wrenched the debris aside, their shape streamlined in a way that no deep-space craft was; sensors would see a bullet-headed spear cleaving the thin haze that had been ceramet and steel and the occasional carbon atom that had started out as a sentient being.

A wolfish snarl echoed across the bridge at the sensation; it meant *victory* in a way that had been a constant of space combat for a very long time.

"Seeker lock," someone said.

That made the small hairs along his spine bristle in a very different way under the sweat-heavy fabric of his uniform. The combat ranges were insanely close now—the enemy ships were throwing themselves at the spearhead of the allied queens' attack and trying to finish off the Commonwealth fleet at the same time.

Which meant that heavy ship-killer missiles were being thrown around like small-arms ammunition. A destroyer had tried to *ram* them, and only a lucky hit on her power plant by the close-defense batteries had stopped it. The antihydrogen flare had been far too close, with secondary radiation sleeting through the carrier's hull giving everyone aboard another uncomfortable hitch towards maximum exposure.

"Tracking . . . by God, one of our Speeds has a lock-on . . . firing solution . . ."

Another expanding globe of white fire against the velvet of space and the uncaring backdrop of the stars.

"Very good," Raeder heard himself say. "Record a recommendation for the Prime Minister's Medal to that vessel."

Invincible shuddered again—he'd gotten enough experience to tell that was a mass launch of counter-missiles. *So much for standing off and pecking at them with our Speeds,* he thought; that was what the manuals said a carrier *should* do. There had never been a fleet action like this before, not in all humanity's recorded history. Probably you could see half a dozen ships at a time out there with the naked eye, and the explosions of warheads were a continuous fireworks flicker.

The figures reeled across the Commonwealth flagship's vision tank, and fresh cones of possible trajectories splayed out.

Grettirson's face went pale, and he blurted: "Oh, my *God!*"

Possibly his first spontaneous utterance since he graduated from the Academy, Scaragoglu thought. His own stomach clenched. Enough heavy metal was coming through to outweigh the present enemy fleet by better than two to one. That turned the odds against Space Command to better than *five* to one. An unbearable situation had suddenly turned utterly impossible.

Then: "Sir! We're getting a Commonwealth IFF code!"

Identification Friend or Foe, Scaragoglu thought. *Why are they trying anything subtle now? They've got enough brute force to do the job, and that seems their style.*

"A trick," Grettirson said, struggling to pull his attention away from a vision of despair.

"Sir, I've got the footprint of the lead ship's engines . . . nonstandard . . . wait, here it is—"

An image flashed into a section of the display tank; a sleek double-hammerhead shape, utterly unlike the mechano-organic shapes of Fibian craft.

Another section of the tank came live, and a face appeared in it; a human face. *Raeder's face,* Scaragoglu realized, and he grabbed at the rail around the display tank. It would never do to collapse. Some calculating section of his mind that never slept realized that a confident smile right now would start a rumor—never to be confirmed or denied—that he'd *expected* this all the time, somehow.

"—friendly forces! Repeat, the Fibian ships with me are friendly forces! Conform to our movements and we can trap the enemy between us—"

"Sir!" the sensor tech said again, his fluting Danska accent strong. "Sir! The new Fibians are opening fire on the old ones . . . ship destroyed, sir! Battlecruiser class . . . carriers . . . they're launching Speeds . . . ship killers outbound . . ."

The fluid shock of bewilderment left Grettirson's face. "Message to fleet," he snapped, every inch the iron man of legend. "General attack; prepare for pursuit! And be careful to avoid any, repeat any, hostile action towards our new . . ." He paused for a second. "Friends," he finished.

Scaragoglu felt an immense grin trying to force its

way onto his face. He tamed it to a suitably mysterious smile. "Madam Minister," he said rising and taking her elbow. "Let's leave the specialists to their work. One of my department's plans has paid off big-time, and I'd like to get your permission— subject to confirmation from the Prime Minister, of course—to . . ."

Marine General Kemal Scaragoglu took a sip of his coffee and listened to the back scratching and the horse-trading of his fellow senior officers with his eyes closed. For the most part he agreed with every word they said. Some things he'd do slightly differently, some subordinates he'd allow to season a bit more before promotion. But he'd pulled enough strings in his career that even he didn't have the brass to criticize when others did the same.

Truth to tell, at this point in time he was grateful simply to be here. He opened his eyes and looked around the comfortable room. It had been a near run thing. A very near run thing. With the whole human race a finger snap away from extinction.

Oh, the remnants of human civilization would have fought on—tried to escape, actually—so that they could make a new beginning. But the general had a feeling that the Fibians were fine hunters and determined killers. They wouldn't have stopped until they'd bagged every human in existence.

He allowed himself a small smile. Only the Fibians could have stopped the Fibians. Especially with the Commonwealth all but out of fuel.

"What's that smirk about, Scaragoglu?" Admiral Grettirson demanded.

The general glanced at the sour-faced Space Command admiral.

"Nothing," he said with a dismissive wave of his

hand. Then he sat up and turned his chair towards the admiral. "No, I take that back. I'm smiling with satisfaction. I'm delighted with the way things have turned out." He gestured expansively. "Here we are again, carrying on with the work of the Commonwealth, making plans, tying up loose ends. Less than a week ago I thought," he tapped the table lightly with his fist, "I really thought that it was all over. And here we are."

His fellow officers grinned back at him. It was a time to be happy, to celebrate, and it was one of those exceedingly rare times when self-congratulation was not completely out of line.

"To the men and women of the service," Scaragoglu said, raising his cup.

"The service!" they answered him, lifting their own.

Grettirson lifted his cup, took his sip, put it down, all the while wearing an expression that implied he was being eaten alive by ants. He suddenly looked across the table at Scaragoglu with a cold blue glare.

"You're happy because that puppy of yours brought home a very meaty bone," he rasped. "The whole situation reflects well on you, eh, Scaragoglu?" He pushed his cup and saucer away with an almost contemptuous gesture.

The Marine general looked back with what was undeniably a self-satisfied smirk. He knew it would drive Grettirson crazy, but he felt he deserved a bit of self-indulgence. He allowed his smile to widen and his head to bob every so slightly.

Yes, he thought, *it does reflect well on me. And it didn't come about by gluing the rule book to my face so tight that I couldn't see anything but the fine print.*

"I've noticed," the admiral said with silken menace,

"that the one fellow *not* under discussion at this table is the very one that any person would expect to top our list. Why is that?"

"To whom do you refer?" Scaragoglu asked, all wide-eyed innocence.

The other officers shifted slightly; some glanced across the table at their fellows, some watched the two antagonists carefully.

"Raeder." Grettirson said the name as though it was sharp enough to cut his lips. "I believe he is your protégé?"

"Captain Sjarhir is my protégé, Admiral, in as far as I have one. Commander Raeder is one of my tools. Of which I have many."

Now the general had gone into wait mode, an inviting blankness that attempted to lure the opposition into indiscretion. The admiral might be a difficult man, but he was wily and knew how to get what he wanted. Of course, so did Scaragoglu.

"Well given your *tool's* influence on current events I'm surprised the man's name hasn't even come up," the admiral snapped.

Scaragoglu shrugged. "Well, now that his name has come up, what was it you wanted to say about him, Admiral?"

Grettirson seethed for a moment. He knew now that the general had been waiting for someone else to bring the subject up. Had he not spoken, the issue of the commander would probably have been handled in some quiet, underhanded way by Scaragoglu. Now, he'd placed himself in the position of looking ungrateful and possibly unbalanced. And yet, he couldn't let the matter lie.

"What I would like to say is that I find him a loose cannon and therefore, potentially, a very dangerous man."

As he took his time sitting forward and folding his hands on the conference table, Scaragoglu noted that none of the other officers seemed disposed to come in on one side or the other.

"We-ell," the general said slowly, "he's young and innovative . . ."

"Innovative! Although he was untrained in any aspect of diplomacy he took it upon himself to represent the Commonwealth to a whole society of aliens. There are rules designed to handle first-contact situations and the commander himself admitted that he was completely unaware of them!" Grettirson leaned back in his chair, meeting Scaragoglu's dark eyes. "Not even aware of them," he repeated. "It's only by the best of good fortune that he didn't ruin relations with these new Fibians."

"But Admiral," Vice-Admiral Paula Anderson said, "not only did the commander *not* alienate," she gave a brief grin at her unintended pun, "these Fibians, he led them into battle as our allies. Against their own kind, I might add, in a war that they could easily have avoided. We can hardly ignore his contribution simply because he was unaware of the rules for first contact. If we made every serving officer take a test on the subject today I'm sure they'd all fail." She spread her hands reasonably. "After all, who actually expects to find a new species?"

"I know I never do," Rear Admiral Bertucci said.

The other officers maintained their silence. They watched Grettirson and Scaragoglu, waiting for the next move. The silence dragged.

"Well," Scaragoglu said eventually with a shrug of his big shoulders, "you brought the subject up, Admiral. What are your thoughts?"

Grettirson looked down and clasped and unclasped his hands. He sensed he'd been outmaneuvered and he didn't like it one bit. But he hated Peter Ernst Raeder, felt he'd been humiliated by him, and that he could never forgive. If he didn't speak now there was a good chance they'd hand that fool the keys to the kingdom and then there'd be hell to pay.

"It's a difficult situation," he rasped out eventually. "Raeder, by sheer luck, seems to have saved the Commonwealth. Obviously the public will expect to see him rewarded in some way." His mouth worked as though he were chewing oak galls. "But we know that this officer, by virtue of his proven record, does not deserve his own command."

There was a flurry of seat shifting around the table. The admiral's mention of the public made them nervous. It was true that the public saw the commander as a bona fide hero and would expect Space Command to see him in the same light.

"You are suggesting perhaps a plaque in acknowledgement of his accomplishments?" Anderson asked, her brow furrowed. "A medal of some kind?"

The admiral shot her a poisonous glare so swift it was almost invisible.

"Perhaps something that honors all of the service equally," Grettirson countered. "Surely the situation is far too big to honor one individual. By picking out one we seem to be ignoring the contributions of all the other brave men and women who have fought in this war." His fingers writhed like worms.

"So you're saying we *should* ignore Commander Raeder's extraordinary actions?" Bertucci asked.

"The war is over," Grettirson said firmly. "The public doesn't need a hero now. What it needs now is to feel that *all* their sons and daughters are heroes. That their dead and their living children are equally responsible for saving the Commonwealth. That way their sacrifices have meaning. If the war were ongoing then perhaps the commander could be some sort of symbol for them. But now rewarding him above others merely makes it look as though everyone else was inadequate. And, as I've said before, he's a shoddy sort of officer; more suited to the Survey Service than Star Command proper."

Scaragoglu nodded slowly, thoughtfully.

"Perhaps the commander does need more seasoning," he conceded. "Would the board be willing to leave the matter in my hands?"

Grettirson's eyes flashed, but he said nothing. This was the very thing he had most wanted to avoid and he'd brought it about himself. Worse, he was about to see it sanctioned by the board. The admiral couldn't believe he'd been outmanuvered so completely.

Anderson studied the general for a moment through narrowed eyes. Then she sighed. Raeder had already thrown his lot in with the Spider. At least he'd have an interesting life, if not necessarily a long one.

She nodded.

"If you can satisfy both the public *and* Commander Raeder," she said cautiously.

"Oh, I believe I can," Scaragoglu said. "I believe I can."

Peter sat in Marine General Scaragoglu's outer office wishing he had something to read. He should have brought some of the report chips he had to read and initial. Heaven knew there was a lot of accounting to do regarding the supplies they'd grabbed for the *Invincible*, not to mention those Speeds he'd lifted.

Not that anyone had yet asked about them, but he knew it was only a matter of time. Right now his stock was high, so no one wanted to ask embarrassing questions. But eventually. As soon as Admiral Smallwood had the leisure to look back on the last few months, or the paperwork caught up with him, or some rat fink tattled to him. Peter stifled a sigh. *Well, the piper must be paid,* he thought.

Raeder was feeling a little lost and lonely right now. It had been over a week since he'd seen Sarah and he hadn't been able to get in touch with her. They were both working double time helping to clean up the mess that the final days of any war must bring. He'd left messages, but had received none in return. *Maybe I scared her off,* he thought dolefully.

He'd seen some of the queens and they'd been as gracious and friendly as anyone could wish. They truly seemed to be enjoying their acquaintance with his species. *Or perhaps they're just being polite.* He only hoped that humanity could be as broad-minded. Or at least as well bred.

They'd been popping their multiple eyeballs over a series of dance concerts the Commonwealth had arranged for them and had invited the performers to visit the clan homeworlds whenever they could.

He checked his watch surreptitiously. It was over two hours since he'd arrived and a solid hour and forty-five minutes since his supposed appointment. Still, this was the first time he'd ever had to wait on Scaragoglu. It probably meant something. Perhaps the general was displeased?

Oh come on, he thought at the closed office door, *I may have stepped on a few toes, but I didn't do that badly. So maybe the human race wasn't quite ready for friendly Fibians. We sure as hell weren't ready for the hostile kind. You've gotta take your friends as you find them, I say.*

He tapped his foot, earning himself a not very friendly look from the receptionist, who returned to his typing in the face of Raeder's glare.

The office door opened and Sarah entered.

"Sarah!" he said jumping to his feet.

He stood grinning at her for a second, then, when she didn't say anything but just smiled back, he gestured at the uncomfortable couch. She sat, he sat, they looked at one another. Peter looked at the receptionist, who seemed oblivious to the fact that she'd arrived.

"This is Lieutenant Commander Sarah James," the commander said aloud.

The receptionist looked up. "Thank you, sir," he said. He went back to his typing.

Peter turned to Sarah and shrugged.

"So, how've you been?" he asked. "It seems like ages since I saw you last."

"It has been ages," she said. "I was out-system. They sent me off to shepherd some WACCIs back from Sreth."

"Why you?" he asked with a frown.

"Why not?" she answered. "I think we can look forward to many strange assignments of that sort. It'll probably be awhile before things settle down and anybody knows just what's going on."

He nodded, looking away. Looking at Sarah was a bit too intense right now.

"I suppose they'll be downsizing the service," he said after a moment, still staring ahead at nothing.

"I wouldn't be at all surprised," she agreed.

After a moment he felt her take his hand. He looked over at her quickly and she smiled. *Yes*, she formed with her lips. Peter turned towards her.

Yes? he asked silently. She nodded. He nodded.

They gazed into one another's eyes while fireworks went off in his head.

She said yes! She said yes! The happy thought went around and around in his brain. Then he thought, *What if she's saying yes to something else? Maybe I'm misreading this yes thing.*

He pointed to his chest and looked at her questioningly. Sarah rolled her eyes and nodded firmly, the corners of her eyes crinkling with laughter. Peter grinned like a fool and took her hand in both of his.

Another thought struck him and he patted his pockets. Finally finding what he sought, he brought out a small box and handed it to Sarah. She accepted it, looking pleased. Upon opening the box she found a thin gold ring with a minuscule stone. Her eyes flashed up in surprise.

"Best I could do on short notice," he explained softly. "They were almost sold out."

She chuckled. "Gee, I wonder why?" Then she held out the box to him. "I think you're supposed to put it on," she whispered.

"Ah." He took the box back and pulled the ring out of its velvet bed. Then, looking into Sarah's eyes he slipped it onto the third finger of her left hand. It only went as far as her knuckle. "Oh!" he said, disappointed. "Damn!"

She held her hand out, checking the way it looked.

"It's a little small," she commented with a smile.

"You're so slender," he said in confusion, "I thought your hands . . ."

"I do not have fat fingers!" she said.

"No! You don't. But they're so long and fine that I suppose I remembered them as being fairylike."

Sarah smiled and sighed.

"You do throw the bull better than anyone I've ever met," she said fondly.

Peter laughed. "Well, better too small than too big."

"Good point," she conceded. Sarah played with the ring, holding it up to admire it.

It was a really ugly ring.

"We can get a nicer one," he said.

"Mm mm. I'll keep this one," she said, her eyes glowing. "This one has a story to it already."

"You can go in now, sir, ma'am," the receptionist announced.

Peter and Sarah looked at one another, almost surprised to find themselves in a waiting room.

"I guess what I was waiting for was you," Raeder said.

He gave Sarah's hand a squeeze, then they rose and walked into the Spider's office.

Scaragoglu had, of course, witnessed the delightful scene in his waiting room. But to offer the happy couple congratulations would be telling. And Scaragoglu never surrendered an advantage.

He returned their salutes casually and gestured to the chairs before his desk. Then he leaned forward, his hands folded before him.

"Congratulations to both of you for a job well done, Commander, Lieutenant Commander. The Commonwealth owes you and the entire crew of the *Invincible* a great debt of gratitude."

Peter and Sarah looked at one another, then at the general.

"Thank you, sir," Raeder said.

Sarah nodded. They both kept their eyes on the general.

Scaragoglu waited a moment, then he leaned back, allowing himself to seem weary and disappointed.

"Unfortunately . . . gratitude can seem . . ." He waved one hand as if trying to find the right word. "Onerous at times." Scaragoglu looked at Raeder with melting dark eyes, full of sympathy. "The official line of the service is that no man or woman is to be raised above another in this victory. That everyone who has served is to be thought of as serving equally and to be held equally responsible for the victory we've enjoyed."

Raeder and Sarah looked at one another.

"O-kay," Peter said slowly. "Sounds good." *If I'm not being blamed and I'm not gonna get court-martialed I guess I'm ahead of the game.* Disappointed? *Me? Nah!*

Sarah looked less than pleased, but said only, "So what happens now, sir?"

"I'm so glad you asked, Lieutenant Commander," Scaragoglu said. He looked a bit amused. He sat forward again, pulling his chair closer to the desk. "I'm sure you've been speculating over the fate of the service," he said.

They nodded.

"We will be downsizing drastically over the next couple of years," the general told them. "I'm afraid that with the black marks against your record," he nodded at Raeder, "your offer to reenlist will be refused out of hand."

"That's hardly fair," Sarah said boldly.

"There's also that unfortunate stay in Camp Stick 'Em Together Again on your record, Lieutenant Commander," Scaragoglu said.

Sarah sat with her mouth open.

"But . . . but that . . ."

The general shook his head sadly.

"It's unfair, I know. You've both done so much, contributed so phenomenally to the winning of this war." He raised his hands helplessly. "But the senior staff were adamant."

Raeder was stunned beyond speech, beyond reaction. *Beached!* he thought, crushed. *It's over, I'll never fly again.* What was left but some boring job on a planet somewhere. He tried to see himself as a salesman and repressed a shudder.

"The senior staff were adamant about us, specifically?" Sarah asked, her eyes narrowed.

Raeder's head came up.

"That is interesting, sir. Just what did the senior staff have in mind for us that they were so adamant about?" Though he hid it as well as he could, Peter fairly radiated hope.

The general chuckled.

"That's one of the things I've liked about you since the first time we met, son. You keep looking for reasons to be optimistic." He leaned back in his chair and folded his hands on his stomach, a very self-satisfied expression on his dark face. "And, as it happens, I can give you reason to be."

Peter and Sarah flashed a look at one another.

"Star Command will be downsizing. There's no getting around that. For one thing the Commonwealth doesn't need the navy to be as large as it currently is to fight pirates and smugglers." He made a moue. "Personally I'd keep it larger than it will be, but no one with the power is asking my opinion."

Peter doubted that. *I wish he'd get to the point,* he thought. *The suspense is killing me.*

"But, one door closes and another opens."

Aphorisms he's giving me. The man is trying to give me a stroke. Raeder schooled his face to show an infinite patience he wasn't feeling.

"I can't apologize enough," Scaragoglu said, leaning forward, a sincerely embarrassed expression on his face, "for the shabby way you're being treated here, Commander. The best that I was able to do was to finagle a transfer for you, and your team if you want them . . ." The general bit his lips as if what he was about to offer was so insulting he could barely bring himself to speak.

C'mon, Peter thought encouragingly. *C'mon!*

"Sir?" Raeder said aloud.

Scaragoglu looked up into Peter's eyes.

"I'm offering you an extended exploratory-survey command in the Survey Service. Out on your own . . ." The general shook his head. "You deserve better," he said.

Don't throw me into that briar patch, Br'er Fox! Please! Somehow Raeder managed to keep from leaping on top of his chair and screaming *"Hallelujah!"* Instead he nodded solemnly. He turned to Sarah gravely.

"What are your thoughts on this, Lieutenant Commander?" he asked.

Her eyes were shining and she was trying to suppress her joy with far less success than Peter.

"What would be the terms of our contract, sir?" she managed to ask.

"The usual five-year mission," Scaragoglu said. "With the standard finder's fees in place."

"I'll want a new ship," Raeder said. "Or at the very least approval on any vessel that's offered."

"As you'll be the first out that shouldn't be a problem," the general said.

"What about supplies and fuel?" Raeder asked. "To be supplied by the Commonwealth?"

Traditionally the ships were provided by the Commonwealth and the supplies and fuel by the captain and crew in a cooperative arrangement. This was because the survey ships tended to become family affairs over time, and the Commonwealth didn't like to interfere in such personal situations. It provided stability for the crews and a good return on investment. There was even an option that allowed the captain to buy the ship from the Survey Service and operate it on his or her own.

"All right," Scaragoglu conceded. "I can't promise that this will be a lifetime arrangement. But for the first two missions at least I can guarantee that ship and supplies and fuel will be provided by the Commonwealth. Try and make it worth our while," he growled.

Peter and Sarah looked at one another.

"In regard to my team, sir," Raeder said. "I have a request."

"Ye-es," Scaragoglu said.

"Chief Patrick Casey, sir. He's an engineer, a New Hibernian. Would you be able to arrange a field commission for him, General? He's more than deserving of one. And frankly I'd need him, but without such a commission I doubt I could get him to come with me."

"Commander, weren't you listening? Space Command will be downsizing, they're not going to be handing out field commissions or any other kind of commission for a very long time." Scaragoglu's displeasure was obvious.

"But he would immediately transfer to the Survey Service, sir. He's extremely qualified, as well as deserving. It won't actually cost Space Command anything but some paperwork. To deny the man a promotion after his contribution to such an important mission, especially when he's moving to another service . . ." Peter shook his head. "It wouldn't look good, sir."

The general frowned, turning away for a moment.

"Just how important is this to you, Raeder?" he asked with a piercing look.

"I'd go to the wall over it, sir." *Well, maybe not to the wall,* he thought. *I'm actually bluffing on that.* He glanced at Sarah. She sat with her calm gaze fixed on the general. Inside he smiled. *With Sarah's help maybe I'd even go that far.*

"They won't like it," the general warned. He sighed. "But I'm owed more than a few favors. I can finagle it. But that's my last concession."

"When will his commission come through, sir?" Sarah asked.

Scaragoglu pursed his lips. "Oh, in an hour, maybe," he said with a twinkle in his eye.

"Then, thank you, sir," Peter said, rising. "I'll be happy to accept this deal."

"And so will I," Sarah said.

"Then I'll have your orders cut," the general said. "Let me know who else you'll be taking with you. Try not to grab too many of our best people," he snarled.

He offered his hand.

Smiling broadly Raeder took it in a firm grip. Then Sarah shook the general's hand.

"We're getting married, sir," Raeder said. "Would you like to come to our wedding?"

Looking genuinely pleased and honestly surprised for perhaps the first time in years, Scaragoglu congratulated them heartily and said that yes, he would very much like to come.

"We'll be in touch with the details, sir," Peter said.

He and Sarah closed the door to the general's office behind them and then threw themselves into each other's arms, regardless of the amused receptionist, laughing like kids. Then, hand in hand, they raced off to tell Paddy and Cynthia the good news.

❖   ❖   ❖

Paddy hastened down the corridor, uncommonly awkward in his excitement; he seemed to be all elbows and knees like a fifteen-year-old, if you could imagine one weighing in at two-hundred-odd pounds of bone and muscle, with callus an inch thick on his knuckles and a nose that all the microsurgery in the Commonwealth couldn't make totally straight again. The huge, awed, world-beating grin added to the effect.

He spied Second Lieutenant Cynthia Robbins climbing out of a Speed and his grin widened to the point where it began to look like a spasm and must have hurt.

"Lieutenant!" he said in a conspiratorial shout that brought heads around across the flight deck.

He waved them all off with a big hand and they turned back to their work, albeit with one eye cocked at the big red-headed engineer.

Cynthia's foot hit the deck and she turned to look at him, lifting an inquiring eyebrow.

"Lieutenant," he said, taking her elbow and drawing her aside. "Acushla," he whispered, pleased to see her blush, though her expression remained businesslike. "'Tis the best day in the world! In the whole of the universe, so it is!"

"What are you talking about?" she whispered.

Cynthia tried to draw her arm out of his grasp and with a fond squeeze he let her.

"Take this," he said and handed her a reader. "And that." And he handed her a chip.

He stood with his hands on his hips and a face-splitting grin on his face as he watched her nervously fit the chip into the reader. The lieutenant started to read, a slight frown between her brows, and Paddy folded his arms. Then he rubbed his face, folded his arms, placed his hands on his hips, changed his stance.

Then she looked up at him and her face lit with a slow smile, like the sun rising.

"Oh, congratulations, Paddy," she whispered.

She reached out and touched his chest just over his heart, and he put his hand over hers, smiling down at her with pride and hope. Slowly his grin faded.

"Ye know what this means, d'ye not?" he asked quietly.

A rare glint of mischief sparked in her dark eyes. "What?" she asked.

The big New Hibernian went down on one knee and Cynthia's eyes and mouth popped wide open. She tugged on his hand to make him rise but she might as well have been trying to lift a Speed.

"Will ye marry me?" he asked her.

"Get up!" she hissed.

"I'm askin' ye girl," Paddy insisted.

"Paddy! People are looking at us!"

"And let them, I want them for witnesses," he said. "Now I'm to be an officer there should be nothin' to stand in our way. So I ask ye once again, lass. Will ye marry me?"

She stopped her frantic tugging and looked him in the eye. After a moment Cynthia took a deep breath and smiled a very sweet and loving smile.

"Of course I will," she said.

He leapt to his feet, caught her up in a bear hug and swung her off her feet while she laughed and the whole of Main Deck broke into whoops and cheers.

Sarah and Peter came in hand in hand while the celebration was still going on. Peter looked at Sarah and raised his brows.

"I guess the Spider came through," he said.

"And in well under an hour," Sarah observed.

"You'd almost think he'd anticipated my demands," Peter said dryly.

"Almost." She winked at him.

With bright smiles they hurried to tell their friends the good news.

Captain Sjarhir entered the general's office and raised one eyebrow questioningly.

"That poor boy," Scaragoglu said with a grin. "He actually believes that he manipulated me into all that!"

THE END